I0690850

Baby Monster

Pensive Horrors from

John S. McFarland

From

Dark Owl Publishing, LLC

Arizona

Copyright ©2024 by John S. McFarland
and Dark Owl Publishing, LLC

All rights reserved.

ISBN 978-1-951716-39-4

This book is a work of fiction. Names, characters, businesses,
organizations, places, events, and incidents either are the product of the
author's imagination or are used fictitiously. Any resemblance to actual
persons, living or dead, events or locales is entirely coincidental.

No part of this book may be reproduced, distributed or transmitted in
any form or by any means without the author's or publisher's written
consent, except for purposes of review.

Cover painting by Gabriel Augusto
Instagram: @gabrielaugustoart
www.facebook.com/gabriel.augusto.796

Interior illustrations by John. S. McFarland

Cover design by Dark Owl Publishing, LLC

Author photograph ©2020 Cindy McFarland

Visit us on our website at:
www.darkowlpublishing.com

Praise for
John S. McFarland

"In *Baby Monster*, McFarland revisits the cursed town of Ste. Odile, where the darkest angels of our souls, all our souls, reside."
- Dacre Stoker, author of *Dracul*
and great-grandnephew of Bram Stoker

"A really unusual and impressive collection—harrowing but frequently quite touching. I very much admire the elegance, the old-fashioned elegance of the writing."
~ T.E.D. Klein, author of *The Ceremonies* and *Dark Gods*

"I genuinely wanted to reread this one for pure pleasure. Some powerful and disturbing imagery lurks within."
~ John Linwood Grant, author of *Where all is Night and Starless*

"The writing is spectacular, by the way. I was drawn in from the first sentence (which is always the goal, right?) and find the language very sophisticated & descriptive."
~ E. J. Hammon, author of *Ted Bundy: Memories of the Beast*

"The stories absolutely absorbed me."
~ David B. Busboom, author of *Every Crawling, Putrid Thing*

"McFarland's stories are like gifts sprung from a dark chest full of wonders. Historical horror... horror against a wide variety of cultural backgrounds... whatever story you pick up, it may remind you of Ray Bradbury or other great masters of the genre, but it contains one thing for sure: McFarland's unique vision and his very own voice! A true master among writers working today."
~ Michael Schmitt, Wandler/Verlag

Also From
John S. McFarland

Collections
The Dark Walk Forward

Novels
The Black Garden

The Mother of Centuries
The sequel to *The Black Garden*

For Young Readers
Annette: A Big, Hairy Mom

Annette: A Big, Hairy Grandma
The sequel to *Annette: A Big Hairy Mom*

Coming from Zagava
The Black Garden
Limited Edition Print Run
www.zagava.de

Visit John on his website at www.jsmcfarlandauthor.com.

All of John's books are currently available through
Dark Owl Publishing.

Also From
Dark Owl Publishing

Collections
The Dark Walk Forward
John S. McFarland

The Last Star Warden:
Volumes I and II
The Phantom World
The Crimson Star Saga Episodes
Jason J. McCuiston

The Brotherhood of Secret Darkness
and Other Cults, Cabals, and Conspiracies
Jason J. McCuiston

Professor Wyrd's World of Wonders:
Miracles and Monsters
Jason J. McCuiston
Limited edition coming August 2024

Tales from New Pangea
Kevin M. Folliard

No Lesser Angels, No Greater Devils
The Aiphace
Laura J. Campbell

The Tension of a Coming Storm
Adrian Ludens

The Nightmare Cycle
Lawrence Dagstine

The Art of Ghost Writing
Alistair Rey

Bad Dreams and Reflections
Trevor Kennedy

Welcome to Scar Ridge
Jonathon Mast

Anthologies
Something Wicked This Way Rides

Novels
The Black Garden
John S. McFarland

The Mother of Centuries
The sequel to *The Black Garden*
John S. McFarland

The Keeper of Tales
Jonathon Mast

Carnivore Keepers
A novel from New Pangea
Kevin M. Folliard

The Wicked Twisted Road
D.S. Hamilton

For Young Readers
Annette: A Big, Hairy Mom
John S. McFarland

Annette: A Big, Hairy Grandma
The sequel to *Annette: A Big Hairy Mom*
John S. McFarland

Shivers, Scares, and Goosebumps
Vonnie Winslow Crist

Buy the books for Kindle and in paperback
www.darkowlpublishing.com

To Cindy McFarland.

Table of Contents

Forward

John S. McFarland:
A Loving Father of Monstrous Misfits

I first encountered the work of John S. McFarland in the pages of the anthology *A Treasury of American Horror Stories* (edited by Frank D. McSherry, Jr., Charles G. Waugh, and Martin H. Greenberg), which collected "fifty-one tales of horror and the supernatural... one for every state in the Union and the District of Columbia." I was nine or ten, more into the magical than the macabre, and still reading *Goosebumps* for my occasional toe-dips into terror. This anthology was my introduction to horror literature for adults, a bloody standout among the disordered deluge of fiction and nonfiction on my parents' bookshelves. McFarland's story "One Happy Family" represented Arkansas, wherein an overworked country doctor attends the birth of a loving but poor couple's fifth freakish child. That story was McFarland's debut, first published in *The Twilight Zone Magazine* two years before sharing *Treasury*'s table of contents with such heavyweights as Stephen King, Richard Matheson, and Robert Bloch. It would later be reprinted in McFarland's extraordinary first collection, *The Dark Walk Forward*, alongside nineteen other harrowing tales.

There and here, McFarland's voice is rooted in the American Gothic while remaining contemporary and original, fashioning familiar forms into strange new shapes like his own Mr. and Mrs. Knoss or the Doctors Treves. Children, parents, and even pets are so transmogrified—sometimes literally—under the often tragic, always unsettling light of McFarland's imagination.

In *Baby Monster*, you'll return to his richly evocative Gilded/Progressive Era small town of Ste. Odile (rapidly becoming one of my favorite fictional locales), but you'll also find yourself in seventeenth-century Spain, the modern American Midwest, and Prohibition Era Florida. Whatever country or age, you'll soon be caught in that shadowed twilight between the everyday and the numinous that only the best writers of dark fiction can reliably invoke.

And you'll meet the ones who call those shadows home.

Living, waking nightmares; monsters and oddities as rare and common as humanity; misfit horrors lurking in the streets and homes of today and centuries past—these are some of what this book contains.

I'll leave you to discover the rest.

David Busboom
Champaign, IL
May 2023

Snake-Head

*B*arthele, my salvation, my deity, you know I can't count the ways I love you. How can that be possible when they multiply by the day? You saved me from Pettibone, got him to release me from St. Mathurin's to your care. You knew as well as I, that I was not sick in the least. Not insane. Since when is sensitivity and insight sickness? Maybe always, as I think back on the sad cavalcade of human affairs.

Yes, you are a cousin, but a distant cousin. I am your last-known relative, which is why you saved me. The love I have found for you is not untoward. I don't consider it wrong, or un-Christian. It is necessary for me and to be fully expected by any reasonable person who weighs the facts. And I believe I was put here in your house at just the right moment to care for you. Who would have expected President McKinley to stop in our forgotten town to dedicate a new train line as he toured the country? Such excitement! The crowd overwhelmed you, trampled you, and we know the resulting back injuries will be with you for the rest of your life to some degree. I had just come to live with you under your care when you fell under my care. God willed it.

As I lie next to you at night for a few moments before I go to my room, watching your face as you sleep, I read your thoughts. They come to me, and I know you are contented. Or were. I know you feel safe and loved, though you have lost happiness for now. The message comes through. This is my gift. Though you can barely move your legs, I place you on the two-wheel cart and push you for outings or just to the street to enjoy the fresh air, and I sense you are happy. At that moment you are happy at least, though it doesn't last. But you are reminded of what comfort and happiness can be. When you have strengthened your will as I have, you will be whole again. I have tried but I cannot do it for you.

You complained too much. You gave voice to self-pity, and I willed you to silence on the subject for your own good. You have barely spoken since. But apparently, I cannot will you to be well. When old Walter, your hound, was gone for two days and returned home jumping in bed with you, I saw in his mind that he knew he was full of ticks. He knew he was sharing his pestilence with you. I saw it in his face. Animals know more than we think. This is to their benefit. Soon the tick bites were everywhere on your body. The bites incited the skin condition which adds to your miseries. I know it is true. They call it eczema now, and even with the limited use you have of your hands, you keep it bloody with scratching. I shot the dog.

Pike, if you would only let me be. Your attentions are well-meant but exhausting. My breathing has gotten so weak I can no longer speak to you. It is difficult to convey my wishes with my breathless words. You think you know best. Your mental state scares me sometimes. I didn't know the full extent of it when I took you in. I think Pettibone just wanted to be rid of you. Your ideas are obsessive. Only a fool or a lunatic never doubts themselves or questions their own beliefs.

This damned itching will be the death of me. It started as tick bites with red centers and red rings around them. After weeks of the itching getting worse, I knew it had turned into something else. I have always been of weak constitution, my body poorly equipped to fight off sickness. The toxins of the bites opened the door for something worse: this insufferable condition I have now. I scratch it raw even in my limited mobility. But I barely have the strength to do it.

Long ago I noticed an interesting difference in the great snakes of the tropics. Of the enormous ones, those that are venomous, the cobras and adders and mambas and such, have a look of evil and malevolence in their hellish faces. They scowl like a bird of prey as if they mean to do one harm or to kill. But the huge constrictors, the nightmare serpents of fetid and dank rivers or the treetops, where alarmed monkeys skitter trying to save themselves, those monsters called anaconda and python, those that slowly and horrifically squeeze the life out of their victims, prolonging their terror—they look dead. Their faces are plated, blank, and emotionless. Their eyes are dead eyes, pale and ghastly, and show nothing but indifference to the death they slowly bring their victims.

This was my familiar thought when I first saw the great snake. It was of the constrictor type, and I was in such shock to see it, I dropped the basket of blackberries I had picked for Barthele. I could only see clearly, its head, some seven or eight inches long and flat. A pale film was folding back from its nose over its dead, blue eyes. It was forcing itself through a fork in a maple tree, shedding its skin. This is from town, I thought. That eccentric fellow, Emlyn, has a menagerie. This thing must have escaped. Either from Emlyn or that Dr. Treves, who experiments on animals.

The old brush hook I had been using the day before was still where I left it, leaning against the shed. It took four chops to cut off the serpentine head completely, but I did it. The great and vile length of the thing writhed hideously without its head for many moments. The movements were violent and raging, but at length, they subsided and stopped. The head lay in the high grass, its mouth opening and closing in a monstrous way. I looked down at it and was all but certain that its dead-looking eye was looking at me. I could not ascertain which subspecies of great serpent this was but assumed it must be one of the Asian types.

Then it spoke to me. It conveyed to my mind, wordlessly, that it would live on despite my violence toward it. It said I must take it up off the ground and keep it near, for it knows many things that will benefit me. No reptile has ever told me any manner of falsehood, so I picked it up.

I suspected you had feelings for me, Pike, when I brought you home from St. Mathurin's that day. I told you it was inappropriate, that we are too closely related, and that in any case, I have no interest in romantic or physical love. Still, God punishes me. Despite my honesty with you, I have had thoughts leading me toward temptation. I admit this only to myself. I have resisted them, but they must be the reason I have been reduced to this state. I can think of no other cause. Prostrate, breathless, and itching... itching constantly.

Our mothers were so close as children. Like sisters less than a year apart in age. You and I, Pike, are only eighteen months apart. I think about those days on your farm. My mind wanders as I lie here. We fed the chickens and the pigs and drew pictures and read together. And, oh, that time I got such a skin rash after walking in the woods with you! Poison oak, or poison ivy. You sat with me as your mother applied the paste she made to relieve the itch.

I remember a day when, after feeding the pigs, you told me the animals knew what was going to happen to them. They knew they were being raised to be slaughtered. Then one morning you let them all loose, saying they asked you to do it. You often did bad things with the best of intentions. You were beaten and locked in the coal bin for two days as punishment. A few of the pigs were never caught and roamed your woods and pastures for a time. They turned wild, killed your old dog, Floyd. A few months after that, you were sent to St. Mathurin's. I thought about you there every day. All through my adolescent years. Every day.

It seems content. Snake-Head does not resent what I did to it, not too much, at least. Reaching me, after all, was its purpose. At any cost. I know it wanted to reach me because I alone can hear it. It has much to convey, I think, and no one but me to hear it.

I placed it on the table under my window and it is content. And I, too, am more content. As I move around my room, I know its dead-looking eyes are on me. In the empty hours of night, when I return to my room after Barthele is asleep, even then it watches and conveys thoughts to me.

Snake-Head wanted to know: "Why did you kill me?"

I said, "I kill every snake I see." Serpents are the only creatures I fear and even... hate. Most people kill any snake they come across if they can. But of course, Snake-Head knew this. The Serpent in the Garden brought this down upon his race, making them the lowliest and most despised of creatures.

Snake-Head continued: "Killing me was of no consequence, so long as I found you. I only ask because it was so violent, what you did. So uncalled for. But such it is in the world God has made."

But you live. You live on because you speak to me.

"Only to you do I live. I am only alive in your thoughts."

What do you have to tell me about God's creation?

"That simplicity... simplicity is the key."

The suicides in Hell never suffered like this. The itching is more than itching. It is stinging; it is painful; it is fire. It stabs me suddenly, making my body twitch, then lingers and lingers as I am barely able to scratch. Those spots I can reach are few and I can mostly only brush my hand across them. I often don't have the strength to claw at them. Pike has treated it with all manner of medicines. Salves he has made, ointments from the pharmacy, ice to numb it. He treats my pain, bathes me, takes me out into the sunshine when he thinks I need it. My suffering is his suffering. Never has anyone so sincerely cared about my well-being.

He does all he can, but it isn't enough. My heart was in the right place to bring him here, but I think now, it was a mistake. Some of his notions, his ideas, are nothing more than delusions. I think St. Mathurin's might be the best place for him after all. And I need professional care. A real doctor. Hildy is coming for a visit sometime soon, Pike tells me. If I can get a private moment with her, I will ask her to make the needed inquiries. Things can get better for both Pike and me if I take the initiative.

In the moonlight, Snake-Head's eyes seem bluer. Anyone else seeing them would think them dead as a stone. I see otherwise. But no one, not even Barthele, may see him. None but me. I lock my door when I leave, and we have few visitors. I fear Snake-Head will stop communicating if anyone but me sees him. Hildy is coming soon, but she has never seen my room. And never will. She didn't approve of Barthele bringing me here, and if she had, the power would almost certainly send me back to Pettibone and St. Mathurin's. And she thinks little of the care I give my dear cousin. She does not understand the power of will, of belief in the good. Of simplicity, as Snake-Head has told me. Barthele will come to understand this as I do. It will be a slow process, but it will happen, and she will be whole again.

Snake-Head said his first night with me: "Self-pity is repellent to God. He wills our calamities. We must accept His will or must recognize He is testing us and then work to help ourselves. Self-pity is weakness and a distraction from acceptance and finding the path to rebirth and happiness and the truth of simplicity."

I understood this to be so. Just this morning I cut myself shaving but willed the bleeding to stop and the pain to subside, and it did, in short order. Snake-Head approved, knowing I had learned and done the right thing. Surely this is the beginning of enlightenment.

Snake-Head said: "Pain is only a perception of your mind. I disallowed it when you struck me, and it was as nothing. This is also in your power, as I think you now understand."

Hildy fears Pike. I can see it in her face. I told her there is no one who cares for my well-being more than she... and Pike. She said she believes that but fears where his tendencies and delusions might lead him. She brought a balm she made and applied it to my legs. But the itching never stops in response to any treatment. It must die down on its own.

I find that I am more distracted the more uncomfortable I am. I tried to figure the household accounts this morning and realized I made a mistake of nearly two hundred dollars. Hildy assured me that she would settle things at the bank.

Hildy brought with her a blueberry pie she baked in the terrible heat yesterday. Enjoying it postponed the conversation we both wanted to have, as did Pike's joining us for a half-hour and claiming his portion of the dessert.

Pike said, "Hildy, I noticed your limp is very much improved since last week."

"It is, yes."

"I am glad to see it. I prayed for you."

"Thank you, Pike."

"I prayed that God would heal you quickly and that you would think thoughts that promoted your healing."

"Well, yes. Dark thoughts never righted a wrong or lifted a spirit."

"That's it in a nutshell, isn't it?" He smiled when he said it. "As simple as that." He went out the kitchen door and began cutting the honeysuckle overgrowing the gate.

Hildy said, "Seems as normal as table salt much of the time, still..."

I told her yes, he seems so, but there is much about him no one knows but me.

I was wrong to revile snakes as I have always done. As I chopped the weeds in the humid sunshine, two garter snakes escaped past me. I was neither startled nor overtaken by an impulse to kill them. They disappeared into the high grass of the yard. Just then I heard the front door open. I walked toward it to find Hildy leaving after her visit. She looked startled to see me.

"Do I surprise you, Hildy?"

"I didn't expect you. You appeared so suddenly."

"Odd. You knew I was here."

"Very good to see you, Pike. You are taking good care of our Barthele."

"I love her, as you know. I am committed to her recovery. Are the two of you hatching some sort of plot? You seem so distracted." I laughed. She was clearly surprised by the question. "I don't know your mind since we are not close..."

"Nonsense!" She smiled and walked quickly away.

I looked at Snake-Head on the table in the moonlight as I fell asleep. It was an unsettled sleep. I had nightmares of fearful creatures approaching me from all directions. To my relief, they did not wish to harm me. They only wished to guide me, enlighten me. Suddenly aware of the dark room around me, I realized I was awake. I felt an object against my left leg under the coverlet. Lifting the linen slightly, I saw a single spot of light next to my thigh. Then a second one. The two small lights were moving along my body, then in an instant, they were gone.

Slowly I turned toward the pillow next to my head. There lay Snake-Head, watching me with glowing blue eyes. I was startled. The jaws slowly opened, revealing the pale, riven mouth and rows of the curved needles of teeth.

Snake-Head said: "It hurts to think I have frightened you. It hurts even more than my beheading."

"I was just startled, not frightened. Nothing more. I promise you, nothing more."

"You have an enemy in that woman. Hildy is your enemy."

"I sense it."

"Barthele keeping secrets with her cannot be good for you. Why would they keep secrets from you unless it was to harm you or change your life for the worse?"

"I can think of no reason."

"The simple answer is the best. Remove the problem by removing the source. You know it. And for Barthele and her suffering, think of my circumstances the day you first saw me. Think on that."

Pike! Pike, such terrible news! Who could have done such a thing? Who is there in this world who did not love Hildy? If I could scream, if I could wail, I would! If I could express how I feel now. She was just here caring for me, treating my condition a few hours ago. The thought of her murder, of the last moments of terror as she faced her murderer! Her throat cut from ear to ear! Pike... Pike... what are you doing? What are you doing? Why are you tying me down like this? What... what do you mean to do with your razor?

You know I live for you, my Barthele. I wait for the day when you can be well again, and we can be happy and equal. You are trying to say something. I see panic in your face. No need. You know I would do nothing to you that I am not sure will benefit you. Hildy was your agent. Her interference would have taken me from you, and the best way to avoid that was to remove her. It was for the best. And your condition, your suffering and torment... I suffer as you suffer. The key is simple, though; I should have seen it sooner. Snakes, my dear. When their skin no longer suits them, they shed it. Whatever parasite or imperfection that old epidermis contained, they leave it behind. What could be simpler than to just remove the skin that vexes you? Leave it behind and in time, start fresh? Start new? You can—you must—prepare for this. I have conquered pain with the power of my own mind. So can you. You can, you absolutely can. I would have given you more time to master this, but Hildy has forced our hand, my dear. She will be found soon. It must happen now. I will help you to relax, to master your thoughts. Only when you are ready will I begin.

The Black Smiles

By late October, Dr. Sirach Treves was certain his experiment was a success. Since the previous November, he had been feeding Gregor, his one-hundred-ten-pound mandrill, a daily diet of sweets and candies. As a control, Treves had withheld any such treats from Mendel, the ape's younger brother. After those many months, Gregor had developed advanced tooth decay in four molars while his brother had not, convincing Treves that there was indeed a connection between granular sugar and dental cavities. Now, with the permission of Pettibone, his casual friend and lodge brother, he could advance to the next step in his investigations.

Pettibone was the general manager, answerable to Dr. Guildea, the Superintendent of St. Mathurin's Home for the Insane in Ste. Odile. There was something indefinably unsavory about Pettibone that precluded Treves from forming too close a friendship with him. Pettibone towered over everyone he met, always dressed in black and nearly totally bald, a fact that made his head look like a malevolent full moon. But he had always been a useful fellow, one to count on when a special favor was needed. Dr. Guildea, a fading and usually confused medical man, gave full responsibility for running his facility to Pettibone.

Pettibone agreed, contingent on the performance of an unspecified future favor he may someday ask of the doctor, to allow Treves to conduct his investigation on three of the asylum's inmates. Having examined the teeth of more than fifty possible subjects in both the men's wing and the women's wing over a period of months, Treves had chosen three friends and inseparable confidants: Maudire Outil, Berenice LaTourette, and Helene deLancre—a girl of about fourteen. Berenice and Helene had been diagnosed as sexual hysterics. Maudire, the most dominant personality of the three, was suffering, it was decided, from acute melancholia.

Treves couldn't pinpoint at first why he had chosen those three women, but he was drawn to them. Maudire seemed very intelligent and creative. She had even been assigned to be assistant to Harrison, the janitor/handyman at St. Mathurin's. She knew something about carpentry, plumbing, and even a little about electricity. Pettibone knew that her energies must be given direction, or she could become aggressive and violent. Berenice and Helene had no such talents or skills but followed Maudire faithfully and always seemed anxious to please her, or anyone they perceived as having authority over them.

Treves suspected that if he could coax cooperation from Maudire, the other two women would willingly follow.

Pettibone designated a small storage room for Treves's use. Treves's needs were slight; he brought a teapot, some logbooks, a Kodak box camera, dossiers on each of the female subjects, and an ample supply of taffy, sweet chocolate, and peanut brittle. He began the human phase of his work officially on Monday, January 2, 1899.

Berenice tentatively entered the study room. She sat in a wooden chair opposite Treves's small desk. She seemed self-conscious and shy and often smiled furtively at him. She wore a hospital shift under a cotton robe. Her hair was in disarray, though she looked generally clean.

"Berenice, how old are you?" Treves asked, though he had her dossier on the desk before him.

Berenice smiled suggestively. "I'm fourteen... No! Twenty-four."

"I am Dr. Treves, and I want to do a study of three typical inmates of this facility."

Berenice laughed as if the statement were a joke. She suddenly realized that it wasn't, and her face went blank.

"You have just been examined by the nurse here."

"Yes."

"Every Monday morning for the next few months, she will examine you. She will record your weight and heart rate and other vitals, and then you will come to me. Please move your chair closer to me."

Berenice smiled broadly and complied. From a cabinet above his desk, Treves withdrew a grotesque device that was all curved metal and threaded bolts.

"This is a jaw opener, "Treves said. "I will use it to hold your mouth open every week so I can study your teeth and gums and make notes. Do you object to any of this?"

Berenice shook her head. "Whatever you need, Doctor. I will do whatever you need so long as it doesn't hurt me. I hate getting hurted." She leaned forward and opened her mouth wide.

Treves smiled. "All right, we'll do it now." He positioned the edges of the device against each side of her mouth and secured it. "Gwynplaine," Treves mumbled.

"Huh?" Berenice sprayed through the device.

"You remind me of a character from a story."

"I like good stories. Good ones."

"Don't try to talk." Treves examined each tooth by its medical number and made notes in a logbook. Then he removed the camera from the cabinet and took a series of photos of the teeth and gums. He reached for a paper bag sitting at the rear edge of his desk and handed it to her. "This is the most important part, Berenice. There is a half-pound of various candies in this bag. You will receive one bag every day. Eat the entire contents every day. As time goes on, you will be given larger amounts of candy. You must eat everything in the bag *every* day."

"I love candy. It is so good!"

Treves repeated these procedures with Helene and finally Maudire.

Maudire was short and stocky. She had cut all her hair off with small garden shears the day before her interview. When asked why she had done this, she said she didn't know, other than she had just sharpened the shears in the custodian's shop. "I am a useful person," she said. "A person who can't fend for theyselfs, can't fix a broken chair or cook a meal... I have no use for them."

"Not everyone is self-sufficient," Treves said.

"God helps them that helps theyselfs. That's the way I bleeve. We have been given the gift of the world to use, to learn its secrets. Use them for our benefit. My grandma was Genevieve the Wildcrafter. She showed me how Nature gives us what we need if we read the signs."

"I see."

"She losted a eye to a branch and knowed to take the eye of a goat to replace it, and it worked. Like she knew it would."

Treves frowned. "She used the eye of a goat?"

"She come upon a goat in a field that a coyote had got to. It was hurted but alive. A crow was before it and ate out one of its eyes. Grandma took it as a sign. She took the other eye. You got to have the faith that God and Nature will give you what you need of the world. That's how I bleeve. Everything that's losted has a replacement. Have faith in that and do not sorrow."

"Yes," Treves agreed. "Sorrow and regret are, in large part, pointless. I agree with that part of your statement. 'Do not sorrow.' Here is your candy, Maudire."

"I don't eat much candy, Doctor, but I bleeve God wants me to help you with your hicksperiment, so I'll do it." She took the bag and nodded at him as she left his office.

All the subjects had healthy teeth, even though none had a regimen of dental hygiene.

At the beginning of the study, Treves only came to St. Mathurin's on Mondays. After a few visits, Pettibone got in the habit of stopping in to check on the progress of the work.

"Still no results?" Pettibone said, entering the small office as Treves was recording information in his laboratory log. "It has been six weeks, hasn't it?"

"Yes. I wouldn't expect to see anything this soon." Treves made an effort to hide his irritation at the intrusion. He wasn't sure he succeeded.

"When do you expect results?"

"Possibly not for a few more months. Maybe never, if my conjecture is wrong."

"It's a very small sampling you are using."

"All I can afford for now," Treves said. "If the results are promising I will seek funding, perhaps from Carthesian. And after that..." Treves pulled a letter from his vest pocket. "This came this morning. It's from Dr. Ostrom. Lars Ostrom in Stockholm. He has heard of this work and wants me to join him with the data I have collected by then in an expansion of these studies next year. I will of course credit you for helping me get started."

"Ah, well thank you. That may be beneficial to me someday. I was wondering... since you have gotten to know them a little, what do you make of these girls? Our three subjects? I spend most of my time in the women's wing. These three stand out to me."

"*Make* of them?" Treves was a little surprised by the sudden change of topic.

"Yes. Your opinion of their personalities."

Treves was puzzled by the question. "Well, they are good subjects. Maudire is forceful... moody. I understand why you want to keep her occupied. Berenice is flirtatious, flighty. What is the word? Kittenish! Yes, kittenish."

"What about Helene?"

"Very quiet and unsure of herself. No wonder she follows Maudire. She's very young. She may grow out of it."

"Sexual hysteric. I suspect she will only get worse. Afraid of men but obsessed by them."

"Hard to say," Treves shrugged. "I see no signs of obsession, but it isn't my field."

"I find her especially... interesting. Interesting." Pettibone smiled slightly, only returning Treves's gaze for a second.

"I see. I hadn't noticed. Very young... and a patient."

Pettibone sat in the interview chair next to Treves's desk. "When you started this, I mentioned I may need a favor from you someday."

"Yes."

"The board is replacing the superintendent at the orphanage."

"Yes, that's right."

"You are on the board. I want that position. I would like to think I can count on your support."

"You want *that* position? The orphanage?"

"Yes. I work well with children. I have a chemistry background as you may remember. I would have more time to work in my field."

"I see. Well... yes, I will support you. I assumed you would want to replace Dr. Guildea here at St. Mathurin's."

"I am not a medical man. They will never give me the position. And I prefer the company of children."

Treves watched him as he left, feeling more certain that his worst instincts about Pettibone were correct. But he told himself that Pettibone's nature and tendencies were none of his business. At least he was cooperating with the dental study.

On May fifteenth, Treves saw the first cavity in Helene's mouth. It was tooth fourteen, a molar on the upper left side of her mouth. Treves was excited to record his first palpable result. He wondered if Helene's age accounted for her developing a cavity before the other women. Helene was restless as Treves examined her teeth.

"You aren't yourself today, Helene," Treves noted. "Are you feeling well?

Locked in the mouth brace, she shook her head no. Treves finished his notes and removed the brace. "Under the weather?" he continued. "Are you menstruating? Young women have some difficulty, I know, learning to cope with that."

"No sir... Doctor." Helene frowned and looked at the floor. "None of the girls here want to be noticed by Mr. Pettibone. Nobody wants to be his special helper. He made me his special helper."

Treves stopped himself before he asked a further question. It was best he did not know any more, he thought. He recognized her expression as indicative of her having more to say, but he turned away from her and thanked her for her help in his investigation.

On a Monday morning in June. Treves arrived at St. Mathurin's to find Maudire repairing the front door of his office. She was sitting on the hallway floor removing a screw from the lower hinge. "This has been loose for a while," she said. "Time to get it fixted. Needs either a longer screw or a more fatter screw to stop the wobble, I bleeve. The hole is stripped."

"Thank you, Maudire. I know you know what you're doing."

Maudire removed a long screw from her overalls pocket, and with some effort, drove it into the doorframe. She stood and pushed on the door. It didn't budge. "That done it."

"Have you been to the nurse this morning?"

"Yes, I have."

"Are you ready for me to check your teeth?"

"I am. I don't know how much longer I can eat all them sweets. I think it's makin' me sick." She sat in the examination chair and Treves positioned the clamp in her mouth.

Treves took many notes as he examined her, then removed the camera from the cabinet and took several photographs. Three cavities had appeared in her mouth in just a period of a week. Treves noted which teeth and removed the clamp.

"See anything?" Maudire asked. "What is it you're lookin' for?"

"Just curious about any changes that may happen. Nothing too unusual here."

"I notice some of my teeth hurts now and then."

"That's nothing to worry about. It will pass."

"Doctor... you're a friend of Mr. Pettibone, ain't you?"

"I suppose you could say I am. Not close friends, though."

"But still, you are his keeper, as the Bible says. As his friend you are your brother's keeper."

"Well..."

"Here, we all think you're his friend. We seen you talkin' to him many times. Some of the womens here asted me to ast you to admonish him."

"He is pretty much in charge..."

"The high and mighty will be humbleded."

Treves suddenly saw an expression come over Maudire's face he had never seen before. It startled him to see her eyes go dead but stare at him with an intensity that, for a fleeting moment, terrified him.

"Helene is our precious girl," she continued. "Pettibone has took her in. Only the latest girl to which he has did this. She is his special girl now. He always has one."

"I have heard as much."

"He is surely abusing her. She don't sleep, she can't eat, and she can't talk to us about it. He has took something from her that must be replaced... or revenged."

"No, Maudire. Don't talk that way. I will speak to him about all this. I will."

Treves hoped that his study would have produced enough results in another month or two that he could call it complete.

The day after Treves's conversation with Maudire, Pettibone took an extended leave of absence to care for his dying mother in Baton Rouge.

Something changed immediately at St. Mathurin's when Pettibone left. Treves noticed that the wails and cries of the insane, which were always somewhere in evidence at the asylum, got louder and more pronounced. It seemed, also, that the orderlies charged with containing the activities of the inmates were more apparent and active. Adding to the chaos, a suspected case of diphtheria put the facility under quarantine for a month.

By August, Pettibone had still not returned. On the second Monday of the month, Treves entered the great front door of the asylum to the sounds of screaming and the dull thud of truncheons hitting flesh somewhere just out of sight. Two naked female inmates ran in front of him along the hallway that the entrance intersected, followed by three orderlies carrying straightjackets. Treves's first impulse was to leave the building and suspend his work until Pettibone returned. But the quarantine had already disrupted his schedule. He knew he must continue the investigation immediately or abandon it, and he certainly wanted to retrieve his records for Ostrom's study from potentially vandalizing inmates. Treves tried to ignore the pandemonium as he made his way to his office in the north wing of the old building.

Treves found Maudire and Helene waiting at his door. Helene's face was bruised and swollen, and the suspicion Treves had been germinating for several weeks was now confirmed: The girl was pregnant. Her left hand was wrapped in a dirty bandage. Beatrice suddenly appeared behind Maudire. When she saw Treves, she smiled a black smile.

Maudire looked at Treves with the same cold stare he had seen before. "This girl has been wrongded and so have us, too," she said, turning Helene's face toward Treves. "I knew Pettibone had his way with her. Now she is gonna find a baby. In a few months' time. And look at this!" Maudire squeezed open Helene's cheeks to reveal a nearly solid band of black craters across her teeth.

"Mine too!" Beatrice said, continuing to smile.

"It's just us three," Maudire continued. "Did you do this with your hecksperiment, Dr. Treves?"

"No, no, of course not," Treves frowned. "It's just a coincidence. One of you must be infecting the others. I will try to figure it out."

"Awww, that's just... nonsense," Beatrice grinned."

"What happened to your face, Helene?" Treves said. "And your hand?"

"Pettibone knows she's in a fambly way," Maudire said. "That's why he still ain't back. She tried to ast the orderly, Pickney, to send him a telegram and tell her what she should do. Pickney hit her and pushed her out of the room. He slammed the door on her small finger and crushded it. Can't be fixted. It will have to come off. See this here? Her pretty little hand is ruint." Maudire slipped the bandage off Helene's hand. The small finger was discolored and crushed flat, dangling uselessly from her hand.

"Oh no," Treves said. "Yes, it looks like it will have to come off."

"God provides what is needed. A replacement. A eye for a eye. You see this here?" She pulled a broad, short-bladed knife from her overalls pocket. "This here's a skivving knife. I was gonna repair the leather on the settee in Pettibone's office with this. Right now, I'm gonna find Pickney and replace Helene's finger."

"No, Maudire," Treves voice was urgent and weak with fear. "Don't be foolish. That is superstition. It isn't real. Your grandmother was a superstitious old country woman. I will speak for Helene. I will go to the board and the sheriff, and we will do right by her."

"Ha!" Maudire puffed. She turned and ran toward the main staircase in the lobby. Berenice and Helene followed her. After a moment, Treves ran after them, past orderlies struggling with screaming patients and other inmates cowering in fear in doorways along the corridor.

Male inmates from the men's wing had wandered into the common room on the second floor, drawn by the noise of the unrest. Pickney, a tall, dark-haired man of about thirty, was trying to usher the male inmates back toward their proper area when he turned and saw Maudire and Helene approaching him. He tried to run past them to the staircase, but two grinning male inmates grabbed his arms. They pulled him to the floor and pinioned him.

"Right is right," Maudire snarled as she knelt on Pickney's left arm. "You will replace what you have took from this girl." In a second Maudire flattened Pickney's left hand on the floor and with one chisel-like plunge, severed the little finger. Pickney screamed. The men holding him released him, and the injured man rolled over on his side whimpering in a widening pool of blood.

Maudire wrapped the severed finger inside Helene's bandages, next to her browning, wet wound. Pickney sobbed on the floor. After a moment he stood. When it was apparent that none of the inmates meant to harm him further, he made his way to the staircase.

"Maudire, what have you done?" Treves murmured. "They will put you in a padded room for this."

"I ain't worried about my own self," she said. "I am worried about Berenice and Helene, though. Like me, their teeth is so rotted they cain't hardly eat. We all ain't nothing but black smiles, now." She looked at the male inmates standing behind her. "I think you done this to us on purpose, Doctor."

Treves suddenly felt a profound threat, and he wondered at not feeling to this extent before that moment.

"Sit, Doctor, sit," Maudire indicated a small oak chair against the common room wall. Two of the male inmates escorted Treves to the chair. Maudire closed her eyes as if in prayer. "Replacement," she whispered. "Berenice," she continued, glancing over her shoulder. "It's a toolbox on the corner worktable in the custodian room. It's a pair of pliers in the top tray. Go fetch them for me."

Anabasis

Great God help me. My strength is gone, but I must somehow escape. I cannot let myself fall into the hands of the mob. I heard them outside, bragging of killing Hungarians in Lesterton and Obli, and Hungarians, Greeks, and a Negro in Bonne Terre. I cannot escape to the west, north, or south. I must make my way east to the river.

Viktor, my only friend, lies dead at my feet.

They call my disease the Vampire Sickness. I cannot tolerate sunlight on my pallid flesh, my teeth appear elongated as my gums recede, and my anemia attracts me to blood. The locals believed this, and so did Viktor.

Those of us who came here from Europe to work in the lead mines became the enemy when the United States, at long last, entered the war and began drafting men into the Army. We Europeans were not subject to the draft, so resentment ran high, and this morning the riot began. Many have been killed; many have been loaded onto boxcars to be shipped out. The violence has come to LaMotte now. As the mob surrounded my house, Viktor slashed his wrist, thinking his lifeblood would calm me and give me comfort in my last minutes. Sad to think that my unhappy friend's journey ends in this lonely and alien place.

An explosion up the hill. It is the home of old Zoltan. The gang of men outside my house can see that another group is attacking my neighbor. Could that have been dynamite? The gang runs excitedly up toward the conflagration. Now is my chance to escape. The Webley I gave to Viktor is still on my table. The company store will not sell us cartridges, but I still have some I brought from Budapest. Six, which I found in a drawer after I gave the gun to my friend. I find these and put them in my pocket. I grab the Webley and the razor Viktor had used from the table and open my front door.

The mob's attention is fixed on poor Zoltan. As his house burns, they drag the helpless old man to the road and beat him. Three of the mob's horses graze across the road from my home. The animals were frightened by the blast but have now apparently forgotten it. I am very weak, and the sun blisters my skin. I need to find the strength to reach the nearest horse.

The old mare is a draft horse. The saddle is far too small for her wide back. I am barely strong enough to climb up, but I make it and the mare hardly notices. I then squeeze my calves together and lean forward and the mare begins to walk toward the road. A shout comes from up the hill: "That Hunkie's gettin' away!" Several of the mob begin running down toward me. I urge the mare on, past the few ramshackle buildings in LaMotte toward the train tracks. I will follow these into Ste. Odile.

The ground along the tracks is level and cleared for a long distance, so the mare can run. I crouch low on her back, struggling to find the strength to not fall off. Looking over my shoulder I see that three men have mounted the two horses left behind and are after me. The horse carrying two men stumbles making the turn from the road to the track clearing. It falls to the ground and the men are thrown roughly onto the rail embankment.

I know I will not be able to outrun them like this. Unseen by my pursuers, I turn the mare into the woods and dismount. Suddenly weakness overwhelms me, and I crave some source of vigor. I must act on it or not... immediately. I remove the razor from my pocket and reaching under the mare's belly; I nick a distended vein. The animal protests mildly, but only for a few seconds. Cupping my hand under the trickle, I collect some of the blood and quickly drink it. This, surely this, has made me feel just slightly stronger. Swatting the mare's flank, she continues running east along the clearing. Riderless, she runs at a high rate of speed. I push leaves across the few spots of blood visible and then move further into the woods to hide myself.

I conceal myself in a clump of undergrowth. I lie on the ground and truly feel that I may not have the strength to rise again if I lie there for too long. In another minute or so, my pursuers pass by. They seem to see my mare far ahead of them but cannot tell that I am not mounted upon her. When they are past, I struggle to my feet. I must continue east.

At Ste. Odile there are always skiffs and other boats moored along the banks. If I can take one of them, I can be out of this region by tomorrow. If I can get to the river. This is the fifteenth of the month. The coal barge unloads at the landing tomorrow or the next day. If I could stow away in it, I could get to Cape Girardeau or even Memphis and seek charity from a church.

The forest floor becomes hillier the further east I move. I can walk no more than twenty minutes before I am exhausted. I sit on a boulder, trembling. There are many exposed boulders here. Pink and gray granite. There are small cliffs and chasms, natural arches where the granite gives way to sandstone. A breeze is blowing. I hear a cow mooing over the hill behind me. The sensations all fade away, though, as my exhaustion overwhelms everything else. I wish I could sleep. I need to sleep, but I cannot imagine when I will have the opportunity again. The sunlight through the trees burns my skin. Even so, I must sit for an hour or more to regain my strength.

As I continue walking, I come to a creek bed and make my way down a gully to the water. I smell sassafras nearby. I wash my face for the cooling effect. I drink. Tadpoles scatter in the water as I submerge my hand. I cross the shallow stream to a gradually inclined bank opposite. I hear the rustling of leaves on a hillside nearby. The sound is too loud to be a squirrel or raccoon.

There is an enormous fallen cottonwood tree in front of me. I hide myself in the huge cluster of roots and dirt. I remove the Webley from my haversack, but I remember I still haven't loaded it. So I take the razor from my pocket. The rustling is definitely footsteps.

Through the cluster of roots I see a young boy, ten or eleven years of age, coming toward me. He is carrying a small-bore rifle, a .22, I assume, looking up into the trees as he walks. He is walking directly toward me. I will not be able to hide from him. He steps past the end of the root bundle and suddenly sees me. Monster that I now am, he screams. He drops his gun and runs back in the direction from which he has come.

I must hurry on, but first, I load the pistol. As I leave, I lean the boy's rifle against the fallen tree so he may easily find it if he returns. I know the creek eventually finds its way to the river. I could follow it and probably more easily avoid detection, but the route would be meandering and difficult. I decide to continue to follow the train tracks.

The track easement is still mostly cleared and level. A fawn up ahead seems curious about me but not afraid. The doe trots out of the underbrush and circles the fawn once, who then follows her into the thicket. The track gradually curves to the southeast. The afternoon train is due at any time. I am not sure what time it is now but assume it must be late afternoon.

I hear the train, perhaps a mile to the west. I have plenty of time to hide. There is a cluster of saplings nearby, along a barbed wire fence. As I step into it, I hear a yipping sound followed by a growl. A coyote is caught in a steel trap and enmeshed in the wire of the fence. Its right forepaw has been crushed by the trap. It is bloodied and a broken bone has pushed through its skin. I cannot disentangle it, and if it is freed, it will not survive long in this condition.

The train passes. The coyote growls at me as I grasp its muzzle to hold it shut. I slash the poor creature's throat with the razor. In a moment it is still. I press its throat to my mouth. I feel slightly but noticeably revived. It is time for a rest. I do my best to stay covered in shade. The few spots where the sunlight touches my skin for more than a moment begin to blister.

I have consumed no food all day. I am concerned about my blood craving. Dr. Treves at Ste. Odile told me most physicians say it is a natural manifestation of porphyria, while others claim this craving is imaginary and appears only within the most suggestible personality. With every passing moment, it feels more real to me.

The walking seems endless, the distance to town, impossible. In addition to exhaustion, I feel pain in every part of my body. The sun is getting low. I cannot stop until I have reached town. I wonder if the men looking for me have doubled back yet. Surely by now they have realized I eluded them along the train easement.

I am past the forest now. There are cultivated fields on both sides of the track and mostly saplings and weeds—very few mature trees. A farmer at the edge of his field does not notice me. He is chopping undergrowth with a brush hook in the last light of the day.

Whippoorwills have begun to call. I hear the distant snort of a horse and see that the men chasing me have returned. They have recaptured the mare I took and all three are mounted separately now. They see the farmer's movement in the field and in the dimming light and must assume it is me. They speed their pace.

A wide drive onto the farmer's field just ahead of me covers a galvanized culvert. It is the only place I can hide. The culvert is wide enough to accommodate me, but just barely. There are rubble, twigs, and water in the culvert, and it is very dark. Climbing in far enough to conceal myself from head to foot, my face is only a few feet from the opposite opening.

I hear the horse's hooves. They are running now. I hear them pass over me on the drive. They are shouting at the farmer and heading in his direction. Then there are hooves on the drive above me again. I hear someone dismount and walk toward the culvert opening. A thin, dirty man in overalls crouches to investigate the culvert. The interior is too dark for him to immediately make me out. With a momentary advantage, I slash across his throat with the razor. No sound comes from him but a faint gurgle. He grasps the wound but quickly falls into the unconscious precursor to death. His lifeblood spills out onto the mud and weeds.

A terrible impulse overwhelms me; I grasp him savagely and hold my mouth to his throat. He breathes his last as I sputter the salty ambrosia. I have taken too much. I cough and spew the liquid and gasp for air. But I feel invigorated. I must get out of the culvert. As I climb past the dead man, I see his tobacco pouch, papers, and matches in his overall pocket. I take these and climb out.

The horse I abandoned earlier is grazing indifferently near the fence. I struggle onto her back and bury my heels in her sides. She bolts, nearly throwing me off. As I speed away toward the east, I glance over my shoulder and see the other two pursuers have dismounted and discovered their dead friend. At a curve in the tracks to the southeast, I turn off the easement onto a footpath through the woods that I know eventually connects to the Belgique Road. The ground is intermittently damp, and hoofprints must be visible near puddles and pools. I am out of the line of vision of the other men, so I hope they do not see the prints and continue along the tracks. If their interest in pursuing me had begun to wane, my actions would have revived it. They will be relentless. And if they catch me, my death will not be a quick one.

It seems they have lost me. I slow my horse. It is dangerous to run a horse on a path like this in the near dark. But even at this pace, I should be to the Belgique Road in less than an hour. It is a clear, warm night and the full moon will be rising soon.

A sudden wave of shame washes over me. I have drunk the blood of a man. The lower creatures—the horse, the coyote—are one thing, but I have now sunk to a depth I have never imagined. What if this becomes an obsession I cannot resist? How will I satisfy it among the innocent? A month ago, I would have never thought this horror could be dormant in my nature. But now I see myself, indeed the world, differently. I see evidence of a vesicle, an artery leading to a stygian region where profanities have received the benediction of a new reality and interpretation.

As I reach the Belgique Road, the whole landscape is awash in silver moonlight. I hear something in the distance behind me. A horse. Two horses. I urge my mare to run to the north, to Ste. Odile and the riverfront. Just as the mare is beginning to get winded, I see the lights of Ste. Odile below me. At the southern end of town, the Belgique Road becomes Levee Street. In veering to the right, I am on the riverfront.

The town is nearly deserted. A few dim lights glow from behind curtains or at the doorways of taverns or restaurants. The moon glimmers beautifully on the wide water of the river. Beyond boats, rafts, barges, and one steam packet, I see the main landing at the north end of the downtown riverbank. A black hulk of a commercial craft sits at the end of the landing ramp, moored with the aft extended out into the water. It is the coal barge. I urge the mare on past dark buildings, quiet houses, and a drunken man asleep on the roadside.

As I approach the barge, I can see the loading doors elevated slightly at the middle of the deck are slid open. The barge has just recently been unloaded.

I stop the mare at the gatepost of the landing and tie her up there. I want to leave her in a very conspicuous place but at a safe distance. I dismount and approach the barge. No one is there. I call down into the hold, but there is no answer. The barge is deserted for the night.

I remove the Webley from my pack and place it on the deck in front of the sliding loading doors. In the moonlight it is plainly visible. The sliding doors are mounted in a raised compartment on the deck. Behind this are wide ventilation flues and an iron post with an unlit lantern on it. There are four glazed panels set in the deck to allow natural light into the hold below. I hide myself behind the compartment.

I wonder if my pursuers will follow me here. Being a draft horse, my mare has left enormous hoofprints. They should be easy enough to track. The men must know my best chance of escape is on the river. I wonder if they will go to the sheriff or keep this a personal affair, wanting to finish me themselves? I light the lantern above me.

In just a few minutes I hear voices and the clopping of horses' hooves. I can make out the two mounted men at the far end of the street. They speed their pace when they see the mare tied up at the gate.

"That's Wilmer's mare all right," one of them says.

"Tie up here. Let's check the barge," the other responds. "Lantern lit. Might be somebody here."

They step onto the iron plate deck. One of the men spots the revolver immediately. "Looky here," he says.

"Bet it's that Hunkie's gun," the other responds. "It's a foreign gun." They look tentatively into the dark hold. "Keep quiet now. I bet he's a-hidin' down there."

"Why would he leave the horse in plain sight?"

"Shuddup."

They both step carefully into the hold. I give them a few seconds to reach the bottom of the ladder. I then move quickly to the front of the chamber and slide the doors closed. I trip the latch. I return to the rear of the chamber. I remove the burning lantern from its post. It just fits into the ventilation pipe. I drop it in.

The explosion from the igniting coal dust tears the roof partially away from the chamber. The concussion throws me off the end of the barge into the water.

I am not sure if I am dead or alive. I am on my back, floating, looking up at the sky. Part of a timber has blown off the superstructure of the deck and I realize I am holding it as I float. I am completely deaf. The water laps at my pallid cheeks as I drift, watching the moon above me. I have no strength left. I hope I am strong enough to hold onto the beam. The blood that must be on my face and clothes is surely washing away. I feel the current moving me. It is strong here. I am quickly being carried away from the landing and out into the main channel of the big river.

Now the stars are more visible. Streaks and smudges of galaxies, gasses, and billions of stars. Unimaginable. I have no place in this wonder. The river is black around me—and under me, where live ancient giants waiting in the depths for my livid corpse to drift down to them. I should join them. Below, in the darkness. I have no place here.

Draco spins above me. Inconceivably distant. Who else looks at it as I am now? What are their circumstances and fears? What hopes course through their bodies? Circulate through their bodies? I will only know once I reach them. Now they wait, dully, in Belgique or Perry or further south perhaps, on a humid, muddy bank. I will know, at length. But I must reach them.

The Plank Road

I

The bull calf had hanged himself. Virgil would have thought it was an act of vandalism by an enemy or cruel farm boys who torture animals for fun if he hadn't seen it before as a boy out at Hopewell. The calf had tried to graze through the barbed wire at the creek's bank, and the bank gave way, hanging the animal whose head was entangled in the wire. The young bull's legs were stiff and extended, the body starting to bloat. It was another setback Virgil could not afford.

Virgil's wife Rina had read bird signs and root magic and predicted they would have no such bad luck this year. She'd done the same last year before their son burned the chicken coop playing with matches. The poorer you are, the more bad luck will likely find you. *If* bad luck was real. Virgil didn't really believe Rina's nonsense anyway.

Virgil managed to pull the carcass up onto the bank and relieve the tension on the wire. He pulled the calf out of it and dragged the body some distance from the edge. He thought for a moment about whether he wanted to bury the animal or leave it for the coyotes and buzzards.

He heard horse's hooves on the gravel a few hundred feet up the creek bed. It was old Horvath, Csepel Horvath, on his mare. The old man seemed to be searching for something on the high dirt bank opposite. Horvath was one of the Hungarians—the Hunkies—who Virgil and the other lead miners had not killed or run out of town during the riot back in 1917. He was a harmless old widower. Retired. He wasn't any kind of threat to the miner's jobs when the conscription started and the Americans were being shipped off to war.

The old man was acting oddly. Virgil stepped behind a cottonwood tree and watched him. Horvath seemed to find the spot he was looking for on the bank. He slid slowly off the mare and looked at the spot for a long time. "Sár Ember," he said, or something like it. "Sár Ember?"

Horvath mumbled some other words which Virgil assumed were Hungarian, and repeated a word, Ordog, several times. The old man removed a canteen from his saddle and emptied the contents on the spot on the embankment upon which he had been focusing. Virgil heard more mumbled words, and then Horvath remounted his horse and returned the way from which he had come.

The immigrants, mostly Hunkies, Osage Lead had brought in

before the war for cheap labor had many odd customs. Their strange festivals and celebrations that didn't seem Christian, their colorful clothes and their way of jabbering in their own language around Americans didn't make them more welcome in Ste. Odile County.

Virgil dragged the dead calf further out into the open. He decided to let the buzzards have it. He removed his pliers from his overalls and began to repair his fence.

II

The Plank Road had been built by Osage Lead during the Civil War to transport processed lead ore from the mine at Lesterton to the landing on the Mississippi at Ste. Odile. It was all oak planks and timbers and bore thousands of tons of ore during the war and remained in service for nearly thirty years afterward. By the time the war in Europe started and demand for lead grew, a rail line had been built. The old road fell into disrepair and rotted over the next ten years or so, until the Hunkies and other immigrants brought in to work the mines started tearing up the planks for firewood.

The lead company had an old easement that ran across the southern edge of the McElwrath family property. A month before the conscription was announced and the riot broke out, Virgil was out riding his fence line, looking for damage that needed repair. When he heard pounding on the planks up ahead in the woods, he dismounted. He checked the Smith and Wesson .44 he always carried when he rode the property. He slowly walked toward the sound. As he moved past a stand of dogwood trees, he could see a young man with an axe and prybar harvesting the planks and piling them on a small cart.

"What the hell you a-doin'?" Virgil called. The young man, whose back was toward Virgil, ignored him. "Hey! I'm talkin' to you. Private proppity! Hey!"

Strangely, the young man continued to ignore Virgil.

"Goddammit!" Virgil said as a sudden wave of rage overtook him, "I tolt you damned Hunkies to stay off my land. Don't you ignore me you son of a bitch! You won't ignore this..." before he realized he was doing it, Virgil raised the revolver and fired. The bullet hit the young man square between his shoulders, and he fell to the easement face down.

Virgil was stunned at what he had done. He could hardly believe it. He was within his rights, surely he was. This man was trespassing. After many warnings to the immigrants, he was trespassing. Virgil ran to the fallen man. The man was breathing slightly. His face was turned to his right and Virgil was horrified to see that it was not a young man he had shot. It was a boy.

Virgil had seen him before and thought he was tall for his age, but he didn't know his name. It seemed the boy could tell Virgil was there but could not see him well. The boy mumbled a few words in his native language. The only word Virgil recognized was Lillafüred. Virgil knew this to be the village from which most of the Hungarians in that area had come.

Virgil stood. He felt completely empty and helpless. On the cart piled with planks, he noticed an ear trumpet. He realized this was the deaf boy he had heard about from the other miners underground. The boy exhaled his last as blood sputtered out of his wound. He was dead.

Virgil felt for a moment that none of this had happened. He had to decide what to do, but his mind went blank. He sat on the Plank Road and thought. He was expected in town. He decided he would hide the body and come back later to bury it. He dragged the corpse into the underbrush twenty feet from the easement. He covered it with leaves, brambles, and a rotted log. He then scattered the planks the boy had harvested in the undergrowth and with the boy's axe, he broke up his wooden cart. Looking to the east, along the Plank Road, Virgil saw that his fence, crossing the old road at the edge of his property, was down. The boy he'd killed must have thought the farm was abandoned.

Virgil restrung the fence as best he could. He had to get back home. It was Sunday. He had a baseball game to pitch. He was expected. He would have to come back to bury the body that night.

"You look like you done put in a day's work," Rina said when Virgil got home.

"A lot of repairs to do. I gotta warsh up and git goin'."

"I heerd a gunshot a while ago."

"Yeah. It was a bobcat up a tree. I thought it might hurt ol' Eugene."

Rina frowned. "Eugene was here the whole time. On the porch. The shot woke him up."

"I meant the horse... Jimmy, not the dog. How come you askin' so many questions? I shot to skeer the cat off. Where's C. O.? He wanted to come to the game today."

"He was a-playin' with that Pirtle kid last I seen. Won't see him for a while. Sometimes I think we oughta start a-goin' to church again. People don't think much of people that don't go to church." Rina was thin and already showing gray hair, although she wasn't yet thirty years old.

"I ain't a-gonna. Damned if I'm gonna spend six days underground and then half of the seventh in church. I'll go to church when I'm retired. If you wanna go... go. Far as I can tell, God don't care that much what we do in this life."

"If we get in that war over yonder and you get drafted... well, I hope you don't find out you's wrong someday." Virgil brushed past her and into their bedroom. "What's wrong with you today?" she said.

Virgil pulled his shirt off at the washbowl and began to wash himself with a cloth draped over the edge of the bowl. "Ain't nothin' wrong with me but too much damn work and too many questions!"

On Sundays when Rina and C. O. went to Virgil's baseball games in Lesterton, Virgil hitched Jimmy to the trap. That didn't happen often. On Sundays when he went alone, Virgil rode the old horse, bareback sometimes, the seven miles into the town.

Virgil was off his game that day. His team of miners, the Lesterton Blues, lost 3-0 to the Louisville Brakemen, a Negro league team working its way to Kansas City.

Just after twilight back at home, Virgil went back out to the woods to bury the dead boy. He thought he would reset the planks the boy tore off. There was no reason to do this, useless and in the way as the road was, except he considered it keeping his word to his father. He found the spot where the planks were torn off the old road, and the rotted log he had covered the boy with, but the body was gone.

III

Virgil and most of the draftees from Ste. Odile County were placed in the 35th Division, 140th Infantry Regiment in 1917 and saw action in the Meuse-Argonne offensive, taking heavy losses. Biz Macke had been a muleskinner and Bill Kopp a blacksmith underground, and both had been Virgil's teammates on the Blues. Both were killed at Argonne. After the Armistice, Virgil and the rest of the returning Ste. Odile County men were bitter and more certain than ever that driving the foreigners out violently before the war had been the right thing to do. Profit was all the lead company cared about, and they knew none of them would have been rehired. After returning from his service, after seeing the wider world and what it could sink to, Virgil swore he would never set foot in a church again.

Virgil's younger brother, Floyd, was too young for the draft. When Virgil shot the deaf boy, Floyd was the one person Virgil considered telling about it, but he didn't. He couldn't confess murder to his little brother. Yet, a month later, when the riot broke out, Virgil participated in the violence like most of the men across the county and encouraged his young brother to join in.

The Monday morning after the Blues's loss to the Louisville Brakemen, the early shift at Number 3 gathered under the headframe to wait for the cage to take them underground. Floyd was just hired after the Armistice and worked on Virgil's crew of hand-loaders.

"You look a little rough today, boy." Leo Whaley said.

"Aw, I'm all right," Floyd answered. He yawned.

"You still keepin' company with that Lou Sparks gal?" Boog Powell asked.

"Not no more," Floyd said. "She ditched me for some damn reason."

Boog smiled at Leo. "Never mind about it," Boog said, scratching his chin with his Masonic ring. "Some other feller in some other ditch was a-waitin' on her, probly."

All the men laughed. Virgil tried not to. He had warned Floyd about Lou Sparks.

"Yeah, yeah," Floyd scowled, "You-uns is real funny."

The cage arrived at the loading deck and all the men moved into it. Andy Demay pulled the gate closed and they started to descend into the shaft. Nobody spoke for a long time. The temperature got cooler as the cage descended.

"Virgil," Norman Insill said after a while, "you 'member that German kid at Argonne was carryin' that gas canister and he got blowed up and burned alive?"

"I ain't forgot that," Virgil said. "I ain't forgot none of it."

"He weren't but about Floyd's age at the time. Germans musta been more desperater than we was, puttin' kids like that out there. I think it was me blowed him up."

"I shot at him too," Delbert Carter put in. "But I'm pretty sure I missed him."

"What we gotta do to beat them House of Davids on Wednesday, Virgil?" Bud Sibole said. Any subject but baseball didn't hold Bud's attention for long.

"I hafta get my arm back, I guess," Virgil said, "and get my brains workin' right again."

The cage reached the bottom of the shaft and the men filed out. They made their way to the locker room where they left lunch pails and water jugs. Virgil and Floyd made their way to Number 8 where a new drift was being cut. The Davies lamps mounted into the walls of the drift lighted the way, and in a few hundred feet they had come to the end of the drift. A mule everyone called Thunderbolt was hitched and ready to haul out the ore the night crew had loaded and be replaced by the day shift cars. When Thunderbolt and his load were out of the way, Cup Eyes Wampler backed another mule named Woodrow Wilson and his empty cars into the drift.

"Why you still a-doin' this backbreakin' job?" Floyd asked his brother. "I would'a bid out long time ago if I was you."

"I don't want to be a shift boss, I don't want nothin' to do with explosives, and I don't want to give this place another thought oncet I'm gone for the day. Just wanna keep it simple. Eighteen tons and I'm out. When I get up of a morning, I know they ain't nothin' I can do in this idiot job to get me in trouble. Long as I score out every day."

Floyd stepped over the shaft and traces connecting Woodrow Wilson's harness to the first ore car, over to the other side of the track. He started loading ore into the car nearest him. "First thing comes along," he said, "I'm gonna bid on it. I wouldn't mind bein' a shift boss one of these days. We'll see if them sons 'o bitches laughs at me then."

Virgil walked to the opposite end of the cars and started loading from his side. Two more men joined them to load in the drift. The brothers said nothing to each other as the first cars were loaded.

Virgil thought of the deaf boy he killed every day. He had killed a man the day of the riot in town. He killed at least two Germans in the war. He didn't know why killing the boy should affect him in a different way than those others. A deaf boy who couldn't hear Virgil's warning, who didn't know he was on private property. A boy, big as he was, who couldn't have been older than twelve.

Virgil's grandfather had helped build the Plank Road. He was proud of it. Virgil's father promised the old man he would not destroy what was left of the road on the easement across their farm. When Virgil inherited the property, he thought the old road was a nuisance and occupying land he could use for grazing or planting. The land was rocky and poor, but there were some areas that he could have planted. Still, it was important to his father and grandfather, and he meant to always leave it undisturbed.

Virgil always wondered when he thought of the dead boy what had happened to his body. Virgil wondered if animals had taken it, or if there was someone out there who had seen what he had done, someone who was going to come forward someday. Killing an enemy in battle was war; killing men in a violent riot could be called self-defense, but shooting a child was just murder.

Virgil wanted a drink. He wanted to drink more now than he did before the war. He knew all his teammates did, too. The Sheriff was against Prohibition, and he didn't put much effort into keeping the county dry. Rina told Virgil he needed to control his drinking, or she and C. O. would be gone. She had been through that with her father; she wasn't going to put up with it from her husband. And when Rina said a thing, she meant it.

Virgil had been hand-loading since he was sixteen. He did the job without thinking about it. Otherwise, the days seemed too long. He would be thirty-five in August. His back was still not bothering him too much, but his right shoulder pained him after an hour or so of loading. That was part of his problem on the pitching mound. The other part was his thinking. He didn't know if he lost his confidence or will but there was a hole in everything he used to value, as if nothing was worth doing anymore. He thought most of the day about how he could get past that—if he ever could. He wanted to remember how to take pride in being a good father, a good husband and worker. And he wanted to stop his losing streak and beat the House of Davids on Wednesday.

IV

Csepel Horvath felt he had lived too long. His sons had come with him and his wife to America in 1913. They knew trouble was brewing in Europe. When the war broke out in the Balkans, the two boys returned home to fight. Both were killed in action. Zsofia, his wife, died in 1917. After the riot of spring of that year, most of his countrymen, the Hungarians, were driven out of the territory. He was a useless old widower, so he was left alone. Now he was adrift and alone in a strange and unfriendly land.

To house the new immigrant workforce, Osage Lead had built villages of detached houses and rowhouses on its lands around LaMotte, Lesterton, and Obli. Csepel and Zsofia and their sons had been placed in a row house strangely situated in the woods a mile from LaMotte. Of the original attached four houses built in the row, all were now abandoned but Csepel's on the west end. Since the purge of the riot, the weeds and saplings of the hardwood forest had begun reclaiming the property.

Csepel found some beauty and comfort in the woods in which his home was immersed, but it did not compare to his home in Hungary, back in Lillafüred. The town was surrounded by unspoiled mountains and scenic valleys. His family's small wooden home was several kilometers from the town, up a mountainside. The property was level enough so that they could subsistence farm. Zsofia provided a small income, from those few who could pay her, with spells and philtres and midwifery. She was Boszarkany—a witch.

The old religion never completely disappeared from the mountains and remote valleys. Yes, Christianity had come to dominate over the centuries, but it never fully addressed the needs of the isolated people of the forests. The spirit, the sentience, the harmonies, and the terrors of nature were never accounted for or understood by the new religion.

Zsofia did not use her knowledge for any evil purpose, although she had great knowledge of evil. Her life work, like her mother and grandmother, was to ward it off. Like them, she never refused help to anyone who needed it, whether they could pay her anything or not. She kept generations-old scraps of paper and animal skins with formulas and incantations for everything from breech birth to infections and made Csepel her Gyam, or guardian of her secrets.

All those immigrants from the region of Lillafüred who were settled in the area north of LaMotte near Csepel, including his family, still used Zsofia's services in the new land. After her sons were killed, whatever gift Zsofia had as Boszarkany disappeared. She lay in her bed for nearly three months waiting to die.

As resentment against her people grew among the Americans, Zsofia decided there was further knowledge she needed to impart to her husband. A defrocked Jesuit had told Zsofia's great-grandmother of the mystical investigations of Athanasius Kircher, centuries earlier. Kircher, also a Jesuit, spent a lifetime researching esoteric clues Kabbala holds regarding the revelation of the Trinity and the mysteries of the name of God. He learned that for this knowledge to survive, its keepers must be shielded from the powers of darkness. In the right circumstance, a corporeal presence of protection, revenge, and terror must be called forth. In the tradition of the old religion, this being was known as Sar Ember.

As Zsofia faded away in her bed, Csepel had no idea what he was to do with the new knowledge she had given him. On the day he was cutting sassafras in the creek bed and saw Virgil McElwrath murder the deaf boy, Barnat Szabo, he began to understand. He knew that the only way there would be retribution for his people would be if he kept what he had seen a secret for now.

He watched Virgil from the bushes until the murderer hurriedly moved away in the direction of his farmhouse. Csepel then dragged the dead boy from the easement, down toward the creek bed. Someday he would tell the boy's family what had become of him.

V

"How come your dad can't pitch no more?" Dickie Pirtle said. He stooped to rinse out his Smile soda bottle in the green water of the Mill Pond. The pond was a shallow, one-acre lagoon that had formed in the hundreds of yards-wide artificial desert made by Osage Lead from dumping tailings sand left over from the ore crushing process. "My dad says his fastball wouldn't bust a window-light."

"His shoulder hurts him," C. O. McElwrath said. "He just gotta get his arm back."

"I hope he gets it back for the House of Davids tonight. I hate it when we lose to them. My dad says we gotta have one or two more pitchers."

"If your dad knows so much, why don't he play baseball?"

"His knee give out. He can't do nothin' like that no more."

"Never could, I bet."

"Aw, shut up. I bet he could if he wanted to." Dickie rubbed his right eye.

"How come you're doing that so much today?" C. O. asked. "What's wrong with your eye?"

"I' a sty in it, I guess."

"Did you piss in the road? My mom says boys that piss in the road get a sty. She knows wildcraft."

"Naw, I never done that."

An injured butterfly flopped on the sand at C. O.'s feet. C. O. pulled some dry fronds from a dead cedar tree sapling someone had dropped on the ground nearby. He made a pile of the fronds and put the injured butterfly on top of it. He removed a match from his overall pocket and lit the small pile. The insect fluttered for a few seconds and was still.

"You're gonna set yourself on fire one of these days," Dickie said.

"Let's head to town. Wanna get there before the game starts. You can cash your bottle at Johnson's."

"You're always mad at your dad. How come you wanna go to his game?"

"Dunno. Somethin' to do. He might win a game one of these days."

The boys crossed the tailings dunes toward the northwest. They passed the dead snapping turtle they had seen earlier, rotting in the sun. C. O. saw these animals often. Snapping turtles and terrapins. He figured they started across the desert and moved so slowly they couldn't make it across before the sun and thirst killed them. This turtle had become too weak to walk beyond this spot but had not died. Dickie said he saw that somebody shot it a few times last week with a .22, but it stayed alive. Every day for four days, Dickie noticed more bullet holes in the animal until finally, on the fifth day, it died. As they passed the carcass, a crow landed next to it and began tearing at the flesh.

"I would'a shot it if I had a gun," C. O. said.

When the boys came to the creek, they followed it northwest. They crossed a narrow strip of land owned by the Wiehardts and then were on McElwrath's back pasture headed for the Plank Road. The snorting of a horse in the creek bed startled C. O. He moved into the bushes at the edge of the creek and Dickie followed him. They saw the old man Horvath dismounting his mare in the creek bed. The old man removed a wooden bucket looped over his saddle horn and filled it with water from the creek. The mare was dragging something like a travois behind her. Horvath said a few words the boys could not make out and then drenched the dirt bank in front of him with the water. He repeated this action twice more.

"He ain't doin' a Christian thing..." Dickie said. "What's he doin'?"

"Dunno," C. O. said, "He usually collects sassafras. We ain't got time to find out. Mom said to stay away from him. She'll whup me if I don't. It's some crazy stuff that don't concern us." He stepped back out to the pasture and Dickie followed.

The boys continued to the McElwrath property, and to the Plank Road. They began to follow it toward Lesterton.

VI

Horvath tied one end of his rope to the saddle horn. He took the other end to the creek bank and cut the rope with two feet of excess so he could tie it. Reaching into the mud he had created he found the leather cord he was looking for inside. He pushed the cut end of the rope into the mud and looped it around the hidden cord. He tied it off. He unhitched the travois from behind the horse and slowly led her away from the bank.

"Sár Ember, itt az idéje felébredni." Horvath said.

Slowly the mare pulled the hulking, mud-slathered anatomy from the saturated bank. Wrists, arms, drooping head, sagging torso, endless legs: all slowly emerged and slid heavily down the creek bank. It lay on its back.

"Sár Ember, itt az idéje felébredni." Horvath repeated. He filled his bucket with water and poured it over the figure. He prayed the prayer of profane rebirth to Ordog. What was once a boy was now a terrible being.

"I have... succeeded," Horvath said.

The being's face was distorted by the transformation. The symmetry of the eyes was lost. The mouth gaped upward to where the nose should be, a black gash in a face incapable of expression. The skin was the reddish color of the clay in which it was incubated and comprised of segments or plates that did not conjoin with each other perfectly. The black eyes, each in its quadrant, opened. The tattered mouth was wet inside, a good sign, and the pink larva of the tongue writhed in it like a snake in a steel trap.

"Sar Ember," Horvath said. "You have come into being. Child of Ordog of old. I am Gyam, the guardian. I direct you to your purpose until the time you speak the name of the man cursed to replace you. If that is needed, you will name him."

Horvath guided the mare to drag the body onto the travois, which he then re-hitched to the horse. He mounted and headed back toward his home, certain that his departed wife was smiling on him from above.

VII

The House of Davids team was always a spectacle. They came through barnstorming once a season, and the crowd for that game was usually three times the crowd size for any other game. By the time they arrived in their brightly painted bus, Daniel Newcomb Park was already overrun with spectators from Lesterton, Oubli, LaMotte, Bonne Terre, and Ste. Odile. A crowd surrounded the bus after it parked near the road and cheered the team as it filed out laden with equipment bags, gloves, water cans, extra bats and balls, and sack suppers. The Davids were dressed in their white with blue pinstripe uniforms, and all wore the waist-length hair and beards their religious sect was known for.

"You-uns looks like cave mens!" a boy yelled as the team pushed toward the field, smiling and waving. A young girl touched the hair of a player as he passed her. Another player made a hoot-hoot ape sound as the team began unloading their burdens in the visitor dugout on the third base line.

Virgil and the Blues had warmed up earlier. Dan Whalen, the manager, had stopped coming to the games a month before. There was cancer in his bones, and he appointed Virgil as player/manager. As the House of Davids took the field to warm up, Virgil made out his roster:

Bird Brain McIntyre RF
Cup Eyes Wampler CF
Delbert Carter LF
Boog Powell 1B
Norman Insill SS
Bones Teeter 3B
Bud Sibole C
Andy Demay 2B
Virgil McElwrath P

The Davids warmed up quickly, the infield taking ground balls, outfielders playing catch, and extra players stretching or doing calisthenics. As they began to slowly return to their dugout, three of the infielders lined up on the third base line and began their "pepper game," flipping the ball overhanded and underhanded to each other, doing sleight of hand tricks and juggling to the delight of the spectators.

"Sure likes to show off, don't they? "Cup Eyes Wampler said.

"Brings the crowd out," Virgil said. "Like with the Brakemen. People wants a show, and they get it."

"You said a mouthful there," Bud Sibole said. "Just a good ballgame ain't enough for 'em anymore. How's the arm feelin', Virgil?"

Virgil shrugged. "Same as always, I guess. We'll see how it goes."

The caretaker at Daniel Newcombe Park, Otto Schmidt, played a recording of "The Star-Spangled Banner" over the loudspeaker, and home plate umpire Tom Banke shouted, "Play Ball."

Since early June after Jasper Phelan broke his arm when he wrecked his DeSoto, Virgil had been the Blues's only pitcher. Dan Whelan had been trying to bring Ernie Riegler over from the Bismark Chancellors, and the deal was almost done when Ernie changed his mind.

The Blues took the field sluggishly. The infielders tossed a ball around as Virgil began his warmup pitches to Bud Sibole. Virgil's first two pitches were high out of the strike zone and Sibole had to stand to catch them. "Down, Virgil," Sibole said. "Not up there where they can see 'em. Keep 'em down or they'll hit 'em all to the Mississippi."

Virgil nodded. He was tired. When he was tired it was always harder to keep the ball low in the strike zone. Virgil scratched at the pitcher's mound with his foot and wondered why he still tried to play baseball. He enjoyed it most of the time, but at other times it seemed like a responsibility he had grown tired of.

He and Floyd shared a room at a boarding house in Lesterton during the work week. His free time was Saturday evening at home and Sunday. He didn't farm much anymore. He had chickens and two pigs and three head of cattle. Rina took care of them. He didn't know how he would spend his free time if he had more of it. He would be inclined to drink, and Rina wouldn't stand for that.

After his last warm-up pitch, Sibole threw the ball back to Virgil. He stood up behind the plate and yelled out at his teammates, "You-uns show some life out there. Let's see some pep!"

The leadoff batter for the Davids was a small man who hit Virgil's first pitch into short right field and got thrown out at second base trying to stretch the hit into a double. The second and third batters both grounded out to shortstop.

In the Blues's half of the inning, Bird Brain McIntyre struck out leading off. Cup Eyes Wampler singled to left field and stole second base. Delbert Carter struck out, but Boog Powell hit a single to second, scoring Wampler. Norman Insill hit a line drive back to the pitcher and the inning was over.

Sibole slapped Virgil on the back as he ran past him as the Blues took the field. "One up. Now let's hold 'em Virgil!" he said.

Virgil always felt more was expected of him when the team was winning than when it was losing. He rubbed the baseball between his hands and wound his right arm around a few times. Glancing at the sidelines he saw C. O. and the Pirtle kid buying penny pretzels from the vendor. He was glad and a little surprised his son had made it all the way in from LaMotte for the game.

Virgil threw a warm-up fastball low in the strike zone, and then another. He dug at the mound and looked toward the crowd again. A tall boy in overalls was making his way to a seat in the back row. A tall, familiar boy. Virgil dropped the baseball. "Can't be... can't be!" he mumbled to himself.

Virgil stood up straight. Sibole was waiting for another pitch, but Virgil shook him off. Virgil walked across the mound, then turned and walked back the other way. He looked to where the tall boy had been a few seconds before, but the boy was not to be seen. Virgil pounded the ball into his mitt a few times and noticed old man Horvath standing at the road's edge a great distance away.

"Keep your head about you Ol' Sling," Sibole called. "Let's keep it goin'. Come on, now!"

Virgil looked at the stands again. He still did not see the tall boy. He thought he must have imagined him. He looked toward Horvath. The old man was walking away toward his horse tied to a tree. He mounted the mare and headed out of town.

Virgil felt he had lost all concentration. He had to focus on the batter walking to the plate and that catcher's mitt behind it. He thought again about the boy he killed. He thought about where the impulse had come from to shoot him. And the terrifying question returned: Where had the body gone?

A thin man with long red hair and beard stepped to the plate. He tapped the plate with his bat. Virgil collected himself for his first pitch. The batter stepped out of the batter's box, stretched, and made exaggerated gestures of checking the wind direction and looking down the length of his bat to make sure it was straight. Some of the crowd laughed and cheered him on. He stepped back into the box and Virgil began his wind-up again. The batter stepped out a second time and Virgil stumbled off the pitching rubber in an effort to stop his motion. "Get in the box and stay there!" Tom Banke shouted at the batter from behind home plate.

Virgil took a moment to collect himself. He made his wind-up and threw the ball. The pitch went over Sibole's head and into the back screen. The batter made a comic surprised expression and put his hand over his eyebrows as if he were looking for something in the far distance. Virgil threw his glove to the ground and charged home toward the batter. "Make fun of me... you son of a bitch!" Virgil yelled.

Sibole jumped to his feet and blocked Virgil's advance, throwing his arms around him. "Calm down, calm down, Ol' Sling. Just part of the show, that's all. Its nothin'... nothin' at all."

The Blues infielders all ran in and surrounded Virgil. The Davids approached from their dugout, but their player/manager stopped them.

"Slow down boys," the manager said. "This is under control. It's okay."

Virgil saw that C. O. was watching him from the stands. Virgil felt his anger fade into humiliation, "It's all right, fellas. I ain'ta gonna do nothin'."

"It's just them horsin' around," Sibole said, releasing Virgil. "Don't mean nothin'."

"I know," Virgil muttered. "Made a damn fool outta myself. Don't know what's wrong lately."

"Can you go on?" Sibole asked.

"Probly not. I need to calm down. I don't want to forfeit," Virgil said.

"We can pull Delbert out of left field," Sibole said. "He can pitch."

"Joe Villner's in the stand over yonder," Andy Demay said. "I shag fly balls with him sometimes. He can still play. See if he'll play in left. Ain't got no uniform, though."

Sibole took charge of the roster changes as Tom Banke joined them from behind home plate and rewrote his score sheet. Virgil never looked in the direction of the stands as he walked away from the group toward the road, and back toward town and his boarding house.

VIII

Win or lose, the Blues always met at Joe Burley's Tavern after the Wednesday night game. The Davids game was a big loss. The visitors scored nine runs in the third inning and four more in the sixth, for a final score of thirteen to one. "I think ol' Virgil's done for," Andy Demay said. "Don't remember the last time he throwed a good game."

"Dan Whelan done and told me makin' Virgil player/manager was a mistake," Sibole said. "He's too high-strung and got that temper... I think after today Dan may kick him off the team altogether."

"Well, sorry to say it, but we won't be losin' much," Boog Powell said. "He been talkin' about the war a lot lately, and the riot we had. His mind is on stuff like that these days. What's done is done. We did right, I think. Thought so then, and I still think so."

"It's old news, but some fellers takes a while before their shell shock shows up, I heerd. Feel bad for him," McIntyre said. "Without the team, I don't know what ol' Virgil will do with hisself."

"Goes for me, too," Wampler said.

After dark, the group started to break up and head home. "Gotta be back at that headframe at seven a.m.," Boog Powell said. He tapped his Masonic ring twice on the tabletop, as he always did when he was ready to leave. He finished his beer and headed for the door.

Powell and his wife Effie lived a quarter mile from the Lesterton city limits on the Pimville Road, just past the point where the road changed from asphalt to gravel. They had no children who lived. Effie gave birth to a stillborn son the second year they were married and never got pregnant again.

Powell was feeling clear-headed. It was too hard to work underground after a night out, so he had cut back his drinking in the last few years. The night was moonless. Powell liked to listen to the whippoorwills as he walked home on Wednesday nights and thought it odd that they always sounded so far away. They were never close by. They knew to stay away from people, he thought. Maybe that was something they learned to do. He used to see them a lot when he was a kid, but no more.

He thought about Virgil, his lifelong friend. He always knew they had different natures. Virgil was more excitable and overthought things too much. He let regrets bother him more than they should. Powell saw no point in that. If you do a thing, you can't undo it. You get on with your life and you live it either happy or sad. Whichever you choose. Virgil's regrets never brought one of those Hunkies back to life.

Powell would wash up when he got home. Effie would still be awake. He hoped to get a few hours' sleep before it was time for work. He passed the stake he had driven into the ground to mark the edge of his property. He had white and red oak and black walnut trees that were big enough now to be worth money to gunsmiths making rifle stocks.

A sound like a grunt resonated from deep in the hardwood darkness. Black bears had been seen in the county in the last year, but they usually kept their distance.

The sound of footsteps in the dead leaves startled Powell. A bear or any animal he knew of in the area should not be approaching him as aggressively as that. As he turned to look for the source of the sound, a great force grasped his shoulder, nearly crushing it. A trap-like hand or claw flung him into the wooded darkness with such power the flesh of his shoulder was torn away. There was only enough strength left in him for a gasp, the sound being suffocated by the cracking of bone and the pop of joints pulling free of ligament and cartilage.

IX

"My dad says your dad is crazy," Dickie Pirtle said.

"Will you shut up?" C. O. said.

"I ain'ta gonna. He cost us another game. Blues is the worstest team in two counties, my dad said."

"He got a lot on his mind. Your dad ain't got nothin' on his ignernt mind."

"At least he ain't goin' crazy."

"Shut up, I told you."

The boys were walking on the Plank Road through Virgil's woods headed toward the open pasture and the creek. "If your dad wasn't crazy, he would'a tore this old road out long time ago." Dickie said.

"It's on our land but the lead company owns it. Anyways, Dad don't want to tear it out. He promised he would leave it be."

"See? That's just crazy."

C. O. saw the pile of planks the deaf boy had pried away years before, still undisturbed in the undergrowth. "All right," he said. "Looky here at these boards. They was part of the road. Let's drag 'em out in the open and have a bombfire one of these nights."

Dickie agreed and the boys dragged all the planks out into the open field and piled them up on a patch of ground that was mostly exposed rock. "Hell, we need more than that," C. O. said. He picked up one of the planks and, taking it back into the woods, began using it to pry up more boards. Most of the square nails were rusted through so the planks pried up easily. C. O. pried four off and positioned his lever for a fifth. Dickie approached him from the pasture.

"That's enough!" Dickie said as he started to pick up the boards. "How big a bombfire you want, anyways?"

"A big one. A great big one..."

"Your dad's gonna whup your ass if he finds out."

"Mebbe. Mebbe he'll just sit on the porch and do nothin', too."

Dickie carried the boards out to the pasture and threw them on the pile. "I think we ought to light this up right now," he said.

"I wanna do it at night," C. O. said. "I'll tell Dad that old Hunkie done it. Or them that lives over by the White Bridge." He kicked at the woodpile. He noticed a gray toad hopping across the edge of the clearing. C. O. caught the toad. He examined it for a moment, then winding up like a pitcher on the mound, he threw the creature as far as he could out into the pasture. He watched it fall to earth.

"Good throw," Dickie said.

"You got any smokes?" C. O. asked.

"Yup." Dickie pulled two cigarettes out of his overall pocket and a wooden match. The boys sat on the edge of the Plank Road and smoked. The heat shimmered over the fields and the dry buzzing of insects came from every direction. "Too hot to sit in this damned sun," Dickie said.

The boys stood and started walking toward the creek. "That old Hunkie Horvath was at the game," C. O. said.

"I know. I seen him too. I didn't think he cared nothin' about baseball."

"They don't. Foreigners don't care nothin' about that. I know where he lives. He's out there all by hisself. I want to see what he does out there."

"Okay with me."

"I know a shortcut."

The boys crossed the creek and cut across a plowed field toward the Pimville Road. They were both drenched with sweat and walked in the shade of the trees overhanging the gravel road as much as possible.

"We got to cut across the field up yonder before we get to the hard road," C. O. said. Something caught his attention on the ground as he turned to see if it was safe to cross to the other shoulder. Something glinted in the dirt and gravel. C. O. stooped and was surprised to find a massive gold ring. He had seen the ring before. "This is Boog Powell's," he said. "This is Boog's Masonic ring."

"Lemme see," Dickie grabbed the ring from C. O. "You gonna keep it?"

"No! He lives right up there. I'm takin' it to him." C. O. took the ring back and the boys returned along the gravel road to the drive that led up to Boog's house. Before they reached the door of the small clapboard house, the door opened.

"You boys heard anything?" Effie Powell said. She was a heavy, short woman approaching middle age.

"About what?" C. O. asked.

Effie looked disappointed. "About Boog," she said. "He didn't come home last night."

"Naw, Miz Powell," C. O. said. He held out his hand and she took the gold ring. "We found this down there by the road."

X

No one had said much to Virgil all day. The miners knew him as a moody man, and they all kept their distance since the Davids game.

Virgil led his mule pulling the seven ore cars he had filled that day to the staging area. He stopped the animal at his accustomed berth and flipped on the electric switch there. "Scored out," he said.

Floyd was waiting for his brother in line near the pay table. It was payday. Floyd had bid on and received the job of drift cutter. This check would show some of his pay raise.

Floyd grabbed Virgil's arm and pulled him into the line next to him. "I heard them Hunkies used to get paid of a Friday and be broke on Saturday!" Floyd said.

"Pretty much," Virgil said. "Lot of 'em drink it away. You wouldn't never do that, would you?"

"Let you know tomorrow night."

Dill Butcher, the shift boss, sat at the long wooden table. Henry Harris, the elderly security man, sat next to him. Dill had a wooden box full of envelopes containing paychecks in front of him. Floyd stepped up to the table.

"How many feet you cut today?" Dill asked. He didn't like Floyd much.

"Six," Floyd didn't like Dill either.

"That's what I hear."

"What did you ast me for then? You hopin' I'll lie about it?"

"To tell you the truth, yes," Dill said. "What's your number?"

"3630."

Dill flipped through the envelopes in the box. He pulled one out and handed it to Henry Harris. Henry checked the number on the envelope against a list on his clipboard in front of him. He made a pencil mark next to the number on the list and handed the envelope to Floyd. "Your doin' a dangerous job now, son," Henry said, "workin' with explosives. Got to be more carefuller than you was in your other jobs."

"He knows it," Dill said. Floyd stepped aside. "Virgil, you're up. What's your number?"

Virgil stepped up to the table. "2627."

"Ought to know it by now, shouldn't I?" Dill said, handing the envelope to Henry. "How you doin' these days, Old Sling?"

"I dunno, Dill," Virgil said. "Off the team, you know. Really don't know what to say."

"Keep an eye on that bohunkus of a brother of yours."

No one said anything in the cage back up to the surface. The ten or twelve men who had been inside made their way slowly across the road to the company store to cash their checks. A line formed at the cash-out cage in the front of the store.

"Deputies still ain't found no sign of Boog," Andy said.

"He wouldn't just run off," Cup Eyes said. "Too big a guy for anybody to jump him."

"When my boy found his ring he wasn't two hundred feet from his house," Virgil put in. "He would'a never left that ring behind."

"No, he wouldn't," Norman said. "Somethin' happened to him."

John Coyne, who ran the store for the company, cashed all the men's checks. "You need to put something against what you owe, Floyd," he said. Floyd gave John two dollars to pay on a bill of eight dollars he owed to the store. Most of the men decided to go down to Joe Burley's for a beer. Floyd went to a speakeasy in town he liked better, and Virgil decided to go home.

Virgil didn't feel as welcome among his old teammates as he once had. At the moment, the Blues were off the schedule for the rest of the season because they couldn't field nine players. If Boog was gone too, that only made things worse.

It was Friday evening. The company was cutting back hours, so they had stopped working Saturdays. There was talk that Standard Oil and others were going to start putting lead in gasoline to improve engine performance in cars. If that happened, Osage would go back to a six-day work week. Until then, everyone was glad for the extra day off.

Instead of taking the short train trip back to LaMotte, Virgil decided to walk home. He had thought a lot about C. O. finding Boog's ring by the road. Virgil wanted to take a look through the underbrush himself. The sheriff and deputies had looked around the woods near where the ring was found, but everybody knew they weren't any better at crime investigations than they were at helping the G-Men with enforcing Prohibition.

Virgil turned northeast onto the Pimville Road and near the place where the pavement ended. He walked onto the shoulder and the ditch beyond it and began to study the ground. He knew Effie Powell was not home; he had seen her walking toward the sheriff's office in town. He wouldn't want to alarm her by looking around her property uninvited if she were there.

He walked up the gradual hillside through the dead leaves and hardwood trees. It seemed that a lot of saplings and low-hanging branches were broken surrounding a glade area about twenty feet from the road. It looked as though spots of dead leaves and undergrowth had been disturbed, either by whatever had happened to Boog or by the deputies investigating the scene.

Virgil sat on a hickory log to think if Boog had ever mentioned anyone he knew or anyplace he might go if he ever wanted time away from Effie. A turtle was pushing away from the log through the dried leaves. A broken branch was blocking its way. Virgil reached for the branch, tugged at it a few times, and removed it from the reptile's path. As he moved the branch, he saw a tuft of white stuck in the loose bark. He pulled it free. It was a scrap of a pinstriped Blues uniform.

"Nothin' left but a ring and this," Virgil said. "Big man like Boog. Whatever happened, happened here. Nothin... natural."

XI

Rina was raised on a farm but didn't care for the country life. She raised two brothers and three sisters and swore she would never marry and have kids of her own. But here she was. Some days she was angry at herself for letting a man change her plans. Other days she thought of herself as contented enough and that she shouldn't complain.

As a girl she learned how to keep a family together even though she didn't want to learn. When C. O. got the chickenpox, she knew to lay him on the ground and run the chickens over him. When he got an earache, she put a knife under his bed to cut the pain. When that didn't work, she knelt in the front yard yelling "doodle up!" at the ground until a doodle bug came out of its hole. She put the bug in her son's ear, and it drew the heat and pain out, like it was supposed to.

C. O. had his moments but wasn't a bad kid. She caught him playing with matches a few times, and he burned the chicken coop last year. There were times he was mean to the dog, and she had to call him on it. He did things his own way and seemed angry sometimes that his father never had a good word to say to him. Rina was a little surprised that she loved the boy as much as she did.

It was near sunset and Virgil wasn't home yet. The company had cut out Saturdays for now, so Virgil should have come home hours ago. She'd made chicken and dumplings, but since C. O. was out running the fields with Dickie Pirtle, she wouldn't wait dinner any longer. She would eat alone. She scooped a plateful and sat at the table. After a few bites, Eugene, their old hound, started barking outside. It was a bark of greeting, not warning.

"Hush up, you old devil!" It was Virgil. The door opened. He looked exhausted.

"I about give up on you," Rina said. "Don't tell me you went to Burley's."

"No. Went by Boog's. I found a piece of his uniform in his woods. Showed it to the deputies and showed 'em where I found it."

"His ring and a scrap from his uniform. He didn't run off, did he?"

"Nope." Virgil scooped himself a plate of the chicken and dumplings and sat at the table. "They don't expect to find him alive."

"Me neither. I just got a feeling. Poor Effie. She must be beside herself. She sure depended on Boog."

"You said a mouthful there. She couldn't find her butt with both hands without him tellin' her where to look."

"Not since she lost that baby," Rina said.

"Yep, that's when it started. Blues can't field a team now with me gone and now Boog."

"Aw who cares about a baseball team when a man might be dead?"

"Nobody."

"Well, all right, then."

The Plank Road

"C. O. eat already?"

"No. He ain't been home."

"Dammit! I told him to be home for supper every evening."

"It don't matter. It's summer. Kids like to stay outside late in summertime. If it was winter, be a different story."

"He got to learn to do what he's told. That's the point."

"He don't think he can do nothin' to please you anyways."

"Don't start this again."

"Virgil, you done had a pole up your butt for two years and it's only gettin' worser. You got kicked off the team, C. O. and me can't do nothin' to please you. What's the matter with you? You ain't the man I married."

Virgil shrugged angrily. He had only finished half his dinner. He took his plate to the front door and set it on the porch, where Eugene was eagerly waiting. The old dog cleaned the plate in a few seconds. Virgil picked it up, closed the door, and took the plate to the sink. He turned and faced his wife and leaned against the kitchen counter. "People is supposed to be their worstest in war," he said. "Supposed to be. That's what brings out the worstest in everybody. If you go into it normal and come out of it tore up and mean and able to do bad things, people ain't surprised."

"That's what God is for. Its why church is there." Rina said.

"No, Rina. No. That ain't true. Religion ain't true. The truth is... it's nothin' there. Ain't nothin' there at all. Out there, I mean. Nothin' watchin' you nor judgin'. Truth is, at the right time and place, even good people can do anythin', any bad thing, and there ain't nobody nor nothin' out there in the dark that cares."

"This is about the war?"

"Yeah, and before the war. Partly. Before the riot, too, when we run the Hunkies out. Few days before. No, a month before. I was out lookin' for that missing calf. I seen that tall Hunkie kid tearin' off planks from the Plank Road in the woods. The kid that disappeared. I hollered at him. I didn't know he was deaf. I just shot him. I don't know why. I don't know why I shot him over that and with not much warning. He was twelve. I only seen him from the back. I didn't know he was that young." Virgil couldn't say anymore for a moment. He looked at the floor. He never raised his eyes to look at his wife. "Then I hid his body and when I come back to bury him, he was gone."

"You should'a told me," Rina said after a moment. "You didn't have to keep that to yourself."

"It's murder, clear and simple. Worser than the war... or the riot."

"I told you to tear out that damn road years ago," Rina said in a sudden rage. "That drawed him in. But you wouldn't listen because you promised your grandpa or some kinda nonsense!"

"Dammit, Rina!"

"Sorry... I'm sorry. That don't matter now."

Eugene began barking again. Another bark of greeting. C. O.

opened the door and looked surprised to see his father.

"Well, there you are. Take a seat and I'll get you some chicken," Rina said.

Virgil suddenly leaned forward and slapped his son, causing him to fall across a kitchen chair. "Your momma tells you to be home at a certain time, you do it," Virgil said. "Ain't up to you to decide when to mind us and when not!"

"Son of a bitch!" Rina mumbled through her teeth. She didn't contradict Virgil in front of C. O.

"Sorry. I'm sorry, but... Dickie told me," C. O. said as he got to his feet and sat at the kitchen table with tears in his eyes, "he stopped me and told me, that Cup Eyes Wampler is gone too."

XII

"Villner said he would come back and play," Dan Whelen said. Virgil didn't have a telephone at home, and he sent word to Virgil to call him on the pay phone at the company store. "Ernie Riegler changed his mind and said he would play here. Two other guys from Bonne Terre is fed up and ready to come over too. You can come back if you promise to work out your problems and control yourself better. That anger has got to go. We can get back on the schedule, play Dittmer Wednesday, and finish the season."

"I'd be lyin' if I told you I didn't miss it, Dan," Virgil said. "I got nothin' to do of a weekend but watch the grass grow. I'll do my best. I don't know what to make of Boog and Bird-Brain disappearin'. What's the chances of that?"

"None, if you ast me."

The next morning Virgil spread the word among his old teammates underground that they had a team again. They decided to have a practice at Daniel Newcomb Park that night to get ready to play the Dittmer Viscounts on Wednesday.

At four o'clock, the men met at the baseball field. They all kept their baseball equipment in the locker room at work for weekday workouts and Wednesday night games. Some of them practiced in their street clothes to keep their uniforms clean.

Virgil and Sibole played catch to limber up Virgil's arm. Virgil felt a little pain in his back and shoulder for the first few minutes, but it passed. After a while he threw harder, keeping the ball low and in a small, controlled zone. "That's it, Ol' Sling!" Sibole encouraged. "That's back on the track!"

Virgil threw batting practice, just lobbing the ball into the batters. That was followed up with infield and outfield practice. Everyone was in good spirits, but subdued, talking about their missing teammates. They were all anxious to get back into the schedule.

Floyd was reading a newspaper in the boarding house parlor when Virgil got there. The two of them walked to Rinder's for supper. They both had the frog legs. Floyd was in a bad mood. He had been trying to court Elaine Caster for the last few weeks, but she let him know she wasn't interested. After the meal, the brothers walked back to their room and went to bed early.

The next morning, Floyd left for work before Virgil. By the time the crew assembled at the cage, Floyd was already underground.

"Good practice last night," Sibole said. Everyone agreed.

"Woosht ol' Boog and Cup Eyes would show up and surprise everybody," Norman Insill said.

"If that ain't the strangest thing," Bones said. "Don't hardly seem right to me to play when they's missin'. Seems like out of respect, we oughta..."

"I'd ruther play than do nothin'," Bones Teeter said. "I think they'd feel thattaway, too."

Virgil got his mule, Woodrow Wilson, from the muleskinner that morning instead of waiting for him to be delivered. He led the animal to his drift. Virgil started his day's work.

He had loaded two ore cars when he heard a familiar pop out in the main tunnel. He heard a man yelling "Get a stretcher," and another said, "Need a tourniquet. Bind it up."

Virgil ran out to the main tunnel. The supply motor was stopped at the mouth of the next drift and men were huddled over a figure on the ground. It was Floyd. Half of his left arm was missing, and the left side of his chest was soaked in blood.

One of the men tending to Floyd, Mel Pickett, picked up the blasted remnant of his bloody forearm and tossed it aside. As he did, he saw Virgil approaching. "Sorry Virgil," Mel said. "He done somethin' wrong with a blasting cap. Lucky he didn't blow all his guts out."

Floyd was unconscious. His wound was bound, and two men carried him on a stretcher to the cage and up to the infirmary next to the headframe. Virgil followed them and sat in the outer office of the infirmary for more than an hour while the surgeon worked on Floyd.

In the recovery room, Floyd didn't come out of the ether until late in the afternoon. Virgil was sitting by his side.

"What... the hell?" Floyd murmured.

"You're a lucky man," Virgil said.

Floyd looked around himself as best he could. He winced in pain. "Yeah, I look real lucky," he said. "I done it this time, didn't I?"

"You'll be all right. They make replacements now that look just like the real thing."

"I can't work underground no more."

"Everything will work out some kind of way. Always does. You can live with us until you heal up."

"You don't need more trouble, brother. I don't want to burden you more."

"Everything will work out some kind of way. I know it will."

Virgil stayed with Floyd another hour and decided to take the last train east home to LaMotte. He was surprised to find Dill Butcher waiting for him outside the infirmary, under the headframe. "What are you still a-doin' here Dill?" Virgil asked.

Dill didn't answer right away. He looked at Virgil sheepishly and removed two envelopes from his vest pocket.

"Oh," Virgil frowned. "You're here to see me."

"Afraid so, buddy," Dill said. "I'm very sorry about this. Never seen the company do this so fast. They want you and Floyd out. Floyd for dangerous negligence and you for leaving your workstation without permission." He handed Virgil the envelopes.

Virgil was speechless for a moment. "They ain't done any kind of investigation. My brother got his damn arm blowed off!"

"They don't want no liability, Virgil. You know how it is. Big company don't give a damn about workin' people. Never have," Dill said. "He can stay overnight here, then tomorrow the company is sending a car to take him wherever he wants to go. I figured you and the missus would look after him for now."

XIII

Horvath made himself a cup of tea in the afternoons. He always sat in his parlor to drink it. He had never experienced summer heat before such as he found in America, but despite this, he preferred his hot tea to a cool drink throughout the stifling season.

The signs showed him his time was coming to an end. The tea leaves read the same every day, and they never lied. He had seen an owl fly over his house toward the west twice in the same week. Horvath saw both relief and regret in these omens, for the Being's time was coming to an end, too. Sar Ember may only be animate for a short time until its energies are desiccated and spent. If its purpose has not been fulfilled, it must speak the name of its replacement to finish the work. The replacement must then incubate until its powers have reached their peak. If this does not happen, the work remains unfinished and justice unsatisfied. Horvath feared that neither he nor the Being would live to see their purpose realized.

Horvath would not miss this life. The struggles and sacrifices he and his wife had made to come here had mostly been for nothing. They wanted to save their sons from the war but had lost them both anyway. They had received no word on what had become of their village. Now Horvath and his wife would rest eternally in unvisited graves in a strange and unwelcoming land.

If their village of Lillafüred was destroyed in the war, he would never know it. It comforted him to preserve it in his memory in the spring of 1913, in their home in the mountain forest, before history and the world disintegrated.

But Horvath's time here had not yet come to an end. He was

Gyam, the Guardian. He still had his duty to fulfill. He arose from his parlor chair and walked outside to the front gate to find his bucket. He began his walk toward the creek.

XIV

"You ain't gonna run away," Dickie said. "You said it before, but you never done it."

"You want me to, don'tcha?" C. O. said. The boys were sitting at the edge of the Mill Pond on a railroad tie left from a trackway the chat cars once ran on to unload tailing sand at the dump.

"No," Dickie said, "but you ort to stop sayin' you're gonna do somethin' when you ain't never gonna do it."

"I was. I wanted to this time, but then Uncle Floyd got hurt. Company car brung him home to live with us last night. Infirmary kicked him out."

"So what?"

"I wanna help take care of him. He's good to me. I like him. Dad's already complainin' he had no choice but to take him in, and it's too damn much responsibility."

"I heard they got fired."

"Yup. We got no money now but Dad's last paycheck."

"If I get any, I'll give you some."

"I'll get a whuppin' if I'm late gettin' home again. Let's go."

The boys walked to the edge of the tailings dump and began following the creek north. The Plank Road on the McElwrath property ended at the creek bank. Remnants of a wooden bridge were still there, all collapsed and stripped by the Hunkies long ago. C. O. hopped onto the road and walked on it toward the woods and the house beyond. Dickie followed him.

As they approached the stack of planks they had meant for their bonfire, C. O.'s foot broke through a rotted board. He howled in pain. He sat on the edge of the road and examined his ankle. It was bleeding. "God dammit!" he cursed.

"Better warsh that out in the creek," Dickie said. "Your mom'll be mad. Hard to get blood out after it dries."

"This God damn thing!" C. O. yelled. He kicked at the base of the Plank Road repeatedly. "This God damn thing in the way! People laugh at us for keepin' it!" C. O. tore the broken edges of the hole he had made away and threw them on the wood pile. He then took a wooden match from his pocket and struck it against his overalls. He pushed the match into the dry grass under the pile.

"Aw, C. O., your old man is gonna whup the life outta you," Dickie said.

John S. McFarland

XV

Floyd insisted that Virgil should suit up and get to town for the baseball game. "It's no point in you missing out since they ain't nothin' you can do anyways," he said. "I just want to rest, and Rina has took good care of me this evening." He had not moved from the only upholstered chair in the front room all afternoon.

"Yeah," Rina agreed. "You need to blow off some steam, Virgil. You go on. Floyd, let's put you in the boy's room. He can sleep on a quilt on the floor. You need rest. Sittin' up, you could pass out."

Virgil wanted to get away from the house. He regretted offering Floyd a room as soon as he'd said it. He felt he was a bad father, a bad husband, and knew he would be a bad nurse, too. He was a good pitcher at one time. He hoped he had some of that left.

He changed into his uniform quickly and saddled Jimmy to ride into town. He could be there well before seven o'clock.

As he led the horse out of the barn, he noticed a glow in the east twilight sky. Sparks flared up. It had to be a fire. Virgil jumped onto the horse's back and filliped him toward the woods. Through the trees, he could see a fire burning out in the open of the pasture. Virgil hadn't checked the property for weeks. He thought he might have hoboes or squatters making a campfire that had gotten out of hand.

As he emerged from the tree line, Virgil could see that the bonfire was very large and unattended. It was a tented pile of planks from the road. There was no one to be seen. He dismounted and began searching through the weeds. "Where are you?" he yelled. "Who's here on my property? Where you hidin'?"

Virgil heard movement out in the field beyond the reach of the firelight. A footstep, a breaking branch. A shadowy, rust-colored figure began to take form.

"What the hell you doin' startin' fires on my propitty?" Virgil's question was cut short by a gasp. The figure approaching him was enormous. It walked slowly, taking uncertain and weak steps. It was the color of the red clay that made most of this withering region barren and useless except for the minerals it contained. The figure's gash of a mouth separated black eyes that seemed to have drifted away from their original placement in opposite directions, up and down. The red/orange skin was ill-matching plates that butted together roughly and incompletely.

"Jesus Lord," Virgil said.

Another much smaller figure emerged from the darkness. It was Horvath. He stopped in the firelight and bent over in exhaustion. "This is the boy you killed," Horvath gasped. "Sar Ember. You murderer. Retribution... is at hand. You and your friends. How many of us did you kill?"

The Being, too, seemed exhausted. It moved its dripping lips. It blew a spray of water from its mouth. It seemed to be forming a word. It made a guttural, wet growl: "Vgg... Vggl," it mumbled. "Muck... muck... rth."

There was a sudden movement in the brush. Virgil was dumbstruck and for a moment didn't realize he was seeing C. O. rushing out of the cover of the weeds. C. O. rammed himself into old Horvath's back. The old man fell into the bonfire. Almost fully engulfed, he rolled away from the fire onto the ground. The burning man somehow got to his feet. He stumbled off, screaming, toward the creek bank.

Virgil felt sick and awash in pain. He was aware that C. O., and now his friend Dickie, were also screaming. Looking at him and screaming. The Being who had once been a boy Virgil had killed stood swaying weakly near the fire. Then it stepped forward and collapsed into the flames. The Being did not move again.

Virgil saw that his son and friend were running from him in horror. Virgil knew this was meant to be. He knew he must make his way to the creek bank. He must climb onto the opposite bank and into the trench Horvath had dug and recently moistened. He must crouch into it and try his best to bury himself under the mud.

Canis Pugnax

For H. G. Wells

Experimental Log Number 38, Feb 4, 1922. Isambard Kingdom Treves, Ph.D., M.D.

My months of collaboration with Fitz-Padgett have paid a valuable dividend. His purine compound has solved the great problem of tissue rejection. I had no intention of continuing my father's investigations as a vivisectionist, but after I heard of Fitz-Padgett's work, I couldn't get the thought of the incredible possibilities out of my mind. This discovery aligned with the apparent success of our unofficially defined protein grafting work terrifies and excites me.

I am continuing parts of my father's work and recording it in his journals. I found no reference yet in these pages to the type of investigation I am here pursuing, but I believe he did such work. He spoke of it, seemed preoccupied with it. He was lacking the purine compound in those days. Did he find something else that worked as well? After the injuries he suffered in developing Dr. Treves's Therapeutic Cuirass and the even more horrific injuries at St. Mathurin's Home for the Insane, his investigations trailed off to nothing.

Dr. Treves closed the dusty logbook and stood. The town of Ste. Odile had forced him to do this, he thought. It had forced him into research and investigation when he had always felt his calling was to help people through his surgical skills.

His surgical practice had fallen off to nothing after he returned from the war. With the loss of his eye, he needed time to reconfigure his conceptions of himself and recover his skill. By the time he felt ready, the town had forgotten him. Or mistrusted him. His squadmate Abel Jarre had noticed the same thing, that the townspeople were ostracizing him. It seemed to both men that their neighbors thought no man could experience the horrors they'd heard of in that war and come home unscarred and with his humanity intact.

Aurore stood by him through everything. Her father, Chabrol, the owner of the lime works, disapproved of the match. Chabrol had told Treves in 1915 not to fight in a foolish European war, but after the *Lusitania* was sunk, Treves's resolve was fixed.

Neither his disfigurement nor his emotional injuries mattered to Aurore. She ignored her father's dislike of Treves at the risk of her own inheritance. She assured Treves she would change her father's mind someday.

Treves noticed, or at least he believed, that Aurore's devotion to him had cost her status, position, and even friendships in Ste. Odile. She was asked to resign her post in the Ladies' Sodality at the Church of the Holy Mandilion and was demoted as acting secretary of the Daughters of de Castres historical preservation group. The name Treves had become suspect in his father's time, and now that he was a scarred veteran, possibly with emotional problems, wearing a grotesque face and eye prosthetic when he went out into the town, he and all allied with him were pariahs.

A loud knock on the front door startled Treves. A surgery room he no longer used now served as his laboratory. He stepped out from behind his desk and hurried to the front of his residence. He pulled open the front door.

Victor Cisco stood smiling on the sidewalk. Beside him on a leash sat an enormous, brutal-looking black dog. "Good morning, Doctor," the old man said. Cisco had supplied Treves's father with test animals in the days of his experiments in vivisection.

"My word, what have you brought me?" Treves was startled by the huge animal.

"This is the dog I told you about," Cisco said. "I thought this would fill your needs... not that I understand them! One hundred dollars!"

"Yes, he will do very well, I think."

"This breed is almost all gone. One less won't be missed. Italian mastiff. Cane Corso, as they are called. Trained by the Romans in ancient times as battle dogs. Ears and tail cut as you wanted. The weight is what you wanted, too. One hundred and thirty pounds. The biggest one I've ever seen."

"It's perfect. I don't have cash in the house today. I will have it tomorrow."

"His name is Pertinax. Let him get to know you a while."

"Yes."

"If you startle him or behave in a way that distresses him, he will tear your throat out."

"Yes, yes." Treves slowly approached the dog. "Where did you get him?"

Cisco shrugged. Pertinax allowed Treves's hand to descend deferentially onto his broad head.

"What are you gonna do with this fella?" Cisco asked.

"It doesn't concern you. Just keep bringing me what I need."

"Your father asked for such a dog once. I don't know what became of him."

"He did?"

"A lot like this one, if I remember right," Cisco nodded.

Treves took the leash from Cisco. "I suspected my father did some such research, but I never found the laboratory records."

"He was burning a book and papers once when I brought him a monkey. A colobus, I think it was. It bit me twice." Cisco touched his hat and turned away. "I will be back for my hundred dollars tomorrow."

"Have you heard from your man in Sumatra? I am still in need of an ape!"

Cisco shook his head no as he walked away.

Treves led the great dog inside and back to his laboratory. Pertinax sniffed the floor and a chair. He looked at Treves with what could have been a puzzled expression. He lay on the floor near a worktable with an audible thud and huffing sigh.

"Good boy, Pertinax," Treves said. "I think I have some scraps for you. Aurore brought me several large filets last night. I have them in the icebox." He stepped out of the laboratory into his living quarters. "I wonder how you will react to the ether?"

In the early evening, Treves met Aurore for dinner at Herve's restaurant. Her face was bright with the excitement of seeing him, and as he watched, her expressions flitting from one bit of news to the next, Treves couldn't imagine loving her more than he did.

Aurore ordered fried catfish and Treves ordered pork and potatoes.

"You said you got the dog you wanted today?" Aurore said, as their wine glasses were placed on the table.

"I did. I needed a dog of a certain size and temperament for the work I am doing."

"Is this something else I shouldn't ask about?"

"It's something else I will tell you about in time."

Aurore frowned a little. "I am nothing more or less than a rational being, Isambard. If you are doing something that will benefit humanity in some way, I understand the means to the end may not be pleasant."

"I know that," Treves said. "Sometimes just wanting to *know* is an end in itself."

Aurore frowned again, looking as if she knew this line of conversation would go no further. "All right, then. Where did you find the dog?"

"Old Cisco found him for me."

"That is a book in and of itself, knowing the old man's reputation."

Their table was at a front window overlooking Bosphorus Street but in a direct line of view to the kitchen. Herve, a fussy little man in evening clothes, stood by the kitchen door, checking orders as the waiters conveyed them to the kitchen and the finished plates of food as they were brought out.

"I wonder how long he will keep doing this?" Aurore said.

"There has always been a Herve's," Treves answered. "He must be a hundred years old."

A large, rough-looking man came out of the kitchen and said

something to Herve, then returned to the kitchen. Herve noticed that Treves and Aurore were finishing their dinner. He approached them with an unctuous smile.

"Your dinners were to your liking, Doctor? Miss Aurore?"

"Very good, Herve, thank you," Aurore said.

"As always," Treves agreed. "Who is that big fellow you were speaking to just now?"

Herve glanced back toward the kitchen. "Ah, that was Udo. Udo Otz. Cleans up, washes dishes. New fellow."

"I wonder if he is available for some odd jobs?" Treves continued. "I have some heavy lifting needs done at the office and laboratory."

Herve nodded. "I am sure he is. He asked me just now for extra work. I'll send him out to you."

In a few moments, the large man ambled out of the kitchen and approached the table. He seemed nervous and unsure of himself and never looked Treves in the eye as he approached.

"Mr. Otz!" Treves said.

"Yes. Udo Otz... Dr. Treves."

"I have heard of your family," Aurore said. "They are over toward Lesterton and Hopewell, aren't they? So many Germans over there."

"Yes, ma'am, they are over there." He didn't seem to be able to make himself look at Aurore.

"Were you born here, Udo?" Treves asked.

"Yes. Mama and Papa too. Grandpa came over here seventy years ago." His voice was deep but tremulous as if his shyness were suffocating him. "Herve said you might have some work for me, Doctor?"

"That's right. I have new equipment arriving soon and I need to rearrange my work area. Moving cabinets and tables and unloading crates when they come. I also now have a dog to care for."

Udo smiled. "I can sure do that!"

"I can give you... three dollars a day. I'll pay you at the end of each day."

"Oh... that would be wonderful! Papa lost his foot working the farm and I support them now. Mama ain't well neither. That pay would be so wonderful! I can work every morning before the restaurant opens! I will do a wonderful job for you!"

"You know where my office is... Come tomorrow at nine or ten o'clock."

Udo extended his hand for a second, then withdrew it as if doing so was inappropriate. He smiled and returned to the kitchen.

"Three dollars a day?" Aurore said. "That's very generous."

"I'm certain he is a hard worker. He will earn it."

***

Experimental Log 38, Feb 5, 1922

Pertinax showed few signs of aggression yesterday and has been most agreeable today. I think in this short time he has learned to trust me. For Canis Pugnax, that is a great deal to learn. I examined his limbs, teeth, and thorax. All are sound and very strong. I tested his reflex responses to small stimuli and commands and have concluded that he is of at least average or above-average intelligence for such an animal. I must decide once and for all how I want to proceed. I still have no definite commitment from Cisco's supplier regarding an ourang-utan.

Since performing the protein graft surgery on the raccoon and gopher subjects in December, both have recovered and prospered. The raccoon has gained two pounds and shown an increased proclivity to digging and burrowing. The gopher, on the other hand, seems more disinclined to digging and has actually developed a preliminary skill at tree climbing!

I have isolated the brain function areas of both Canis familiaris *and* Pongo pygmaeus *I intend to consolidate...*

***

At nine a.m. exactly, a tentative knock on the laboratory door was followed by Udo opening it and stepping inside.

"Good morning, Doctor," Udo said. "I saw you inside, so I just came in."

"That's fine, Udo. Good morning to you. Let's get started."

Pertinax greeted Udo cautiously at first but seemed to take to him quickly. Over the next two hours, Udo transferred cases of medical and experimental records from the laboratory to a large shed at the back edge of Treves's property. By eleven o'clock he had cleared a large space in a corner of the laboratory and nearly filled the shed.

"How are your parents today?" Treves asked as he gave Udo three silver dollars.

"Not too well, Doctor. Thank you for asking. They can't take the cold weather. My mama coughs a lot. She has the consumption."

"Very sorry to hear it. Maybe you can get her to a warmer climate someday soon?"

"That is what I am hoping for. Would be a wonderful change for her. I have to get to Herve's now. Thank you again, Doctor."

Pertinax butted Udo's hand with his head and was rewarded with a pat between his ears.

"I will see you tomorrow, then."

In the afternoon, Cisco returned to collect his one hundred dollars. Pertinax growled and charged him, and Treves had to put the dog in his kennel.

"There is now a ban on exporting ourang-outans," Cisco said, counting his money. "The Sumatran government has outlawed headhunting by the tribal peoples, so they have taken to headhunting apes. The apes are solitary beasts and reproduce sparsely. The Office of Resources fears their extinction."

"A very reasonable fear, I would say."

"And I would not be able to get African apes until late in the year when the collectors go into the bush again."

Treves said nothing as Cisco pocketed his money and left. It looked as though Treves would need to switch to one of his alternate plans for his experiment. It would change the terms and design of the work greatly and push his schedule back by two years or more if things didn't go well, but he had always known he may need to prepare a direction for his research that might take him on an entirely new path.

Treves released Pertinax from his kennel. The enormous dog was always hungry and thirsty. Treves gave him a goat's leg he had bought that morning and refilled his bowl of water. "You may have just got off the hook, old boy," Treves said.

Udo worked diligently for Treves for the next two days, completely clearing a large space to be dedicated to new research.

By ten o'clock on the third day, Udo had still not arrived at the laboratory. Aurore dropped off some cleaned lab coats and linens and Treves decided they should lunch at Herve's. Seated at their window table, Treves glanced around for Udo, but he was not to be found. Herve brought menus to the table himself.

"I didn't see Udo this morning, Herve, is he here?"

"No. I haven't heard from him. Most unusual for Udo. I recommend the onion soup today, and the catfish."

After lunch, Aurore walked home. Treves returned to his laboratory, fed Pertinax again, and decided to ride out to Hopewell and look in on Udo. He stopped back in at Herve's and asked Herve and his dishwasher how to find Udo's farm. Back home, Treves saddled his old horse Mnester, disagreeable in the cold stable, and headed west out of town.

At LaMotte, Treves took the Pimville Road southwest toward Hopewell. In a couple of miles, the oak and cedar forest thinned out to meadows and cultivated fields. Directly to the west, Treves saw a column of black smoke rising at a distant tree line. Treves urged Mnester to a trot. Halfway down a long, gradual grade that stretched toward the column of smoke, the old horse became agitated. There was a disturbance in the grove of dead weeds and saplings to the left.

"Doctor! Dr. Treves!" Udo burst out of the thicket and onto the road. His face and hands were covered with soot and his expression was wild and disoriented. Mnester nearly reared but Treves steadied him.

"Udo! Good God, what happened? I was coming to look in on you. You're nearly frozen through."

"He wasn't even grinning at us," Udo gasped. "He just looked at us like he was asking the time. He couldn't have cared less, which is worse than laughing."

"What? What happened?"

"Tancredy from the bank stopped by. He's my cousin... Mama's nephew. Papa borrowed money against the farm when the sorghum didn't come in two years ago. We are two months behind on the payment. The bank is taking the property. I mean, Tancredy is. Was. He always wanted it. His house on the river flooded and he wants the old family property."

"Is that your house burning?"

"I put Papa and Mama in their room so's I could talk to him, to Tancredy. His mind was made up and he was gonna put us out. I hit him before I knew it, with a skillet. He knocked over the stove when he fell. The whole kitchen and front room went up. I know he's dead. I couldn't get to Mama and Papa. I couldn't get through the fire. They're dead too. I gotta run. I gotta leave town."

"Jump up behind me. I'm going to get you to my place, and we'll decide what to do."

Udo climbed up behind Treves. Treves turned the old horse around and headed back toward Ste. Odile at a gallop.

Aurore had planned to come to Treves's home that night for a light dinner. Treves called her, saying he had a headache, and promised they would reschedule their evening. It took many hours for Udo to calm down. Pertinax watched Udo and whimpered. Treves removed the great dog from his kennel and, seeming to sense distress, he would not leave Udo's side.

"We will have to find you a lawyer," Treves said, offering Udo a cup of coffee. Udo shook his head.

"They'll hang me," he said. "And I have killed my parents. I can't live with that. I don't want to." He stood and walked across the laboratory. He looked out the back window.

"Let me get you something to eat. I'll warm up some pork from yesterday for you." Treves walked into the kitchen and found a slab of pork loin in his icebox. He placed it in a skillet and lit the burner. As he searched for a clean plate in his cupboard, a shot exploded from the rear of the house. Pertinax yelped and whimpered. Treves rushed back to the laboratory.

Udo lay dead near the back door. He had found Treves's Enfield revolver in his worktable drawer and shot himself in the chest. Pertinax barked and whimpered and skittered in a frenzy around the room. Treves put him in his kennel with great difficulty.

The Enfield was still in Udo's right hand. It looked as though he had shot himself through the heart. The blood had not yet stopped flowing. Treves heard Mnester whinnying out in the stable. His first thought was to go to the sheriff's office and report the suicide. Then he realized that probably no one heard the shot. The Founder's Festival was being celebrated on the riverfront that week. Most of the town gathered in the old Osage warehouse for food, music, and celebration. And no one knew where Udo was.

Treves was ashamed of the thought that overwhelmed him, but he knew he could not constrain himself. He pulled Udo's body by its left arm toward his surgical table. The corpse was surprisingly heavy. Treves knew he could never lift it onto the table alone.

Pertinax had calmed down but was watching Treves intently. The enormous dog would have to be sedated before Treves continued with what he was now compelled to do. Treves pulled his examination table alongside the surgical table. From a storage cabinet, he wheeled out a cart holding twin canisters: one of oxygen and one of nitrous oxide. He placed this near the surgical table.

Treves opened Pertinax's kennel door. The dog lowered and raised his head in uncertainty. In a cowering attitude, Pertinax slowly emerged from the kennel. Treves stroked his head and in a few moments the dog seemed reassured. Treves cut a strip from the pork he had meant to prepare and gave it to Pertinax. He cut another strip and placed it on the surgical table. Placing a wooden crate near the table, Pertinax jumped onto it and ate the strip of meat. Treves slowly placed the inhaler cup from his canisters over the dog's snout and opened the valves. In a few seconds Pertinax was unconscious. Treves knew he was risking a bad reaction by coaxing the dog with bits of food before sedating, but he hoped the morsels were small enough to minimize vomiting or choking.

Treves pulled two leather straps over Pertinax's body, securing him on the table. He then went into the kitchen and found his large cimeter butcher knife hanging on a wall. He returned to the laboratory and knelt at the side of Udo's corpse. It took a few moments to gather the resolve he needed. He placed the blade on the dead man's neck and began sawing with all his strength. Passing between two neck vertebrae, he had the head severed in a few seconds.

Treves felt suddenly lightheaded and nearly blacked out. When he felt steadier, he lifted the head from the floor and placed it on the examination table. He removed a straight razor from his storage cabinet and carefully shaved the top of Pertinax's head. He then washed the bare skin. He returned the razor to the storage cabinet and removed his hand-cranked osteotome, two sterile dermaplaning scalpels, surgical gloves, and a device of his own invention he called filum novacula.

Time was short, so Treves didn't shave Udo's cranium. He cut the hair short in several spots over the frontal lobe and on both sides with scissors, then cut the skin away with one of the dermaplaning scalpels. Positioning the brace of the osteotome against his abdomen, he quickly sawed away a large rectangle of bone extending from the forehead to the top of the skull and two smaller squares above each ear. He removed the cut pieces of skull and discarded them. Then, after sterilizing the osteotome, he used it to cut a rectangle of bone from Pertinax's skull an inch or more above his eyes.

With a micrometer, Treves measured the distances from the edges of the left and right hemispheres of Udo's exposed brain to find the areas he needed to harvest. With the filum novacula, he set to work.

***

Experimental Log Number 38, Feb 8, 1922

Was too exhausted to update log yesterday. Surgery appears to have been a success. After I was certain of the accuracy of my measurements, the harvesting took no more than a half hour, with the removal of the amygdala being the most difficult. When I had located to my satisfaction the proper regions in Pertinax's exposed telencephalon and incised the needed voids, I adjusted the filium novacula for its protein grafting function, referenced in the November 11 entry, and after three hours or so, completed the procedure. I then seeded the wounds with the purine compound.

Then I set about the grim business of burying Udo's body and head. I waited until dark; the digging was exhausting due to the ground being mostly frozen. He now lies behind my storage shed in the bushes. May he rest in peace.

I was awakened before dawn this morning by growls and coughing barks. I went into the laboratory. I had somehow managed to place Pertinax's enormous bulk back into his kennel after the surgery. The great dog had still not come out of the sedative. He seemed, as I watched him, to be dreaming and reacting physically to the images in his head. His body jerked and shuddered. He coughed and barked repeatedly. Then his eyes slowly opened.

***

Treves had tightly bandaged the wound on Pertinax's head after the surgery. The dog's eyes fluttered open and closed for several minutes. He tried to stand but seemed too weak. Treves opened the kennel door. Pertinax barely acknowledged him. Treves brought in meat and water, but the dog ignored them. Treves knelt and examined the wound and bandage. Everything looked dry and undisturbed.

Treves made himself a cup of coffee and sat with Pertinax for several hours. At length, Treves began to doze. He was startled awake when Pertinax jumped to his feet and began eating the food left for him. After a minute or so of ravenous eating, the dog came to Treves's side. Treves stroked the massive neck and back and examined the bandage on his head again. A trace of pink seepage was showing now. Treves would change the bandage later in the morning.

Pertinax walked to the spot where Udo's body had lain the night before. Treves noticed that the dog stumbled and seemed to hesitate as if he were remembering how to walk. He fell to the floor several times, always struggling to stand again. Pertinax sniffed the browning spot on the floor, looked at Treves, and sniffed the floor again. He whimpered and growled.

Pertinax scratched at the laboratory door and the doorknob as if he wanted out. When opened, Pertinax ambled out the door, and Treves followed him. A light snow had fallen overnight. In an irregular lope, stumbling once, Pertinax moved back toward the old storage shed. To Treves's horror the great dog began digging on Udo's shallow grave, pulling dirt and rocks toward himself, in the normal manner of dogs, but also oddly pushing it aside. Treves ran to the spot and coaxed Pertinax back into the laboratory.

Back in the kennel, the dog seemed exhausted and fell into a deep sleep. At eleven in the morning, Aurore stopped by unexpectedly and asked Treves to lunch.

"You missed a wonderful meal at the Osage last night," she said. "I hope you're hungry now."

"A kind of emergency," Treves responded. "I noticed an irregularity on Pertinax's skull. It was a tumor. I removed it."

She looked at him quizzically. "Oh my. Odd I didn't notice it the other day. Must have become apparent very suddenly. I hope he will be all right."

"Yes, so do I."

Treves and Aurore were seated at their usual table at Herve's. Herve seemed to be in a particularly bad mood.

"We have had a report this morning," he said as he took Treves and Aurore's menus, "that Udo's parents are dead. Died in a fire that burned the house down. No one has seen Udo."

"They didn't find his body?" Treves asked.

"No. Only two dead bodies."

"How terrible," Aurore said.

"That's awful news. Strange Udo was not found too."

"Tancredy from the bank was found there also," Herve added. "He is a cousin. Alive but badly burned and with other injuries. He is at the hospital. They barely saved his life."

Treves picked over his lunch and barely ate anything. "I have to tell you something," he said to Aurore after a long silence. "I rode out to look in on Udo yesterday. I found him on the road. Tancredy had come to the farm to give them an order to vacate. Udo fought with him. The stove was turned over and the old people and Tancredy were trapped inside. Udo was on the run when I found him."

"Oh no..." Aurore said.

"He killed himself in my lab. Shot himself in the chest. I buried him at the back of my property."

"*You* buried him? What do you mean?"

"I... I harvested segments from him first. From his brain."

Aurore seemed in shock. She sat in silence for a long while, not looking at Treves's face. "I don't know what to say to that," she finally said. "It seems... immoral or blasphemous or... I'm at a loss."

"I won't defend myself." Treves stared into his coffee. "It's indefensible. I wanted an ape subject as you know. This... happened and he killed himself. I had a compulsion I could scarcely control. The opportunity would never repeat itself..."

Aurore stood. "It's too much for me. I need time to understand it." She didn't notice Herve nodding as she walked past him. She exited the front door and was quickly out of sight.

***

Experimental Log 38, Feb 20, 1922

Pertinax's wound is healing well. Oddly, the fur around it and on the top of his head has fallen out and now is just bare skin. He has become more active, and his hunger is unabated. As a function of the spliced brain segments, rewiring of the dog's telencephalon, and the protein graft, his morphology is adjusting and changing. His shoulders have widened a little. His elbow joints have dropped by at least an inch, as have his knees. His forepaws are flatter and wider as are his rear paws. He quite often now stands on his rear legs against tables or countertops.

I hired carpenters to build a high pine fence around my property. They finished the task in a day and a half. I needed the freedom to bring Pertinax outside from time to time, unseen by passersby. Pertinax can stand on his rear legs against the fence and nearly see over it. I brought him out this afternoon and he again made for Udo's grave and began digging. I pulled him away by his collar and he growled at me in a most savage manner. I have never seen that response in him toward me before. The expression on his face was markedly not dog-like. And he made a gurgling sound in his throat sounding almost like an attempt to form a word.

***

Ten days after their separation, Aurore agreed to see Treves again. She arrived at the laboratory at ten in the morning. Treves prepared a late breakfast for her. They sat at his table in the kitchen, sipping coffee after the light meal.

"Has it been worth it?" she asked. "Has the result of your experiment been one you foresaw? One you hoped for?"

"Much, much better. I really can't believe the results I am getting and how quickly they are coming. In the past, artists and anatomists had to break the law by dissecting bodies to educate themselves in anatomy. There was no other way. Their work set the stage for modern surgery. But they had to *break the law*."

"But to what *use* will you put this success?"

"Well," Treves said after a long pause, "we could... engineer organs for human transplant, or..." He stood. "Come, let me show you."

Pertinax was asleep on a cot at the far end of the laboratory. Aurore gasped when she saw him. "Good God, how... different he is now," she said. The beast's back and shoulders had widened, his snout had shortened, and his front toes had lengthened into proto-fingers.

"Let's not wake him," Treves said. "He is like an infant in that he needs sleep. I think the changes going on inside him demand it. Every day his expression is more human-like than dog-like, and there is more comprehension in his eyes. Every day I see that he understands what I say to him in a more complex way than a dog does."

Aurore walked away from the cot. "What have you done to him? How will he live? Will you hide him here the rest of his life?"

"I don't know. The consequences mean little to me. The work is all that matters."

Aurore collapsed into a nearby chair. "If only Udo had lived," she said. "Mr. Purviance the lawyer told me there would be a case against the bank and Tancredy for Udo to keep the property. Extra funds were paid at the beginning of the mortgage that are not accounted for. Tancredy is back home now. His house is at the landing on Front Street, and it nearly flooded last spring. He will build a new house on the farm."

"Haarruuff! Rrrrrrrdy. Errrrdy. Rrrr..." The sound came from the cot. Pertinax sat up and slowly stood. The expression on his face, the glint and knowledge in his eyes, the tenseness of his lips, were markedly and undoubtedly human. Treves felt a fear and uncertainty he had never known with his creation before. He moved to place himself between Aurore and the beast. Pertinax pushed past Treves, slamming him with great force against Aurore. Aurore's head hit the wall behind her chair. The chair fell on its side.

Aurore was conscious but injured. Treves tore off his lab coat and placed it under her head on the floor. He saw Pertinax wrench open the laboratory door and run outside.

"Aurore, Aurore, are you all right? Can you hear me?" Treves implored.

"Yes... yes," she mumbled.

"Lie still. I may need to get you to the hospital." Treves stood. He ran to the laboratory door. He could see Pertinax digging at Udo's grave again. The beast tore savagely at the ground. In a moment he reached into the hole he had dug and with newly formed fingers, ripped the nearly frozen carcass from the ground. Pertinax held a gray arm in his hand for many moments, with a nearly unrecognizable headless torso attached to it. His face went blank and then transitioned to a confused, disoriented look. Suddenly the beast ripped a stringy section of meat from the arm. He chewed it slowly, then scowled in an expression that could have been either disgust or recognition, then spit it out.

Treves wanted to return inside and care for Aurore, but he couldn't take his eyes off his creature.

Pertinax suddenly dropped the corpse. He moved to the far-left side of the storage shed and with a burst of violent energy, crashed through Treves's pine fence. Treves lost sight of the great beast as it ran onto the street toward the northeast, toward Front Street, toward the landing.

The Long Dead Sister

This moment is unique because I never think of you. I make certain I don't. My self-contempt cannot tolerate acknowledging the qualities and traits we shared, so many of which made you a spectacle and laughingstock. Yes, I was disgusted by you, no doubt because I hated myself and you reminded me—too much—of that.

These things have only just occurred to me. New psychological fancies? For years I have tried to understand this revulsion. I have never visited your grave even though it sits at the far end of our family property. I never go back there. I never think of you.

Our family fortunes continue to decline. Or mine, I should say, since I am the only one left. Mr. Schiller, the coppersmith, continues to conceive of inventions no one wants. I financed his perpetual irrigation system and the soil repository for gravediggers, neither of which have been patented. I am finished with him. He has left the repository here on the property though I have complained to him and to the sheriff for its removal. I will sell it for the copper and brass in it if there is no response.

You have missed very little since you've been gone, Lilibet. I am still a bachelor. This would matter to you. You always cared about my well-being, though I never returned the sentiment. I thought, how can any family be excused for producing a child like you?

As I was saying, Elise ended our engagement, though I begged her not to. She called me too compliant, too desirous to please, too weak for her. "You want to be led around by me," she said. "You'll do anything I say." She was bored. I don't see how being forever agreeable can be boring, but there it is.

After this, of course, I fell into a terrible state of melancholy and more self-hatred. I thought about suicide, since my failings, it seems, are irreparable. I will never be good enough, so why continue? But I haven't yet found the strength to face the end. When I try to step outside myself and see what others see, I completely understand.

Even you found a mate, Lilibet, the reportedly near-impotent imbecile that he was. Ajax Carl Windt. Your Tristan. He couldn't write his own name until he was ten or eleven. The spectacle of the two of you out together—you, fat, clumsy, stupidly emotional, and shrieking every word at top volume, and Ajax, a grinning, uncomprehending Gwynplaine following you like a puppy, was a source of mortification for me.

Somehow our parents let you marry him. Somehow his parents agreed. You lived with us so they could watch over you, I suppose.

Ajax fell into a ditch dug for sewer repair while absentmindedly walking Bucephalus Street, trying to reset his pocket watch. Killed instantly. But not before you were pregnant. The little thing died inside you, and I felt some pity. It came out of you in fetid pieces. Yes, that was a sad day.

We all continued to live together, Mother and Father, you and I. Mother maintained her indifference to Father and he raged and fretted over it, depending as he did on her affection for his notion of self-worth. This fostered an anger that he directed at me. Insults, trivializations, mockery, wrath. You, he protected but ignored. He didn't understand how he had produced two such as we.

My first fiancée, Irma Sedgewick, ended things soon after your loss. I offered to convert to Methodism and oppose the Gold Standard if she wanted me to, but to no avail. I was depressed and shattered for months. Father told me to join the Army or the priesthood because no one else on earth would have me. He thought the Army might miraculously make a man of me, but the priesthood would at least cause less unease to womanhood.

At about that time, we found out how sick you were. The rashes, the pain, the fatigue—these were symptoms of systemic lupus erythematosus. There was little the doctors could do. We kept a nurse but saw no improvement in your condition. I saw a compassion for you growing in Mother that I had never seen before. That change prompted a change in Father also, who instantly developed a concern and affection for you, unpredicted during the whole course of your life until then. Their example affected me. I began to see a change in myself toward you, too.

Then your friend Nelly moved in. Nelly lived with you in your room and took scrupulous care of you. You showed some improvement, but Mother was not comforted. She suspected there was something "unnatural" about your friendship, and the idea obsessed her. With uncharacteristic empathy and insight, Father suggested that whatever the nature of your relationship with Nelly, at least you were getting better.

It was anger and outrage that killed Mother, unless, of course, it was jealousy that a friend was more important to you than she. Either way, while resisting Father's calming embrace, she fell down the stairs and, like Ajax, broke her neck. After a day of inconsolable grief and wailing that he had never been good enough for her and would never again be accepted by any woman who was her equal, Father shot himself. Enough said.

I rejoiced privately. And you rapidly declined afterward. In two months, you too were dead. I buried you on our property and forgot about you. I felt reborn. Yet, I am no manager of money. Our finances were declining under Father, and I only made things worse. I invested in foolishness like Schiller's inventions, and nothing came of them. I started to wonder how, with your many failings, did you come to be happy?

Every hour I sat alone in that big house began to seem emptier than the last. The silence became nearly unbearable. How is it your life was happier than mine? How is it you attracted more affection, if only a molecule more, despite the fact you were laughed at?

Sitting in the parlor one afternoon, I was dumbfounded to realize I missed you. I had often felt, from time to time since your death, that you were perhaps sending me little messages of encouragement and support. A flicker of an idea here, a wisp of contentment there. At those moments, I knew I was right. This was part of a journey of personality I needed to make. I never in my life expected you to be the key to it all. But I became certain you were. I came to count on, to depend on these.

I should not have ignored or disregarded your affection for me in the old days. I should have sought it out and valued it. How stupid of me to not have understood that it was all the affection the world had to offer me. Perhaps it should have been me who died, not you. If I had gone first, perhaps Providence would have spared you. You deserve to have found your rightful place in the human race, even if I never did.

For the relationship we never had, Lilibet, I now truly grieve, especially since I feel your presence and hear your words now more acutely than ever. Sitting in the front parlor this afternoon, looking out on Mal Ardents Street, I saw an old stray dog carrying a puppy. The old bitch was dirty and starving and mange-ridden. She stopped in front of the house and laid the pup on the ground. I saw immediately that the small creature was dead. The mother nudged it a few times, then picked it up again and slowly continued on her way. Though the dead infant's decomposition is assured and underway, the mother is in denial of this, and her love for the little creature continues until such time as it too falls into fetid pieces when she tries to lift it. She perhaps hopes that her love alone will keep it whole.

And what of you, my sister? If I had returned your affection, would you have gained some strength from it? A person of faith knows all things are possible. I once doubted this, but now I don't know. I do know that I miss you terribly these days, and if you were sitting here with me, in this evening's gloom, I would do anything to earn your kind deference again.

I had an impulse that grew into a conviction, and I did it. I hope you approve. I think you do. Pushing Schiller's contraption to your grave would have been much easier if the wheels were bigger. Perhaps if he made that change, he could sell it to churches and funeral directors. I finally got it out there under the willow trees and set the scoop in "receiving" position and locked it with the release catch. After some searching in the gardener's shed, I found a shovel. I began filling the scoop with the dirt from your grave. It was arduous work, especially for one as sedentary as I have become. Fortunately, we only dug a four-foot grave, and so after a couple of hours, it was done. The inexpensive wooden coffin in which I had buried you was revealed.

The wood was damp and beginning to rot. I inserted a crowbar at the right edge of the lid and pushed. There was a loud pop as the lid separated, and it blew away from the coffin. Chunks of brown muck splattered out against the wall of the hole, my trouser leg, forearm, and even on my chin. The released gas smelled horrific, and I coughed as it enveloped me. But there you laid, damp and blackened, flesh sliding away from muscle and bone. The dress in which we had buried you looked intact, though it was stained and saturated with seeping fluids and appeared stuck to your flesh.

Your body was limp and wet. As I lifted you, your left foot fell off, and your right arm. I am sorry, it couldn't be helped. All else stayed together as I got you up onto the ground above. Carefully, solicitously, I carried you into the house.

And here we are. You, situated in Mother's chair. I, on the divan, so we may truly be face to face. So, I ask: will you forgive me? Will you forgive my cold and shameful treatment of you? Will you forgive the disgust and mockery? As a child your hair was blonde and fine. Now it is dark and the little that is left is plastered to your skull. There is some sort of mass in your eye-sockets, though I wouldn't call it "eyes." Even as you are, you outshine me. You are more radiant, made so by your love and selflessness. How may I appease you? According to your nature, I believe I can win back your goodwill.

All night, you have conveyed nothing. I wrapped you in a shawl and built up the fire for you. All I sense, if anything, is disdain. The bad opinion, the disregard and dislike of everyone else, I will live with, but I am determined to subvert these things in you. If, as I suspect, they are there.

It is hard to divine your feelings. But there must still be love in you for me. I am certain of it... if I adopt your misfortunes. If I take onto myself your suffering and sad memories, I will show you how selfless I am regarding your happiness. Think kind thoughts, affectionate thoughts of me, and see what sacrifice I will make. Even now... just see.

The backyard of this property is long and wide, and so overgrown. I have let it decline as our family has declined and as I have been pushed ever more deeply into loneliness and self-hatred by the world. But you, Lilibet, abided these things. You kept bitterness out of your heart, though I saw moments when sadness overcame you.

I have the rope in my hand that releases the scoop. I lie as best I can on the lid of your rotting casket. Ah, the smell. Lingers for weeks, I am told.

The lid collapses and I am lying in the brown ooze you left behind. The sooner the better, a strong pull on the rope releases the dirt back to its rightful place.

Hopewell

Bessie looked across the dry grass and red clay of the backyard toward the tree line of oaks and scrub cedars and thought how her small world had shrunk even more when Fat got sick. She'd had enough of farm life as a girl and was happy in their small house back in Lesterton. But after Fat got promoted to shift boss at Osage Lead and the accident with the blasting caps happened, nothing would do for him but to move out of town and live on a farm again as he had done as a boy.

He didn't take her feelings into consideration, which was usual for Fat. There was a small community of Swedes back in Lesterton, brought in to work the mines when World War I broke out. Bessie considered them all to be her people and where she belonged. Her grandmother Ahlqvist had lived with her family after her grandfather died in an ore car accident. As a girl, Bessie enjoyed the immigrant stories about the old country, and their tales about superstition, trolls and monsters, and the spells of old Mrs. Larssen the *häxa*, or witch-woman.

Fat didn't seem to care that Bessie wouldn't know what to do with herself out on that dry, useless little farm all day while he was at work. There was nothing to Hopewell but a general store a mile down the gravel road and three other larger farms scattered off in the distance. She had never learned to drive, anyway. "Ye got yer television, yer radio, and housework," Fat said. "I don't know what else ye need to fill up yer time."

Bessie did have her programs and her stories on the television. She liked to watch *Queen for A Day*. In yesterday's program, a Mrs. Ponder from Battle Creek, Michigan who had breast cancer and eight children to raise alone was given a day at a beauty parlor and a new wringer washing machine. When Jack Bailey put the crown on Mrs. Ponder's head and called her Queen for a Day, the lady cried and so did Bessie. "What wonderful gifts to brighten her day," Bessie thought. And Bessie never missed *The Guiding Light* every morning.

But there wasn't a lot to choose from on the radio. The one station that came in best was KDDY from Potosi, thirty miles away, and it didn't carry much other than farm reports, local news, and information on who was expecting visitors this week and from where they were coming and how long they were expected to stay. Despite that, Bessie almost always had her radio on to keep her company while she did her housework or her canning. It was the dead silence of Hopewell she couldn't stand.

Rex, Bessie's old black and white collie, scratched at the back door.

He wanted to be fed. She scooped some dry dog food into a pan along with some table scraps she had saved and took them out to him. Rex's bowls were on the edge of the concrete slab back porch. Bessie filled his food bowl, and he eagerly ate. His water bowl was still half full. The sun was starting to set, but it was still humid and hot. She knew she had another sticky, restless night ahead of her, trying to sleep under the box fan.

The grass in the backyard was sparse and dying. Browning patches of it receded across the cracked red clay of the lot, as Bessie had given up watering it weeks ago. "If the grass is dead, I don't have to cut it," she thought. It seemed to her that everything you do in life starts to fall apart immediately, anyway. She was tired all the time now. It was easier to let the decay of the world happen rather than keep fighting it to no lasting result.

She wiped her brow with her apron. As she turned to go back into the kitchen, she thought she saw a movement in the tree line off at the edge of their pasture. It could have been a deer, but her impression was it was too dark a color. She watched the spot for a few moments more but saw nothing.

Back inside she could hear Fat coughing. It was time for his treatment.

Fat was a small man. His nickname was a joke and was given to him by the other ore hand-loaders in the mine forty years before, when it was obvious he couldn't keep up with them. He was lucky to be promoted to shift boss when "Cupeyes" Wampler died in a cave-in.

Now Fat was completely helpless. As his emphysema and heart condition worsened and he slowly became an invalid, Bessie had started sleeping on the couch so that his wheezing, coughing, and gurgling struggles to breathe didn't keep her awake all night. Most of the time Fat seemed to hear nothing but shouted instructions to roll over, sip through a straw, or take his medicine.

Fat's bed was against the wall. Bessie was waiting for a hospital bed with rails that the Lesterton Church of the Nazarene was trying to buy for her. Then she would not have to worry about Fat falling out of bed as he had done in February. The oxygen tank stood next to him. A clear, plastic cylinder bubbled on top of it, and plastic tubes ran up over the headboard and were taped into Fat's nostrils. He was wheezing shallowly and seemed to be semi-conscious.

"Time fer your treatment now," Bessie called out to him loudly. He was on his right side, facing away from her with his knees drawn up and a quilt tucked between them. She pulled the bedclothes down to his waist. He was shriveled and thin-skinned and naked like a newly hatched bird. His legs and arms were thin, their veins blue and clustered like grapes. She had washed him a few hours before and he still smelled of talcum powder. Bessie pushed a chair to his bedside and sat. She pulled his arm, useless under white, sagging skin, toward her to expose his side, and began to gently and rhythmically pound on his exposed ribs with cupped hands.

Fat began to groan. He tried to pull his arm back to cover his side, but Bessie easily pinned it down with her knee as she did twice every day. Fat mumbled something about Bill Larsson coming to the farm. Larsson died in the mine soon after Fat's promotion. Fat hadn't mentioned him for months.

"Leave go of me, ye damned ole bitch..." His voice was weak and thin and full of congestion. "Leave go my arm. Stop a-whackin' me, ye damned ole whorey son of a bitchin'..."

"Lay still an' quit a-fightin' me! Ain't nobody a-pickin' on you now." She shook his arm like she would have done one of her boys' arms years ago. The arm was dry and soft like bread dough sprinkled with flour. He couldn't respond. He was helpless.

When she had finished with his side, she pulled him over on his stomach and began to pound on his back. Every few minutes he would cough into a rag she would hold to his mouth as the congestion broke loose. Then he would gasp for breath and quiver a little as he did, sometimes mumbling things she knew she didn't care to hear.

When he settled down, she sat back in her chair. Her knees hurt and her ankles were swollen and isolated spots of pain higher up on her legs marked the blue-violet smudges of varicose veins she thanked her husband for. Before he got on in the mines, when they still lived in town, Fat only worked when he felt like it. Some winters he would sit with his feet on the stove all winter long, smoking one cigarette after another, never lifting a finger to help around the house. Bessie had to take up the slack: piecework, the meat cannery, the drill press at Lowell Manufacturing, dry cleaning, making four dollars a week to Fat's eight during the Depression, when he chose to work. Still, she considered herself robust and was thankful for that.

The whippoorwills had started calling out in their small strip of woods. Bessie was a little surprised it was that late in the day, although her body felt it was. Out in the backyard, Rex had started barking. There were often rabbits or foxes on the other side of the pasture fence who knew the old dog could not reach them. Bessie thought it was funny how the animals seemed to be mocking Rex and smugly enjoying his helpless excitement. Rex would occasionally catch a rat or mole or black snake, only because they didn't stay out of the yard.

Rex suddenly growled and yelped. Bessie thought she had better check on him. She found the dog cowering on the back porch. He had a jagged cut across his snout.

"Aw, dammit Rex," Bessie said, "When are you gonna learn not to put your snout through the fence? That was a fox, wasn't it? Or a coon. I better clean that up."

She stepped back into the kitchen and dampened a cloth. She

carefully cleaned the old dog's snout. "It ain't too bad," she said. "Leave them varmints alone!"

She glanced back out at the tree line, gloomy in the gathering dusk. A wisp of white moved behind some tree trunks and vanished.

"I bet that's Fred Otz," she mumbled, "pokin' around our proppity, a-keepin' a eye on me." Fred Otz and his momma Hulga were Bessie's nearest neighbors. They had come from Germany twenty years before and bought the small farm down the road. Momma barely spoke English. Fred was a short, massive man with a red face, who Fat had always called "retarded." Fred used to show up for a visit many nights at suppertime and Bessie always felt compelled to invite him to stay. She had put an end to that practice earlier this year. She had always been a little afraid of him. Bessie refilled Rex's water bowl and closed and locked the kitchen door.

In the bedroom at the front of the house, Fat was asleep. Bessie opened the closet door in the room and rummaged around behind her winter clothes until she found Fat's old Iver Johnson shotgun. It was a single-shot twenty gauge. She broke it open and saw that it was unloaded. A half box of shells sat on the closet shelf. She brought the gun and ammunition into the living room where she slept. She put two shells in her apron pocket and loaded a shell into the gun and leaned it into the corner behind the couch.

She thought about turning on the television. It was time for Perry Como, her favorite nighttime program, and they were going to salute Missouri in the Fifty Nifty United States segment, but she was tired. She decided to lie down on the couch a while.

It was because of what happened to Bill Larsson that they moved to the farm. When Fat hired on at Osage Lead, they put him on the hand-loader crew like they did all new hires. Each hand-loader had to load fifteen tons of ore a day to score out and go home. Fat could barely do it. Bill Larsson was Bessie's third cousin and a big man. His branch of the family and Fat's parents had been in a dispute about the bottom land on the River Aux Vases a generation before, and there had been bad blood between them since. The other loaders said that Bill bullied Fat and laughed at him until Fat got promoted to shift boss over the drift cutters and hand-loaders.

One of the first things Fat did as boss was to shift Bill over to the drift cutter crew even though Bill knew nothing about explosives. One day in drift 32, Bill was offloading a crate of blasting caps alone. He mishandled them or dropped them, and they blew, cutting Bill in half. Bessie had heard that Henry Pfaff, the aged company doctor, took photographs of the dead man's eyes as he always did after a fatal accident, to see if the last image before that man's death had been preserved to help solve the mystery and absolve the company from liability. If a man was looking at another worker or distracted in some way when he should have been concentrating, the photo might provide evidence for the company's benefit. Bessie believed that this was possible, and she often wondered what secrets Henry kept from grieving families.

After a few weeks of complaining that the town was blaming him and judging him, Fat moved his family out to the farm. Pretty soon Fat started to get threatening phone calls from Larsson's family. That's when he had the telephone taken out.

Bessie resented how women and kids have to pay the price for the foolishness of men. Bessie remembered her mother and Swedish grandmother complaining of this. She remembered when her grandfather ran over a man with a carriage in a drunken rage at Obli, and her grandmother nailed a horseshoe upside down above the door to keep the revenant, or *draugr*, from seeking revenge away from the family.

It wasn't only Bessie who didn't want to move out to Hopewell. Her boys, Walter and Chet, moved back to town as soon as they were old enough. They married and had families and never visited anymore. At forty, Bessie got pregnant again and had her "change of life baby" Elaine. Both she and the baby nearly died at birth. Dr. Crabtree, smelling of whiskey when he examined the child, said she would never develop normally. The baby died at eight weeks old one evening when Fat was working second shift, and Bessie, with no telephone, could do nothing but wrap the tiny corpse and sit in the silent house, waiting until her husband came home from work.

Bessie still had family in Lesterton, Obli, and Belgique. Her great-uncle Jubilee died in Ste. Odile a year earlier. She wanted to go to the funeral but knew that was out of the question. Bessie couldn't go anywhere. Now she had to care for Fat. Her duty was to put off his death as long as possible because there was nobody else to do it. The boys were done with him. There was nobody left in the world who even thought of him anymore, but her.

Her eyelids were heavy. It was still early but she thought she would lie back on the couch and nap a while. The clicking drone of the cicadas was starting to die down, meaning evening was coming on. Maybe later she would watch a little television, although she was too late for Perry Como. She heard the train off in the distance down at Hopewell. It was odd to her how far that train sound carried over the hills and through the hardwood forests.

She felt herself dozing off but awoke to the sound of Rex barking. As she sat up on the couch, the barking became more urgent and suddenly ended with a yelp. Bessie reached for the Iver Johnson. She hurried to the back door and stared out the window. She could see nothing in the small bowl of illumination from the porch light. She opened the door.

"Rex!" she called. "*Rex!*" There was no answer. She walked over to his doghouse just inside the pasture fence. The light was bad there, but there was no sign of the old dog she could find except for a wisp of fur on the fence wire nearby. "Rex!" She stared off at the horizon to the southeast. She could see the spotlight on at the Nixon's barn about two miles away. She looked toward her own tree line across the pasture. A pale flicker passed through the trees.

"Fred!" she called. *"Fred Otz, is that you?* What did you do to my dog? I got a gun, you German son-of-a bitch. I'll git the sheriff after you and git you deported. See if I don't!"

She went back into the house and locked the door. She decided she would go out and look for Rex in the morning. She put a pot of coffee on. She knew she wouldn't sleep anymore that night.

The next morning was hot, and the dry fields were humming with insect sounds. After Bessie gave Fat his morning treatment and got him to eat a little, she put a few more shotgun shells into her apron pocket, took the Iver Johnson out from behind the couch, and crossed the backyard to the pasture gate. Outside the fence across from Rex's doghouse, the milkweeds, briars, and sprigs of alfalfa were smashed down. She saw scattered strands of black and white fur and on a few dandelion leaves, spots of blood.

Following a new path of broken weeds a few more feet, Bessie spotted the mangled remains of her dog. Rex's throat and thorax had been torn out and his left front leg was missing. Bessie gasped and dropped the shotgun. She covered her mouth in shock and disbelief. As she recovered the gun from the weeds, she lost her balance and fell across the carcass. The old dog's dead eye, placid and enduringly vacant, seemed to simultaneously look at her and at nothing at all.

Rex had been Chet's dog. They had gotten him from the Nixons when he was a puppy. For many years the old dog had been the only companionship of her empty days. Bessie was surprised at how suddenly and severely she felt his loss and at how utterly alone she now realized herself to be.

"God! My God!" Bessie gasped. She felt lightheaded and knew she needed to steady herself. "Might be... could be coyotes," she whispered. "Or red wolves. Nixon saw one last year."

She turned and looked at the tree line across the parched field, already shimmering in the heat. The black oaks, cedars, hickory trees, and black walnuts were motionless. Many were showing the distress of the drought. The buzzing of the insects came from every direction. Bessie looked at the barrier of trees for many moments. Nothing moved, though she *thought* she could hear movement deep in the dark undergrowth. Squirrels or a raccoon, probably. She considered whether she wanted to continue into the woods or go back to the house. She glanced down at Rex's shredded carcass and started toward the tree line.

Beyond a small rise, Bessie came upon what was left of their half-acre pond. Nearly all the water had evaporated, leaving a muddy red pool no more than ten feet across. The banks, once submerged, were now cracked, red clay. The few perch and bass Fat had stocked the pond with years ago were now all dead, fly-covered and rotting in the sun.

The weeds thinned out as she approached the woods, and an erosion gully cut a severe gash across the pasture. She veered to her right to avoid this and disturbed two crows scavenging something. Bessie couldn't tell what the carcass was, but this time of year, it was likely a fawn.

The tree line was a few feet in front of her. She stood for a moment at the barrier. The bleached, sweltering field behind contrasted sharply with the shadowy wall in front of her. As she stepped forward, a loud pop resonated off the tree trunks like a thick, fallen branch breaking under a covering of leaves. She stopped. The woods seemed to exhale a breath and a muffled word was carried on the breeze. "*Gaugeup*," she thought she heard, then something like "*burt upp.*"

Bessie decided she could go no further. "If that's you, Fred Otz, I swear I'll blow your foreign head off," she murmured. She turned and made her way as quickly as she could back to the house.

When she got back inside, she could hear Fat groaning in the front room. She kept the box fan on him most of the time, but she could see he was suffering in the heat. She dampened a cloth and wiped his face and neck.

"Ain't gonna be pushed around," Fat mumbled. "No hireling is gonna..."

"Ain't nobody a-pickin' on you, lay still," Bessie, roughly pushing him against the mattress as she wiped his chest and stomach. "Settle down, now."

Bessie remembered she had left the back door unlocked. She rushed back to the kitchen to lock it. She leaned the Iver Johnson against the couch nearby. Fat was mumbling something barely coherent about the mines: payday and quitting time.

"Gaugeup," She heard him say. It could have been the same word she thought she heard among the trees. She hurried back to the front bedroom.

"Fat, what did you say? What did you just say?"

His voice was vague and irritated. "Quittin' time. Cage up. Ever'body out."

Fear prickled across Bessie's body. Cage up was work talk. Miner talk. Fat was remembering ordering the hand-loaders into the elevator cage at the end of a shift. But she had heard the same phrase out in the trees. Or he thought she had. Her grandmother's old *Alla Helgon's Dag* stories, repeated once a year in her childhood, told of *draugr*, the vengeful spirit, of which she was genuinely terrified, of apparitions and revenants who always whispered their intentions to you when you were distracted or fearful. "If you do na listen to them," the old woman would say smiling, enjoying the reactions of her grandchildren, "what happens to you then is your own doin'. And never harm the family of a *häxa*. Bring down revenge and kill everything in the way before it kills you."

Bessie locked the door on the front wall of Fat's room, which led out to their screened front porch. Neither she nor Fat had ever locked the door before. Bessie checked Fat's forehead. Despite the heat, he was clammy and cold, and he seemed to be growing restless. He was mumbling things she could not make out. She pulled the sheet up to his shoulders and decided to make herself a pot of coffee.

The television was on in the small living room area all afternoon, but Bessie scarcely glanced at it. She sat at the kitchen table in the breeze of her little green countertop fan, sipping her coffee for hours. She had no appetite, but as the dry drone of insects in the fields gave way to the calling of whippoorwills, she made herself a head cheese sandwich.

As the sun was going down, she heard a sound like branches from their elm tree scraping the roof. She looked out the kitchen door window and saw no sign of a breeze in the growing darkness. She checked to make sure she had locked the door.

"He made fun of me!" Fat yelled from the front room. Bessie walked back to quiet him.

"Be still, now," she said. "I'll feed you and you can go back to sleep."

"Said I was a skinny little tater-bug, that I had to stand up twice to make a shadow!"

"Be still! Shut up, now. I don't want to have to rassle you through your treatment again. Don't git all worked up."

An exasperated breath gurgled out of him, and he began to snore.

Bessie saw the front window in Fat's room was open. She closed and locked it. She heard the scraping branches sound on the roof again. She could see through his window that the trees were all still. There was a pop of metal as if a gutter had bent. She moved back into the kitchen and looked out the window over the sink. She could see nothing but the darkening fields. Sometimes raccoons or opossums dropped from the branches onto the roof. It had happened many times before.

For many minutes there was no sound of any kind except Fat's snoring. Bessie sat at the table a moment and thought she might make herself a cup of tea. She preferred tea to coffee when she wanted to calm her nerves. She filled her old copper kettle, rough as a lunar landscape inside from the minerals in their water, and set it on the stove. After a few minutes of thinking nothing, of staring at the kettle spout, steam began to roil out. Just as she stood, a crashing, violent knock at the back door stabbed through her torso and head and nearly sent her reeling into the stovetop flame.

"Iss eet zuppertime?" a husky voice laughed. Through the back door window, the small cone of the porch light only touching his large belly, Bessie saw Fred Otz. He was laughing at the sport of startling her. Bessie grabbed the Iver Johnson leaning against the couch. When he saw the shotgun, Fred's smile faded.

"Did you kill my dog, you son-of-a-bitch?" Bessie screamed through the door.

"Nein... no, no," Fred insisted.

"You bin sneakin' around my propitty, a-watchin' me?"

"No... no. I usse to come by for zupper. I was yust playing a yoke..."

"Oncet an' for all, I got no time for your jokes nor your freeloadin'..." As Bessie opened the door, Fred took a step backward. He made an odd yipping noise as some great force pulled him suddenly and violently back into the enveloping darkness. Bessie heard a slight scream and gasp out in the night. She quickly stepped back inside and locked the door.

For a moment she was afraid to look out the window. When she did, she saw nothing unusual.

"What happened? What happened?" she whispered. "What... *did that?*"

Still holding the shotgun, she ran back to Fat's room. The room was dimly lit by one small table lamp. Shadows spread into every corner and at an angle across the small room. Fat was snoring fitfully. His oxygen tank bubbled on the headboard above his pillow. A rattling sound grew out of the silence and Bessie gradually comprehended, almost against her will, that it was the kitchen doorknob being tested and shaken.

She lifted the shotgun to her shoulder and walked tentatively back toward the kitchen. She watched the doorknob slowly rattle back and forth as she approached, but she could see nothing through the window. Her legs were weak, and she realized that she had stopped walking and could not make herself take another step.

"Who... *who is it?*" she croaked through a dry mouth.

She took a step. And another. When she passed into the middle room, she switched off the overhead light at the switch near the doorway. The small light over the kitchen sink was still on. She wanted to turn all the lights off so whoever was outside could not see her. She moved quickly to the sink, watching the back door as she went. As she reached for the switch behind the sink, there was a great crash against the sink window. Bessie screamed and squeezed the shotgun. The gun fired, blasting a hole in a lower kitchen cabinet. She dropped it. Bessie fell backward against the kitchen table.

She saw only darkness beyond the small kitchen window, but the panes began to rattle and shake violently as if they would break. Bessie plunged toward the light switch and quickly turned off the kitchen light. All the house now was in darkness except for the dim lamp back in Fat's room.

Bessie felt for the shotgun in the gloom and found it. She stood silently for a few moments, listening. For a long time, she heard nothing. Then a low, guttural murmur grew out of the silence. It was coming from Fat's bedroom. The sound of breaking glass nearly caused Bessie to drop the gun again. She moved toward the sound and tripped over a kitchen chair in the darkness. She fell to the floor, cutting her shin against the leg of the chair. The murmur in Fat's room grew into a low, wet voice, the voice she had heard in the woods.

"*Cage up,*" the voice said. "*Bur upp.*" Bessie realized after a second that the last two words she'd heard were Swedish.

Bessie struggled to her feet and painfully hobbled back to Fat's room. A crashing sound was heard, and his small bedroom lamp was thrown against the front wall. In a matter of a second, the room was still.

When Bessie entered the bedroom, she saw by the faint remaining light that the window and part of the wall beyond Fat's bed had been nearly destroyed. There were glass shards spread across the bed, and splinters of the wooden window frame, and Bessie saw that Fat's small body was still and lifeless, his glassy eyes open, as the image of the last form he saw in his life surely faded away.

Renatus Sum

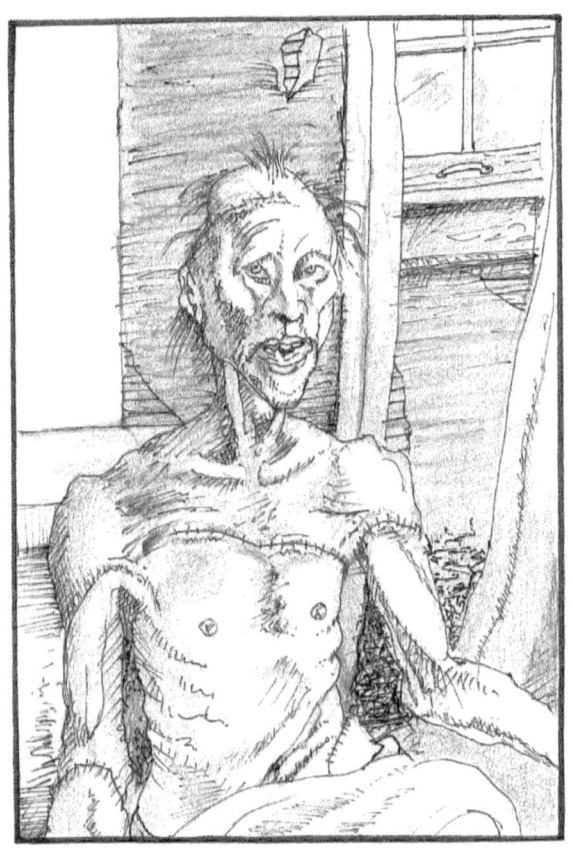

I am aware of the room around me. All was darkness before, but now I am aware. I recognize a table for a table, chairs for what they are, windows, doors. They are all new, yet familiar. I still do not know where I acquired the words though, the words I am using now. Somewhere from my past experiences, they are reborn. As I am. As my thoughts travel, the words just appear to frame them. I will understand where the words originated someday, I hope.

And I am aware of pain. The pain of healing, all over my body.

Sameh is my keeper. I learn from him when I am aware, and not in darkness. At first was the great darkness stretching back into an infinite past. Before my being. Then there was awakening. Awakening with memories. And words. A flood of words. Then from time to time more darkness from which I awaken and find I am changed. My body, my being, has changed. *"Renatus Sum,"* Sameh says, but I do not know what he means.

He talks of the blessed saints Damien and Cosmas, Arabians, creators, and keepers of the great medical discoveries of the Arabic world. *Antidotarius Magnus*, the ancient eastern tome of medicine, names *Opopira Magna* as the creation of the two saints. Sameh says his extractions from the kidneys of swine and two other creatures added to the *opopira* have made his work, have made *me*, possible. I do not think I know what he means by this, either. He says it is the work of twenty years.

Whatever all of it means, it must be true. Sameh knows all. I know nothing more of the world than dim memories. Sameh tells me what I need to know. He prepares me. Someday I will be ready to see it all for myself. I will be ready to create memory again. Until then, Sameh is my keeper. My protector. Twenty years of working alone, he has said, scorned by his teacher, determination drove him. He isolated, sacrificed all in his lonely seacoast retreat, and has proved his detractor wrong.

He experimented with dogs over the years, and pigs to middling success. Finally, he had the opportunity to work with a foreman at a sawmill who lost a hand in an accident, and Sameh was at last vindicated. He proclaimed a great boon to humanity and surgical science, and what he learned led to the great test of his work. It led to me.

As time has gone on, he has fixated more and more on revealing that vindication to his teacher from long ago and discrediting that researcher's contradicting theories.

He decided we must come to this village, a new place, Ste. Odile.

Our hermitage in the north on the gray seashore suited me very well. It was where Sameh had worked for years. Twenty years, as I have said. It was where I first became sensate. I do not know if we will ever go back. Whatever he decides is best. He knows what is best for me far better than I.

I hear the name Treves every day. Sirach Kingdom Treves. The name is almost always spoken in anger now. An anger that grows. It is the name of Sameh's teacher, his mentor from long ago. I know Treves is an old man now. I know he lives in this village of Ste. Odile. He is why we have come here, I suspect. Whatever Sameh's intention, I know it to be just and correct.

I do not remember my name. It doesn't matter because Sameh has named me Oriax. It is a name that means something to him. My incomplete memory was caused, Sameh has said, from blood loss. Blood loss affected my brain. He repaired the damage. My blood was restored. He promised to make me better than before and he kept his word. As my brain repairs, these words return. The words I use now. They are a wonderful gift coming from the skill of my creator.

There was an explosion at the Council House in Linden Ford, Massachusetts. An anarchist's bomb. I was severely injured. Some of this I remember, and some I have heard from Sameh. I often confuse the two sources. With the sawmill injury, he had solved the mystery of the *opopira* of Saints Damien and Cosmas and experimented with adding the extra elements those martyrs themselves must have used. Having arrived in Christian lands from Arabia, the saints heard of a man with a gangrenous leg that needed to be removed. They undertook this task but replaced the leg with one harvested from the body of a recently deceased Moor. The recipient recovered and prospered with the newly grafted limb. Nothing like this had ever been seen before. Sameh learned the secret, and I became the beneficiary. It is said that the subject of that surgery felt no pain. I feel pain constantly. Movement is agony.

My legs were lost in the explosion and essentially, my arms. Seizing the opportunity, Sameh replaced these with the limbs of a larger man, recently deceased. Part of my skull was missing and my lungs and liver damaged. He worked for four days, he said, in an ice chamber, to reconstitute me. My wounds still seep and bleed. They are always wet as the healing crust is broken because Sameh insists that I move to regain strength. The pain is constant.

Traveling was terrible. Nearly 1,300 miles, Sameh said. Mostly by train. I had to be concealed in a long crate for most of it. Sameh said the public must not see me. He fed me when he could and looked in on me at night in the baggage car. Terrible. Now we are in what Sameh calls a farmhouse. It is a few miles from the great river and the town called Ste. Odile.

It is a very old farmhouse, from the look of it. There are open fields and hills nearby and forest in the distance in every direction.

There is a weathered old pony trap near the house, and Sameh has rented a horse from a farmer beyond the woods. There are two sleeping rooms in the house. I have the smaller, darker one. I rest much of the day. It is important that I heal. My pain subsides a little after I rest.

Sameh rode the horse to a general store somewhere to the south. He went to buy food and bandages, pain powder, and other things. I have no appetite, but Sameh says I must eat. He says it is important for my healing.

It is late autumn, and the sleeping room is cold. I must get warm as best I can. Sameh will be gone for several hours. He built a fire in the stove before he left. He cares for me so well. I only hope I can be as benevolent as he is when I am able.

I lie in the near darkness thinking of a time when I will no longer feel the pain. Sameh says his concoction is generally working to prevent my body from rejecting those parts he has grafted to me, but there is still the threat of rejection to a small extent, and the possibility of infection. He will do his best for me, I know, and someday I hope to meet other souls and find acceptance in a human community when the time is right. This, I know, is why Sameh has done what he has done for me.

A tiny knock on the door. I am startled. I am always to bolt the door after Sameh when he leaves, but I know I forgot to do it this time. I hear a chicken cluck and the small tap is repeated. I arise and step into the front room. I will move quickly to the door and bolt it and listen to hear if the chicken alone is tapping on the door.

Before I reach the door, it pushes slightly open. "Hello?" It is a child's voice. I stop. Before I can retreat into my room, the door opens further and a little boy of about six steps in. The chicken runs past the boy toward the kitchen. The boy chases it and as he picks the bird up, he notices me.

The child is startled by my appearance and takes a step back. "Hello," he says timidly.

"I see you are afraid but have overcome it," I say. "That is a good thing, I think."

The boy shrugs.

"I am sorry if I startled you. But you know you should not come into someone's house without being invited. My protector will be unhappy."

"Yeah. I shouldn't."

"What's your name?"

"Vernal Ivey Quested. We live up the road. I seen you moving in. I raise my own chickens. I keep 'em as pets and for eggs. I brung you one since you got a coop out there. A few more and a rooster and you can have eggs and new chicks if you want 'em."

"Well, thank you... Vernal. I don't know how long we will be here. That was very kind of you, though."

"What happened to you? You got lots of operations. You got a dent in your head."

"I was in a bad accident and the doctor who lives here is making me better. I nearly died."

"So that man saveded you. Where did you come from?"

"I don't remember very much. I am starting all over again. I have to relearn everything. Sameh says I need to recover and learn about... everything again. I don't even remember my name. Sameh calls me Oriax."

"That kinder sounds like a devil's name. You can sit down if you want," Vernal said. "You look tired."

I sit. "You are very thoughtful," I say. "Do your parents know you are here?"

"No. They's at a revival in Lesterton. I think they come home tomorrow. They leave me on my own to take care of the animals when they go to testify."

"What is 'testify'?"

"To go witness to the Lord. It's a prayer meeting."

"It is religion, then? It's praying to God?"

"You wasn't joking me when you said you forgot everything!" Vernal seems surprised by my ignorance. "Yeah, it's religion. It's how we thank God for making us."

The chicken Vernal has brought struts around the kitchen, pecking at seeds and insects on the floor. "Thank God for making us?" I repeat. "Then it is a good thing."

"Yes, I think so. I go with them sometimes. People get moved by the Spirit and hug each other."

"I hope to see it myself. I thank Sameh for saving me. I should thank God too, then."

"Yeah, you really ort to, unless you choose Hellfire."

"I don't know about Hellfire."

"You're probly makin' God mad, then, but He'll forgive you and let you into the community."

"Yes... the community. I look forward to the time when I can join a community."

Vernal picks up the chicken and sits in the other kitchen chair. "I call this chicken Nancy, but you can call her whatever you want to," he said. "I don't like to eat animals but 'cept for sometimes, even though God gave us the whole world to use as we want. My pop taught me that. My pop was on the wrong path when he got saved."

"The wrong path...?"

"But he learnded to love God's chiggen and he got in the community then."

"And that is a good thing."

"You said a mouthful, Mr.... Oriax."

"Wonderful."

"The chiggen of God are good, Pop says. They just get losted sometimes."

I smile a painful smile at him. I find it odd that I am comforted by what he has said. I want to heal quickly and learn much more.

"How come you moveded here?" Vernal asks.

"Sameh wanted to come here. I am not sure why, except an old teacher of his lives in the town. It has something to do with Dr. Treves."

"Dr. Treves ain't doin' good. He got hurted real bad at the insane asylum. The crazy people done it to him. He can't get outta bed no more."

"That's terrible, but an insane person can't be blamed. Or called bad...?

"God let it happen." The boy says this as if it were a lesson often repeated to him. "I'm gonna put Nancy in the coop and see if she likes it." The boy picks up the chicken, which makes no effort to escape him, and carries it out the front door.

I watch him from a kitchen window. He opens the wire gate of the fence surrounding the coop and steps inside. He places the bird on the ground. The door to the coop is blocked by a rusted farm machine of some sort. Vernal tries to move it but he cannot. I must decide whether to go outside to help him. I have never been outside except for short distances with Sameh, and always covered by a sheet or blanket.

I walk slowly out the front door and around to the back of the house. Every step is painful, and I must brace myself as I walk against the outside walls. "I didn't think you could help me," Vernal says.

I am shirtless, as I always am when I rest. The sun burns my pale, ribbed flesh. I notice that the sutures in my chest and abdomen are wet. They have broken open again. I brace my hands against the rusty frame of the machine and push. I easily move it away. Pain rings my arms where Sameh attached them. Blood trickles out of the sutures.

"You're strong!" Vernal says in amazement. "I didn't think you was strong with all them operations."

The boy puts the docile chicken inside the coop, and she remains there. I need to get out of the sunlight. I return to the house and Vernal follows me. I am spent. Exhausted. I sit at the kitchen table again. Vernal sits too.

"You look sick," he says.

"Why weren't you more afraid when you first saw me?" I ask.

"I was a little, but I seen you was afraid, too. There's goodness in everyone and I seen it in you. I seen fellowship."

I smile at him. I feel in a way I would call... reassured. I am certain Sameh will like this child as I do. I stand. "I need to rest, to lie down..."

"Okay." He continues to sit at the table.

I quickly drift off to sleep.

I awaken to the sound of the horse's hooves. Sameh has returned. I rise to greet him. I am anxious to introduce him to our new young friend. I hear footsteps moving past the side of the house, then the cackle of the chicken. I hear the front door open.

"I brung you a chicken for your coop," Vernal says.

"Who are you? What are you doing here?" Sameh says.

"What are you doing?" Vernal shouts.

As I enter the room, I see through the front door that Sameh has tied the chicken's feet to a clothesline post in the yard. In a second, he has twisted the bird's head off. The headless body flutters grotesquely for a few seconds, spraying blood everywhere nearby.

Vernal is speechless for a moment. "I brung her for a pet, to get eggs!" he protests. He seems stunned by what he has seen.

"It will make our dinner instead," Sameh says in a gruff voice. "Who are you, boy?"

I was confused by Sameh's tone. He seemed to be hostile toward our guest and frightening to the child. "He is a neighbor," I say. "He meant the bird as a gift. It was his pet."

Sameh wears a dark expression I have never seen before. He walks brusquely toward me. "You were to remain unseen!" he says. "I brought you here *hidden in a box*. You were to remain unseen!"

"I... He just came into the house..."

"I didn't give you my chicken to kill her!" Vernal was near tears.

"You stay in the house! Rest!" Sameh shouts at me. "I will see that this young man gets home."

I close the door. This is very confusing. I feel something like fear and regret. I remember these feelings now. Through the window, I see that Sameh has remounted the horse and placed the child on the saddle in front of him. They ride off. At that moment I remember another feeling. I call it dread.

I am unfamiliar with anger, though I remember the word. If I knew of it before in my earlier life, I have little memory of it. It worries me that I do not understand where the anger comes from. I have a sense that I should be concerned with what actions it can lead to...but how much will the goodness of humanity allow? The comfort I felt when Vernal was here is gone. Abruptly, I have doubts about his well-being.

I try to rest but find it impossible. Dread oppresses me and confusion... confusion about my perceptions of all I have seen of the world so far, and the nature of man. It is more than an hour before Sameh returns. He does not come into the house immediately. He cuts the chicken carcass from the post and begins pulling the feathers from it. After he has cleaned and gutted the bird, he boils it in a pot. As he sits to eat, he has still not spoken to me of the boy. He has long since stopped insisting that I eat when I have no appetite.

"I have never seen anger in you before you started speaking about this town, and Dr. Treves. Anger is the right word. You are preoccupied, fixated now." I say at length. "You took Vernal home?"

"Yes, I took him. He should have never seen you."

"I think he keeps his word. If you asked him to stay silent, I believe he will."

"Yes, he will," Sameh says, never looking at me. His tone releases strange feelings in me, and troubling suspicions. It is as though I suddenly see that there is a darkness afoot that I have not heretofore imagined. I feel supremely foolish and vulnerable. I see my creator in a new way. For a time, I resist the suspicion that I have never understood his true nature. It seems to me important to resist.

Sameh finishes eating quickly. "Tonight," he says, "we will do what we came here to do. Tomorrow, we leave this place. You will finish your healing and then... the world will know what I have done."

***

The moon was long risen before we set out. Sameh hitched the horse to the trap. I had climbed into the back seating area, and he drove us out onto the moonlit road.

"Where are we going?" I ask, after deciding that Sameh does not intend to volunteer any information. "Is this the time when we will see your teacher?"

"An old score is to be settled. I was insulted and mocked years ago. You are my vindication."

"I know the word. In what way am I? Why do you need vindication?"

"I won't bear an insult."

"In what way does vindication affect... or change the insult?"

"It gives satisfaction to the offended. That is all you need to know. You will ask no more and do as I say."

I have never before desired to do anything other than what Sameh required of me. I have always been unerringly grateful to him as my protector and creator. Perhaps I have misunderstood his moods. Surely Vernal is now safe in his home, awaiting his parents' return...? I don't know why I should doubt this. It is what Sameh said he would do.

I quickly find the jostling of the trap painful. The compartment is too small for me, and as I struggle to find a less painful position, I must move a cloth sack Sameh has placed on the floor. I push the sack out of my way as best I can.

The road passes through woods for a short distance and then opens to moonlit fields and then hills. At the top of a hill, the town is visible, as is the dark river beyond. Sameh says nothing as we approach the town but the words, "Rouen Street... Rouen Street."

It is very late when we enter the town. There are few streetlights, and it is difficult to see the old street sign that reads ROUEN STREET. We turn north onto it. The houses along the street are large and were once impressive compared to the more modest ones we passed along the way. Midway along the block, Sameh seems to recognize one of the houses. "This looks like it," he says.

The house is stone, three stories high and with a large porch. The grounds are very unkempt, the grass overgrown, and a flower garden is immersed in weeds.

"He told me in his last letter that he lives alone," Sameh says.

"Why are we here?" I ask, to no response.

Sameh climbs out of the trap and helps me out of the back. He removes the sack he has brought. The streets are completely empty as we approach the front door. I am limping. There is much pain in my legs from the cramped trip into town.

"Why are we here?" I ask again. "Why would we come at this time of night?"

Sameh says nothing. He pushes the front door open, and we step inside. The feeling I had when Sameh rode off with Vernal returns. If I must believe the child is unhurt, I must also believe that Sameh has no bad intentions. He said he would not bear an insult, but I do not know what that means. Nor do I know Sameh, it seems.

There is a staircase just inside the entryway of the old house. To the left of this is a hallway with parlors on either side. At the end of the hallway is a closed door with the slightest suggestion of light under it. "There," Sameh says. He walks toward the door, and I follow him.

Sameh my creator, my protector, my sainted benefactor, is transforming. My memories of him expand as I enter the house. I am remembering more. Every gesture and movement reconstitutes another fact of his nature I had forgotten. Before my creation there *was* anger. I knew him slightly in my old life at Linden Ford, Massachusetts. Anger and resentment, I think are the words. And the ascendancy of his own needs.

Sameh opens the door. A bedroom door. A maimed and weakened old man lies awake in a large bed. A dim lamp burns at his bedside. He is shirtless and his entire torso is covered in scars. His head lolls toward us. He looks neither surprised nor fearful. His mouth and chest are wet and it is apparent that he has no teeth.

"Dr. Treves," Sameh says. "My good Dr. Treves! My dear teacher."

The old man grunts.

"You are not surprised to see me," Sameh continues. "Your research has not gone well. I see the results, the wages of your inquiries. The scarring from your investigations into treatment of *cutaneous larva migrans*, and the revenge of the lunatics you used to test your hypotheses on tooth decay! No, your research has not gone well. Let me show you the results of mine."

I step from behind Sameh. My scars are seeping and wet. Treves looks upon me in horror.

"You mocked me, Dr. Treves," Sameh says. "In fact, you mocked all Arabic medicine. I succeeded in reconstituting the ancient compound and discovered the other three elements. This is Oriax, so named. Oriax of Hell. I rebuilt him after an explosion and harvested arms and legs he had lost from a corpse. He lives, he moves, he has use of the new limbs."

"It... it isn't healing..." Treves wheezed. "Wounds not healing."

"You knew I never forget an insult, Dr. Treves," Sameh continues. "It is fitting that my creation will kill you. He will do as I command. My research will murder yours. Then I will burn your notebooks. You will be forgotten." Sameh pulls a pillow from behind Treves's head and hands it to me. "Cover his face. Kill him."

"You were always driven by anger." Treves mutters. "You were always a step away from madness."

I do not take the pillow. I look at Sameh and see no vast expanses full of possibility. I see only short, insipid spaces, petty, vengeful distances.

"No," I say. "No, I will not. I was not made for this. To gain knowledge. Not for this. My obeisance must end here. This was not your intention. I will not."

After a few moments, in anger and frustration, Sameh himself presses the pillow to the old man's face. I see no reason to intervene. I do not know what evil this old ruin has done. I know in this moment that retribution does not involve me. Retribution is a real element of the world, but here and now, it does not involve me. I now know that is important. Very quickly, the old man is still.

As he tosses the pillow aside, Sameh accidentally topples the bedside lamp. The chamber is dark but for moonlight streaming in its two windows.

"Dr. Treves!" It is a woman's voice. It is coming from the foot of the front stairs.

"Housekeeper!" Sameh whispers. He is visible in the moonlight. I am in shadow.

"Who is it?" the woman screams. A pistol shot rings out, and Sameh crumples to his left side. He stands and rushes forward and I hear him struggling with the woman in the darkness. There is another shot, and the thud of a body falling to the floor. Sameh returns to the bedroom. Blood flowing from his wound trickles black in the moonlight. He falls to the floor.

"I need help," he whimpers. "The bullet is in my liver. I need help compressing the wound."

I watch him from the shadow. I will leave him where he lies. I remember this is in my best interest. I remember the world is unrelenting, self-preserving, merciless. I think of the boy, Vernal. He has been spared the eternal disillusionment of knowing this... perhaps. Unless Sameh burdened him with it in the last moments of his life.

The Emperor of Ice Cream

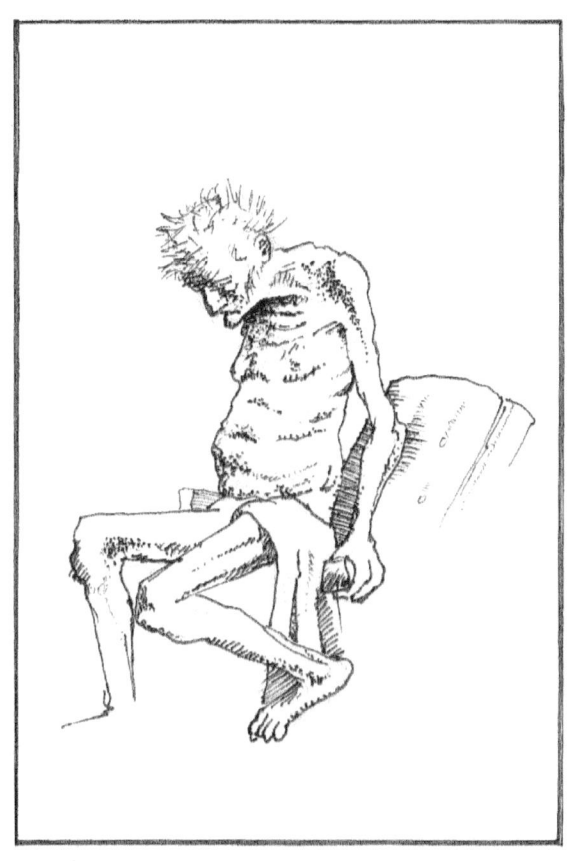

He must be hungry. When he looks at me as I pass by, head lolled to the side in his recliner, mouth open, watery blue eyes watching me, he's hungry. And he's always hungry. Ignoring him at least makes him put out the effort to speak. I ignore him.

I am trying to not regret my decision, but I mostly do. My brother and sister just said to put him in a home and be done with it. He will hate it, but he will adjust. They wanted nothing to do with him. I put him in a home for a while. I wanted nothing to do with him either.

On my best days, I just disliked him. But I have always hated him. In fact, I doubt there is anyone left in the world who loves him. Maybe a niece or nephew who only saw him on holidays, but no one who knew him well. But if they could see his weakness, his bitterness, his fearfulness, and hear his mumbled resentment, every day of the week, any affection would fade away.

These weaknesses, his terror of facing his last year or two alone, are what made me take pity on him. My brother and sister had no sympathy for him after Mom died. Put him in the home and be done with it. Don't take all that responsibility for him, they said again and again. But when I saw his sniveling, sobbing, pigeon-toed, tiny little form hunched and wailing on his Coca-Cola café chair, I decided I had to move him in with me.

The power is still out. A tornado hit Belgique and St. Mary just south of us, and the power has been out for two hours. I have two battery-powered lanterns going and I put his ice cream in a cooler full of ice cubes. He is still looking at me. One of the lanterns on the floor to his right illuminates his withered face from below.

"If it ain't too much trouble," he mumbles through the blockade of congestion constantly in his throat, "can I have an ice cream bar?"

"You had one with dinner."

"Okay. Can I have another one please?"

His blood sugar was below 180 this morning. "Oh, I guess it doesn't matter. I guess at ninety-one you can eat whatever you want." I remove a bar from the cooler and walk it over to him. "You are the Emperor of Ice Cream."

"The what? I don't have my ears in."

"THE EMPEROR OF ICE CREAM. It's an old poem."

"That don't make no sense. It's nonsense, ain't it? Nobody never paid a power bill writing a poem, did they? Nonsense."

He isn't asking those questions as real questions. He is stating his obnoxious opinion as fact or as an observation of undoubted truth and common sense and insisting on immediate agreement. He has always done this. "Of course. Of course it is. Foolishness. A big waste of time." I hand him the ice cream without touching him. I care for his needs but touch him as little as possible. The thought of touching his withered, cold skin or the sharp bones under it disgusts me. I was surprised to realize that. I have been told I should be ashamed of this fact, but I am not.

"When was the last time you got up from the recliner?" He has been using the recliner as a bed for many weeks because of his back pain.

"Huh?" He screws up his nose and upper lip to take a bite of his ice cream bar. A large flake of chocolate coating breaks off the bar and lands on the blanket covering his lap.

"When did you stand up last?"

"I don't want to stand up. My back hurts too much."

"You're in that chair all day and all night. You have to get up sometime."

"My legs are too weak. You don't want to help me wash so I do it by myself when I feel like it. I got my bag and bedpan..." The blanket slips off his shoulder and I see he doesn't have a shirt on. I lift the lower edge of the blanket and see he is naked under it. A horrible smell wafts up from under the covering.

"Why don't you have any clothes on... again?"

"I forgot. I forgot to do it. Too hard to do, though. Too hard after I washed off last time... if you won't help me. It hurts a place on my back and hip to get them clothes on. Do you want to help me?"

"You can... you need to do it yourself. You need to do things for yourself."

He looks up at the black TV screen on the wall in front of him. "Get *Death Valley Days* or *Rio Lobo*. I want a cowboy show."

"The power is out. No electricity."

He drops the wrapper from his ice cream on the floor. He does this as unselfconsciously as a tree dropping a leaf. I pick it up.

"I like shows that have Audie Murphy and... and Dan Duryea in them."

"I know."

"I'm hungry."

"I'll make you a sandwich."

"I don't want that. I want chicken strips."

"I don't have chicken strips. I'm not going out again and you have goddam chicken strips almost every day. And you just ate an hour ago."

"Well... I'm ninety-one. I like them with barbecue sauce."

He lolls to his right side and watches me. His mouth is open. He is breathing through it, grunting every few seconds. I can't look at him for more than an instant. I make him a sandwich just to stop him looking at me.

"I wanted ham," he says.

"You got salami. I can't believe you are hungry this much. You are just bored. Stop looking at me all the time... okay?"

"I like to watch cowboy shows."

I give him his sandwich. I know he will stop watching me while he eats. I walk away into the darkness. I won't watch him eat. Or listen to it.

He was an angry little man before he became weak and dependent. Small town boy. Short and red-headed, clumsy and learning impaired. He was slow to understand things and couldn't read situations quickly, which triggered his short temper. He married my mother after she got pregnant at sixteen, believing that he didn't deserve her. He believed nothing in his life more thoroughly than that she was too good for him.

As a young woman married early, my mother felt she was missing out on the fun and irresponsibility of her friends' lives. The old man told me stories of her flirting with other boys in front of him. He was short-tempered but cowardly and convinced himself, undeserving of her as he was, that this was something he was going to have to put up with in his marriage.

I don't know where compassion comes from, but I have none for him. Always unconvinced from day to day if my mother still or ever loved him, he was only brave enough to take out his anger on his kids. We hated him then and hate him now. But I took him in. I found compassion and so I did it. I can't remember how it happened. It seems so unlikely. Then, I couldn't foresee the sense of disgust and revulsion I am wrapped in every day. I never hugged him as a child and the thought of touching his cold, moldering flesh now is abhorrent.

He stands unsteadily. His blanket is wrapped loosely around him and doesn't look as if it is likely to stay there. He has lost sight of me and looks around. There is something in his hand that I can't quite make out.

I decide to stay in the darkness and move away from him. I have had enough of caregiving for one night. I know I shouldn't feel this way. Maybe I am ashamed after all. I don't want to hurt him or abuse him. I just want to be *away* from him.

I move into the living room in the darkness. I see him looking around for me.

"I want an ice cream," he says. He doesn't see me, so he looks toward the cooler containing the ice cream. His blanket falls off and he is naked for a moment, his spindle legs and sagging, splotched body fully revealed until he picks up his blanket and slings it carelessly over his shoulder. He makes his way tentatively to the cooler with tiny steps and removes an ice cream bar from it. The wrapper falls to the floor.

"I need to talk to you," he says wetly as he eats. "Where are you?"

The stairs are carpeted so I climb them silently. I am not sure why

I am doing this. I can only avoid him for so long, but I know at that moment and for moments longer I want to avoid him. I sit at the top of the stairs. He can no longer climb steps. In a little while, I will go downstairs and put him in his recliner for the night. I just want to be *away* from him for a little while.

It's raining heavily outside now. The tornado watch is not over, according to the weather feature on the radio. I don't hear the old man moving downstairs. Surely, he didn't go outside in the storm. Storms are another thing he is afraid of.

I built him a ramp outside for his motorized wheelchair to the second floor of the house when he first moved in and was sleeping upstairs. As his legs failed and his back deteriorated, he decided he wanted to sleep in his recliner in the TV room. The wheelchair battery is dead. He could get upstairs on the ramp if he wanted, but I can't imagine he has that much strength.

For a long time, I don't see or hear him downstairs. The lantern I left on the counter only illuminates part of the kitchen, and I don't see his lantern anywhere. A cold hand on my shoulder sends an electric shock of fear through me. I jump to my feet. He is standing behind me. He has turned off his lantern. He turns it on again. He is wet and the blanket on his shoulder is drooping off him.

"I turned off the lantern so the rain didn't short it out. I didn't mean to scare you. Had to hold my ice cream under the blanket in the rain."

"Why did you come up here?" I step down one stair, looking up at him. He is finishing his ice cream, which has just dripped onto his distended stomach and down his forearm.

"I didn't know where you was at. I wanted to talk to you. You kinda hid from me." His legs are skeletal and bowed. His feet are gnarled and flaking, and his thick, yellow nails are each growing in a different direction.

"You shouldn't be on the stairs. It's not safe for you. You stay where you are a second. Get your bearings and I'll help you. Don't do anything like this again." I step down another stair. He carefully descends a step, too. "Very slowly. You'll fall." He stumbles a little, and I reflexively reach out to steady him, but I don't touch him.

"You don't want to touch me. I know that," he says. "I might feel the same if I was you. You was always like that as a kid. Skittish and put off by things. You couldn't stand blood or animal guts if I tried to show you how to skin a squirrel, or sickness neither. Too much for you."

His thin legs were trembling with exertion. "You're walking too fast. Slow down."

"I 'member the time they was a dead possum out by the hard road. I told you to get rid of it. It was pretty far gone with maggots and rot, and you couldn't do it. I whopped you in your head, I 'member."

"Yes. I remember that too." He has ice cream at both edges of his mouth.

"And the time when you was ten or so and your buddy Chris was throwin' firecrackers into Virgil's beagle kennel next door. I know you didn't do nothing bad, and you tried to stop him, but I strapped you anyway, because... only because Virgil expected me to."

"Yeah, I know. Slow down now." He descends two more stairs.

"I don't know why your mother picked me," he continues. "All I wanted was to hold onto her when I knew what she coulda had. I don't think... she ever did care for me that much."

"I don't either, to be honest. You need to get back in your recliner."

"Aw, I ain't goin' back to my chair." I see that he has his old razor knife in his hand, the one he used to use to cut drywall and open boxes.

"What are you doing with that knife? You'll hurt yourself." I realize that I have backed into the kitchen, into the corner of the countertop. He approaches me surprisingly quickly. Now I can't get past him without touching him. That seems to be what he intended. "Why do you have that knife?"

"Because I know about myself better'n you might think."

"What?" I am watching the knife. His hand is limp and weak. It doesn't seem as if he intends to use it against *me*.

"No one remembers me kindly, and I deserve it." He is speaking through the congestion in his throat, which, as always, he does not clear. "You kids were in the way, something I had to put up with. An expense that kep' me workin' at jobs I hated. All I wanted was to know your mom thought I was good enough and wouldn't leave me. All I cared about. I would have put up with anything, even a pack of brats, to keep her."

"She was never going to go anywhere," I say. "She was never a woman who would take her kids and strike out on her own."

That's what you kids always said. She was un...."

"Motivated."

"And lazy. I know she was. So I took everything out on you'uns."

"Yeah. Let me have that knife, okay?"

"No, I need it. You didn't want to, but you took me in. I thank you for that. I ain't nothin' but in the way. Nobody wants me around. Never did." The blanket drops to the floor. My body goes tense as I resist the urge to choke. "You know I'm a coward. Cowards take everythin' out on the weak. I always did that. I'm finished. I seen on TV if you want to cut your wrist you do it longways. Jab at the wrist and pull upwards toward your elbow. That's what I want to do but I'm afraid. Too cowardly to do it."

I am lightheaded. "That's nonsense! Stupid. You'll do no such thing."

"It has to look like I did it, not you. The knife has to have only my fingerprints on it, like I seen in *Matlock* oncet."

"I'm not going to do any such thing. You are doing okay. I will try to take better care of you. I will try not to act so..."

"Put off. You are put off by my body, my skin, my bones, my sores, my smells—and I don't blame you. You can't help it. You just need to stand behind me. Behind me so the cut looks right. I will hold the knife and you move my hand. Jab in and pull." He is now only a foot from me. He turns his back to me and edges closer. His lantern reveals gaping sores I haven't seen before. Bedsores I have allowed to happen. There is an open one at his right shoulder blade, glistening and red, revealing the edge of the scapula and the spindly muscles attached to it. Below, at his right hip, is a larger sore oozing green, gelatinous pus. Starting at the top edge of his pelvis and continuing to a cavernous opening beyond, the wound spirals into the darkness of his fetid guts. A terrible gangrenous smell wafts up from the great lesions. I cough and nearly vomit. I can't bear to touch him to push him away. I want to turn toward the wall behind me, but I can't move.

I feel delirious but manage to see the knife he holds above his thin, dry forearm. There is no way I can see to get around him, no way to get away from him but one; there is nothing left but to jab and pull.

Toads on Her Face

Alsace, 1348

Guarin knew that even a scourge of God could produce an opportunity for those imbued with the capacity to seize it. The opportunity must first be identified and then energetically pursued. Then one may prosper, even in a time of devastation. Even in times of God's wrath. Surely if one may profit from tragedy and horror and find no impediment to success, then that success must be God's will and meet with Heavenly approval. Guarin comforted himself with that thought.

The basic material of Guarin's new enterprise was plentiful. To put it to use must be a good thing. He had been a baker by trade in the village of Zellenberg. He made a comfortable living, which improved when old Eudes, the other baker in town, died. Guarin raised his prices, of course, because he saw this as another opportunity God had given him. When the pestilence arrived in the spring, Guarin's wife and daughter succumbed immediately. Lothair, his apprentice, soon followed. In another month, there was scarcely anyone left in the village to buy bread.

For the Festival of Ste. Odile, Guarin stacked most of the loaves he had, which were few, onto his cart and pulled it down the hill to the juncture of the Riquwihr Road. He thought he might sell some of the last of his loaves to pilgrims on their way to the festival. But few pilgrims passed by.

After an hour or so, having sold none of his wares, Guarin removed the loaves from the cart and stacked them neatly by the side of the road for anyone to take. The death cart was approaching him from the south. Having discharged its morning load of corpses into the nearby burial pit, it was returning to Riquwihr to await its evening round. Puzzled by his own inclination, Guarin decided to visit the pit to see if any familiar souls had recently died.

He pulled his bread cart past the withering vineyards toward the circling ravens just beyond a small hill. The smell of rot reached him before the pit was in sight, suggesting that the death cart driver and sextons had not scattered lime on the carcasses for a while. The ravens, jackdaws, and other birds tearing at the pallid flesh filling the pit scattered as Guarin approached, but soon settled back to earth to continue their scavenging.

The stink was overpowering but shifted with the wind. Three fresh bodies tied within shrouds must have been lately left by the death cart. Guarin expected that some sentiment of respect or contemplation of the brevity of life, of the vanity of mankind's endeavors, must surely come to him as he surveyed the mass of rotting humanity. But nothing came. No reflection, no sorrow, no musings on mortality. Nothing.

The only thought that eventually entered his mind at that moment was how Nature accommodates everything. Every devastation visited upon God's world by man is somehow accepted and absorbed into the natural order of things. Flies swarmed over the bodies before him, taking from them whatever they needed. Birds fed on the flies as well as the carrion, worms bored into the gray flesh, slugs undulated across the putrescence, absorbing it, and toads, everywhere in evidence, feasted upon the slugs and worms.

Then abruptly, it occurred to Guarin that putting to use the materials at hand must be what he was meant to do. How is it, he wondered, that worms and slugs may feed on corruption, and toads, in turn, eat those creatures, and thrive? Why does the pestilence not kill those lowly creatures? Could the toads, for example, act as a membrane or gauze to nullify or filter the pestilence? Could something in their bodies purify and destroy the contagion? And if that were true, then could not that same agent protecting the lowly toads not also protect mankind?

A cart's length from the edge of the pit, just beyond where the new corpses had been dumped, Guarin spotted the body of an older woman whose wrapping had mostly fallen away. The pallid, damp flesh of her face seeped the liquids of advancing decay, and worms and slugs industriously made their way across cheek and chin, in and out of passages created by their consuming of the fetid flesh. Sitting atop the forehead of the corpse were two toads, tongues darting out irregularly to catch and swallow the verminous scavengers.

Guarin carefully stepped across the edge of the pit. He tried to find a solid place to step through the layers of the dead. As he shifted his weight to his forward foot, there was a muffled popping sound and his foot broke through an unseen ribcage to the wet cavity within it. A terrible odor engulfed him and he nearly swooned, but he steadied himself and reached for the corpse of the dead woman.

He slipped his fingers through the still intact wrappings around her neck and pulled her toward himself. The cold, separating flesh of the neck under the wrapping slid against his fingers and hand as it separated from its attachments, making Guarin's gorge rise. The toads did not relinquish their positions on the dead face.

Guarin carefully pulled the body out of the pit and dragged it to the rear of his cart, lifted it inside. He then returned to the pit and gathered several more toads from other cadavers and placed them in a wooden implement box he always kept in the cart.

Guarin pulled his cart back up the hill to Zellenberg. He dragged the cart into his vacant stable behind his shop and carefully removed the corpse, placing it on the floor. He then found a wide oaken plank he had saved from building a roost for his chickens. In an hour he had constructed an elevated platform extending from the front edge of the cart to the back, upon which to display the cadaver.

He carefully lifted the corpse onto the platform. He smiled to note that the two toads had still not abandoned their positions on the rotting face. He wound a rope around the body, securing it to the plank. He lifted the lid on the wooden box and saw that the toads he had collected were all still alive. He was ready to proceed.

Since Zellenberg was nearly abandoned, Guarin knew that he had better opportunities in the larger town of Riquwihr nearby. The pestilence had become very active in that town, and there were still some residents remaining who had money to spend. It was still early in the day, so he decided to waste no time.

The day grew much hotter in the afternoon. Riquwihr sat on a minor prominence to the north, which formed a subtle preamble to the mountains further on. The shade of the South Gate was a welcome respite from the sun and Guarin considered stopping there, but he had resolved to find a very conspicuous location. He chose the fountain in the South Square. He stopped his cart, sat on the fountain's edge, and waited.

The square was nearly empty. An old woman swept in front of the guild hall, and several nuns moved in and out of the infirmary as they gave what comfort they could to those dying inside. The canon, walking toward the church, stopped for a moment, looking at Guarin suspiciously. "Are you taking that one to the burial pit?" he asked.

"No, Father," Guarin said. "This one is harmless. The contagion is gone from her."

"Why do you bring a corpse inside the city walls? The dead must be removed immediately."

"I tell you, there is no danger. I have discovered a miracle, a talisman against infection."

"You miracle workers!" the canon scoffed. "We'll see what the sheriff says."

"The sheriff is away, Father." A voice came from behind Guarin. It was a tattered young man of perhaps twenty with a satchel over his shoulder. He sat on the fountain's edge near Guarin.

The canon said nothing more and continued on his way.

"Good afternoon, sir," Guarin said to the young man.

"And to you. I am Merton."

"Merton. What is your family name?"

"I am just Merton. Merton of Riquwihr."

"One can be whomever one wants these days," Guarin said. "Start life anew as a new person. Are you interested in what I have to sell?"

"I have no money. I am looking for a way to earn a living. I have several possibilities but wanted to ask you about this enterprise."

"I am selling hope in a hopeless time."

"You mean the pestilence?" An old man carrying a bundle of

kindling interrupted.

"I do. Yes, I do," Guarin said. "I have found that these toads," he stood and plucked one of the toads from the face of the corpse, "make themselves protected from the contagion by consuming the vermin feeding on the dead. All one need do is fry the toad to a crust, crush to powder, and mix the powder into any liquid to drink. I promise that by so doing, one will never be afflicted."

"Hmm," the old man scowled for a moment. "I don't know you, but do you swear this is true?"

"By Saints Peter and Paul, I swear. Do you have money?"

The old man seemed hesitant to answer. "A little. I am a poor man. I am sure your charity extends to the poor in times such as these."

"I do what I can," Guarin said. "What money do you have?"

The old man examined his battered purse. "I have *lire*." He then held up four fingers: "*Denari.*" Then one finger: "*Sou.*"

"Two *denari.*" Guarin said, holding up two fingers.

The old man smiled in relief and gave Guarin two coins. Guarin dropped the toad he still held to the cobblestones and crushed its head with his foot. He then handed the creature to the old man. "Remember," Guarin said, "crush it to powder."

The old man nodded in agreement and hobbled off toward the North Courtyard. Guarin removed another toad from the wooden box and placed it on the corpse's face.

"That seemed easy enough," Merton said. "If any splinter broken from a fence post can be sold to the ignorant as a relic of the True Cross, anything is possible."

"Yes, Guarin agreed. "My first sale in this enterprise."

"I was on a pilgrimage to Ste. Odile in the mountains once," Merton said, "and an old woman there, a wise woman, told me of a similar practice. She said eating some part of the body of a good man who has never been infected will also stave off the contagion. Barbaric, I know."

"That sounds like witchcraft to me," Guarin said. "Nonsense and superstition. I have seen for myself that this method *must* work. My conscience is clear." Guarin had brought one of his loaves with him. He tore it in half and gave a portion to Merton.

"Thanks to you," Merton said. "You are a generous man. I agree with you. If you believe in your heart that your medicine works, then you are right to sell it to others. You are doing a kindness and earning money from it. But I must ask you, if this plague has been sent by God to punish our sins, is it then agreeable to God to protect oneself? After all, these people are fallen and wicked. I have no doubt they deserve suffering and death. Humanity is surely disgusting to its creator."

"A fair point," Guarin responded. "But I must in turn ask you, if God opposed my actions, if they met with His disapproval, why would He allow me to proceed? Certainly, He would punish me."

"True," the young man agreed, "unless your punishment is yet to come. All are fallen. We must make our way as best we can until our retribution arrives."

A starving dog approached the men from a shadowy alley. Merton picked up a flake of stone that had fallen off the lower part of the fountain's edge and threw it at the dog, striking it below an ear. The dog yelped and disappeared back into the shadows.

Guarin sold two more toads to peasants in the next hour. Merton remained at his side asking many questions about the baker's life and profession, his family, his travels.

"You ask so many questions," Gurin said at length. "I never thought myself to be an interesting man."

"I say you are. Interesting in your way and generous in your way. A good man such as you can be a model for me. I am clay to be molded. I have no family, no father to teach me. I have collected information in my travels and soon am determined to settle on a trade or means of income."

"Very good," Guarin said. "You have ambition. You will make something of yourself. Now, I need to replenish my toads. If you would care to accompany me...?"

The two exited the South Gate and made their way toward the burial pit. "You say you have traveled?" Guarin asked.

"Yes," Merton said. "I was a sailor. I have been to Majorca and Naples and the Kingdom of Genoa. I hoped to make a life of it, but it became disagreeable to me. Difficult to be enclosed on a ship with so many filthy men."

"I hope to make a pilgrimage to Avignon someday. I have traveled little."

"I am glad to have done some of it before settling on my profession. I particularly favored the Kingdom of Genoa. On the north shore of the old harbor, there is a fish seller who sells many unusual things to be found in the sea in addition to fish. Things you cannot find elsewhere."

"Yes?"

"Extracts from fish and other sea creatures that are said to do such things as improve hearing or eyesight, cause paralysis or forgetfulness in an enemy, or reduce fever in children, or incite love."

"Can a living be made selling such items?"

"It seems so. You have shown me that many things are possible. I think it is providential that I have met you! Possibly for both of us."

The sun had sunk well below the hills by the time they reached the burial pit. The barren trees were full of birds roosting for the night. Guarin stepped gingerly out into the pit and plucked four more toads from the corpses. These he carried to his cart and put into the box. Merton gathered twigs and sticks, and, removing a flint from his satchel, started a fire. He sat on a stone and watched the flames.

Guarin sat on a log nearby. "We can rest here if you like. For a short while. Unpleasant spot to rest, but as you wish. My home is just up the hill in Zellenberg if you wish to stay for the night."

"Certainly, many thanks." Merton's eyes never left the flames.

"You know, my young friend, that there are opportunities everywhere. Saint-Hippolyte, Ribeauville, even Strasbourg if you care to wander that far. If we can find you a cart, and any abandoned property nearby will have one, we could carry this enterprise all across the plain. Every town has a death pit and citizens fearing the pestilence."

Merton smiled and looked at his friend. "Yes, that is true. A glorious idea. I don't care to save them, but only to profit from them."

"You go your way, I go mine," Guarin continued, "then we could meet from time to time to pool resources, since this is my conception, or not, if you want to be on your own. It doesn't matter to me. I have enjoyed your company today and would like to call you friend, but if you wish to press on alone, so be it."

A soft thud on the ground next to Merton startled him. An injured dove had fallen from a branch above. Merton picked up the helpless bird. "How cruel this life is," he said. "Who ever thought death would become so common that we would become numb to it?"

"Very true," Guarin agreed.

"This one has been attacked by one of the other birds," Merton studied the injured creature who watched him, terrified and helpless. "Kindness and gentleness are not what one should expect. The cruel survive, wouldn't you say? You, I think, are a good man. I say that without knowing what a good man is. I am not certain. I saw a doe in a field once, trying to escape a pack of dogs. She was also birthing a fawn. She could not run far. She was soon exhausted. The dogs caught her and pulled the fawn out of her. She collapsed onto the ground, witnessing the butchery of her small one being torn to pieces, and awaited her own inevitable death afterward. How can one be gentle in such a world as this?" At that moment Merton tossed the live bird into the fire.

"Great God, man! That was uncalled for!" Guarin gasped.

"Nothing is either called for or not called for," Merton replied. "How can one judge anything that is possible in Nature that way? God allows it. We should not judge God's handiwork or choices, should we?" Merton removed a wineskin from his satchel and tossed it to Guarin.

"Where did you learn such a philosophy?" Guarin said, taking a sip from the wineskin.

"I think it's obvious. In times like these, certain basic and foundational things become obvious. Do you think lower creatures, animals, are sensible? Do you think they feel pain? I have heard that a living goose slowly cooked in heating water feels a sort of ecstasy in its death."

"Did you learn this from your parents?" Guarin tossed the wineskin back to Merton. "The dog you hit with a stone cried out, the dove in the fire suffers now as she is consumed."

"My mother died at my birth. My father was an ignorant peasant like so many others. Like those who pay trifles for your confection here. He was cruel, if there is such a thing. If anything in this life can be judged. Forbade me to go to sea. It was in my power to do so, so of course, I killed him. Then I could do as I wished. A necessity." He smiled.

Guarin was speechless. Merton placed the wineskin back in his satchel. Guarin saw that the eyes of his companion were looking at him in a way not hinted at in all their hours together.

"I have found my profession. My trade, my friend," Merton said. "Meeting you today decided the question."

Guarin felt fear course through his body. He must leave this strange young man behind. He tried to sit up but found he could not. Neither his legs nor arms nor neck would move.

"By now you can no longer speak," Merton went on. "It's the extract from Genoa I told you about. You are, I suppose, a 'good man,' whatever that may be. It doesn't matter. Most souls are willing to believe whatever you tell them if they are desperate for comfort, as nearly all are these days. The old wise woman told me that any part harvested from the corpse of a good and uninfected man can be roasted and eaten to prevent the great sickness. She said in Colmar or Strasbourg the wealthy will pay two florins for such. It was providential that I met the old hag and she told me this. Certainly, I am meant to profit from it."

Guarin's terror was imprisoned within him. He could not move or scream. Merton reached again into his satchel and removed a curved harvesting knife. He stood. "That you are alive and not a corpse is unfortunate," Merton said. "Somehow I can't bring myself to kill you. But again, it must be as God wills. Unfortunate, too, that I cannot wait for the toxin to wear off. Tongues are most highly valued in this trade because they speak the prayers of a blessed man to God. The unfortunate difficulty, of course, is what I have to do to your jaw to get to it."

The Monster of the Palace

Though it may be whispered otherwise, *I* am not the Monster of the palace. I am seen as such by some, I know. My nearly deaf ears have heard it. No. I am Charles, second of that name *Magnus Rex Hispaniae,* undoubted and supreme King of Spain. The Bewitched, yes. Bewitched. My head is over-large not from water oppressing my brain, as the physicians say, but because of my secret intelligence, which no one may see. My head must be large to contain my great awareness.

With a swollen tongue and diseased mouth, I cannot speak clearly. I mumble and drool, and as I try to articulate, lose my path of thought and am regarded as stupid. I do lose my path of thought. Many are the ideas that die in my head before they are spoken. The stink of their corpses must rival that of my mouth.

But I am not stupid, surely. Or inept? I am *not* stupid. A stupid, inept king could never rule for so long. He would be assassinated. But I am still here. Against all expectations, against all murmured jokes and comments. The physicians are nonplussed. My half-brother was angry. Died angry. But I have survived. My swollen tongue, my pitted face, my clublike jaw, my limp member (long-dead cockroach that it is), my gnarled, silted-up guts, have survived.

So I deserve to be commemorated, though no subject chooses to do it. I at least deserve entertainment. Where is my Monster? Where is the real Monster of the palace? Where is the one who is more grotesque than I? Where is my Eugenia Martinez? Ha... the bladder with a ribbon in her hair.

My chamber door opens and there stands a surprised Mistress of the Linen, come to change my bed.

"I beg your forgiveness, Majesty!" She looks at the floor as she speaks. "I was told you were out of your chamber this morning."

"Where is my Eugenia Martinez?" I say it several times before the old woman understands me.

"Ah, the Monster!" she understands. "Word is she is ill, Majesty. Weakness of the heart, so say the physicians. She is too weak to rise from her bed."

"Nonsense!" I mumble. "*Nonsense!*" This time the woman understands me. "Tell her to meet me in the Patio del Rey in a half hour. I am in need of amusement!"

The woman sauntered off. I am not sure if she understood me.

The walk to the Plaza is a long one and painful to my knees and feet. The hallways of this old Alcazar seem endless. I pass ministers and servants. Some stop in their tracks and speak to me. Some walk

The Monster of the Palace

past me, unphased and showing no respect. When I gain my strength, they will pay a price for their insolence. I just have to remember their faces. I must try to remember their insolent faces. This, so they will pay a price for their insolence.

When I reach the Plaza I see a boy, I believe he belongs to the stables from the way he is dressed, and a girl, perhaps from the kitchen. They are kissing on a stone bench. His hand is up her skirt. Startled, they jump to their feet and run away, even as I shout at them to stop. Such insolence! I am not sure I will recognize them again if I see them, but if I do, they will be punished.

I lay my loaves on my customary stone bench in the sunlight.

In very little time, of course, I am uncomfortable. The bones of my backside and the seepage of guts coming out of it make repose impossible. I knew this ahead of time but forgot. In a moment, Sorolla, an underminister of some sort, notices me alone on the Plaza and comes out to me.

"Majesty...?" says he, as he comes out to me.

"I have commanded the presence of my Monster. Send her out immediately! I am being treated like a page in my own palace! I won't have it! All will soon see! Where is my Monster?"

"Sire," Sorolla whimpers once he has understood what I said, "she is very ill. Villareal was supposed to tell you, Majesty. She cannot rise from her bed. The doctor says her heart is failing her. She is dying."

I am surprised to feel a stab of fear shoot through me from stomach to fundament. "Nonsense!" I say. I stand, with Sorolla's aid. "I will see for myself!"

Sorolla nods in deference and offers to take my arm. I let him, as my legs are weak. Another endless corridor. We come to a corner, then turn right... left, rather, and find ourselves in a region of humble unpainted doors. A scullery woman is shocked to see me, as I have never been in this region of humble, unpainted doors before now.

"Here, Majesty," Sorolla snivels. "Will you need me further?"

"No."

He skulks gratefully away. Skulks, or slinks, or slithers, or flops. Quickly away. I push open the unpainted door. A simple room. Dark and barren. One small bed. It looks as though a bull has climbed onto the thin mattress and been covered by a sheet. But it is just my Monster. Eugenia, my Monster.

I close the chamber door, but the sheet mountain does not move. I smell her odor immediately—the sour smell of sweat and other things mixed in. I remember that from my marriages.

"Are you no longer my subject, my Monster who entertains me? Are you now, too, turning insolent?" That is what I say, or meant to say, in my head. I know when I say it that it sounds nothing like those words at all. Gibberish. The sheet moves. A pained exhalation. A pink melon of a head is visible beyond the top of the sheet.

"The king visits!" she wheezes. "You are the king!"

How can she be so stupid, I wonder? So fat and stupid together? Surely God hates her even more than He hates me!

"I am the king." I say it slowly enough that it is understood.

The sad mound of flesh starts to wriggle. She is trying to rise, encumbered by bulk and weakness. Her stomach is her enemy. The mound of a stomach. She is a continent unto herself.

"Did no one tell you I demanded your presence in the Plaza? You are not even dressed."

"Not...?"

"Dressed... *Dressed!*" Spittle sprays from my mouth but she understands.

"No, Enormity, Majesti... cal. I am sick. Weak." She tries to rise again but is quickly exhausted.

Her struggle vexes me. The quaking waves of her flesh under the sheet I find most unbecoming, even though I have laughed at them so many times before. In merriness and hilarity, before. Not now, somehow. "Stop! Lie still." She lies still. "What is wrong with you then?"

"My heart is failing," she whispers. "Dr. Alvarado says so. I can't hardly breathe, and I hardly have the... the strength to lift my arm up."

"That tree trunk of an arm, you mean? Who could lift such a log? Samson would have to pray for strength to do it! Gluttony is your sin. Did you think there would be no price to pay?"

"I..." It is obvious she doesn't understand me. I approach her bed and seat myself on a stool near it. Her head is like the giant egg of a great African bird on her thin pillow. Her face is bloated, pale, and covered with sweat. Where can compassion be found for such a creature? I find little of it for myself, after all. She is gasping in air, struggling as she breathes. Her lip trembles. I am an exalted personage, and I am seeing this lowly misfit at her worst. Even she understands this.

Her eyes are as dark as the far bank of the River Styx. Her lids flutter as she looks at me timidly. In her dark eyes I see fear, yes, and shame. The shame for doing whatever she has done so that God has punished her with a cursed life. Her expression shifts a little and I imagine I see the taunts of the court—the ministers and servants and clergy as she saw them with those eyes. I see the taunts of her village and the long-lost respite of her parents, the only people on this earth who love her. They love her, I have heard. There are those who love the thing lying there. And I see something more, something familiar I don't recognize as yet. Familiar, though...

"How old are you, girl?"

"How...?"

"Old." The impatience I felt a moment ago has gone for a moment.

Now I want to talk slowly. Wait for her to understand. "How old?"

"I don't know, Enormity. I don't know numbers. No one ever told me."

"You don't know your age?"

"No, sire. I am stupid."

"I know words inside my head," I say slowly. "I know them in my big head..."

"Full of water, they say, your big head, but I don't believe that."

"Only brains can be in my head, can't they?"

"Yes."

"But I can't read words well. Or speak them. I can't write but only to write CARLOS REY on documents."

"I can't do either one of those things."

"Tell me Eugenia, my Monster, am I ugly?"

"Oh yes, sire."

"So very ugly, truly. It is only the truth you have spoken. And yet I had my Marie Louise. The beautiful Marie Louise who loved me. When I think of her, I think... *think* she loved me. I could still function as a man then. At least somewhat. I was somewhat a man. Do you know what I mean?"

"No, I don't."

"I could still fire my round, but too quickly, alas."

"My father fired an arquebus once. He said he did in the Army."

"I could never wait for her. I was ashamed, but she was patient, though the ministers blamed her for our childlessness. Diplomatically blamed her. They looked at me, saw me every day, saw my repulsive limitations, but blamed *her*. How could that be possible? How could the fault not lie with a grotesque like me?"

"I... don't understand." Her upper lip is slick, glistening with the mucus running from her nose. She coughs. Her eyes, her dark eyes are encrusted. Looking into them, I see she is not comprehending. I am saying too much, and the flopping of my thick tongue is not to be deciphered. Unknowable. Still, she tries to listen and understand. I could command her attention, but I won't do it. I am tiring her.

"Your face is pretty enough if you weren't so fat. I have never seen anything like it. Such fatness. I smelled your odor when I came in. They need to clean you better. I was repulsive as a younger man— more than you. Filthy. Stunk like the cesspit under a garderobe. My half-brother refused to confer with me about matters of state unless I was cleaned. I refused. If the king stinks, it is what God wishes, I thought. But then, one possessing the divine right *cannot* stink, I thought. Stupid, stupid. I only agreed to have my hair washed to meet my dear brother. Only that. Stupid."

The Monster coughs again. There is congestion and wetness in the cough. She smiles at me and seems distressed that I am seeing her in such a state.

"When did you see your parents last?"

"I don't know numbers but... so long ago. Longer ago than my thinking goes to. My thinking doesn't go back very far on most of things. I do remember some things, though."

"What? What do you remember?"

"Ribbons Mama tied in my hair. I liked yellow but she liked red more. She would put one on both sides sometimes. Here and here. If I went to the market with her, she put a black dress on me so I didn't look so big, she said. But everyone wanted to look at me. She said they looked and laughed because I was so pretty."

"Yes, people will stare."

"She had to go to the market every day because of I was hungry all the time. When I came to the palace, the money they got helped them, Mama and Papa... very much."

"I heard of you, the baby monster, but I had to see for myself."

She is exhausted from just a little talking.

"When you met me as a child, you thought I was ugly."

"Oh yes, Majesty." Always has she been unmannered and honest when asked. "Your face was crooked and your tongue and lips too large for your mouth. Your skin was covered with red holes. I was frightened."

"So you remember that much."

"Those red holes, oh my, and you smelled so badly. I am not hungry."

"Not hungry?"

"I am hungry... always. But now I am not. Why?"

"Marie saw past my ugliness. She saw my mind and my soul. Always did she have a smile in my royal presence."

"The linen mistress said she mocked you. One of the queen's ladies agreed, and another said she felt... felt disgust."

Such immediate anger overtakes me that I think I might strike the helpless girl. I stand and look down at her. Her eyes glisten and look back at me with so much benevolence and affection that I find myself verily disarmed.

"That is gossip, the gossip of rabble!" I say.

Eugenia's eyes flutter closed, then open again. She is struggling to show deference.

"I know gossip when I hear it," I continue. "The hateful gossip of jealous underlings. When you are the king, the king of all Spain, of all Spanish domains, all you encounter are underlings. I have all. All, save strength and beauty. I am all things, and they wish to deny me the one simple need all seek: to be loved. They would deny me that."

"Yes," she whispers. "If you have only one thing... they would take that, too..."

The words she speaks invade my wet brain, surround it as if in a siege. They envelop my memories and my great awareness, the awareness of which I spoke before. Simple words but rife with understanding it seems to me. Am I imagining it? It does seem so to me, though only I will grasp it. Understanding. Commonality. She understands all I understand, it seems so to me. She alone, it strikes me, *knows*.

Yes, I have mocked her, demeaned her, and brought her to tears before the court. Hundreds laughing at her at my direction. Stupid and fat, I repeat again and again. Fat as a sow. Fat as Saturn after he has eaten all his children. All the abuse has left nothing but benevolence behind in her, knowable and apparent in her dark eyes. I must see it in her eyes again. I look at them as before. But now, she is gone. There is nothing but emptiness in those depths. The wisps in the void, fluttering off, are the ribbons in her hair, her memories of early kindness and her mother holding her hand. I will hear no more of these things from her as these wisps abandon me to these endless corridors and this small room.

The Temptation of St. Antonia

Doctor Hess seemed too young to be a professional man. His complexion was bad, and in those areas not erupting in pustules, his skin looked soft as a child's.

"Your name, Mrs. Surin," he said, "your first name is *St. Antonia,* not Antonia?"

"Yes, Doctor," St. Antonia said. "Named for Saint Antonia of Constantinople. My mother was very devout." She had begun to feel uncomfortable in her oaken examination chair. She was not used to sitting so long. In addition, she had dreaded having a new doctor, especially someone so young, looking at her body so intimately. Perhaps the tension of her body was why she was feeling so tired.

"I'll just call you Mrs. Surin, if you don't mind," Hess said. "Well, you were right. It is a tumor. Breast cancer. To be safe, your left breast should be removed, or part of it if we want to be conservative. Several inches of it, at minimum." Hess pointed to a spot on the exposed breast. "At least to here," he said.

"Oh, my," St. Antonia's face shriveled into a frown.

"I can do it today, if you wish," Hess continued. "This afternoon. The standard fee for mastectomy is thirty dollars."

"Well...I don't have thirty dollars, Doctor. That's a lot of money. I could pay it over time if you will let me."

"I am sorry, Mrs. Surin. I cannot conduct my practice that way. I am just starting out here. I can't set that kind of precedent."

"But we don't have the money."

"I understand. I was warned before I moved here that people would want to pay me in chickens and turnips. I am here to establish a practice and earn a living, not to prepare a Sunday dinner."

"Doctor...please," St. Antonia implored. "There is no real surgeon in town anymore but you."

"Yes. That's why I am here."

"But I'll die! I ain't afraid of death, Doctor, but I'm not ready. Since I was a girl, I been a medium. I have always had a link to the other side, the world of the dead. Years ago, we had old Father Condell who was a exorcist. Since he's been gone, I found that the power was in me to do it. I can summon and drive out the demons. It may sound like backwoods nonsense to you, but it's true. All those demons and spirits are waiting for me for their revenge. I am not ready to face them. I haven't found out yet how to protect myself when I travel over to their realm. If you would just let me pay you over time. I *need* time."

Hess shook his head. "Absolutely not. You are right, Mrs. Surin. It is backwoods nonsense. This is 1894. I will not get off on the wrong foot like that and become a poor small-town doctor. You have a few months. Save the money and come see me again."

St. Antonia felt numb in every part of her body as she stepped out onto Gentian Street. She watched a carriage and a dray wagon pass in front of her on the street and children rolling a hoop on the sidewalk in front of the pharmacy. She thought nothing except that she may never see these simple sights again.

She turned south toward the livery to fetch Linda, her old mare. As she walked past the Dei Gratia hotel, she saw her old friend Roberta Wallis still working the front desk. A terrifying notion flashed through St. Antonia's brain, and she stepped into the hotel lobby.

"St. Antonia!" Roberta exclaimed," I'll swan you're a sight for sore eyes. I haven't seen you in a coon's age!"

"Roberta, it's good to see you. I been busy. Very busy out to the farm with Frank and the kids and all."

"Are you still talkin' to spirits? I told you once to leave that alone. You look plumb give-out. Are you all right?"

St. Antonia stifled a sob. "I don't see the evil spirits and the dead as much as I did. I feel I got to leave the darkness alone and prepare to meet it myself. I am give-out, to tell you the truth. I'm near done. To the end of my rope... but it's nothing a little rest won't help."

"You said a mouthful there, old girl."

"I need a rest. Maybe a week to myself."

"Just what the doctor ordered!"

"I had this idea to spend a week here in town, away from Frank and them. How much could you give me a room for? Say for five days?"

"For you, hon, nothing. I keep the books. It'll be our secret! When you want to check in?"

"I have things to do at home. Let's say Monday."

St. Antonia's oldest daughter Juanita met her mother at the front door of their farmhouse on the Pimville Road. The girl was taller than her mother but looked much younger than her age of seventeen.

"I'm so glad you're home, Mamma," Juantia said. "Daddy's leg is hurting real bad today. And I can't keep the twins fed."

"Hey, sweet girl. I'll tend to it. I need to show you how to, though. You'll need to know. Did Peter and Paul wash today? Hard to make ten-years-olds see the importance of keeping clean."

"Yes, they did. And the strangest thing," Juanita continued. "The dutch oven fell off the shelf in the pantry. I put it back in its place and what do you know, it fell off again, all by its own self, me looking right at it."

St. Antonia did not respond to this news. She dismounted her horse. "Take old Linda and see to her. Get her fed, will you?"

Juanita took the reins and led the old mare toward the barn.

Frank was sitting in his rocker near the stove smoking one of the ragged cigars he liked to make for himself. He tried to rise when St. Antonia entered the front door, but she motioned for him to stay seated. Frank had lost his right leg below the knee in an ore car accident at Osage Lead twenty years earlier. St. Antonia kissed the top of his head as she walked past him toward the larder.

"Well, what did the doctor say?" Frank asked.

"It doesn't look like anything to worry about. He said we will just check it now and then." She opened the larder and inspected the contents. "I seen my brother in town."

"Which one?"

"John the Baptist. He says Verna is real sick. Been in bed a few days. I thought I would go visit a while until she's on her feet again. Juanita can take care of things here, all right?"

"Well, that's fine. Do what you can do. I don't do nothing but sit here and smoke anyways."

"You got a supply of them cigars made?"

"I do."

"So you won't be making any more for a while?"

"Don't expect to." Frank looked a little puzzled by the question. "Is it anything I can do to help with Verna?"

"No. It's women's work. Today I am more sure than ever that it takes women to do the nurturing and caring for the sick. I'll go alone."

St. Antonia spent most of the next day preparing the components of two stews for Juanita to prepare over the next week. She brought in several jars of vegetables she had canned from the spring house. In the evening she packed some clothes and toiletry items, and after Frank was asleep, went out to the barn to find things she would need in the next few days.

***

St. Antonia set out before dawn the next morning. It had rained a little overnight, enough to settle the dust on Pimville Road but not enough to muddy it. The old mare plodded along dutifully, needing little or no guidance or encouragement. In less than two hours, she had reached Ste. Odile.

At Aristide's Livery, Linda knew which stall was hers. She walked into it and St. Antonia dismounted. Pulling her carpet bag off the old mare's back, she paid Jean-Joseph the attendant and walked across Gentian Street to the pharmacy.

"Good morning, Mr. Boldoc," St. Antonia said.

"It's Mrs. Surin...?" The pharmacist asked.

"That's right. I would like to purchase one of your small bottles of cocaine. The liquid kind. Also some carbolic solution and tincture of laudanum."

"Will you need cotton with that?"

"I will, yes."

Bolduc turned to a shelf behind himself and selected a small brown bottle from among many, two larger ones on the shelf below, and a handful of cotton. He wrapped these in brown paper. "That will be fifty-five cents, Mrs. Surin."

Roberta had just arrived at work at the Dei Gratia. She greeted St. Antonia gleefully. "Oh, hon, I got the finest room for you," she said. "Just come available last night. Second floor, front room overlooking the street. Room 201."

"Thank you, Roberta."

"You got your hands full there," Roberta nodded toward the heavy carpet bag St. Antonia carried. "Can you manage?"

"I can, yes. Thank you again. I just want complete privacy for a few days."

"Just what the doctor ordered!"

"Would you send up a sandwich or some fruit or something a couple of times a day? And just leave it outside the door for me?"

"I will take care of it, sure as the world! You get a good rest, you hear me?"

"I mean to try." She started to walk toward the stairs but stopped. "It's so much darkness in this life, if people only knew. So many folks don't care if you live or die, so long as they get what they want. And evil...it's a solid, living thing. We make it real by our wicked nature because we are victims of our own nature. This life is bad, but the next is so much worser. If people only knew."

"You said a mouthful, hon."

Room 201 was at the end of the long hallway and overlooked Gentian Street. It was a larger room with a table and two chairs, a wash basin, shelves with some cups and saucers, and a brass bed. St. Antonia placed her bag on the table and sat on one of the chairs facing the street. She thought about what she had to do and hoped she would have the strength to do it. She decided today would be a day of preparation only.

From her bag she removed several clean, white cloths, the bottles of carbolic solution, laudanum, and cocaine, a packet of catgut, and a curved needle, along with a bastard file and a whetstone she had found in the barn. She placed these items in a neat row across the table. She then removed a change of clothes and a few toilet items she had brought and draped the things over the adjoining chair. Finally, she took out another tool, cumbersome and heavy, that she had found in the barn: a disc of red oak, sectioned from a tree trunk to make a base. A crude iron hinge was bolted at one edge. Attached to the hinge was an iron blade with a handle. It was Frank's tobacco chopper.

St. Antonia lifted the blade and checked it. It was dull, nicked, and had traces of tobacco leaves on it. She reached for the file and began to slowly sharpen it. For more than an hour she worked methodically on one side of the blade. For another hour, she worked on the opposite side.

She then poured a little water from her ewer into a teacup she found on a shelf, and dampening the chopper blade, worked at it with the whetstone for another hour or more.

In the late afternoon, she found that Roberta had left an apple and some meat and bread outside her door. St. Antonia had little appetite, but she nibbled at the meat and the apple as she watched the street below. By this time tomorrow, she thought, she would have done what she needs to do. It was hard to think of the intervening hours as she knew she would not rest that night. She must just try to calm herself and be at peace with what was to come.

***

The night was hot and still. St. Antonia removed her dress and underclothes and lay naked on the bed. Not since she was a child had anyone, even Frank, seen her naked body. She herself, in private after a bath, admired it and thought it, despite the rigors and difficulties it had known, to be perfect. Bearing her children had not scarred and stretched her skin, and she had not gained weight afterward. This was the form God had given her. It was truly a temple of the Holy Ghost. But vanity, even secret vanity, was surely offensive to the Creator. Her form was His handiwork. For her to claim it and take pride in it was a sin. What she had to do should be met with no regrets, anger, fear, or sadness. God had placed her in this position, and accepting His will was the only path toward grace for her.

She tried to rest but lay awake on the bed for hours, praying. She thought of her boys and of Juanita caring for them. She knew her daughter would take good care of the family. Frank would be horrified at what had transpired when she returned home. Horrified and angry she had kept it from him.

Well after midnight, she heard shouting on the street. She walked to the window and saw it was coming from Le Coq Galuois, a tavern just down the street. Raul the proprietor was throwing what appeared to be a drunken man out the front door. The man, probably in his forties and disheveled, fell onto the cobblestones of Gentian Street as Raul slammed his front door shut. The man lay still for a moment, then tried to stand and discovered his knee was injured. He grunted and whimpered as he hobbled toward the sidewalk.

When the man reached the sidewalk, he glanced upward toward St. Antonia's window. She was standing naked behind the sheer curtain. She could tell the man was not sure of what he was seeing. She pushed the curtain to the side and stood motionless, staring down at him for several seconds. She suppressed her breathing to hide even that small indication of movement. The intention, which suddenly

The Temptation of St. Antonia

came over her, was to convey to this stranger no indication that she was a real, mundane thing. Her perfect skin glowed in the dim lamplight and this anonymous man was now closer to her than anyone had been in her life. No one had ever had this connection to her, and no one ever would in all the days to come. To this stranger only was given this sensate moment. In the instant when she drew back the curtain, her choice was to share it with this man, or with no one, forever keeping it her secret. She felt a tinge of gratitude pass through her.

The man gazed at her, spellbound, stumbled backward, and fell against a wooden fence. As he did, St. Antonia retreated back into the shadows.

She sat at the table for the rest of the night. As the sun was coming up, she thought there was no more reason to delay. She poured water into the washbowl and washed her whole body. She then sat at the table and threaded a length of catgut into the curved needle. She spread a white cloth over the tabletop. She dampened another cloth with carbolic solution and cleansed the needle and her hands as well as the blade and handle of the tobacco chopper. Opening the bottle of cocaine, she doused a wad of cotton in it and swathed the liquid around her left breast above the point Dr. Hess had indicated. Then she sat and waited for the numbing effect of the drug.

After a few minutes, touching the swathed area, she could feel nothing. She knew though, that it was likely she would still feel sensation inside the flesh if not on the surface. She pulled the chopper toward herself and put the breast into position.

"I must be resolute," she whispered. "I must not hesitate. The Lord helps them that help theirselves. To think of the suffering He endured and His blessed mother and all the saints hated by the ungodly..." With both her hands she smashed down on the chopper handle. She gasped at the slicing fire of the cut and a sound, a horrible nightmare of a sound she would only describe as a crunch. She gasped again and shrieked a stifled shriek. Tears filled her eyes as the internal pain rose to her notice. The severed tissue flopped onto the floor, and St. Antonia gagged to see it fall.

She breathed heavily and rapidly until she thought she could faint. Blood spread across the white cloth, and she knew she must suture. Thankfully the curved needle piercing her skin did not hurt as much as she expected. The cocaine was effective there. She grew so lightheaded, she had to steady herself against the table edge. Her hands trembled as she stitched the wound. The sutures were irregular and haphazard, but they were holding. Thank God they were holding.

She washed the wound and bound another white cloth around her torso. The cloth spotted with blood but didn't become saturated. St. Antonia washed her hands and sipped a dose from the bottle of laudanum and then settled herself cautiously into bed.

She felt a glow of injury around her wound. It burned and pained her and seemed disoriented at the horrific and violent loss of itself. Soon the sensation faded into nothing, and she felt herself getting drowsy.

Her sleep was a murky, viscous sleep. She drifted toward consciousness repeatedly then fell back into the glutinous depths. At half-conscious moments, sleep seemed like a miasma she couldn't climb out of; dim awareness always gave way to impenetrable darkness again and again. Eventually she fell into a paralyzing and dreamless oblivion.

She slowly awakened to a burning sensation in her wound. She felt feverish. Night had fallen and there was the faint sound of activity in the street. She was terribly thirsty but wasn't sure she had the strength to rise from the bed. She struggled to sit up. The area of her wound and her left shoulder felt much more feverish than the rest of her body. The pain and burning of her struggle were too much. She lay back down.

In the morning she found she could still barely sit up, but she was so incredibly thirsty she felt she must get to the water pitcher on the table somehow. As she sat up on the bed's edge, she blacked out for a second, and as she teetered to the left, she regained herself and stopped her fall. She barely had the strength to pour water into the glass and spilled much of it. When the glass was full, she drank all the water down, barely taking a breath as she did so.

She crept slowly to the door and found Roberta had left fried fish and green beans for her in the hallway. St. Antonia did not trust herself to bend to pick up the plate, so she pushed it along the floor with her foot toward the table. Once there, she sat and then carefully retrieved the plate from the floor.

She was hungry. She took a bite of the fish, swallowed it, then instantly felt her gorge rise. She vomited across the tabletop. She knew she should not attempt to eat again that day. She stared at the sky from her chair until the sun arced overhead and she could see a few stars in the indigo sky above it. Carefully and painfully, she lifted herself from the chair and slid herself into bed. She fell asleep almost instantly.

After a few hours of fitful sleep, she heard scratching at the door. The hotel kept a cat to catch mice, she knew, so she assumed the cat was outside in the hallway. The scratching grew a little louder, then suddenly seemed very close to her. She tried again to rise. She thought somehow the cat had managed to get into her room. Steadying herself against the edge of the mattress, her right hand slipped off and hit the floor under the bed. Before she could right herself, she felt something brush her hand. As her pain allowed, she tried to sit upright. When she did so, her fingers brushed what she immediately recognized as the wet sleeve of a mouth. She gasped. She drew her hand and feet quickly back into the bed.

"Scat!" she hissed. "I don't know how you got in here, but scat!"

At that same moment, across the dark room, something shattered on the floor. A teacup and saucer. The cat couldn't be in two places at once. It must be something else. There was a flopping, wet sound on the floor, then something like a gurgle.

"Jesus, Lord," St. Antonia whispered, "please do not abandon me to the devices of the demons I have defied and drove out in your name..."

She tried again to rise from the bed, but the pain in her wound was intense. She lay still to regain her strength. Slowly she understood that the pressure against her left calf was not her pillow. She became as rigid as death and dared not move. A cold prod at the top of her thigh, a probe against her groin, a paw, a snout, the brush of coarse fur. She screamed a muffled scream. Forms writhed under her blanket and, against her, side to side. They chittered, growled, nipped at her flesh. With a pain-seared wail, she threw herself over the edge of the bed.

She thought her wound must be bleeding again. She felt a trickle of liquid channeling toward her breastbone. In an instant, she realized she was at the same level and just a few inches from whatever was under the bed. "Away from the bed. Away from the bed!" she whispered. As she struggled to move toward the center of the room, she felt something brush the hair on the back of her head. Suddenly, something grasped all her hair spread out on the floor behind her and pulled violently. As she was dragged toward the opposite wall, a rough hand grasped her ankle and attempted to pull her back toward the bed.

She screamed. Another appendage descended alongside the one grasping her hair and touched her face and chin. It was not a hand. Its edge undulated along her cheek. It felt like the underside of an enormous slug. The appendage moved across her chest and touched her wound, gently, it seemed. It positioned itself under her right arm as the hand from under the bed released her ankle. She was too terrified to make any sound but whimpering. Senseless, immemorial whimpering. The realization of the moment, the acceptance as valid of each sensation she needed to muster a scream, was beyond her.

As the being dragged her toward the far wall, she felt its touch leaving a wet trail across her flesh. Her bare legs, her stomach, her injured and uncut breasts glistened in the faint light from the street window. Her body was lifted back toward the wall and held vertically against an undulating, glutinous mass. It partially enveloped her and, oddly and suddenly, her fear drifted away and evaporated.

She felt herself wrapped in a viscous cocoon and saw the dim movement around and under the bed in the darkness across the chamber fade back into the featureless gloom of night and shadow. Soon there was nothing in the room but the thing enveloping her in its inscrutable embrace. She felt the skin of her back, legs, and stomach come alive as it seemed to welcome the touch of its enveloper.

She felt a tingle in the pit of her stomach that radiated outward and played upon the surface of her thighs and groin. Her breathing quickened and she felt a warm elation that she welcomed against her will, promising as it did, ecstatic connection and completion she had never imagined before. Her impulse was acceptance of these sensations: to surrender to them and the joy and release that accompanied them.

But pain would not be forgotten. The pain, when it came, was the price for the life she lived. For Frank, for Juanita, for Peter and Paul, a small price.

"I won't be mocked by you or tempted!" St. Antonia screamed. "I won't abide in darkness where I sent you. I won't submit to lasciviousness..." Something like a tentacle encircled her throat. With tremendous pressure it choked her, squeezed out wisps of exhalation that she could not replace. She felt the room spin and darkness overtaking her.

***

"Land o' Goshen girl, what a state you're in!" Roberta shook her gently. "You're feverish and drenched! What did you do to yourself?"

St. Antonia was too weakened to move. "Roberta..."

"My Lord, what has happened here? You didn't eat the food I was leaving. I waited as long as I could, but Sweet Jesus what did you do to yourself?" She held a cup of water to St. Antonia's parched lips.

"I had to do it. The doctor was fixing to let me die. I had to do it."

"I can't believe it. I just can't hardly believe it. You was screaming and yelling so I came in to look after you..."

"A little more rest," St. Antonia breathed. "Help me wash, and I need a little more rest. Juanita does her best at cooking, but if they have ate up the meals I made, she can't do it all on her own. I have got to hurry back to the house, to the kitchen and the canning and the dirty faces of my boys," She looked at Roberta's face with a grateful smile and watched her friend's expression change as she looked at the implements left on the table, the dried blood, and the mass of shriveling, brown flesh, starting to dry and attract flies, still lying on the floor.

Obasute

"You are the man of the house now... your house," Emi said. The old woman was out of breath from the cold. She placed the bundle of sticks she had gathered out in the snow against the wall and closed the door. "I must honor your will; Naoto and Kana's also. She is your wife and now the true mistress of the house."

Naoto moved behind his grandmother and pushed the door completely closed, as she always failed to do. He latched it.

Emi shrugged. "It is winter, the time of *Yuki-onna*, but your wishes must be carried out."

Naoto watched his grandmother as she struggled to unwrap her shawl from around her small body. He stopped himself from dismissing her superstition. How could he cast off one ancient tradition while allowing another? *Logical inconsistency*, as Professor Hidaka at the university would have called it. "I don't think you need to worry about the snow ghost, Grandmother," he said.

"Worried? I am not worried. I am just saying a true thing." Emi looked at her grandson sorrowfully. "I wronged you, Naoto. This is my doing. I was too indulgent of you. You were an orphan and I grieved for you. You are weak now because of it."

"Grandmother..."

"You lost discipline and resolve. It's why you failed at university and why you have agreed to this terrible tradition. The only benefit of your education was to keep you out of the war with Russia."

Kana pushed between them impatiently, carrying the tiny bundle of their newborn son, Aito. "He has just gone to sleep," she said. "Keep your voices down. I am blessed he is a sound sleeper, but I am exhausted. I don't want to test fate." She lay the child on a mat in a far corner of the small house. She stood and covered her swollen breasts with her *nagajuban*. "Grandmother," she said. "You know we love you. You brought our little son into the world. I am sure I could not have done it alone."

"No, as a breech he would have died."

"Perhaps so. Who can say? You have been a great help. You made the *wasanbon* pouch that comforts him so and has made him a sound sleeper. And you have always..."

"Thank you for your acknowledgment, Kana. I hope you will be a good wife to my grandson and a good mother to our Aito. I have prayed for it and performed a purification ritual to appease the *onryō*, the spirit of my dead son. He is satisfied. He will not bring harm to you or the child. Now my congress with these spirits must change. I am ready, if this be the time."

"I am sorry, Grandmother," Kana said. Naoto looked as though he meant to speak but said nothing. "I did not make this decision lightly," Kana continued. "I know I must be mother, wife, and sole mistress of the house you have given us. I have prayed about it, and this is the answer I was given. *Obasute*."

Emi nodded in acceptance.

"I have put *anpan* buns and dried fish in this satchel for you Grandmother, as you may take one remembrance of your home with you."

"Thank you. Seems an odd thing to take food, child." Emi said. "Why would I prolong the end?"

"Naoto, you must prepare to take her," Kana said as she took her husband's arm and guided him into the back room. Emi could hear her speaking lowly to him as she rewrapped herself in her still-cold shawl. She then wrapped her *kakebuton*, which lay folded on the floor nearby, around herself. In a few minutes' time, Naoto emerged from the back room, wrapped in his warm *hanten*.

Naoto opened the front door and gently took his grandmother's arm. They both stepped carefully out into the snow.

"The old tradition is you must carry me," Emi said.

"Yes, Grandmother," Naoto said. "If we are doing this, I suppose we must honor all of the tradition." He helped his grandmother step up on a large rock under their pine tree. From the boulder, the old woman climbed upon Naoto's back. "Can you hold on?" he said.

"Yes, I think so. We must climb the mountain trail past the shrine. I wish to go to the Forest of Suicides." Emi wasn't sure how long her strength would last. She clasped both her arms over his shoulders and around his neck. Her grip wasn't strong, but she felt well-supported by his arms under her knees.

"Grandmother," Naoto said as he climbed carefully up the shrine path in the deepening snow. "You have said I am a weak man."

"I have said I made you so."

"I would have defied Kana's wishes, but you seemed resigned to accept it."

"She has a strong will. This is what she wants and will have. It is her house now. She was a younger daughter and always wanted a home of her own, as you said. She has one now."

"I will keep you home if that is what you want. I will refuse."

"There will never be peace in the house, nor a day without resentment. I think the time has come."

The teeth-like ridges of blue and violet slate jutting up on either side of the path were almost completely covered in snow now. The paving stones, laid in ancient times, were slippery and treacherous. At the entry to the centuries-old shrine, a priest was sweeping snow away from the *sando*. The priest stopped his labors as Naoto and Emi passed. Naoto nodded. The priest scowled in an unmistakable attitude of disapproval and continued his sweeping.

"He knows what we are doing here," Naoto said.

"Yes," Emi agreed. "It has been many generations since this was last done."

Naoto followed the path to the left. It became steeper and more treacherous. "Few use this path in winter," he said. "All dread the Forest of Suicides, but more so in the winter. Many still fear the snow ghosts."

"For those who would end their lives, the impediments here are few and there is nothing left to fear," Emi said.

Naoto said nothing for a long time. At length, the few ginkgoes, cedars, and maple trees gave way to pine forest higher up the mountain. The path was uncared for at this altitude, and it appeared no one had been up that far for a long time. A pair of ravens flew overhead and landed on the bare branch of a dead tree. One of the ravens held a morsel of meat in its beak. It allowed the other bird to eat its fill as it held the food, then it swallowed the rest.

"Naoto," Emi's voice was weak.

"Yes, Grandmother. I'm going to stop a while." Naoto was breathing heavily.

"Naoto, how will you feed your family now that you have left the university?"

He settled the old woman carefully onto a fallen pine log. "I will do what most uneducated men do in this prefecture. I will be a fisherman."

"You know nothing of this work. Your grandfather is long dead. He could have shown you."

"Yes. I have spoken to Daichi. He and his son will teach me. I will go out on the water with them for a while. Grandfather's oars are still strong and the *Hakudo Maru* is still watertight. I will learn."

"Will you be satisfied with such a life? I would not have foreseen it."

"I have no other options."

"You have never been out on the open ocean at night, Naoto. Alone, collecting your nets at the end of the day. All your fears live out on the dark water. The spirits of dead sailors and fishermen are there. Angry ghosts as your own father was, raging for revenge and purification. There are also the monsters of the deep. There is *Namazu* and many others..."

"You know I don't believe in such things." The slight smile that flickered over Naoto's face was one of affection, not condescension at the old woman's superstition. "I am not going to take you up the mountain, Grandmother. This is barbaric. I won't abandon you according to *obasute*."

"You have already done it, boy. You agreed when your wife demanded it. I know where your heart is and that I would always be a source of anger in the house. We must proceed."

She was looking toward Naoto but seemingly at something far away from that moment, and frightening. Her look changed to one of acceptance and resolve, and she closed her eyes.

"I think I know why you want to go to the Forest of Suicides," Naoto said. "The tradition says you may take a soul with you for company in the next world. Grandfather's burial vase is near there. You believe you will be with him forever."

"A good thing in life to give comfort forever."

Naoto did not ask her to clarify what she had just said. He gathered the old woman onto his back and stepped carefully back onto the path to continue upward. The two ravens circled above them. Anytime they appeared, it was likely there was a fresh suicide in the forest ahead, or there was soon to be one. Emi had said many times to the young Naoto, "Nature fills every need."

The villagers often debated whether the birds foretold the future.

"Grandmother, you must be hungry," Naoto said after another hour on the path. "We can rest again if you like, whenever you like, and you can have your fish and *anpan*."

"No, I am not hungry." She glanced at the huge black birds overhead. "Soon, I would stop to pray, though."

"Would you like me to carry the satchel?"

"No. It is no burden to me."

The trail got steeper and more indistinct, and soon Naoto was struggling with every step. He stopped at a large violet slate boulder and brushed the snow from it.

"You can pray here, Grandmother," Naoto said. He placed the old woman carefully on the cleared spot. She seemed exhausted and a little confused.

"I will not make a full prayer," she said. "I will only address one *kami*. I only wish to purify myself and ask forbearance of *Shinigami*, who rules the land of the dead." Emi eased herself onto the snowy ground. She stood as straight as she could stand with a spine that had grown crooked over the years. She bowed deeply twice, then extending her arms straight in front of herself, clapped twice. She then whispered her prayers. Naoto thought he heard his name mentioned, and his father's and grandfather's. As the old woman finished her devotional, Naoto clearly heard the word *Yuki-onna*.

Emi finished her prayers and dabbed a tear from her eye. Naoto felt a rush of warm sentiment and pity for the old woman. She surely believed that the terrors of her superstitions were soon to be met. She had raised him and delivered his own son. He put his hand on her shoulder. "I am taking you home," he said. "I will not take you further up the mountain."

"Yes, you will!" Emi said sternly. "It is *decided*. Nothing will be undone now." She nodded her head in resolution and dabbed another tear. "I have prayed about it, and all is settled. I don't know why I weep. Think nothing of it. I am resolute."

She climbed onto her grandson's back, and he slowly and wearily continued his uphill trek.

The sun had long since passed the peak of the mountain and was starting to set. The penumbra of trees and rocks and snow was getting almost impossible for Naoto to navigate. The two ravens had preceded them up the path and awaited on pine branches ahead. Naoto was exhausted.

"My life with your grandfather was a good life," Emi said weakly. "We knew each other as children. A good man. Stubborn in some ways, but a very good man. When your father drowned at sea, our spirits were sucked out of us. We were as lifeless ones for years. You were our responsibility and our joy. In a weak moment, you cast me out, and your wife will not have me near. Little Aito, your helpless newborn son, is all the family I have left. He should not be exposed to your weakness."

"Grandmother..."

"We are here."

Ahead, though the falling snow, could be seen the Chasm of Souls. A dilapidated rope bridge, strung generations ago, led across the chasm to the Forest of Suicides. In the gathering darkness, a gray forest covered the plateau that was the summit of the mountain. Emi slipped slowly off her grandson's back. A small village cemetery to the left of the trail was quickly being buried by the snow.

"Grandfather's urn is here," Naoto said. "Do you wish to pay your respects?"

Emi shook her head. "I must go across," she said.

"The bridge looks dangerous; I had better help you across."

Emi smiled at him. "I am here to die," she said. "I will be dead by morning. If I fall into the chasm... what does it matter?"

Naoto said nothing. Emi pulled her blanket more tightly around herself and began walking toward the bridge. She was limping slightly. "These legs have but one more task to do," she said.

The wind began to howl through the chasm. The snow blew across the small plateau. Naoto could barely see the old woman from moment to moment.

"Grandmother," Naoto called after her, "You will be safe soon. Don't fear the snow ghost! Don't fear *Yuki-onna*."

"There is no reason to fear what can't be changed. I cannot fear my own nature. My prayer will be answered." She stepped onto the bridge and made her way slowly across the teetering ruin. When she at length reached the other side, Naoto watched her turn and face him. She pulled an object from within her sash. A knife. She cut the ancient ropes of the bridge and the far end collapsed into the chasm.

"Grandmother?" Naoto called. He ran to the edge of the precipice. Emi seemed to be lost in thought or meditation. She swayed slightly as if she might fall. A whimpering sound drifted through the howl of the wind, then a tiny cry. The cry of a small child. Terror grasped

Naoto's body. Emi, a wisp of presence through the driven snow, opened her satchel. A gust obliterated her for a moment. Then Naoto could see that she held next to her aged bosom the swaddled bundle of his infant son.

"Grandmother!" Naoto screamed.

"One soul may accompany me. One soul saved from cruelty and weakness."

Through the growing darkness and gusting snow, the old woman appeared to collapse to the ground. In another moment, a dim and insubstantial form arose from the spot. Through the gloom, Naoto could barely make out an emaciated anatomy, skeletal and wizened, carrying its small burden into the dark woods, the country of the suicides.

The Girl With the Timorous Smile

Wilhelm tells me I had better not smile in the photograph, but how can I help it, as pleasant a boy as he is? One needs to smile in a place like this, and who may know what will lead to it? The smile, I mean. Twice when I have seen him out in the yard, Wilhelm has smiled at me. They were smiles of friendship and encouragement, not effrontery. Never that. He is not that kind of boy, I am sure. I think he might be five or six years older than me.

I think he must be kind and thoughtful. The second time he smiled at me was the day after my mother died, just a few weeks ago. I was so lost and so sad. So alone in this terrible place. But God put the thought in my mind that at least she is free of the camp and will see me again someday.

The first time Kapo Rose beat me was my first day here in December. My hair had just been chopped off and I was given my striped uniform. I stepped out with some other children into the cold yard with the terrible smells just as Kapo Rose was crossing in front of me. I smiled—a slight smile, only to show that I have no hatred in me. I did not understand what was happening and I still do not, but I will not resist or object. Kapo, I think, thought me impertinent and she beat me with her stick. I cried and cried for hours afterwards. My mother and the women in the barracks comforted me and insisted I must stop crying. For the longest time, I could not. I could not imagine there was someone I did not know who hated me so much, so suddenly, and that she should want to hurt me.

"She knows you are not a Jew," old Adah, one of the Krakow women, said. "Your people brought this on us, and she hates you for that."

"But I am a Pole," I said. "They brought us here, my mother and me. Why would you say that, Adah?"

"I don't believe it," the old woman assured me, "but she does. She is from Lodz. All her people were killed as soon as they arrived. You are not a Jew and since you have no power over her... stay out of her sight."

"Be nothing. Be nobody. Be unseen," Ida said. "You are a little too pretty for your own good."

I didn't know what she meant by the first thing she said, but her compliment made me feel a little better.

I will soon be fourteen, and since there was no more room in the newly opened children's barracks, they put me in the women's camp. Though the conditions were cramped and filthy and the smells terrible, I had some comfort here while my mother was alive. But on the day of a medical check, she disappeared. I never saw her again, and the rumor among the women was that she was dead. I feel it is true, now. I know she would want me to try to find hope and some small happiness here, so, I try. Every day I try.

In the second week, they put me in the Kanada area to sort the belongings of the new people coming into the camp. The building was freezing. I had my mother's shawl to cover myself with and a scarf for my head, which was made colder when they cut off my hair.

Wilhelm asks me most politely to place my head in an iron brace to steady it for the first photograph. A guard steps into the room and whispers something to him. He does not answer. The guard steps back outside. Wilhelm seems sad now. I know I am not presentable. My face is dirty, and I know I have scabs where Kapo Rose slapped me. I can feel them. I must look a sight.

At Kanada, I sort through piles of jewelry and other things to remove anything made of gold. There are so many beautiful ornaments. I am amazed by some of the beautiful rings and pins and things I sort through. I opened a locket yesterday and inside were photographs of a baby on the left side and the parents on the right. Suddenly, I burst into tears. These people must be dead. The owners of all these things must be dead. The officers look them over quickly when they get out of the boxcars. Many are taken away and never seen again. I was ashamed of my silliness for admiring the pretty things when each is a leaving of death.

This morning, I was assigned to piles of jagged gold shapes. Gold from the teeth of the dead, another girl told me. Some of it extracted from living mouths, she said. My hands began to tremble as I touched the bits before me. I struggled to hide my tears until the guard brought me here for the photos.

Wilhelm can see I am thinking sad thoughts. He asks me to make my expression a blank one. He says to cancel sad thoughts with thoughts of how happy we will be when this terrible war is over. He said "we," not "you." Does he mean himself and me? Does he mean all the suffering people? I am not sure. He is so kind to me, I think he must mean the two of us. He looks at me so warmly.

"How will we forget all this when the war is over?" I ask him.

"God help us if we do forget it," he says. "But life will be good again for us. Don't forget that."

I feel like smiling, but I make my expression as blank as I can. He takes the photograph.

"I see people here who have made this... normal." I say. "It doesn't seem horrible to them anymore."

"They already consider themselves dead. It is not a thing to be accepted."

Mother told me that every terrible thing that happens will end someday. I have faith in God that He will save me if I have strong enough faith to survive this test and if I pledge to serve Him. I do pledge.

I pray that Wilhelm survives, too. He is not a Christian, but I think his goodness will redeem him. In a few years, our age difference will mean nothing. If I am not being a silly girl and find he does have affection for me, we may live in a world without the cruelty and hate of the Nazis. Surely God wills the Allies to defeat this evil.

Wilhelm tells me I am lucky to have been placed in Kanada to work rather than outside in the mud and snow. I tell him despite myself I do not know how much more of it I can take. I want my spirit to be unbroken, but when I consider that all the original owners of the things I handle have been murdered...

Wilhelm tells me the next photograph will be a profile of my right side. As he moves into position, I cannot stop myself. I burst into tears.

"What is it, girl?" he asks quietly.

"I am filthy. I smell bad," I sob. "I am bruised and scabbed and my hair is hacked off, and this is how you see me. These are only the second photos ever taken of me, and I hate that you or anyone should ever see them!"

"Don't worry about that. Only the Nazi bureaucrats will see them, and soon, I expect, they will be wiped from the earth."

I feel heartened at what he said. I feel encouraged though he still looks sad. I wonder if there might be something I could say to lift his spirits. Now in position, Wilhelm takes the photograph.

I don't remember much about my father. I was three years old when he died. There was a calmness in our house before that, and an emptiness after.

We had goats and a small vegetable garden and chickens; my mother tended to these. My father was a skilled machinist who made threaded metal fittings.

When my father died, my mother said she could not imagine a greater disaster befalling us. Then the Germans invaded our country. Mother said it was the end of contentment. The end of history.

Oddly, it was after the Germans sent everyone from our village here to this Hellish place that Mother regained her faith and her hope. I wonder if she did it just for me, her only child, as a thin, sad kind of protection. I think she wanted me to have something of goodness to cling to.

But I believe it, whatever her intention. I do believe it. Horror truly cannot last forever. I know hope is not foolish.

Now Wilhelm is ready for my last photograph. He wants me to look up and to the right. He wants me to wrap my scarf around my head. "The guard told me," he says, "that when we are done, you are to join the other children in the yard." His voice breaks a little. How largely he feels things! His spirit must be very good. "You must all have a medical procedure and an inoculation. The inoculation must be in your ribs. Do not be afraid. All right? Many diseases to fight here."

"I won't be." I wrap my scarf around my head. I must look a bit exotic! Perhaps a bit Orientalist! I smile at this. I must show my lack of bitterness and resentment as I did on my first day. I will show I can willingly accept my circumstances and place my life in the hands of a higher and loving power from whom I have begged protection.

I remember smiling is not wanted. I must only smile within myself, and timorously at that! It will from now on be especially important to me to be happy on the inside. I look up and to the right as if looking toward God and perhaps toward a wonderful future I may share with as caring and kind a spirit as the boy before me.

The Testament of Cleander

Cleander Redburn Weatherill sometimes thought that his father had brought him and his mother to Oscola, Florida to be buried alive.

They had been perfectly happy in Newton, Massachusetts while his father was away at war, then finishing his military service in the demobilization effort at Fort Dix afterward. But in 1922, when his retirement came through and his pension started, Floyd Weatherill thought the time was right to claim his small part of the burgeoning paradise of the state before the wealthy put all land ownership out of reach of the middle and lower class. His plan was to buy a patch of land on a small, isolated lake, and as he could afford it, buy lots in the area, develop them, and sell them for a profit as more northerners discovered the tropical promised land.

Cleander was about to begin his first year of prep school—Prescott, to be exact—when his father announced the move. Although Cleander didn't particularly relish the idea of going outside his home to attend any school, his tutor and friend Edmund Corey had graduated from Prescott ten years before and was excited at the thought that his protégé would follow in his footsteps. With Edmund's guidance, Cleander hoped to finally test the waters of the wider world outside his home, from which his mother had shielded him his entire life.

He had always been a sickly child. Constitutionally weak and consumptive. At age ten, the family doctor told his mother the boy may not see another five years. Edmund was hired that year as his tutor, and as the son of former missionaries in Tibet, he convinced Cleander's parents, especially his mother, who had dabbled in Transcendentalism and The Golden Dawn over the years, that it could be life-changing to educate the boy in the mysteries of *Vajrayana*, a Buddhist tradition of tantric practice. Seeing the limitations of medicine and doctors, Cleander's mother was open to anything.

Edmund had seen great promise in Cleander from the first. The boy was exceptionally bright and sensitive. He loved history and literature and had an irrepressible curiosity about cosmology and the natural sciences. They shared a love of weird literature, of the works of Arthur Machen, Joseph Sheridan LeFanu, Lord Dunsany, and M. R. James. Cleander mused about founding a journal of weird and dark fiction to be called *The Stylus* in honor of Poe's unrealized magazine of the same name. Edmund was excited to help his protégé in this venture.

And as his revelation of *Vajrayana* to the boy proceeded, Edmund was in awe of the potential he saw. He recognized that his young charge had within himself the spiritual energy to achieve *mahasiddha* and become a true adept. This was Edmund's wish for him: to gain mastery over his own weak flesh and animate it to self-healing.

On a February evening after a year's study and meditation, Edmund stayed late after lessons to keep Cleander company when his parents were out for a Knights of Columbus dinner. Edmund had assigned Cleander to read LeFanu's *Carmilla*, and the tale was to be the subject of the evening's discussion and analysis. Edmund sat in the north parlor by the fire, looking over notes he had made. He was surprised when Cleander entered the room shirtless with a wet towel draped across his shoulders.

"What is all this?" Edmund said.

"I want to show you something," the boy answered. "Feel this towel. I want you to verify that it is dripping wet." His skinny, pale torso was also wet, as were his suspenders and the top of his trousers.

"Yes... yes, it is. You're dripping all over the floor!"

"Wait here. Don't move." Cleander disappeared down the hallway toward the rear of the old house.

Edmund smiled. He returned to his notes on LeFanu, his thoughts occasionally drifting back to the image of Cleander's emaciated torso. Bony and pale. He regretted coming to the opinion that the New England climate was not best for the boy.

After twenty minutes, Cleander had still not returned. Edmund stood and dropped his notes on his chair. He walked toward the rear of the house.

Cleander was not in the kitchen. The back door was slightly ajar, freezing air gusting in. He looked out the small window on the door. Cleander was sitting cross-legged on the back porch, eyes closed. He appeared to be in a meditative state. The towel wrapped around his shoulders was steaming as the moisture was evaporating out of it.

"Cleander!" Edmund ran onto the porch. "What are you doing? *Cleander!*"

The boy did not respond. Edmund gathered up his tiny, bony frame and carried him back into the kitchen. He placed the unresponsive Cleander onto a kitchen chair. After a moment, the boy appeared to be coming back to his senses.

"What were you doing? What were you doing out there? That sort of trick could kill you, you know?" Edmund felt the boy's cheek. It was warm.

Cleander blinked his eyes a few times and smiled.

"I shouldn't be able to do this yet. I shouldn't be able to," he said. "Look at the towel. I made it dry out. I did that through meditation."

Edmund touched the towel still draped on the boy's shoulder. It was completely dry.

When Floyd announced his plan to move his family to Oscola at dinner one evening, Cleander suddenly found himself unable to breathe. His head spun and he fell on the floor. As he came to his senses after a few minutes, he began to wail.

"I can't move away... I *can't!*" he cried. "I can't live in a tropical place so far away from Edmund. I like it when everything is gray and cold. The winter! I see things differently and stories come to me in the winter! There won't be a friend for me there. Who will I talk to? Edmund is my friend!"

Floyd looked at his son sternly. "I have a business opportunity down there. Once in a lifetime. We're going and that's that. And I think it's time to get you away from Edmund."

Cleander remained inconsolable. Floyd confined his son in his room for several days and refused to let Edmund see him. His mother, Hestia, brought soups and bread to her son's room but he didn't eat them. The boy sat in his window seat watching what was probably the last snowfall of the winter falling in their backyard.

"This is a venture your father has to try," Hestia said. "It may not work out, and if it doesn't, I imagine we will come back here. It is our home. I don't really want to go either, but his mind is fixed on it, and he has to try it."

"Why can't I see Edmund?"

"I think your father feels Edmund has served his purpose."

"But he teaches me. I am still learning from him. He is helping me with my new story, *The Death-Messenger of Neferneferuaten*, and he has new research to show me from the Boylston Street Library..."

"Your father and I have become uncomfortable with his relationship, his attachment to you."

"I don't understand..." Cleander frowned.

"Edmund is a grown man. He should be out in the world on his own with a wife and family, not living with his mother. He should have friends his own age. Not young boys."

"But... why? I have so much to share with him. He taught me about so many things, about *Vajrayana*, and..."

Hestia embraced her son and brushed the hair back from his forehead.

"We will not discuss this any further."

Cleander refused to come out of his room for two more days as his parents prepared for their move.

On the morning of the second day, he noticed a large knot had developed over his right eye. It was discolored and scaly but did not hurt. Instead, it was mostly numb and almost seemed to vibrate slightly when Cleander focused his attention on it for any length of time. Hestia was alarmed and planned to take the boy to see Dr. Keane, but when Cleander calmly assured her it was nothing and would go away on its own in a day or two, she felt oddly reassured as she often did when someone provided her a simple answer to a difficult question, and she believed him.

The day before the long drive south, a letter arrived for Cleander with no return address. It was from Edmund. Cleander read it privately in his room.

My dear Cleander:

I hope you have a safe journey. My spirit will travel with you. Be sure of that. And it will be with you as you explore your new life in Florida. You see, we have made a connection that no interloper may break. It has been the most valued of my life and losing it is therefore out of the question. Do not despair, for I know we will be together again not only in spirit but in person. Wait and see. The void will close, the gyre of being will complete its orbit, and we will be together again. We will talk of the great issues, publish your journals, write fictions, explore the beauty and terror of that yawning chasm of time and space. Together. There is a brilliance and power in you that sustains and inspires me, and sometimes even frightens me. Meditate. Think. Write.

Yours,
Edmund

***

The family had always lived frugally and had few possessions. Floyd decided they would pack what they could into the Model T truck he traded for their touring car and leave the rest behind. Chifforobes and chairs can be replaced, he said. He thought it might take them five days to drive to Florida on the Boston Post Road and Atlantic Highway, allowing for any breakdowns and problems. He thought they would camp along the way to save money and stay in hotels only as a last resort.

The morning they left was frigid and it took Floyd an hour to start the truck. Cleander sat between his parents and Hestia covered him and herself with a blanket to try to keep him warm in the draughty, freezing cab. She reassured her son.

"We only have a few days of this, and it will be warmer in the South," she said.

"That's why everyone goes there," Floyd said. "Including us."

They were well beyond Hartford when Floyd decided to stop for the night. The weather had turned colder, and Floyd thought they would have to find hotel rooms on their first few nights until they were much further south. In a small village, Latrobe, Connecticut, he found a clapboard hotel called The Skelly.

Their room was shabby and contained an iron bed and military cot. Cleander sat on the floor near the radiator until he felt warm enough to unwrap himself from the blanket his mother had covered him with. He stood and folded the blanket. Hestia opened their large leather suitcase on the bed. Cleander found his red journal in it. He had written *The Journal of Aeons* in black ink on the cover. He sat at a small wooden table in front of the room's only window and opened the journal to the page marked by his pencil. He wrote:

> *This is Day One of my journey to oblivion. I think we must have gone two hundred miles today. The cab of the truck is cramped and freezing cold, and the seat, hard and uncomfortable. The jostling rattles my bones, and I wonder how I will make it another eight hundred miles. The highway is mostly paved, but not completely, and I am led to understand that the road will get more primitive as we go further south.*
>
> *I found I was able to put myself in a meditative state today, in spite of the noises and vibrations around me. I can warm my body as I did when I dried the wet towel, though it is difficult to maintain the state for hours on end. Edmund would be proud. I am hoping that when we arrive, or somewhere along our path, I may be able to find a telephone and call him. Nothing would be more soothing than to hear his voice.*

Over the next few days, the weather warmed considerably. At Virginia Beach, the truck's right front tire went flat, and while Floyd hitchhiked to a gas station to get it repaired, Cleander and his mother walked the boardwalk. The wind was brisk and cold coming off the gray ocean and as Cleander watched the rising surf, he removed his red journal from his coat pocket. He opened it to the back where he noted ideas for stories or essays as they occurred to him. He jotted, smiling to himself:

> *Use the phrase 'my Oceanic mood and mind,' in a story somewhere.*

In two and a half more days they reached Jacksonville, Florida and headed southwest toward Chobeetaygee County and the tiny settlement of Oscola. The roads deteriorated from concrete or asphalt to gravel to muddy ruts as they went, and it took an entire additional day to get to Oscola.

Floyd's map of the county showed Lake Chobeetaygee at the end of the dirt road they were on, but it seemed as though no attempt at settlement had ever been made in the area. There were spots where the palmettos and scrub oaks were overtaking the road and where the road became a path, and branches and leaves that had fallen across the ruts looked as though they had been undisturbed for months.

The road crept past a wet area full of bald cypresses and then became more well-defined and substantial. In another hundred yards, the forest opened to a glade, beyond which could be seen a small lake with a few deteriorating wooden buildings scattered around the shoreline, along with one small, reasonably tidy house with a dilapidated mailbox out front. Floyd parked the truck near the front porch of the small house.

"Number 4 Chobeetaygee Road," he said. "Home sweet home."

"I thought it wasn't supposed to be cold here," Cleander said, climbing out of the cab.

"Far cry from Massachusetts," Floyd said as he and Hestia began to unload their few possessions. Cleander gathered his box of books and papers, his pillow and blanket, and carried them into the house.

The house was in reasonably good repair but starting to show early signs of deterioration. The floors were pine boards with spots of linoleum in the kitchen and hallway. Wallpaper in the front room and bedrooms was starting to peel, and there were a few scraps of furniture left behind, including two small tables, three chairs, and an old walnut wardrobe. Cleander claimed the front bedroom for himself. He pulled the smaller of the tables into the room and positioned it in front of the single window, which overlooked the lake. Floyd dragged Cleander's thin mattress into the room and let it flop onto the floor. A moment later he brought in his son's bookcase, which, along with the mattress, were the only two items of furniture Cleander had been allowed to bring. He lined up his books on the bookcase, as well as his issues of *Dread Tales* and *Hutchinson's* magazines.

As his parents were arranging things, Cleander wandered out the front door and down to the lakeshore to look for kindling and firewood for the old kitchen stove he'd heard his mother say she would need. He walked along the shore picking up twigs and branches, glancing now and then out across the cold water. He thought he might write a story someday about an aquatic monster that terrorizes a small rural community. Something like *Negotium Perambulans*, which he had just read in *Hutchinson's*. He dropped his kindling and removed his journal from his jacket pocket and opened it to the back. He wrote:

Reread E. F. Benson.

He realized that he had wandered near the collapsing wooden buildings he'd noticed when they first arrived. There was some sort of livery building, a general store, a cottage, and the remains of a hotel with the words OSCOLA ARMS peeling away above the front door. Cleander stepped onto the porch of the hotel. It was decaying and moss-covered. One of the double front doors was missing. He stepped into the lobby. A large part of the floor had rotted through, revealing a cellar. Broken remnants of lobby chairs and a sofa were scattered around, and moss and creeping vines covered most of the teetering north wall. A part of the roof had rotted through over the lobby, and squirrels could be seen skittering in and out of the opening. The old front desk was still intact, as was the oak key cabinet on the wall behind it. Small birds had made nests in two of the key compartments. An enormous copper planter containing a dead palm sat near the end of the desk.

The moldering rot of the primeval forest! Cleander thought. *Time, Nature, and travail may reclaim and rot away mere flesh, as the Earth calls back all material things unto herself...but NEVER may she destroy an idea! A thought!*

Cleander smiled and quickly scribbled the passage into his journal.

He looked around the cavernous lobby and decided this would be his hermitage, his private place. Through the front door and across the lake, he could see his parents bringing the last few boxes of clothes and odds and ends in from the truck. They would be to blame if he never saw Edmund again. Floyd and Hestia.

Cleander sunk to the floor at the base of the front desk. He sat for a few moments, thinking about the loneliness and isolation he could expect in this wilderness. Whoever tried to live here before, whoever built this small settlement, had given it up and abandoned it. He wondered how his father planned to attract people to this fetid lake.

Cleander could feel his distress and anger roiling within him. He knew he needed to meditate, to refocus his energies to some neutral point in the void. He climbed up on the hotel desk and sat, crossing his legs. He slowed his breathing and emptied his mind. He felt his body gradually becoming lighter and warmer. He felt a painful pressure grow in waves above his brow where the knot had appeared before. Soon he became calmer and lighter still, and he felt a sense of connection to his surroundings and some glimmering of contentment. He opened his eyes.

He was surprised at how weak he felt. Meditation had never had that effect on him before, at least not to this extent. He breathed deeply a few times. He caught a twitch of movement in his peripheral vision.

Next to him on the desktop, glistening in the muted light, was a gelatinous, dark mass, some five or six inches in length. At first, Cleander thought it might be some sort of plant secretion, like a viscous sap that he somehow hadn't noticed when he clambered up onto the desktop. But it had thickness as well as width and length, and as he watched it, he could see a slight shivering along its wet surface. The thing seemed to be breathing. Though no part of it could be clearly identified as a head, it had an opening like a mouth and seemed capable of locomotion. With a slight undulation, it moved toward Cleander a little. Slug-like, he thought, but more nondescript.

Cleander felt no revulsion toward the creature and had no impulse to move away from it. In fact, he felt an odd attachment to it, a connection, as though it were in his charge and had appeared here so that he may care for it. He reached toward it tentatively and touched it. It felt predictably slug-like but seemed to sensuously respond to his touch. It rippled its flesh upward against his finger as he stroked it.

He opened his journal and wrote:

My dear Edmund: Let this be my testament. There will be no better executor of my story than you. For expediency I am writing this in my journal, hence the cut pages. I wanted to write it all down as quickly as possible!

Cleander described in detail all that had happened that day. At the bottom of the third page, he drew a reasonably accurate representation of the creature, which had hardly moved on the desktop the entire time he'd spent writing his account. He touched it again, and again it seemed to welcome the contact. From across the lake, he heard his mother calling.

"Cleander! I need that firewood! Where are you?"

The creature had moved slightly toward him. He didn't want to leave it as it was. He climbed over the desk to the back of it and carefully cupped the creature in both his hands. He placed it in a lower compartment of the key cupboard on the rear wall. It lay still and after a few moments, it seemed to Cleander that the thing would be content to remain there. He slipped his journal into his pocket and gathered up the collection of twigs and sticks he had left on the front porch.

Floyd had also placed his and Hestia's thin mattress directly on the floor of their room, as he'd considered the bedframes they'd left behind to be luxuries taking up space in the truck that they would replace when they could afford to. Soon after the three of them went to bed that night, Cleander could hear his father snoring. He wondered if his mother would be able to sleep in this new place.

Moonlight was streaming into the single window in Cleander's room, and he found it bright enough to be a distraction. He heard sounds far off in the dark, mourning swamp that must have been birds because it seemed too cold, to him, for frogs and insects to be active. He crawled off his mattress and looked out his window at the still lake reflecting the moonlight. He looked toward the dark, ruined buildings at the opposite end of the lake. He thought of the odd creature he had left in the hotel key cupboard. He couldn't imagine what it could be. He had always had an active interest in biology and taxonomy, and he had never heard of anything like it. He wondered if it would still be there in the morning.

It was still dark when he awoke, but the moon had just sunk below the tree line. As the sky began to gray a little, he dressed, put on his jacket, and walked down to the lakeshore toward the old hotel. He startled a pair of raccoons as he stepped onto the front porch of the Oscola Arms.

Everything seemed rotted, cold, and damp as he stepped into the lobby, even more so than when he had first seen them the day before. In the gray light across the room, he could see that the creature was still in the cubicle in which he had left it. He hurried to the desk and climbed over it and examined the thing more closely.

He could see respiration and it responded welcomingly to his touch as it had the day before.

Then Cleander noticed something in the dark box behind the creature. He carefully lifted the creature out of the cupboard and placed it on the desktop. At the rear of the cubicle, barely visible in the dim light, Cleander could just make out what appeared to be fur and blood and red meat. As his eyes adjusted to the gloom, he realized that he was looking at the carcass of a freshly killed and partially devoured squirrel. He looked at the thing on the desktop and saw traces of fur and blood near the mouth-like orifice. What was this thing? How could it consume a creature nearly its own size?

Cleander climbed back up onto the desktop and sat himself next to the creature.

"I think you are something new. Something unknown. I need to give you a name," he said. He pulled his journal out of his jacket and opened it. "I will call you *Parum Daemonium*, the Little Demon."

He scribbled the name in the journal under the drawing of it he had done for Edmund. He turned the page and wrote:

> *This odd creature, which I have just named P. Daemonium, as you see, is a mystery that I need to share with you. I found it this morning in the cubicle in which I had left it and saw that it had nearly consumed an entire squirrel's body at some time during the night. It seems so docile to me and yet is fearfully voracious. What do you make of it? What can it be... a new species, as I suspect? Why can you not be here with me to study this small horror?*

Cleander closed his journal. He felt overwrought and knew he must calm himself. He crossed his legs, closed his eyes, and began to meditate.

It took a long while for his mind to clear. When it did, dark impressions overtook him. They washed through his mind and body and soon expressed themselves in a weight and pain in his brow above his eye, the same pain he had felt before. He felt a sudden urgency to remove himself from this meditative plane. He opened his eyes, weakened, diminished, and disoriented.

He jumped down from the desktop and as he steadied himself against it, he saw that there were now two additional *Parum Daemonium* next to the first one.

Cleander could not believe what he was seeing. He touched the painful spot above his eye.

"It's me," he whispered. "*I* am making these things!"

The two new creatures lay motionless next to the original one, acclimating, it seemed to Cleander, to a new state of existence. He opened his journal and quickly wrote an addendum to Edmund, describing the morning's incredible development.

I will do my best to mail these pages today or tomorrow if possible. It is essential that you know of this as soon as ever you may, and try to find a way to join me here. Truly essential to me. It is a secret for just the two of us. Something I am resolved to share with no one else until I have shared it with you.

Cleander placed each creature in a separate compartment of the key cabinet. He slipped his journal back in his pocket and hurried back to the house.

Hestia had a fire raging in the kitchen stove and was preparing to make breakfast. She barely noticed when Cleander passed behind her, walking toward the kitchen sink. Floyd's straight razor was in a shaving mug behind the faucet. Cleander used the razor to carefully cut the journal pages comprising Edmund's letter and folded them.

"Do we have any envelopes and stamps?" he asked his mother.

"Envelopes in the box on the front room floor. One stamp in there too, I think. Are you mailing a letter?"

Cleander didn't answer her. He found an envelope in the box on the front room floor and the stamp, which he affixed to the envelope. He put his folded pages inside and sealed the flap. He wrote Edmund's address from memory on the front and carried the letter out to the dilapidated mailbox at the end of the drive. As he closed the box, he saw his father approaching with a bundle of sticks and branches.

"Mailman don't come out this way anymore," Floyd said. "We have to let the post office know we're out here. What're you mailing there?"

"It's nothing. Just a letter back home. Nothing much."

Floyd opened the mailbox and removed the letter.

"That's what I thought," he said. He crumpled the letter and stuffed it in his coat pocket. He continued to walk toward the house. Cleander followed him.

"Dad, my letter..." he said. "It's important. Very important!" He thought now may be the time to tell his father about *Parum Daemonium*, the secret he only wanted to share with his friend. He almost said the words, but he could not make himself speak. This great discovery, this dark new dimension of nature, must not be trivialized by sharing it with his parents before the one being on earth beside himself who could truly grasp and understand it.

"We told you, made it clear, that you were done with Edmund. A grown man that wants a boy for his best friend is up to no good. I won't tell you again!"

Inside the kitchen door, Floyd dropped his bundle of sticks on the floor. Then he took the crumpled letter from his pocket and stuffed it into the blazing stove. Cleander watched helplessly. He looked at his mother whose face had an expression of either indifference or resignation.

"I wondered if that was what he was up to," she said. She focused her attention more intensely on the potatoes she was slicing.

Cleander began to sob. He ran out the kitchen door and up the lakeshore toward the Oscola Arms. He heard his father calling him, angrily demanding he come back home. The gray-green winter swamp absorbed the calls and dispersed them into distance and irrelevance. Cleander knew his father would not follow him.

He stood inside the cold, rotted hotel lobby thinking of how trapped he was. He was a prisoner in this place, cut off from all the things that mattered to him in the world. In a rage, he ran to the large copper planter at the end of the front desk and dumped it over. The dried palm tree trunk snapped as it fell, as the planter crashed against the floor. Cleander felt drained and weak. He knew he needed to collect himself. He climbed up on the desktop, crossed his legs and closed his eyes.

As the darkness overtook his mind, an incandescent pain crept up his neck and into his head. The distraction was so great that complete meditation was impossible. After a few minutes, he opened his eyes. Behind him and next to him on the desktop were four more *Parum Daemonium*.

Cleander was so weak, he fell off the desk and onto the floor. The pain in his head was intense. He stood and looked at the four new creatures. He looked at them dispassionately, without his previous sense of amazement or disbelief. They were no longer odd or miraculous. Now they just *were*.

"They must all be together," he said. "They are all intended to be put together."

He ran to the overturned copper planter, dug out the remainder of the soil left inside, and uprighted it. He ran back to the desk and gathered up the four new *Parum Daemonium*. He carried them back to the planter and dropped them in, then collected the three creatures from the key cupboard and placed them in the planter with the others.

A wet, kneading sound arose from the copper vessel. Steam began to waft from it. Cleander looked inside. He saw two of the creatures press hard against each other. In a moment, the two had melded into one being. Then that being melded into another individual, and soon all the creatures had coalesced into one large *Parum Daemonium*.

Cleander suddenly absorbed all that had happened. He would need to write it all out again and somehow secretly get the account to Edmund. He needed his friend to be there with him, to understand it all.

"What the hell you a-doin' here?" It was a high, reedy voice. Cleander turned to see a tall, thin boy of about sixteen standing in the back doorway of the Oscola Arms. "Nobody tolt you that you could be in here."

"We just moved in. I didn't think any of this belonged to anyone."

"I say it belongs to me. Little Carl Stepney. I been here since I was borned. Didn't just move in."

"It don't belong to you.

"If you don't plan on gettin' a whuppin', callin' me a liar is gettin' off on the wrong foot. What're you a-doin' here?"

"Nothing. Just getting away from my parents. Nothing much."

Little Carl took a few steps toward Cleander. Cleander walked toward him to stop him from approaching the planter. Little Carl seemed surprised by this. He grabbed the sleeve of Cleander's coat.

"I'm needin' some money," he said. "You got anythin' in them pockets?"

"I don't have any money."

"Well, we'll see..." Little Carl thrust his hand into Cleander's jacket pocket. He pulled out the journal. Cleander grabbed for it, but Little Carl held it high above his head, laughing. He pushed Cleander away.

"*A Journal of Aeons.*" Little Carl grinned and opened the book. "What the hell is all this nonsense? '*Prospectus for my literary magazine to be called The Stylus.*' '*My oceanic mood and mind,*'" he read. He flipped back a few pages and read, "'*The Death-Messenger of Neferneferuaten. The Horror of the 18th Dynasty.*'"

Cleander grabbed the journal from Little Carl.

"You wouldn't understand any of this. You keep your hands off it! It's all about things that will never be revealed to you or any of the low orders like you!"

Little Carl grinned. "You're kinda Aunt Mary, aintcha? A sissy?"

"You're a low-brow ignoramus."

"You're a sissy-boy. I can tell by your book. You look it, too. You ain't gonna do too well here. Like ole Willis Reed. He was thattaway. Some fellers knew what to do to him. They could do it to you, too." Little Carl furrowed his brow in thought. "I think you work for me now. I think if you want me to keep quiet about you, and you want to keep a-comin' to my hotel, you're gonna have to work for me."

Cleander brushed his hand across his journal as if wiping off impurities visible only to him.

"Proof is in here," he said, holding up the journal. "Proof in here that you're wrong and proof about lots of other things besides. Things, information, you could never figure out on your own."

"Let me see it," Little Carl grabbed for the journal. Cleander tossed it into the copper planter nearby.

Little Carl grabbed for the book as Cleander threw it. He hurried to the edge of the planter and reached in before he saw its contents. When he saw the now massive creature inside, he withdrew his hand.

"Land O' Goshen, what's *that*?"

Cleander ran up behind Little Carl and pushed him hard. Little Carl fell forward, and his right arm reflexively stiffened to catch himself and thrust into the planter. In a second, *Parum Daemonium* had grasped his arm and begun the process of positioning it near the mouth orifice. It began to devour the flesh. The thin boy screamed and struggled until, as Cleander watched in growing excitement, Little Carl's head was drawn down into the ravenous cleft, and he was dead.

Cleander felt a sense of exhilaration unmatched by anything since the days when he had mastered the *Vajrayana*. Now the world was reborn. Now everything was possible, and nothing could prevent him from sharing these things with Edmund. With all his strength he pushed the copper planter over on its side. The half-eaten carcass of Little Carl flopped onto the floor; its legs crossed as it came to rest near the desk. The creature undulated a bit toward Cleander, who stepped toward the front door.

"Just a short distance along the lakeshore for you to follow," he said. "Slow going. Might take all day, but I am patient. The house is close by."

Cambion

The law had to be followed. The sheriff and coroner had to be called, which Mesmin Gothard did, without understanding the necessity of it. His wife of fifty-seven years, his Genevieve, was dead. Certainly dead. No official county person needed to tell him that. He could have easily buried her himself immediately, but the law is the law, and Mesmin had no wish to defy authority.

The coroner and sheriff took the body away. Two days after the official verdict, "death by stroke," and having been prepared for burial by Aubert the undertaker, Genevieve was returned to Mesmin in a pine coffin. He put her in the glade west of the cabin they had shared since Genevieve inherited it after the death of old Euphrosine the wildcrafter in 1882. Over the grave he placed a stone he carved himself, inscribing only Genevieve's name and date of death on it.

Fifty-seven years. They moved into the cabin a week after the inquest following Euphrosine's death, the old woman, along with her enormous dog, Potiphar, having been killed by unknown wild animals. Euphrosine, foreseeing her end, filed a will the month prior naming Genevieve, her *protégé*, her sole beneficiary, and so the newlywed couple quickly took possession of the property.

Genevieve had been the old woman's occasional pupil from the age of eleven, although she'd nearly been denied the opportunity, as Euphrosine, at first meeting, decided the child was already too old to be taught. But Genevieve's mother was persistent. She'd been helped herself by a philtre provided by the old wildcrafter, and she was determined that her daughter would continue the tradition after Euphrosine was gone.

Genevieve mastered the craft very well. She provided philtres and powders, unguents and elixirs. She could smell a mother's head and belly and predict the sex of the unborn child. She could read tea leaves and coffee grounds and cure most female complaints. Most importantly, she was schooled in her primary responsibility as *La Mere des Siecles*, in the doctrine of Circe and eternal conflict with Balphoroth the incubus.

The myth, repeated over many generations in Ste. Odile, was that Balphoroth, the parasite spirit, inhabited the body of the town's imperious hermit Orien Bastide. Over two continents and since Roman times, they had been the adversary of Euphrosine. Through her craft as an ancient sorceress, she had extended her life to fight this evil across the ages, but in the end, Balphoroth, within his host Bastide, had finally won. Together they killed the old woman, the Mother of Centuries, and then it was left to Genevieve to oppose them and their assaults on the women and girls of Ste. Odile and wherever Bastide traveled.

Superstition and peasant tales brought from the old country by the earliest settlers, Mesmin scoffed. But he knew Genevieve believed it all, and the legends about Bastide persisted in the town.

Bastide disappeared the same year Euphrosine died. There was a collapse in an old mine shaft where he stored some of his art treasures, and he and a teacher, a Miss Perdita Badon-Reed, were both presumed killed in the cave-in. A friend of Miss Badon-Reed's had pressed to have the county excavate the shaft and retrieve the bodies, but the executor of Bastide's estate blocked this action, saying that the great danger and expense involved would lead to a result that was already a foregone conclusion.

Still, Genevieve remained wary. Euphrosine told her that if Bastide should vanish, even if there is no trace of him for twenty years or more, she should not assume he is gone. He has survived unimaginable things over the centuries, she said, and you must consider the possibility that he continues to do so.

In the afternoon after he buried his Genevieve, Mesmin sat on a granite boulder facing the sunset. He watched the fading rays flicker through the wings of the gathering mosquitoes above the grave. Beyond them, the fireflies were starting to appear down the hillside that was covered in the stunted oak and cedar forest that continued unbroken until it opened in the distance at LaMotte and Lesterton, many miles away. Genevieve's herb garden was just down the hillside from the cypress tree above the grave. She had used it thousands of times over the years for her remedies and cures. Now it would weed over, as Mesmin had no use for it and no knowledge of his wife's craft. Genevieve had not made the time to train and prepare a successor. She would be the last Mother of Centuries.

That evening, Mesmin decided to light a fire in the hearth. A small one. It wasn't uncomfortably cold yet. He wanted the light, the brightness, more than the warmth. He had come from a large family and married Genevieve when he was eighteen, more from a desire to get out of his house than out of love for his bride.

Until Genevive's death, he had never lived alone. It had been three days since her death, and he found he had little appetite and no desire to sit alone at the table. He thought this odd because he did not consider himself lonely. It must be because his routine had changed. It shamed him to realize he didn't miss his wife as much as he knew he should. His daily life would be quieter and emptier, and the life he was used to and comfortable with would change. He would need to adjust, and he knew he would. But he believed he would not miss the companionship or the responsibilities of caring and affection.

Soon after sundown, Mesmin lit a lantern. It was chillier now. The light from the fireplace alone was too dim to read by. He had started reading *The Private Memoirs and Confessions of a Justified Sinner* by

James Hogg a month before Genevieve died. In the evenings, he would open his book and read for an hour or so until he became too sleepy to go on. Genevieve would knit or stitch repairs in his trousers and shirts, speaking occasionally of her craft, her remedies, or the danger of being a woman or girl in Ste. Odile.

"The darkest days," she said the night before she died, "was the time of old Euphrosine's death. The last time Orien Bastide was known to be here and living at Jardin Noir. The demon in him attacked many women."

"Yes," Mesmin said, "everyone knew about Marie Delaporte Chardin and Sister Solana and Perdita Badon-Reed. Terrible. Terrible."

"Worse than the attacks were the offspring of them—*Le Vorace*—the familiars of the demon that only lived a short time."

"Yes. Thank God."

Mesmin's attention always wandered when Genevieve spoke of demons and familiars and Bastide, but after all their years together, he always made an effort to appear serious and concerned.

"I've never seen one, and all who did died in the attacks by Bastide... the demon. There were harbingers, signs that the demon had chosen that woman. I always suspected that it was *Le Vorace* that killed Euphosine and old Potiphar, not some wild animal. What animal could have overcome that dog?"

"The Ravenous. I've heard of them."

"But Euphrosine said not all the offspring die off quickly; rarely, there is a cambion. One that survives to perpetuate the line. If such a thing comes into being, it will find you, she said. She warned me."

"But Bastide is dead. Years and years ago. Maybe all that is in the past for Ste. Odile...?"

"I don't know. Take nothing for granted, Euphrosine told me. Nearly every day she repeated this."

Now there would be only silence in the evenings. Mesmin would make the best of it. It was God's will that he live alone in these, his last years, and the thought of that was not unappealing. The companionship he shared with his wife had shriveled to almost nothing over the years, and though their love had been long dormant too, now the vague sense he carried with him to express it occasionally would never trouble him again.

He found his book on the floor under his chair and opened it. His eyelids were already heavy, and he found it difficult to focus on the page. As he sat up straight in his chair and began to read the same sentence for the third time, a stick of kindling fell from the top of his stack of firewood onto the floor. This woke him up a little. He thought he might skip the rest of the chapter he was reading and see if the next chapter held his interest more. There was another slight sound of wood falling against wood, and then, quickly, a log fell to the floor.

Mesmin looked at the stacked wood for a few moments. He wondered if he had brought a mouse or rat inside when he carted in his logs a few days ago. People sometimes gave away kittens or puppies at the farmer's market in Ste. Odile on Saturdays. He would walk into town on market day and see if he could find a kitten. After a few more minutes of drowsy reading, he decided to go to bed.

The sun was already up when he awoke the next morning. That was unusual. He was normally awake by four or five in the morning, hours before dawn. During the night though, he had been awakened by the sound of skittering movement in the front room. He thought his mouse or rat had become active in the darkness. It took him an hour or more to go back to sleep. This was Friday. Yes, tomorrow he would go into town and to the farmer's market for a cat.

For a few years after they were married, Genevieve owned a grandson of old Euphrosine's huge dog, Potiphar. Genevieve's dog was also enormous and named Potiphar. Mesmin liked the dog well enough, and buried him solemnly when he died, but he found he liked cats better. Their indifference and distance appealed to him. Mesmin thought he might not mind having a cat around his home for a while. When the cat had done its job, he would give it away.

It had rained a little during the night. Mesmin knew he must have slept better than he thought he had, because he didn't remember hearing any rainfall. On chilly mornings like this, he was especially glad he had moved the plumbing inside the cabin years ago. He put a pan in the sink and ran water into it for coffee. He was startled by the sound of stacked wood falling in the front room. He looked cautiously around the corner toward the fireplace.

At first he saw only the eyes, and the terror in them. Terror and desperation froze the small face. The creature's terrified gaze was fixed on him from behind what was left of the woodpile. The being was mostly hidden in shadow and indistinct, except for the eyes.

It was the size of a large rabbit or opossum. Its skin was gray and mostly hairless, sagging into folds under the neck and around the thin arms. Some coarse hairs grew on top of the small head and down the back of its bony neck. The eyes were large and orange, slightly too large for its face, as was the mouth. Its face was slightly prognathous, and its expression wizened, terrified, and seemingly compressed into too small a space.

Mesmin gasped. He stood motionless for a long time, as did the creature. When he stepped into the front room a little farther, the creature tried to hide itself in the kindling. When it failed at this, it lay cowering on the floor, and trembling, staring fixedly at Mesmin. The creature's abject fear emboldened Mesmin a little. He watched it there, helpless on the floor, fearing for its life. This was, Mesmin sensed immediately, this must be, the being of which Genevieve had spoken. There was nothing else like this in the natural world. What else could it be but the demon offspring known as the cambion?

"Genevieve," he whispered, "I'm sorry to have doubted you."
Genevieve mentioned over the years that there was always a possibility in Ste. Odile that this creature, the offspring of one of Bastide's victims, could appear and that as the *La Mer Des Siecles*, it would be drawn to her. She was, after all, the adversary—the one who knew of the creature's nature, strengths, and weaknesses. The cambion, alone in the world, with no ally or powers of its own, would seek her mercy.

Mesmin walked further into the room, giving the creature a wide swath so that it would feel less threatened. He sat in his chair near the fireplace, never taking his eyes off it. It returned his constant gaze. His first thought was how to drive it out of his cabin, but he considered that if he did this, there would be no guarantee it would leave him alone. Its instincts had brought it here and it likely had no conception of any other action to take. Mesmin thought he would have to kill it.

He decided not to make a sudden move to grab it. It had substantial claws and teeth. He could get his .38 from the bedroom and shoot it. That made the most sense. But he was fascinated by the look of it and transfixed by its constant gaze upon him. He didn't know if he could kill something so helpless. Odd to think that its only instinct seemed to be to come here, yet it was almost too terrified, hiding in its corner, to move. As he continued to watch it there, it seemed more curious and sad and nothing like a threat to him.

After watching it for forty minutes or more, Mesmin rose from his chair to return to the kitchen to make his coffee and decide what to do with the creature. It watched him walk past and out of the room. He put his pan with water on the stovetop and lit it. His heavy white coffee cup was draining in the sink. He removed it and set it on the edge of the stove. He turned to see the creature cowering under the icebox against the opposite wall. Its gaze never left his eyes.

"What poor soul brought you into the world?" Mesmin whispered. "Genevieve was right about all of this. She would be horrified to know that Bastide has come back again. I can't have *you* here. I'm sure I can't tolerate this." He walked quickly into his bedroom and removed his Smith and Wesson from his top dresser drawer. He returned to the kitchen. The cambion had moved out from under the icebox but scurried back under it at the sight of him. Mesmin raised the gun and pointed it at the creature. The terror was still evident in its eyes, but now there was more: He recognized a look of not only complete helplessness, but also dependency. He lowered the gun. "What am I to do with you?" he said.

When he had made his coffee, Mesmin walked back into the front room and sat in his chair. The creature followed him back into the room, remaining near the woodpile and fireplace. Mesmin sat uneasily for an hour. He realized that at moments when his attention wandered, the creature would move slightly, bit by bit away from its hiding place. It was slowly moving toward him, and it gave the impression, as it moved so gradually, of flattening its body, or compressing it as it crept along, as if its bones could be displaced or softened and then reconstituted.

In another half-hour the creature was nearly at Mesmin's feet. It had never stopped watching him, and only when he returned its gaze intently, would it avert its eyes. After a few more minutes it became apparent to Mesmin that the creature meant to touch him, that it wanted and needed contact with his foot or leg as he sat. He stood and walked across the room. He didn't want it to touch him. He opened the front door and stepped outside. He still held the Smith and Wesson. He thought he would let the creature follow him outside, then he would shoot it.

Mesmin stepped off the front porch and into the yard. The cambion soon appeared in the open doorway and stopped there, watching him. It seemed unable or unwilling to move through the open door. It would move a front foot forward then bring it back again, unable to cross the threshold to the outside. It mewled and cried in growing frustration, but it could not make itself move forward. Mesmin thought he would have to shoot it where it sat if he were going to shoot it at all. He raised his gun. "I can't have it around," he thought. "I don't want it... or anything here with me. I don't want it touching me."

The cambion grew more agitated, flopping helplessly in the doorway. It stretched its neck forward and its mewling and crying became more desperate and panicked. Mesmin lowered his gun and put it in his pocket. He knew he could not make himself, for whatever reason, kill the creature.

"I'd swear," he mumbled to himself, angry, as he moved back toward the door, "that this thing loves me."

The weather turned colder in the afternoon and Mesmin built up the fire in the fireplace. The creature had become a little bolder. It lay on the edge of the rug, a few feet from Mesmin's chair, always watching him. "You trust me more now," he thought. "Not so fearful. I wish you didn't watch me all the time. If you get to trust me completely, maybe you'll stop."

He thought of Genevieve telling him the long history of Bastide. It was as the young Roman, Medullinus, as he was known then, that the parasitic demon chose him to be its host body. The demon kept the host alive for two millennia to continue its attacks on women from Asia Minor to France to Ste. Odile, until, it was assumed, Perdita Badon-Reed brought an end to his obscene existence. Mesmin thought of how the entity entered the body of Medullinus and how it kept him alive over the later centuries as Bastide, even as his body slowly and inevitably corrupted, despite its demonic interventions.

Mesmin felt himself falling and he realized he had dozed off. His right hand drooped over the arm of his chair, and he became aware that his fingertips were touching a cool, velvety surface. He looked down and saw the cambion, looking up at him fearfully. Mesmin quickly pulled his hand away and stood. He crossed the room and stood by the kitchen door. He shivered a little. The touch of the creature was repellant. Not for its texture or temperature, but for its intent. There was an abominable affection in it that Mesmin found appalling.

"You stay away from me," he whispered. "Just keep your distance. I'll shoot you. I will shoot you."

The creature seemed to flatten itself and partially wrap its body around the leg of Mesmin's chair. It looked at him mournfully. Longingly. Mesmin hurried past it and into his bedroom. He had returned his gun to his dresser drawer earlier. He removed it again and went back into the front room. "I have to kill this animal," he thought. He aimed the gun and put his finger on the trigger. The yellow eyes never looked away from him. He saw thought processes in that look. This was no creature familiar to zoology on earth. He didn't know if it could reason or solve problems. All he knew for certain was that it felt fear and attachment. Abject fear and loathsome affection. Mesmin felt a pall of defeat and hopelessness in his body. He tossed the gun on his chair.

Nearing midnight, Mesmin was so exhausted that he knew he would, against his better judgement, have to sleep soon. He put his gun in his pocket. There was a simple wooden latch on his bedroom door. It wouldn't be that difficult to force it open or slip under or around the door since it was a poor fit in the door jamb. He had always meant to fix it but had never gotten to it. Tomorrow he would do it. He hurried into his room and closed the door behind him, latching it and pushing a ladderback chair against it for a brace.

He fell into bed. For a long time, he heard no sound of movement outside his door. He missed Genevieve tonight, more than he had since he'd buried her. She would understand all this and help him through it. Or maybe none of this would have happened if she hadn't died. Maybe her departure opened the door and made the way safe for the entity to find him. He placed his gun on his nightstand and felt himself drifting off to sleep.

He dreamt of Genevieve, of her doing small things for him and for others whom she helped with her craft. He thought of Bastide, though he had never seen him or heard an account of his physical appearance. He pictured Bastide's ancient self, Medullinus the Roman, adopted son of a Roman governor in Gaul. How did the demon defile him? And how did he face the dread and drudgery of unending life, to be conscious and aware through decades and centuries, sustained by a parasite through a hellish existence, yet still fearing the gift of death?

His awareness slowly arose out of sleep. He struggled for a breath and noticed a velvety, cool texture spreading across his face. He gasped for breath again. To his horror, he realized the cambion lay across his mouth and neck. It mewled contentedly and warmly, and its claws seemed to be working their way across Mesmin's teeth. They were slowly opening his mouth. Mesmin struggled to move, and he found his body mostly frozen as in a waking dream. He labored to stretch out his left hand to his nightstand. The gun was there. He was hardly strong enough to grasp it. He tried to lift the gun, but it fell to the floor. Mesmin knew he had to move, to throw the mewling monstrosity off him, but he could not.

Too close to him to focus his eyes, the cambion was a blur of slow movement and its contented mewling had become something like a loving purr. It seemed to flatten itself against Mesmin's jaw and cheeks as it wedged open his mouth. Mesmin choked a little and gasped for air as the creature slid itself inside. Mesmin saw the blurry form disappear below his range of vision. He could no longer see anything in the room, and he thought he might be losing consciousness. The blur of years replaced the dark forms in his mind. There might be a night a century from now when he remembered this night's suffocating, choking horror, and there would be thousands of nights between this night and that one when the life he had lived as a child, young man, and husband would seem like someone else's. He saw years and decades of subservience to the will of the being. He saw himself helpless against the decline of his body and the terrifying progression of years, and helpless, too, against the oppression of inescapable devotion.

Innumerable Radii:
A Conversation

March, 1842

"Gray day. Gray, windy day." I mumble this to myself alone, or so I think, as I look out the large window of our room, a room which I would call decidedly palatial. This is the United States Hotel in Philadelphia, and I am gazing down at Chestnut Street, and at the Custom House building across the busy avenue. "I was hoping for better weather, but this might be appropriate."

"Appropriate for what?" Catherine startles me as she enters the front room from the bedroom, tying her bonnet. I recognize her sharp tone. She is wearing her wine-colored Carrick coat. The mayor of Hartford, whose name I have already forgotten, insignificant functionary as I found him to be, called me 'Charles Dickens, the most famous man in the world!' Fame is fatiguing to no end, and my wife is showing the effect.

"My visitor. I have a visitor this morning. Do you remember?"

"I do wish you would stop asking me if I remember everything, or noticed something or forgot something. All this is so exhausting, this traveling. One gets tired. I am tired, not irrational."

"Of course."

"I certainly don't wish to go out today, either."

"Well, Kate, I am having some dark brandy sent up. You could brace yourself, or... you can refuse, you know." I am wearing a dark blue suit, freshly made for me in New York. This I realize has no bearing on my narrative, but I recalled just now the new and satisfying smell of it.

"So *you* say. These people are already looking for reasons to dislike us. Some of them, at least. I have promised Miss Hepworth, and the Ladies Sodality are awaiting me now in the lobby. I do wish you hadn't begun that copyright business in Boston."

"I'm sorry to hear it because I am far from finished on that subject."

"Oh, dear," Catherine unties and reties her bow. "Won't you come out and look at the mastodon skeleton with us? The city is quite proud of it."

"I told you last night, and again this morning..."

"You led me to believe you *wanted* to see the museum."

"No, Kate, I did not. I merely gave you my full attention when you spoke of it. I do enjoy curiosities, but we have seen other skeletons in other cities."

"I need to hear about the children and home. I'm desperate to hear of them. I do hope Katey is showing less temper."

"Little Lucifer? I doubt it."

"Yes... so do I." Kate walks toward me as I return my gaze to the window. She hugs me. "I am so tired of these literary people and ladies' groups. I don't see how you can abandon me today for the sake of another parochial editor. You've put them off before. Why not this one?"

"He is the editor of Graham's. I showed you its latest number last night."

"Yes."

"Edgar... Poe. You've heard me compared to Bulwer back home?"

"Yes."

I remove some papers from a packet on a nearby console and read, "'Mr. Bulwer, through art, has almost created a genius. Mr. Dickens, through genius, has perfected a standard from which Art itself will derive its essence, its rules.'"

"It's all very true about you, of course." Kate considers. "I hadn't thought about Mr. Bulwer that way. Your guest wrote that?"

"Yes, he sent it yesterday morning, with some other things. You know they have just finished the serialization of Barnaby Rudge here?" I remove a clipping from the packet and hand it to Kate. "Here is a review," I continue, "published 1 May 1841, nearly a year ago, in the *Saturday Evening Post* in which our Mr. Poe predicts the outcome of the book! In fact, he implies that the solution was not so terribly difficult, since my book bears such undeniable similarity to *Caleb Williams!*"

"What nonsense! I don't see any similarity..."

"But there is more," I say. "In addition, he has sent me an article of his authorship on how to write a mystery novel! Can you imagine? My suspicion is he thinks I sacrificed art for obscurity."

"These people are astonishing." Kate sniffs, retying her bonnet.

"With everything else, he sent two volumes of his own tales. Brooding, Germanic things, mostly, but difficult and quite memorable. One hardly knows how to take some of them."

"He sounds like a boor to me. I shall be glad to *not* meet him."

"I think an egoist of this magnitude has not become such out of a secret doubt of his capabilities, as lesser ones have. This man has no doubt of his superiority."

"I think he protests too much." Kate approaches me and kisses me on the cheek. "Don't let him trap you here all day. I hope to be back in an hour or so. And remember what happened in Hartford; don't mire yourself in arguments with these people about abolition or copyright laws."

"Mr. Graham is coming later. The magazine's publisher. I promised to meet his niece." I follow Kate to the door. "I'm sorry you have to go," I say as she steps out.

"I'll do my best to wear out old Miss Hepworth and her biddies as quickly as possible. Shouldn't be too difficult. I doubt any of them are younger than fifty. I hope to be back by one or two at the latest." She closes the door gently behind her.

I return to the window and sit in a chair nearby. I pick up one of the volumes of Poe's tales and leaf through it. In a moment, the door opens again and Kate steps back inside.

"Have you forgotten something?" I ask.

"No, your visitor is here. Mr. Poe. He is just outside."

"Why didn't you let him in?" I say, rising. It is my tone now, that is sharp.

"He asked to be announced. He thought it more polite."

"Well, you've done it. Let's not leave him in the hallway." I approach the door.

"Perhaps we should make sure he is who he says he is," Kate says, stepping in front of me. "His clothes look none the better for wear. He could be... an... anarchist representing himself as Poe, or one of those radical slavery advocates."

I slip past her and open the door. "Good morning, Mr. Poe. Come in, please."

Poe steps into the room; there is something at once regal and deferential in his manner. He extends his hand as he enters. I take it and gesture toward the chairs near the window. Poe carries a beaver skin top hat and wears a somewhat threadbare black cloak. His complexion is pale, nearly sallow. He reminds me of a man of fallen circumstances who has put himself together as best he can, an appearance I recall from my father's worst days.

"Since I first heard of your visit, I have had no greater wish than to take you by the hand!" Poe says. "It was most gracious of you to see me."

I shrug. "After receiving your parcel yesterday, I could hardly have left Philadelphia without meeting you. You've met my wife..."

"Yes!" Poe bows courteously.

"Goodbye, dear, and Mr. Poe. Forgive me for rushing away like this." Kate nods as she exits through the hallway door.

"Let me take your things," I say. Poe hands me his hat and cloak which I hang on bronze hooks near the door. "I'm a bit surprised to find it still so cold here."

"Interestingly," Poe says, "Philadelphia is within a few degrees latitude of Constantinople, so yes, logically, it should be warmer. Or I would assume as much. One usually assumes Mohammedan regions are warmer."

A tentative tap on the front door. I open it and find an older man holding a silver tray with the brandy I requested. I can't help but notice Poe studying the man closely.

"Your brandy, sir," the man says.

"Please, place it on the cupboard." The man, with a slight limp, carries the tray to the cupboard and places it there. I notice his interest has been attracted by the urn of umbrellas and walking sticks near the front door. Poe notices this, too.

"A moment, if you don't mind, Mr. Vernet—I believe that is your name," Poe says. Vernet seems stunned.

"Why yes, sir. Vernet. Israel Vernet at your service." He bows slightly.

Poe places his hand on Vernet's shoulder. "I believe you will find your stick in the lobby, in the large porcelain umbrella urn near the front desk."

Vernet's jaw fairly dropped. "Land O' Goshen, sir, how did you know...?"

"You were a military man, Mr. Vernet? A veteran?"

"Oh yes, sir."

"U.S. Regiment of Rifles?" Poe seems to not doubt his speculation. If speculation it can be called.

"Sir!" Vernet gasped. "You must be in touch with some higher..."

"Such a shame that heroic group was disbanded," Poe interrupts. "Pressed into the regular Army. I could not help but notice you still wear the boots of the riflemen. Yours have an old repair at the ankle."

"Wounded at the Big Sandy Creek action."

"Dear fellow," Poe bowed slightly. "I was in the Army. I recognize that nearly thirty years on you still wear your service boots and those unmistakable green trousers."

"Pension wouldn't support a dormouse," Vernet frowns, "as you must also know as a veteran, sir."

"As I came in from the street I quite coincidentally and accidentally noticed the umbrella urn against the wall near the desk, and my attention was struck by a brightly painted stick. I found it interesting enough to take a closer look. An inscription said *I. Vernet, Big Sandy Creek 1814*. A parting gift from your company?"

"It was, sir."

"Perhaps you set the stick down when you arrived at the hotel today? Inadvertently? And maybe an errand boy or someone noticed it and not recognizing it, placed it in the urn?"

"I think that's it in a hen's egg, sir. Thank you, sir! And Mr. Dickens!" Vernet nodded thankfully and exited.

Poe smiled at me. "Poor old fellow," he said. "Must hobble around on duty all day without the stick. He is of no use to the hotel if he cannot carry a tray or luggage."

"Gloriously perceptive of you. You had Mr. Vernet quite nonplussed. I wonder why he did not consider looking in that urn for his stick?"

"That urn is for the use of the guests. I think Mr. Israel Vernet thinks those people to be a league apart from himself and his working fellows. I suspect it would be some time before it would occur to him that his battered possession could be found among the finer ones used by those he serves."

"That is probably true."

"I usually do not admit to my time in the Army. I am not sure why I did just now." Poe rubbed his hands together. "I am nearly frozen, through."

"Let's sit by the fire, then," I proffer the chair nearest to the grate to Poe. He sits. "I have just had this dark brandy sent up. That should take the chill off."

"Nothing for me, thank you," Poe says.

"Very well." I sit in the chair opposite Poe. "I'll wait, too."

"I hope Mrs. Dickens hasn't gone out on my account...?"

"No, no. I've had quite as much tourism as I can manage for a while. I consider myself to be a man of considerable energy, but we've been in a whirlwind since Boston: balls, lectures, receptions. For six years I've barely put my pen down, and I thought it time for a rest. I'd always wanted to see America, to evaluate its great accomplishment. I have been duly humbled; I can tell you. But to return to your question: I needed a day away from the crowds. Kate does too, but she declined to put Miss Hepworth and her ladies' group off. Are you married, Mr. Poe?"

"I am," Poe holds his hand near the fire. "Very happily. I am fortunate."

"I'm not sure Kate should have married a writer. She isn't much comfortable with celebrity. I wonder if it ever crosses her mind that she should have married a parson or banker."

"Not every writer is Charles Dickens." Poe smiles at me. "I have some small celebrity. Notoriety might be a better word. Virginia handles it well. She isn't strong."

"No? I am sorry to hear it."

"Notoriety or fame carry with it some burdens, even at my level. There are many enemies I can count, and then there are followers, hangers-on. Like Miss Hepworth's group, I imagine."

I stand and walk to the sideboard. The subject being touched upon often requires some bracing for me. Removing the stopper on the crystal decanter and a goblet from the cabinet, I pour myself a measure of dark brandy. I return to my chair. "There are always women if that's what you mean. Yes, that is a fact."

"Important to keep one's wits and priorities in mind," Poe says. I sit and begin sniffing my brandy. After a moment, Poe shifts his chair closer to the grate. He seems almost thankful for the warmth.

"I couldn't stand the thought of hurting or betraying Virginia. She has every dear quality of every woman I have loved or admired since my infancy. I never forget that. That is to say, I always come back to that."

"You said she isn't strong?"

"Consumption. I am glad the warm weather is coming. The cat sleeps on her breast now for warmth. But summer is coming."

"Oh dear. I do hope she regains her vigor as the weather warms."

"Several loved ones have succumbed to the disease. A terrible scourge. I suppose that is why I come back again and again to the tragedy of the wasting death of a beautiful woman in my work, as you noticed if you looked through my volumes. In Virginia's case, I wonder sometimes if the writing life I live isn't making her worse." Poe stops himself. He smiles. "Ah," he says. "I'll leave that subject alone."

"I do understand," I agree, sipping the brandy. "I can hardly say if it is worse for a marriage for a man to be a struggling unknown or somewhat famous. Both are difficult. It is taking its toll on Kate. That, and the children. Women often drop into a state of melancholy after a birth. Kate is scarcely out of hers when she is expecting again."

"We have none as yet. Children. Circumstances will warrant it someday, but not just now."

"Still," I am scowling into the fire like a falcon studying a field mouse from afar. "When a woman is in that depressive state and her husband finds himself... set aside..." I cross my legs and my foot strikes the grate slightly, sending tiny embers up from the iron.

"Have you noticed," Poe interrupts, almost urgently, watching the embers, "that the solitary firefly will gather with others into a mass of some considerable density, then suddenly fly off into the darkness, into innumerable radii?"

I scowl again. A point I was trying to make seems deliberately derailed. And in the most florid language. "Into many different directions? Yes, I suppose so. You are a man of great imaginativeness, as your work reveals."

"I'm sorry; the embers reminded me of that just now. I remembered that phenomenon as a boy in Virginia. I have always had a wild interest in trifles."

"Just as well. I was letting my conversation drift off into an inappropriate region. My apologies."

"I suspect you have few opportunities to talk casually with another man on a tour such as this. In any depth, I mean."

"Few or none!" I laugh. "Of course, I have met some of your writers. Mayors, political people, clergymen, and many, many women. Most of the conversations are brief and trivial. Rarely do I have the chance to sit with an intelligent, well-read man such as yourself and just converse at ease."

"Then in commemoration of that, there should be no barrier or obstacle. I would feel honored to be a partner in your unfettered discourse! And into whatever region you choose."

I finish my brandy and rise and walk to the sideboard to refill my glass. "Kate has already warned me," I say, returning to my chair, "to avoid the topics of abolition and copyright."

"I read they weren't kind to you in Hartford."

"I mentioned copyright infringement and the newspapers called me a mercenary scoundrel and said I was no gentleman."

"A novelist in this country can scarcely support himself, and a writer of tales and poetry cannot. Longfellow is a professor, Emerson a minister, Hawthorne works in the Boston Custom House, Irving has been a lawyer, merchant, and diplomat. I am a magazine editor. Provincial taste has always preferred the established English author to a lesser-known American one. That is why I believe the copyright problem is more difficult for us than it is for you."

"Our popularity is a compliment paid by greedy publishers. I don't get a farthing. I do see signs you are developing a national literature, though I found no reference to America or democracy in your work."

"I don't care at all about developing a 'national literature.' I care about developing a legitimate, serious literature that is *native*. And yes, my friend, I do have an opinion about democracy."

I sip the brandy. "My opinions on that subject were shaken by my visit here, if I may say. Not certain what I expected, but it must have been some egalitarian Utopia. Perfection of a human system of governing, at last. The primary fixture of my disappointment is the cuspidor. The spittoon. All else is concentric circles radiating away from the spittoon."

Poe laughs.

"Such filthy things!" I continue. "And they are everywhere. I can't imagine a more disgusting habit. And to see it as widespread as it is here is unimaginable."

"And these men vote," Poe says. "How may the ignorant, the unlettered, the willfully uninformed sustain a democracy? They cannot... for very long."

"Well, I choose to believe that most men, if not all, will do the right thing eventually. It may be a long time coming."

Poe shrugs in disagreement. "I feel that with time, our anger, obsession, resentment, and an inexplicable urge to perversely do the things not in our best interests, those things we know will destroy us, can take ascendancy. I believe that we inevitably—ordained by fate and our nature—do the wrong thing. Many of us, at least."

"The pessimist's point of view," I raise my glass to my guest. I am enjoying the first engaging conversation I have had since Boston.

"Laid against the optimist's," Poe says. "I hope I'm wrong. I would be glad to admit it. I hope Virginia will get well, but how many consumptives do?" Poe stands and moves toward the cupboard. His manner is almost petulant. Almost shameful. "May I?" he says.

"Certainly."

Poe removes a glass from the cupboard and half-fills it with brandy. He quickly drains it down and refills the glass. He seems to have no interest in savoring the liquid, but rather only in getting it into his systems as quickly as possible.

He returns to his seat but doesn't sit; instead, he begins a soliloquy. "A cold winter's day it was. January just past. We were happy. Virginia was singing and accompanying herself on the pianoforte. It was Heaven's music as she has always been to me its most radiant host sent to Earth. Then such a look came over her face. Such a look of terror in her as I hope never more to see. Blood, dark arterial blood spattered forth from her lips staining her face, breast, and the keyboard."

"Terrible, how terrible." This description dismays me more than I would have predicted.

"She collapsed." Poe drinks half the brandy in his glass. I see now he is not a man who employs wine as a pleasure of life, but rather as a carapace against pain. "I carried her to her bed," he continues. "Muddy and I—my aunt and I—cleaned her and sent for a doctor. She has never been the same." His speech becomes louder, faster, and more impassioned.

"How dreadful, my friend."

"My mother, my adopted mother, and my dearest friend Mrs. Stanard—all taken by one terrible disease. Now Virginia." Poe sits in his chair again. He seems to realize he has become more animated. "I am sorry. But when faced with the possibility of losing her..."

"I well understand."

Poe places his glass on the floor beneath his chair. "And brandy is no solution to my distress."

"You seem overheated," I stand and move to better survey Poe's suddenly reddened face. "There is water. Would that help?"

"No, thank you. I do not want to embarrass myself. Perhaps I should leave? Gather my thoughts?"

"Oh, no, no, not at all," I insist. If expressing his thoughts will comfort him, it is the least I can do. "Think nothing of it. I am a passionate man also. How can a man of feeling and passion not rage against such misfortune? Such injustice?"

Poe relaxes in his chair. "It is misfortune indeed," he says. "In my darkest moments, I wonder, how long will the coming tragedy be kept in abeyance?"

"They say warmer weather and cleaner air will help," I say helpfully. "Keats went to Italy..."

"Keats died there."

"Of course... He did."

"That is why I mentioned the copyright situation being more dire here. Certainly, it is for me. Royalties would help. Being a literary man is my passion. But it may be killing Virginia." Poe reaches under his chair, retrieving his half-glass of brandy. He finishes it, rises, and refills the snifter. "Mr. Graham is a good man, but he is also a businessman. All my publishers have been businessmen." Poe's voice becomes louder. "What good is earning a penny if you have to part with it? Good men or not, all are miserly."

"That they are. Without exception."

"Graham's silly niece is visiting him now. She is a follower of my work, and yours, of course."

"As we said, there are always women."

"There is something about the girl. Something familiar, but I can't pin it down. Edmontia Chantrey-Wallis. Barely fifteen."

His face slowly fades from its flushed hue back to its original pale aspect. He remains agitated. He looks at his snifter but hesitates. Then his resistance abruptly fades, and he finishes his brandy. He rises and refills his glass. He walks back to the window, making a slight stumble on a rug, and gazes down on the busy street. As he does this, I return the decanter of brandy to the cupboard. My brilliant companion, it seems, has a weakness.

His expression is a little wilder, a little more disorientated than before. "I was very interested," I say, in an obvious attempt at distraction, "in your tale, 'The House of Usher.'"

"Thank you." His face brightens a little. He sits. "I do favor it. Have you read Rees' papers on 'Atmosphere?'" Poe asks.

"No. I don't know of them." I say.

"Atmosphere, he writes, is the sphere formed by effluvia or minute corpuscles emitted from solid or consistent bodies, and he notes how this idea so amicably accords with the metaphysical precepts of sentience in inorganic matter." Poe's voice has become louder again. He stands and walks aimlessly across the room.

"I haven't heard of this," I say. "I am not entirely certain of what we are talking, in fact."

"Think of it—the actual literal awareness of stone, mortar, trees, and sedges, and their suggested complicity in malevolence in the sapping and annihilation of a family, the Ushers, and more importantly, in the delusion and suggestibility of the narrator."

"Ah, I see." None of this has occurred to me in considering the tale. I think that is because hearing it now, it seems nonsense to me.

"My interest was in the *supposed* effects of these elements on the diseased imagination of the hypochondriac as his soul decays, and their influence on the perceptions of his friend." Poe has become more agitated again and the flush has returned to his face.

"It is a brilliant piece of work, certainly," I say. He seems to have not heard my comment.

"Although the miasma which arises from Usher's tarn," he continues, "is intended to recall the well-known gas, febrile miasma, which has, as its effect upon the human mind, nearly identical delusions to those which characterized the disease of Usher; this association is purposefully unspecified. It is better unspecified; the workings of the mind and imagination, especially when in desperate decline, are of more interest in literature than a simple chemical reaction."

"Infinitely." I agree.

"One has to wonder if there is a limit to what the mind of man can know. I value logic and investigation but lament the loss of imagination and spirit which science may encourage."

"Do you think so?" I ask. "I would think they might go hand in hand."

"Let me ask you to imagine something incomprehensible." Poe's excitement seems affixed to a high point. "Is it conceivable that all the matter in the universe, now spread across the cosmos in the form of planets, stars, comets, and all heavenly bodies, was at one time in eons lost, compressed into one singular point? And at a titanic moment, this indescribably dense point exploded and dispersed the matter across the void? Stars and planets were formed, possibly out of the action of gravity, and continue to expand outward from that single point even to this day?"

"It is indeed incomprehensible."

"In addition, at some moment the outward expansion of that matter will reach its apex, gravity will lose its influence, and all will begin to contract. This action will continue across untold ages until all becomes compressed again as it was in the beginning. And then, the process will repeat."

I take a moment to absorb what he has said. "This all seems incredible."

"And what else in nature compares to that expansion and contraction?" His excitement borders on the manic. When he also notices this, he tries to calm himself. But his excitement quickly returns. He finishes his glass of brandy. "Why, nothing less than a *heartbeat*! This could be the heartbeat of creation, of God, if you prefer!"

"It could be," I agree. "But isn't it a human tendency to confer human traits upon things that are not human? An angry sea, for example, or an obdurate weed in one's garden? Could the universe have a heartbeat?"

"I feel it is true," he persists. "Science may never prove it, but I feel it is true, regardless." He turns toward the cupboard and notices the brandy decanter is missing. He places his empty snifter on a table nearby. "There are moments... when realization and epiphany come from feelings alone. Logic, ratiocination as I call it, must give way to intuition."

"Of course. These are interesting flights of conjecture, you describe."

"I have always had a wild interest in trifles."

I join Poe at the window. "I wonder how Kate's expedition is progressing with the Ladies Sodality."

"She will either have much to say on the adventure or not wish to discuss it." Poe conjectures.

"I sometimes think," I take Poe's empty glass from the table and with mine, place them inside the cupboard as I speak, "that I underrepresent women in my own work. That I don't attach enough complexity to their characters."

He watches me remove the glasses and seems distracted for a moment. "What do you mean?" he asks.

"Perhaps I idealize them too much, make them only agents of comfort and supplication to the male characters."

Poe frowns. "They cannot, in my opinion, be idealized too much. The ethereal, the pure, the vulnerable abides in them in my work. This is as it has been in my life as well. I think of my mother, my stepmother, Mrs. Stanard, Elmira Royster..."

"Kate reminded me today that she is a rational being. I try to portray the harsh judgments of the world touching women as well as men. But upon whom do *they* depend for succor? How many women roam the East End every night, scratching out an existence in the alleys and on the quays, perhaps slightly surprised if not grateful each morning to still be alive to see another dawn?"

"You are the conscience of civilization, my friend. I can only fix on one diseased soul at a time."

"Well, that is the universe in a grain of sand, isn't it? If I idealize women as you do, I am certain to resent their inability to fulfill my illusion. It's an odd thing I have only recently noticed. Unfair to be sure. Kate has borne four children, traveled the world with me, been a specimen in a cage for six years, yet I find myself annoyed when she is weary, and when I notice that her figure is becoming, let me say... vaguer. Why is that, do you think? What would you say as a student of the darkness of human souls?"

"Perversity. The perversity of ill-treating that which is of aid and comfort in our lives, for the opposite. A phenomenon unexplainable except as a... tumor of the spirit."

I smile. I feel the need to keep him distracted. "Tumor? Perhaps it is true. My sensibilities are a tumor affixed to my happiness and satisfaction. Or rather a pustule. Yes, a pustule, more like. Kate's too, I suppose."

Poe walks back to the grate and extends his hands toward the warmth. "When I look at Virginia, I see the effects of her illness, of course," he says, "but what I predominantly see is a... sweetness that will transcend this world. Whatever ravages her body does not taint her spirit, but only serves to make it more precious to me. I mean to honor that sentiment and that purity, but I have not always succeeded."

"Nor have I."

"Sometimes," he continues, "memory is the enemy. The ideals of love lost in those years of innocence. One wonders how differently love may have developed." Poe turns quickly, moves to the cupboard, and opens it. He removes the decanter and his glass. "Do you mind?" he asks.

"I thought perhaps we'd had our fill for today," I say, but he has already poured the brandy. He drinks it as quickly and joylessly as before. He braces himself against the cupboard.

"Are you all right?" I ask.

He doesn't speak for a few moments. The brandy takes immediate effect.

"I make such a spectacle," he says angrily. "I humiliate my dear ones, my employers, myself." His face has reddened again. "This is a curse, my friend. It shames me to think you have witnessed it."

"None of it. It is painful to see how these things torment you."

"They do!" he says in a loud voice. His eyes have a far-away quality now. He returns to his chair near the grate and sits. "All the more as I sit with you in this comfortable room, all the more because I think, I truly *think* I have killed someone!"

I am not certain I have rightly heard him. I return to my chair opposite. "Killed someone?"

"Elmira!" he says sadly. "Elmira Royster. Strong drink is a sedative, yes, but often... often there are phantasms. The light of day may distinguish these from reality, but sometimes they are so mixed together, like the vortex of a maelstrom... it is impossible to say."

"Who is Elmira Royster?"

"The daughter of a wealthy man who disapproved of me. She and I were engaged in Virginia. Her father forbade the union and destroyed my letters to her. I was away at the University then." He seems out of breath and is perspiring. "She thought I had forgotten her. I have always wondered how our life together would have been. The other day, yesterday I think it was, I *saw* her. After all these years, I saw her again."

"Saw her again?"

"She was unchanged. Miraculously unchanged. She was the same brilliant girl, fearful and expectant as yet of what life has to teach her."

"Well, that is impossible, isn't it?"

"It was too much for me. I stayed late at the offices and consoled myself and what should occur, but that she appeared again?"

"No, my friend. No, Edgar."

"She meant to gather me back to her bosom. I screamed at the figure, be she real or apparition, that I have a young wife now, shivering under my Army cloak for warmth, wasting away to nothing. *I will not abandon her!*"

"Calm yourself. This is the drink talking."

"She was set against leaving me in peace and cared nothing for my helpless, loving wife. Nothing at all, as if to say, 'sacrificing her life is the price of my happiness.' I struck at her, and she fell. With my fists, with my walking stick, I do not remember. I struck again and again as the notion of betraying one so loyal and loving, and the memory of having often been tempted to do just that, enraged me." He bursts into tears. He is certainly quite lost and inconsolable for many minutes. "How can one entertain for a second such a temptation?"

I say nothing. There is no reasoning with one adrift in this wine-dark sea. A sense of mortification emanates from him like the warmth from the grate. I pity him. I remain silent. I wish him to retain what he needs to of his dignity. Comforting him may only patronize, as I can of course, only manage conjecture at what he feels. The creative force in the sensitive, in those greatly attuned to the cruel ironies of Nature, can exact a terrible price.

A knock on the door. I rise and open it. There stands Graham, a prosperous middle-aged man with a young girl in a red bonnet. The girl smiles timidly and quickly averts her eyes. She holds a copy of *Oliver Twist*.

Graham extends his hand. "Mr. Dickens, thank you for seeing me again," he says. "This is my niece down from New York. Edmontia Chantrey-Wallis, a great admirer of yours!"

A sob attracts Graham's attention toward the grate.

"Poe!" he says abashedly. "Poe, what have you done?"

Poe looks up. Terror seizes his features as he fixes upon Miss Chantrey-Wallis. "Fiend!" he wails. "You have come back to torture me!"

The girl is confused and frightened.

Graham moves quickly to Poe's side and grasps him firmly by the shoulders. "It's Edmontia, my niece!" he says. "You try my patience so. If you have no aim to control this weakness, I must be done with you! You have embarrassed yourself as well as the magazine and *me*!"

"It was my honor that he chose to speak frankly to me of things troubling his mind," I say. "It was too much for him. I am to blame."

"We had an occurrence just yesterday," Graham rages on. "I warned him. His work is brilliant, but I don't know what will become of him. Incorrigible he is. Incorrigible. I must get him home. Please accept my deepest apology, sir!"

I turn and approach Miss Chantrey-Wallis. She seems a bit ill at ease at my approach. I extend my hand. She meekly takes it. "Let me have your book, may I?" She hands me the volume she holds. "Very proud of this one. Let me inscribe it for you."

"Thank you, sir," she says. "I meant to ask you if you would!"

I take the book to the desk nearby and sign on the title page: *To my dear new friend Miss Edmontia Chantrey-Wallis, your approbation ennobles my efforts. Many thanks, Charles Dickens.* I return the book to her. She beams with delight as she reads my inscription. "Edmontia," I say, "If I may call you Edmontia?"

"Oh certainly, certainly!"

"I wish to ask if you and your uncle might join my wife and me for breakfast tomorrow morning."

The girl is taken aback.

"I am occupied just now but wish to know you better. Mr. Graham, would you be so kind as to join us? Eight o'clock?"

"Of course, sir. For now, I must get Poe safely home. His aunt will be very angry with him."

"If I may, I will sit with him a while. I wish to see him recovered. I will arrange with management here to see he gets home when he is himself again."

Graham nodded in agreement. "As you wish, Mr. Dickens. This is very kind of you, to be sure." Graham returns to the door and with a touch of the shoulder, guides his niece out into the hallway. "Tomorrow at eight, then."

Poe remains in his chair. He glances painfully up at me. The flush is draining from his face somewhat, though his eyes are bleary and irritated. He looks like a man accustomed to the aftermath of self-degradation. "It wasn't she," he says miserably. "Why did I think it could have been she?"

I stoke up the fire a bit. Kate should be back soon. I retrieve Poe's cloak from the hook and cover him with it. I sit in my chair near him and watch him rise by degrees from what must be a familiar dark depth.

Those the gods would destroy, they first make mad.

I say nothing more for there is nothing more to be said. Soon my friend will be well enough, and he will return home. Home to his dying wife and admonishing aunt. I hope to talk with him again. At home he will complete his recovery. He will make of this whatever his sensibilities direct him to. The darkness will harry him, and if he glimpses a brighter world over a shoulder, will he aspire to it? Or is he wise enough to know that having once achieved transport to a brighter world, he would find for himself no place in it?

Phrygia House

Prologue

Everyone agreed that the devil was in George Pettibone. *Superintendent* Pettibone. The children didn't dare to be so familiar as to call the Superintendent "Mister." Even the staff of Phrygia House—the teachers, nurses, custodians, and vocational trainers—all called him by his full title, Superintendent Pettibone, as if to say only "Superintendent" would be somehow impertinent.

Pettibone's anger always seemed to be ebbing and flowing inside him. All tried to read his mood on the face towering above them. Far beyond six feet tall and nearly bald, slim as a sandstone spire in the desert, his head was a malevolent full moon floating imperiously above the masses. There was resentment in him, the staff said, for failing in his chosen profession of chemist, and being "reduced to playing nursemaid to a pack of grubby jackanapes and urchins, and the illiterates who ride herd on them."

Mary Whelan was only nine years old, but fully understood that she should go to any length to avoid displeasing the superintendent. Mary had tried to escape Pettibone's notice. She didn't want to become his helper, as Virginia Elizabeth McConnachie had been. As soon as Pettibone noticed Virginia and made her his special helper, Virginia's life changed. She became quiet, sickly and sad—everyone noticed it—and began having nightmares nearly every night.

But Pettibone did allow Virginia to have a pet. A large, and as it turned out, fiercely loyal stray dog wandered onto the grounds of Phrygia House from Bucephalus Street one Saturday morning. The animal was enormous and most of the staff guessed it was a mix between a wolfhound and a mastiff. Its back was as high as Virginia's chin, and its rough fur was coarse and brush-like. None of the other children could have a pet, but if Virginia allowed it and they patiently waited their turns, they could pet Enoch and maybe even help with his food and water.

Having Enoch was Virginia's only benefit to being singled out for attention. She had always told Mary she considered herself to be different from the other children. She was not really an orphan. She had foster parents, if not real ones. Virginia had come to Ste. Odile on the Orphan Train and Phillipe Labardemont and his wife Cecile had claimed her. The Labardemonts were landowners and their holdings included the Phrygia House property, purchased at auction after the New Phrygian community abandoned it. Virginia lived with the old couple for a year on their farm until Cecile became ill with consumption. As Cecile's health deteriorated and her care became all-consuming for Phillipe, he decided it would be best for Virginia to not witness the slow death of her foster mother, and that he was too preoccupied to care for a child. Phillipe arranged to place Virginia temporarily in the Phrygia House orphanage.

For the first few months, Phillipe visited Virginia twice a week, when he could arrange for Ruth Kraft, his neighbor, to sit with Cecile. But as time went on and Cecile became sicker, Phillipe visited Virginia less and less. It was soon after this that Virginia became Pettibone's special helper, and as she was becoming more detached from the other children, she was given Enoch, and the loyal dog instantly became her constant companion.

As Phillipe's visits dwindled to nothing, Virginia began to show signs of an odd illness. She grew melancholy and pale as winter came on. The few happy months she had known with the old couple had been replaced by the life she thought she had escaped at the orphanage in Boston. Her hair began to fall out and her hairline receded past her ears. Her eyes started to bulge and protrude like those of an anencephalic newborn. The symptoms only became worse as she took the medicine Pettibone directed the staff to give her. Enoch became even more fiercely protective of her, especially against Superintendent Pettibone. Within two months of Virginia first falling ill, Enoch wouldn't allow Pettibone within thirty feet of Virginia, and at the end, the dog would growl and his fur bristle at the mere sight of the superintendent. Then, on the Monday before Christmas, Enoch was found dead, stiff and grimacing, on the hillside behind the Reliquary Chapel.

"Strychnine," LaPointe, the custodian, said. "We used to poison red wolves and coyotes. I know the look of it." He buried the dog at the edge of the old cemetery of the Sisters of Perpetua, where lay buried generations of nuns who had taught the daughters of Indians and freed slaves before Phrygia House had become an orphanage. It was still known as the Academy of Perpetua.

On Candlemas, February 2, Virginia died while Labardemont sought treatment for Cecile in St. Louis. Dr. Remarque, a close friend and lodge-brother of Pettibone, conducted a brief autopsy and declared Virginia had died of infectious diphtheria, and ordered the child buried immediately. She was unceremoniously laid to rest in the old cemetery next to Enoch.

After Cecile died in St. Louis and Labardemont returned to Ste. Odile, he tried to open an investigation into Virginia's death. Sheriff Aubuchon was old and sick by that time, and Dr. Remarque was a respected physician, so county officials let the matter drop.

Mary Phelan had seen all of this happen, observing it from the camouflage of shadowy hallways and stairwells, and being lost in crowds of other children. A child, a friend, had sickened and died alone in the world. Adults had taken charge, and having many grim, serious conversations, had come to some resolution, and told the children to put the tragedy behind them. Mary was more than willing to do this and to continue to live unnoticed and out of sight.

But long before the gray morning when she first realized it, Pettibone had noticed her.

"Mary Phelan," Pettibone called as she slunk past him in the hallway outside the great dining room after breakfast that morning.

"Sir," Mary said as a stab of fear pierced her stomach. "Superintendent Pettibone."

"You were a friend of Virginia's, weren't you, Mary?"

"Um... well, not really, sir. We played sometimes. She didn't share like she was told to do."

"You have no family, Mary. No connections."

"No, sir."

"Your cheeks look very rosy today, Mary. I'd say the angels kissed you in the night. That would account for it."

"Would it, sir?"

"Did Virginia let you pet her dog?"

"She only let me pet Enoch if I did her favors. I should be getting to my class, sir."

"Virginia had family and connections. Important ones. It was stupid of me not to consider that, but... there it is."

"Sir?"

"You are alone in this dreadful life. You deserve companionship more than she did. Would you like a dog, Mary Phelan?"

Mary was speechless for a moment. A pet. A dog of her own. A dog to sleep with her and protect her from the other children. But accepting the dog would make her the special girl. If she agreed, from that moment, she might begin to slowly die as Virginia had done. But was it *possible* to say no? Once chosen by Pettibone, could a girl refuse?

"You think it over, child," Pettibone smiled. "A man on his own with no wife needs help putting the details of his life in order. From personal things to business, all females have a knack for that, that men lack. Did you know I did once have a wife, Mary? A wife who took care of those things?"

"No, sir. Superintendent."

"Her name was Mary too. She died of the consumption a few years ago. Only sixteen. Even the young are susceptible, you see? You could help me, Mary. You could be my helper and special girl."

Pettibone smiled, patted Mary's head, and nudged her on her way toward class. She ran off down the hallway in a panic, mouth dry, and did not hear a word spoken by Miss Moss, her arithmetic teacher, for the entire class.

Over the next week, Mary felt more and more that she had

become the special girl. She still had no dog, and Superintendent Pettibone didn't bring up the subject again. She could not put her finger on whatever it was she dreaded or feared from Pettibone, but whatever it was, it had not yet happened. His attention was on other things.

Two men, accompanied by the sheriff, had come to Phrygia House twice in the last few weeks. They were due to come again tomorrow, Mary knew, and Pettibone seemed lost in thought, irritable and more distant than usual.

He awakened her that night from a sound sleep with his signal lantern in his hand.

"Mary, wake up," he whispered. "I need your help. Take the lantern and go to my office. Fetch the folio of papers in the top desk drawer and meet me in the attic. I must go up there now!"

"Why do I have to get up?" Mary mumbled, confused. "Why do I have to get the papers?"

"Do as you're told!" Pettibone snapped. "I must find kindling and make a fire in the stove up there and get some papers out of the shed. Go!"

Mary followed the lantern's strong beam down the stairs to Pettibone's office on the first floor. The top drawer of the desk stuck. She tugged on it a few times until it opened. The drawer was nearly empty but for the brown cardboard folder full of papers. Mary pulled it out of the drawer and tucked it under her arm.

The hallway was freezing as she made her way back toward the stairs. A strong wind was blowing outside, and cold air gusted through the mullioned windows at the landing. Branches from the cypresses in the garden slapped against the diamond panes with a violence that Mary thought must surely send glass and lead crashing to the floor at any moment.

She passed the second floor and thought of her warm bed just a few feet away. She hurried up the third flight of stairs hoping that Pettibone would need no more of her after he had his papers, and she could quickly return to her dormitory.

The attic of Phrygia House was abandoned, dark and freezing. Oaken planks in the floor were warped in some places where the roof had leaked over the past few years. Barefoot, her toes numb, Mary kept the lantern beam focused on the floor to avoid splinters, which would hurt more severely as her feet warmed. There was no lantern lit in the main garret room. As she entered the room, she saw no light at all except for a faint red glow from the front vent of the Franklin stove against the far wall.

"Mr. Pettibone? Superintendent?" Mary said.

There was no sound but the wind outside and the sizzle and pop of hardwood logs in the stove.

"Mr. Superintendent...?"

Mary decided to leave the folder near the stove and go back to bed.

The floorboards of the garret room were even coarser than the ones in the hallway, so Mary focused her light on the floor and started to make her way carefully toward the stove. After walking a few feet, something soft and pliant brushed her right shoulder in the dark. She gasped and jumped backward. Unwilling to direct her light beam toward the object, she reached out tentatively into the black void. A fingertip brushed the object again and Mary quickly withdrew her hand.

"Hello?" She spoke in a near whisper.

No answer.

She reached out again and found the object. It was cloth. Perhaps there was a drape or curtain hung here for some reason. But the cloth seemed to be corduroy. Not a fabric for curtains. Mary slowly moved her fingertips downward along what seemed to be a crease, and quickly encountered a more solid object which seemed to jut out from the fabric at a right angle.

"Feels like... leather," Mary mumbled. "A shoe."

Reluctantly Mary grasped the signal lantern with both hands. Quickly she directed the beam upward from the spot she had originally touched, toward the ceiling.

The glassy, staring eyes had found Mary in the dark. They bulged from a face gone purple from the rope around the grotesquely stretched neck. The lips were rubbery, black and dripping, and almost looked as though Superintendent Pettibone was trying, at the moment of his suicide, to issue one further, irresistible order.

I

August 10, 1936

Miss Adelina didn't seem to be breathing. Iseult continued to grasp her hands, and though her grip remained tight, almost painful, her fingers seemed to be growing colder by the second. Miss Adelina scowled, then gasped for breath. Some nights, the wall could not be breached. Some nights the spirits resisted human attention and were indifferent to mortal needs. This had been true throughout the month of July. Iseult would try to come again the next day and hope for a better result.

At least twice a week since April, Iseult rode the Grand Avenue streetcar south eighteen blocks to visit Miss Adelina. She would leave her young son, Octave, in the care of Hugo, her husband, in their sweltering third-floor apartment on Laclede Avenue, as often as she could get away. More than twice a week whenever possible. She could feel Hugo's disapproval growing as her preoccupation with the realm of the spirits overtook her. She had been interested in Theosophy and Madame Blavatsky long before she met Hugo. Her father, the medieval scholar and academic Russel Aubrey Pearse, himself an early Theosophist and follower of The Order of the Golden Dawn, encouraged his daughter's growing interest in the occult.

After her mother's death in 1911, Iseult had witnessed seances held by her father in their large home near the university, and she'd heard the medium speaking in the voice of her dead mother, assuring Pearce and the terrified Iseult of the gorgeous existence that awaits them on the other side.

In the spring of 1926, Pearse discovered, by accident, a slim volume acquired by the university library the year before and quickly forgotten: *The Sorrows of Cuchulain.* It was a lyrical, imaginative account of the personality and inner conflicts of the mythic Irish hero, and the first novel of Hugo De Giverville, an American expatriate living in Paris.

Pearse began correspondence with Hugo through his publisher, and within a year had convinced Dr. Gardner, the head of the English department, and the trustees at the university to offer the young novelist an associate professorship. Hugo gladly accepted the post. His second novel was proving harder to write than the first, and his publisher had given up pressing him for a completed manuscript.

Hugo rented a room on the third floor of the house Pearse still shared with Iseult. From the first, Iseult recognized that her interest in Hugo grew out of her father's interest in him. Soon, though, her regard took on a character all its own. He had left his country six years before for the sake of his art with forty dollars in his pocket and moved to a tenement in Dublin to feel more fully the influence of his subject and the moods and dialects of the race who created the Celtic myths. When the novel was finished, at the urging of his publisher, Hugo moved to Paris to be amid a more vibrant and cosmopolitan literary scene. His advance and small royalties quickly evaporated on the Left Bank, and, finding himself somehow unable to flesh out the complexities he had originally foreseen in his proposed second novel, *Deirdre and Concubar,* Hugo quickly found himself as one of the countless nearly penniless Bohemians scraping together an income in any way he could, while watching his creative ambitions fade in an increasingly desperate effort to keep body and soul together.

Iseult was stunned by the courage of this, of his willingness to abandon comfort for art. Ultimately a failure, but a courageous one. Living a secure and comfortable life with her father, Hugo's perambulations were far beyond any adventure she would have ever planned for herself. To her, he seemed to be an almost heroic figure: a disregarded, mistreated, and undervalued genius, raging against the indifference of an insipid world.

Iseult and Hugo were married on Saturday, June 2, 1929, and they moved to an apartment on Laclede Avenue to be near the university, and to Pearse. The following March, Octave was born, and the next week, the Board of Trustees at Carthesian University and Dr. Gardner informed Hugo that due to his intractable nature and insubordination toward his department head, his services would no longer be employed.

For the next three years, as Hugo searched for a post at other universities and colleges around St. Louis, Pearse helped to support the young family. In October 1932, Pearse suffered a massive stroke and died four days later at University Hospital. Pearse had, unfortunately, never rewritten his will from the days long before his daughter was born, and he had left everything to the Carthesian Library. Hugo and his little family were soon nearly destitute, and when it became obvious to him that his difficult reputation had spread across the local academic community, Hugo had to take work spraying straw hats with lacquer at a factory on the riverfront for six dollars a week.

At the death of her father, Iseult became despondent. She could no longer care for her husband, her infant son, or herself. She tried working as a tutor, a housemaid, and a canning factory worker, but was dismissed from all these positions for being moody and unreliable. She began to have a dream in which her father had fallen into an icy river and attempted repeatedly to climb up the girders of a bridge to save himself. Again and again he would lose his grip, fall back into the water, and narrowly miss being swept away downstream. In the dream, Iseult tried to climb down the girders and grasp his hand, but she never managed to reach him.

"You *must* save me, child," Pearse said as he slipped back into the water. "I am your only parent now, your only real family. Your only connection to all who came before you..."

The dream meant something to Iseult: Her father was urging her remembrance, insisting that she keep alive the bond they had shared across the threshold of death. For four nights in a row Iseult had the dream, and she barely slept at all for another week following. In the afternoons, she sat sobbing in the window seat looking down on Laclede Avenue and the edge of the University quadrangle. Octave, now three years old, developed an earache and wailed in pain from his pallet on the living room floor. His mother barely heard him.

Hugo took Octave to the infirmary at University Hospital on the streetcar after work. Back home he made potato soup while his wife paced the floor in the living room, still oblivious to her son's crying. When Iseult looked at Hugo, he could see nothing in her eyes for him, no glimmer of concern, regard, or love. She was lost to him and Octave in her mourning.

"I want you to see a doctor," Hugo said. "You are not well. Octave needs his mother."

"It's not a doctor I need," she answered sharply. "We have seven dollars to live on this week. How would we pay for a doctor if I wanted one?"

"We have money to spend on seances and psychical readings..."

"It's *contact* I need. My father is desperate for contact with me. I feel he is lost without it. Only that will give him comfort."

"Your father is *gone!*" Hugo shouted, "lost to us! *Dead!* He needs nothing any longer. We can do nothing for him now but remember him."

Iseult turned away from him in exasperation. "How could you *ever* understand?"

"Even if what you believe is true, is that more important than your son? Are his needs *less* important?"

Iseult turned to face her husband.

"Octave is here with us," she said. "He is not lost... lost in the darkness like my father. Lost and terrified!"

"Pearse is neither of those things. He is dead. Just dead!"

"How can you argue with someone who believes in nothing?" Iseult said.

"I believe in here... now. I believe we must concern ourselves with what is real, what we can see and touch. We have a son to raise. Do you think I wanted this? I never wanted a kid. How can I write, how can I *think* with all this?"

Iseult looked coldly at Octave, still crying on his pallet. She sighed. She faced the window overlooking Laclede Avenue and the university quadrangle beyond.

"I know that Octave was born to replace my father on this earth," she said quietly. "I wonder if Octave had not been born, if my father would have lived longer..."

"That's crazy. Completely crazy."

"Perhaps Octave was born too soon," Iseult continued. "Miss Adelina has wondered about it, and I believe it is true. She said that Octave was born to replace my father and that because you came into my life... he was born too soon. He pushed Father into the darkness and shortened his life."

Hugo was speechless for a moment. "There's no sense in this."

"That is why my father abides in terror. He was not ready to go. That is why I must resolve this debt to the next world. I must help him find peace. Find comfort. Only I..."

"We are going to see a doctor." Hugo interrupted. "I still have friends in the medical school. I won't raise this boy alone."

Iseult walked to the hall tree near the front door. She removed her peach-colored hat from it and pinned it to her hair. Her purse was on the small table next to the hall tree.

"I will be home late. I have an appointment with Miss Adelina."

II

Phillipe Labardemont's life's work was finished. He knew few men could say that, and many might not recognize when it happened, but Labardemont knew it. The promise he'd made to his dying wife and their adopted daughter Virginia, who had died so mysteriously many years before, had been kept.

Cecile Labardemont loved the land she married into. Her father was a tanner whose livelihood vanished as the red wolves and beaver disappeared from the county. He gladly gave Phillipe permission to marry his daughter. Cecile's family owned no land other than a tiny plot on Constantinople Street in Ste. Odile where her father's shop had been. There was barely enough space for a family garden. Both her parents had hoped one day to buy a small farm, but her mother fell into a decade of hysteria and melancholy, and the cost of keeping her in a sanitorium in St. Louis claimed the small family savings.

The Labardemont family had originally been granted 3,100 acres by Zenon Trudeau, the Regional Commandant in August 1801, and unlike many French and Spanish families in the territory, their claim was honored by the new government of the United States in 1804 on condition that five hundred acres be leased in perpetuity to the county of Ste. Odile for use as a poor farm. The Labardemonts also acquired property in town to generate income, including the rambling Gothic brick and stone complex of the Academy of St. Perpetua, which in the 1890s had become an orphanage known as Phrygia House. Soon after the death of Phillipe and Cecile's daughter Virginia and the disgrace and suicide of the superintendent George Pettibone, the orphanage closed and had been an abandoned, deteriorating shell ever since.

These town affairs had only been Phillipe's concern. Cecile loved the land. She oversaw the management of the Labardemont acreage and returned it to moderate profitability within a few years of their marriage. Unlike many of the old families in the area, they did not have to sell off any of their property during drought or hard times.

Cecile insisted that five hundred acres of woodland be left intact and untouched, allowing another five hundred to be subject to sparing harvests of hardwood. She forbade the trapping of animals upon which her father's livelihood had depended, and made Phillipe promise that if he outlived her, he would maintain her preservationist philosophy and build on the land a testament to nature for all to see—some memorial to the beauty and mystery unnoticed by those only concerned with land as a resource, as a means of earning a living.

It was toward the end of Cecile's long illness that Virginia, their daughter, died. Phillipe didn't tell his wife the tragic news. For the few months they had been a real family, Cecile had found in Virginia an eager inheritor of her passion and commitment to the natural world, and someone to manage the land long into the future after she and Phillipe were gone. Phillipe feared learning of the child's death a few days before her own may have hastened his wife's passing even more.

For two years after Cecile's death, Phillipe considered what he might do to fulfill his promise to his wife. Eventually, it occurred to him to build a museum of their life together, and to the things she had collected and loved from the land itself. He would build a tower in the high pasture where all could see it—a tower of field stones and timber and limestone slabs that fell or could be pulled from his riverbank by his strength alone. He must do it all himself and it must be built only of naturally occurring resources from their land and filled with objects found there. It would be Cecile's museum of the natural world. It would make people notice what was all around them. Phillipe was sure that Cecile would tell him if she could that it was her greatest wish.

He sold off all the livestock and gave away his favorite colt, a roan stallion he named Vern. Then he went to work. With his crosscut saw, his wedges, and a sledge, he cut beams and planks from red oaks and lodgepole pines that had been growing on his hillsides for generations. He pegged the timbers together like the ribs of a ship and built a sturdy spiral staircase of polished, wide walnut planks. He mortared and set the stones over the next year, carefully shaping each one for a perfect and permanent fit. By the third anniversary of Cecile's death, the structure, a square, medieval-looking tower some forty feet high, was finished.

He immediately started to fill the tower with objects Cecile had collected over thirty years of wandering the acreage: snakeskins, skulls of foxes and coyotes, fungoid growths on tree trunks, dried wildflowers, fossil fishes and shells, a mastodon thighbone, and the fused skull of a two-headed calf. And at the very top of the tower, in a small vestibule that led out to the roof and observation platform, Phillipe built a shrine to his departed family. On an oak table in a dark corner, illuminated by candles, was displayed a small oil portrait of Cecile done by an itinerant artist twenty-five years before. And next to that was the death photograph of Virginia, her bulging, distended eyes closed and her balding pate, fringed by thin, brittle hair, resting on a satin pillow.

There was no neighboring farmer and few townspeople who did not know the purpose of the tower, and when Phillipe finally finished it, many of them came to see it and to climb the dark, polished stairs for the most expansive view of Ste. Odile County to be had, short of the promontory of the Jardin Noir estate north of the town.

The townspeople saw a great eccentricity in Phillipe's monument. Many of them looked at each other and whispered back and forth as they climbed, looking from one oddity to another, and ultimately to the shrine at the top. Phillipe could see it in their faces and hear it in snippets of their conversations: first, the death of Virginia, for which he must have felt ultimately responsible, then the death of his wife, were too much for the old man. He would fade away into insanity, as his father and uncle had done before him. Surely the isolation of the farm was not good for him. He had a nephew in St. Louis, Hugo, who had visited once, one of the DeGivervilles, who should be contacted.

He was a university professor, and Father Maeys, the parish priest at St. Perpetua's, had met him once. Perhaps Father should try to find Hugo and encourage him to visit his Uncle Phillipe and determine whether the old man's state of mind should be of concern.

III

A junk-hauler's horse collapsed in the heat on the streetcar tracks on Grand Avenue. The old animal, slathered in foam, gasped for breath for a few minutes, shuddered, then died. The street department brought in a draft horse to pull the carcass to the curb. Hugo could have walked home from there but decided to stay in the car and watch the small tragedy play out.

It was a short walk from the corner of Laclede Street to his apartment building. He had bought Mary Janes at the market, along with the bread and ham and fresh carrots Iseult had sent him for. He needed to get the candy upstairs to Octave before it softened too much in the heat. But there were to be strangers in his rooms tonight.

At Iseult's invitation, Miss Adelina would be conducting a séance on this, the fifth anniversary of Pearse's death. That night's company was also to include four of the medium's other devotees. The group had recently named itself The Golden Confraternity of Neferneferuaten and dedicated its members to establishing a conduit to the unseen world. Hugo wasn't anxious to join their company but wanted to occupy Octave in another room, away from the spiritualists. He really wanted to go to Paddy's Bar until the company left, but he was concerned about how Iseult's behavior and beliefs were affecting their son. And she would hear no criticism of her activities.

Hugo climbed the sweltering stairs to the third floor. His apartment door was ajar. He pushed it open. All the electric lights in the apartment were off. The dining room, between the living room and kitchen, was lit by a dozen or more candles. At the dining room table sat Miss Adelina, Iseult, and the four other members of the confraternity.

"Excuse me," Hugo said as he moved through the dining room into the kitchen. No one at the table noticed or acknowledged him. Miss Adelina sat at the head of the table, her eyes closed, swaying from left to right as if in a trance. Iseult stared intently at her, as did all the others assembled.

Hugo put the ham he had bought into the refrigerator. He placed the other items near the sink and put the Mary Janes in his pocket. As he reentered the dining room, he saw Octave standing in his bedroom doorway, watching the séance. The little boy held his nose against the incense Miss Adelina was burning.

"All clasp hands," Miss Adelina said as Hugo passed through into the living room. All those at the table complied. He walked across the living room and picked up his son.

"That smoke is stinky, Dad," Octave said.

"You're right about that, *lutin*. Let's go into your room so we don't smell it so much." He carried the boy back into his room. They sat on his small bed. "What do you make of all these goings on?"

Octave shrugged. "It's odd. They want to talk to ghosts. To Grandpa Pearse."

"Yes. A strange thing to want to do, don't you think?"

Octave shrugged again. "Maybe. They won't be able to do it."

"Oh? Why not?"

"He can't talk to them. He told me."

Hugo switched on a small lamp at the boy's bedside. "He *told you*?"

"Yes. Grandpa Pearse talks to me."

"I see. I think your mother talks to him, too."

"It's harder for her. She tries too much. I saw him above the table just now, like smoke from a candle, but he will only talk to me until she stops trying so much. It makes her sad that it doesn't work. I think I could help her."

Hugo nodded in agreement. Octave had had invisible friends before. "Well, maybe we can find a way to tell her that," he said. Miss Adelina's voice drifted in from the dining room, louder now.

"All must empty their thoughts. Think only of the mind of Pearse. We must try to think his thoughts."

Octave moved closer to his father.

"All remain silent," Miss Adelina continued. "Pearse... Russel Aubrey Pearse, hear me. Your daughter grieves for you, as you know. The company here assembled has such love for her we have joined together tonight to seek your mercy in relieving her suffering, the suffering of your despondent daughter, your dear Iseult. Will you not speak to her?" After a minute of silence, she continued. "Iseult believes you abide in terror in the afterlife. She wants to know you are at peace. Will you tell her you are at peace?"

"He won't talk to her," Octave whispered to his father.

Miss Adelina began to moan. "The boy," she wailed. "The boy prevents him. He says it's the boy!" There was a thud and cries of concern. Hugo stood and looked out the bedroom door.

Miss Adelina had collapsed on the floor and the congregants were crouching around her limp form, trying to revive her. After a few minutes, she sat up. "We must go," she mumbled. "We must all go now. Nothing more to be done here." The congregants helped her to her feet. When all were certain she was fully recovered, they gathered their things and filed out of the apartment.

Iseult returned to the chair she had occupied and sat. She sobbed into her hands for many minutes. Octave stood next to his father in the doorway. It took Hugo a moment to decide to comfort his wife. He had felt less inclined to respond to her in an affectionate or supportive way in the last year. He walked slowly toward her and put his hand on her shoulder. She looked up and saw Octave, small and frightened, in his doorway.

"It's him," she rasped. "It's *him*!"

IV

Phillipe scarcely visited his property in town anymore. It was rare for him lately to think beyond the loss of his wife and daughter and the land they shared together. The grounds of the old Academy of Perpetua, renamed Phrygia House when the New Phrygian spiritual community purchased it, were in ruin now. The lawn and old cemetery were overgrown and nearly impenetrable, and the avenue of cypresses was covered in weeds, moss, and rubble. Exposed roof timbers were visible on the chapel, gymnasium, and main dormitory. Saplings grew in the gutters and bats roosted in the attic, made accessible by the rot of centuries-old timbers.

Ronald Estes, the newly appointed city engineer for Ste. Odile, had been concerned about the condition and future of the Phrygia House property since he took his position. Two letters to Phillipe had gone unanswered. The third was hand-delivered by a county deputy, who awaited a response. Estes insisted that Phillipe join him at Phrygia House to either describe his plans for its future improvement and use or work out the logistics of demolishing it.

Phillipe drove himself into town the next morning. At nine a.m., Estes met him at the front gate of Phrygia House on Constantinople Street. Estes parked his weatherbeaten DeSoto across the entry drive and emerged from the car carrying a clipboard. "It's good to finally meet you, Mr. Labardemont," he said, extending his hand. Phillipe looked at him grimly and shook his hand. "I am sorry you had to come all the way into town, but we need to keep track of derelict properties," Estes continued. "You are current on your taxes, but the property is in a sorry state."

"Yes," Phillipe agreed, "This place had a special meaning to my wife. My dead wife. I can't imagine what use I would ever put it to. It could be salvaged. It *could* be."

"I wanted to walk through it with you and assess its condition and see if that helps you decide one way or another."

The two men began walking toward the old buildings. Phillipe handed Estes the heavy iron key to the convent door. The avenue of cypresses was overgrown, but to the left of the avenue could still be seen the old headstones of nuns who had operated the original girls' academy from its inception until its closure nearly forty years before. The cornices and rosettes of the old building were crumbling in many places, and ivy had overtaken the south wall of the chapel, nearly obscuring what Phillipe remembered to be a beautiful stained glass window. The old stone statue of St. Perpetua in the center courtyard had lost a hand, and a lion at her feet retained only the stump of a tail.

A slight vibration could be felt under the paving stones. Estes was startled. "What was that?" he said.

"Tremor," said Phillipe. "Terrible earthquake back in about 1811. Changed the course of the river. Still feel a tremor now and then. A miracle, I am told, that these old buildings survived."

A shadow of movement at a rear corner of the building caught the two men's attention. The old Reliquary Chapel, built into a hillside at the rear of the property nearly two hundred feet away, was partially obscured by a wide mulberry bush. Sitting half-hidden behind this was a large, wild-looking dog. The animal was gray and black with matted, splotched fur, almost appearing to have mange, except that no part of its body was totally without some fur. The dog's eyes were yellow cabochons, almost glowing in the morning sun in the black sockets surrounding them.

"That's an ugly old fellow," Estes said as he moved to the front door of the old convent area and endeavored to unlock it. Phillipe glanced back toward the dog and thought he saw the creature stretch its body upward like wafting smoke. Then, though the dog remained sitting, it leaned its body to the right, obscuring its upper half behind the foliage. For an instant, it seemed to Phillipe that the beast's head was visible at the opposite side of the bush, at least five feet away. After a moment, the impression passed, and the dog trotted away up the wooded hillside.

Estes pushed the massive door open, and the two men stepped inside. A moldering vestibule lay just inside the door, connected to a wainscoted waiting room. The wallpaper above the wainscotting was peeling away from the wall in most places, revealing damp, crumbling plaster and lath underneath. A large, old fish tank still partly filled with murky water sat against an opposite wall. "Must be a leak somewhere for there to still be water in that," Estes said.

"It's been so long since I was here..." Phillipe mumbled. Stepping into the hallway from the waiting room, the two men turned to the left toward a large open gathering room. "This looks in better shape," Phillipe said.

The floors were sound and intact, and a slight water stain near the ceiling looked like a plumbing problem, not a roof leak. The wallpaper in the large gathering room was generally tight with the only staining visible being under one of the many broken windows.

Estes made some notes on his clipboard. "It's salvageable," he said. "Upstairs will tell the tale."

Phillipe studied the walls, ceiling, and what was visible of the kitchen from his vantage point. "So much happened here," he said. "So many girls passed through. Our little Virginia died here. Healthy as a mastiff when I put her in. I was caring for my dying wife. Before long they claimed she had signs of thyroid disease. I couldn't get back from St. Louis. Poor little Virginia died. Scarcely knew ten months of happiness in her life. We got her off the Orphan Train—not to work, but to be our real daughter. I put her here temporarily when Cecile got deathly ill, and she died. Our new little daughter died. So many bad memories here, bad thoughts about what happened. Nothing can be gained by saving this old ruin. Who would want something like this? I see no reason... Mr. Estes, no reason at all not to pull it down."

"Very good," Estes nodded. Both men were startled by a piercing yowl behind them. They turned to see the large gray dog at one of the broken windows. The beast stared at Phillipe for a moment, then was gone.

V

Iseult sat at the large window overlooking Laclede Street. Hugo returned from their bedroom with a handkerchief and handed it to his wife. He sat on a dining chair near her. "I don't know why I can't put it out of my mind," she said. "I know it isn't right. It's an awful thing to admit. I just... can't find any love in me for my own son."

Hugo had long suspected her coldness toward their child but had never heard her say it. He moved his hand to place on her shoulder to comfort her, but he could not make himself do it. "I have heard mothers sometimes go through a melancholy period after the birth of a child," he said. "They say in some cases it can last years."

"I have never felt any affection for him. I can't feel anything but anger. Half the time I am ashamed of myself. The rest of the time I feel justified. I never wanted children. All I wanted was the life I had with Father."

"Now wait..."

"The boy has displaced him! I know father was taken to the darkness to make room for the boy!"

"That is such nonsense. 'Make room for him?'"

"Yes! I've learned; Miss Adelina revealed that we are only allowed a select few, only a few souls to commune with in the next world. Father was pushed out by the boy."

Hugo looked at her for a long while. They'd had this argument four or five times in the last month. He could see resentment and sometimes even hatred in her face when she looked at Octave. This evening when he'd come home, he heard her screaming at the boy as he came up the stairs. He stepped into the apartment just as she broke the handle of her broom to hit him with it. At the last second, she noticed the sharp end of the broken shaft and turned that end toward her son. Hugo grabbed her and she went into hysterics, finally collapsing into tears on the floor.

"I barely got to you in time this evening," he said. "What would you have done? Killed him?"

"Something comes over me." She sobbed into the handkerchief. "Sometimes I see him as my worst enemy on earth. I never know when it's going to happen."

"He is a little boy. He is terrified of you. He needs his mother. I can't be... What a pair of parents he has!"

"I don't know if I can ever be what he needs. He is the agent, the demon, keeping the one dearest to me out in the darkness. Miss Adelina told me he will always be in the way." She stood, walked into their bedroom, and closed the door. In a second, Hugo heard her turn the latch.

Octave had fallen asleep shortly after his mother attacked him. Hugo sat at the table, looking down at Laclede Street until full darkness covered the city, except for insufficient pools of illumination under scattered streetlights.

He resented his wife enormously at that moment and dreaded what he felt he had to do. There was nobody else in the world to do it. In the dark, he finally stood and found his large haversack in the living room closet. He went into Octave's room and packed a few clothes into it, along with some books, and money he had been saving for his son. The boy stirred under his blanket. "Dad, what are you doing?" he said.

"Get up now boy," Hugo answered. "We have to go."

VI

Phillipe was wealthy by the standards of Ste. Odile; still, he hated ostentation. The house he had shared with Cecile and Virginia was a simple brick farmhouse of two stories. The yard was small and unkempt, and he had long ago given up his pigs and cattle, his favorite horse, and most of his chickens. Everything was returning to the state Cecile loved, back to untouched nature. On a hill a quarter mile away, in what had once been a pasture, the stone tower monument Phillipe had built for his wife could be seen.

Curious neighbors had stopped visiting the tower. After a few months, it was no longer a curiosity. It seemed that the community had forgotten about the grieving, eccentric old man.

Phillipe visited the monument several times a week and climbed to the shrine at the top to pay his respects. Otherwise, he filled his days with tending his kitchen garden, walking his land, and reading, rarely and only under the greatest necessity driving into town.

Two days after the meeting with Estes, as he sat on his porch having coffee he had re-heated from the day before, Phillipe heard a yipping coming from the north. On the hilltop, pacing around the base of the tower, he saw a large coyote or red wolf in silhouette against the empty sky. Phillipe stepped into his front room and found his 12-gauge shotgun leaning against the north wall. He quickly grabbed the gun and took it outside into the yard. He fired it once into the air. The animal stopped its movements and looked toward Phillipe. In a moment it vanished below the far side of the hill.

Phillipe walked to the rear of the house and saw that all his chickens were accounted for. He watched the ridgeline for another half hour but saw no further sign of the animal. Coyotes were common in the area, though this animal was exceptionally large. If red wolves hadn't become so rare, he would have assumed that was what he had seen.

Phillipe slept lightly that night. He expected commotion from the chicken coop but heard nothing until dawn. He had hoped for rain that evening but none came. His almanac predicted that 1936 would be a very dry year, and that forecast was proving to be true.

The next morning, he fed the chickens and sprayed the small garden with the hose. As usual, he wasn't hungry for breakfast. He made coffee and sipped it on his front porch, looking out toward the dusty road. For more than an hour the road was empty.

After another twenty minutes or so he was starting to feel the heat. As he stood to go into the house, Lem Amoreaux's flatbed truck turned into Phillipe's dirt drive. Lem pulled up a few feet from the porch and waved to Phillipe. "Another hot one," he said. "A little rain wouldn't kill us."

Phillipe nodded. Lem's thirteen-year-old son Eminence jumped out of the passenger side of the truck. The boy was a messenger for Western Union in town. "Dad takin' me into work," Eminence said. "Sorry, but this come day before yesterday. I been sick with the chicken pops, so..." He handed Phillipe a folded telegram and ran back to the truck.

"Have you fellas seen a big coyote around?" Phillipe said. "Big one. Looks like a dog I seen in town the other day, but must be a wolf or coyote out this far."

"Nope, I ain't seen it," Lem said. He looked over at Eminence who shook his head no. Lem waved again and backed out onto the drive.

Phillipe unfolded the message. It was from his niece-in-law Iseult, whom he had only met once.

Hugo and Octave disappeared. Probably coming your way. Stop.

Phillipe went back into the house. He sat at the table and read the telegram again. He hadn't thought abought his nephew Hugo since he remade his will. He had never seen the boy, Octave.

In the early afternoon, Phillipe felt himself nodding off. He thought about Cecile. The telegram from Iseult made him suspect there was discord in the young couple's marriage. Phillipe had never had that with his wife. He decided to walk up to her tower and pay his respects to her shrine at the top.

The grass in the yard was long dead and brown, but the milkweed, lamb's quarter, and other weeds in the fields were thriving. Grasshoppers hopped and flew in every direction as the old man waded through the dry growth. A garter snake lay across a small bare spot before some blackberry bushes, but it vanished as Phillipe approached. Climbing the hilltop to the tower had grown noticeably more difficult for him in recent months. At the top of the hill, he rested a moment before taking the stairs inside.

He progressed slowly up the stairs inside the dark structure. Only the occasional windows he had built in the walls illuminated the collections of oddities and natural objects that decorated the passageway. At the top of the tower, he walked out into the vestibule that contained the likenesses of his dead wife and daughter. He lit a candle there and whispered a short prayer. When he had finished, he stepped away toward the wall to look out across his unspoiled property.

"You would want me to move on, Cecile," he whispered. "This is the monument I have built in the memory of my family, to you and Virginia. That old ruin in town is a monument to suffering and tragedy. I will tear it down, wipe the memory of it away, and allow the town to forget it was ever there. Tear it down!"

An insidious growling behind him startled Phillipe. He turned quickly to see the hideous dog he had seen at Phrygia House snarling at him and blocking the stairway. The beast appeared as if it were in a haze or fog, seeming both substantial and insubstantial at the same time. For a moment Phillipe doubted he was really seeing it.

"No," he mumbled. "How did you get up here without..." The animal stepped slowly toward the old man, frozen against the shallow wall. "It's the building, isn't it?" Phillipe whispered. "It's that building..."

The mottled beast lunged at Phillipe, who instinctively flinched backward. The old man felt himself roll against the top of the tower wall an instant before he fell over the side.

VII

"Dad, are we running away from Momma?" Octave was too exhausted to walk anymore. Hugo picked the boy up. He was tired too. He wasn't sure how long he could carry his son and the haversack on his back. He was really in no hurry. He would rest as often as he needed to now that he was away from the apartment and Iseult didn't know where they had gone.

Hugo looked at his pocket watch under the streetlight: 4:20 a.m. "Momma is not well," he said. "Something is wrong in her mind, and she isn't herself."

"Shouldn't we stay home and take care of her?" Octave rested his head on his father's shoulder. "We should stay if we can help her. I should stay! If she is afraid and I can help her, then I am supposed to do that. It's the right thing for me to do."

"Being with us makes her worse. Being with us makes it harder for her to get better. I told a doctor at the university about her. I think he is going to help her. I hope so. She needs to learn that she shouldn't be angry at us."

"But why is she angry at us?"

"It's a hard thing to explain. She is still sad because your grandpa is dead."

"But that's not our fault."

"No, it's not. She will understand that someday."

"Then we will go home?"

"I hope so, but we'll see."

Grand Avenue was completely empty. Hugo walked north on the intermittently shattered sidewalk, from one dim pool of light to the next, seeing no signs of life other than occasional rats rummaging through garbage in the alleys as they passed, or scarce police cars crossing intersections many blocks away. He would keep walking north to Choteau Avenue then east toward the river. There were trainyards there. He hoped to jump a boxcar heading south.

Octave felt completely limp on his back and Hugo could tell his son had fallen asleep. At Choteau, he turned east. The long, straight avenue was deserted and offered an unimpeded view to the trainyards and the warehouses on the riverfront. Hugo's feet were starting to hurt, and keeping his objective in view, it seemed impossibly distant. He thought if he had only stayed in Paris, he might have broken through by now, and there would be no family drama to distract him.

As he approached Broadway, Hugo could see a freight train on the western edge of the trainyard would be southbound. Several boxcar doors stood open, and in the dim light, he could see figures, hobos, climbing into the open doors. Hugo stopped. "This is not for you, my boy" he mumbled to his sleeping son. He remembered if he turned south on Broadway, it eventually turned into a county road or even a highway, Highway 61, he thought, where they could hitch a ride.

After another hour of walking, the buildings behind him were towering hulks of gray in the dawn, and those in front of him, smaller, more dilapidated, and trash-strewn as he neared the city's edge. Empty lots covered in weeds and grass were more common, and small brick and clapboard houses were intermingled with markets, gas stations, and pawn shops.

Hugo needed to rest. Octave was stirring, and he was sure the boy must be hungry. On a streetcorner to the right, he noticed a neighborhood market with a sign above the door: *Lupke's Groceries and Sundries*. Hugo crossed the street. He slid Octave off his back and sat on the sidewalk on the north side of the building. He leaned his drowsy son against his arm. He just needed to rest a moment.

Hugo wondered if Iseult had awakened yet. He didn't leave a note. He wanted to give her no idea of what his intentions were, and no clue about where she could find them. She might be glad they were gone. Maybe Dr. Winternitz, a long-time friend of Pearce at the university, could help her and the family could one day reunite. Hugo doubted this and wasn't sure he wanted it. He knew he could not take a chance with his son's safety or emotional development, even though he often had the urge to put his own needs first. He thought of Iseult's last words to him: *He will always be in the way.* This was an unmistakable threat.

Hugo heard the front door of the little store open. Then he heard sweeping, first inside the shop, then moving out onto the sidewalk. He saw an old man in an apron, barely five feet tall, broom in hand, apparently preparing for his business day.

The old man glanced in Hugo's direction and looked startled. "I don't let no bums zleep on my zidewalk!" he spoke with an accent Hugo decided must be German.

"I'm not a hobo..." Hugo said as he stood.

"What you doing wid a kid out here? Dis ain't no life for a kid! You got to move on, or I call the cops!"

"Sorry. We're not hoboes. I just need to get my boy south. I have family."

"Well...no loiterink here..."

"Just resting, that's all. I've been walking since four. My boy will be safer down south."

The man whom Hugo assumed was Lupke shrugged. "I don't ask no question if it not my buzinezz. Zo many bums now."

"I have some money," Hugo said. "We need to eat."

Lupke studied him, then said, "Come in, den." He turned and walked into his store as Hugo helped the groggy Octave to his feet.

Lupke stepped behind a wide, old-fashioned counter that held glass cases of muffins and biscuits and other bread, fresh fish and meat, and small prepared meals. There was a white grocer scale and jars of hard candy and bubble gum surrounding a brass cash register. A small, round table and two chairs sat in front of the shop's only window. Rows of shelves carrying canned goods, hardware, clothes, and shoes lined the walls.

"Zit," Lupke said, and Hugo helped Octave into one chair before he sat in the other.

"Where is this?" Octave said.

"Does he like Veaties, I mean *Wheaties?* Do you like Wheaties, zon?" Lupke asked.

Octave shrugged.

"How about Farina? Zometing hot?"

Octave nodded yes.

"I got egg zamwich for you we make, unless you want zweets?" Lupke said to Hugo.

"Sandwich sounds good," Hugo said.

Lupke stepped into a back room and in a moment reemerged with a large white mug of coffee that he placed on the table. Hugo smiled at him gratefully. Lupke returned to the kitchen and reappeared with a tray containing a plate with a sandwich and slab of ham on it, a bowl, and a glass of milk. He placed these on the table. The rattling of pots and pans could be heard in the back room.

Octave looked at Lupke solemnly. "Your wife can talk to spirits," he said.

"Son, be still," Hugo said.

After a moment Lupke spoke. "How do you know that? We keep it a zecret. People here don't trust immigrants, you know."

"Her brother Helmet died," Octave said.

"*Helmut*," Lupke corrected.

"She's still sad." Octave continued.

"His mother is about spiritualism. He says he sees things," Hugo said.

"He iz right!"

"It's... why we are leaving the city," Hugo said.

Lupke nodded in understanding. "It vill follow him everywhere," he said. "No ezcaping."

"He just needs to be in a safe place for a while. I think I did the right thing. I hope..."

"Yes, it iz good you left." An old woman no taller than Lupke stood in the kitchen doorway. "I tink dere was a danger in your home."

"Analize," Lupke said, "I tought you might want to meet diz boy."

Analise approached the table with a slight smile. She extended her hand to Octave. He shyly took it, not seeming to know what to make of the gesture. "Very pleased to meet you, young fellow," she said. "You zee tings you don't wanna zee and know tings you don't wanna know."

"I do," Octave agreed.

"Zo do I," the old woman said. "Do you fear doze tings?"

"Sometimes. I think they might hurt me."

"No one can zay. Try not to fear. Fear can make you weak. De dark zpirits don't want you to know deir intent. Fear ztrengthenz dem."

"I know your intentions are good," Hugo interrupted. "And I thank you for your generosity, but I don't want to encourage him in these supernatural things..."

"Zure, zure," Lupke said. "You don't owe me nothing here. I give the boy zome hard candy if you don't mind."

"Thank you. You've been very generous."

"Zo you going zout? Where?"

"Ste. Odile. I have an uncle there."

Lupke and Analise looked at each other.

"Ve ztarted out deir when ve come to dis country," Lupke said. "My cousin helped us. Lots of Germanz deir now."

"It'z a place of zhades and darknezz," Analise said. "Not a place I would take a child like him."

"We have no place else to go," Hugo said.

Lupke put his hand on Hugo's shoulder as he rose. "It izn't our business, Analize," he said. "Keep going zout from here. Zoon you will find the *fahrbahn*... the highway. Number 61."

You can hitchhike a ride."

"Trust in God," Analise said. "Do not fear."

VIII

It was late afternoon by the time Hugo and Octave reached the two-lane highway. Just off the shoulder on the right side, a deserted produce stand stood in the shadow of a partially destroyed Indian burial mound, the pinnacle of which was catching the last orange glow of the setting sun. "I can't go any more today," Hugo said. "We'll spend the night here."

Octave released his father's hand and looked at the shack, the mound, and the weeds. "But this is *outside*. We have to sleep outside?"

"Maybe just one night. I hope just one night. If we get lucky tomorrow, we might get a ride the whole way. It's sixty or seventy miles. There's a little roof here and it looks like it could rain." Hugo removed a quilt from his haversack and spread it out on the ground underneath the roof of the produce stand.

As night fell, Hugo built a small campfire well off the shoulder of the road. Tree frogs began to burr, whippoorwills called, and Cygnus spun coldly overhead. The black monolith of the Indian mound blocked out much of the horizon.

Octave sat near the fire throwing twigs into it. "There are bugs here," he said.

"I know. I can't do anything about it. They are biting me too. Hope we won't have to do this for more than one night. We might get to Uncle Phillipe's tomorrow. You know, this area used to be covered in these mounds. They tore them all down one by one to build the city."

"It's a sad thing," Octave said, "but the people in them are all still now. They have been still for a long, long time. Now there is nothing in there but bones."

It didn't rain overnight, but the morning was damp and humid. A steady stream of southbound traffic had awakened Hugo.

"Wake up, son," he said. "I think we can catch a ride." In a moment he had repacked the haversack and they were standing at the side of the road, thumbs out.

A pickup truck and roadster sped past them, causing Hugo to step back from the road by a few inches. Headlights positioned high above the level of the pavement appeared in the mist, approaching at a much slower rate. A large, odd-looking truck appeared. It looked to be a truck cab with a second cab stacked on top of it. The vehicle pulled onto the shoulder and stopped. The long trailer it was hauling was loaded with bound bundles of rebar. The passenger door was pushed open.

"You boys are out early," a gravelly voice said. "Climb up."

Hugo lifted Octave to the level of the seat and climbed up after. "Thanks for stopping," he said.

"You don't see too many hitchhikers with kids," The driver said. "I'm Angelo."

"Hugo, and this is Octave. What kind of truck is this?"

"I never seen one like this," Octave said, seating himself on his father's lap.

"It's a Dearborn Cabover. Brand new," Angelo said. "Drivers love them."

"So high up!" Octave said.

"They don't like us to pick up hitchhikers," Angelo said, "but I can't leave a kid on the road like that! I'm way ahead of schedule anyway. Where you goin'?"

"Ste. Odile," Hugo said.

"This load is headed to Belgique, so I can drop you. Mind if we get some breakfast?"

Forty-five minutes later, Angelo pulled into Fat Sammy's Café just north of a town called Festus. The restaurant was busy, but Angelo found them a table in a far corner.

Hugo and Octave ate little, but Angelo had an enormous breakfast. As Hugo sipped from his cup of coffee, he noticed a woman alone at a table across the room glancing at him repeatedly. Hugo thought the woman looked familiar and suddenly wondered if she could have been an attendee at Iseult's séance.

Hugo didn't look at the woman anymore. After his third refill of coffee, Angelo was ready to continue the trip. Hugo paid the bill, and the three of them climbed back into the truck.

IX

At the juncture of the highway and Lesterton Road, Angelo pulled to the shoulder and let Octave and Hugo out. Hugo thanked him and Angelo wished them good luck and thanked Hugo for his breakfast. As he pulled away, Hugo looked to the west and thought he recognized the modest Labardemont house in the distance. "We only have to go that much farther," Hugo said, pointing at the house. Octave reached up and took his father's hand.

The road was dirt, gravel, and exposed limestone strata. Dust covered the milkweeds and scrub cedars along the roadside. There were vultures and crows in the sky. It was early afternoon, so the day was not as hot as it would be in another couple of hours. "That looks like a castle," Octave said as they passed Phillipe's stone tower.

"It does," Hugo agreed. "My old uncle was an odd bird."

Octave struggled to keep up with his father as they walked toward the house. Hugo slowed his pace and finally stopped and picked up his son and carried him the rest of the way.

Phillipe's old Ford was parked at the south end of the house. On the front porch, Hugo knocked on the door. "Uncle Phillipe, it's Hugo." After a minute or more, there was no answer. Hugo pushed the door open. "Uncle Phillipe!"

The house was not in too disordered a state considering an old man lived there alone. Hugo had heard of the deaths of his Aunt Cecile and their adopted daughter Virginia. He expected Uncle Phillipe to be living in grief-driven squalor and chaos. "He must be around somewhere," Hugo said. "His car is out back."

Octave collapsed into a living room chair. Hugo looked around the house for a clue to the whereabouts of his uncle. On the kitchen table, he found Iseult's telegram.

Hugo and Octave disappeared. Probably coming your way. Stop.

"She'll come looking for us here," Hugo mumbled. He walked back into the living room. "You rest here a bit, son," he said. "I am going to walk up to the tower to see if Uncle Phillipe is there." Octave shook his head yes and settled into his chair, closing his eyes.

Hugo dropped his haversack on the floor and hurried outside. The tower stood silently on its hill. A few birds were visible at the top roosting or squabbling, it seemed, over a morsel of food. Hugo would tell Phillipe to expect Iseult and perhaps some of her companions to appear at his door very soon. Hugo and Octave would have to slip into town unseen and find a place to wait things out for a few days. He knew Phillipe owned the old girls' academy now known as Phrygia House.

Hugo found the climb up the hill upon which the tower sat to be exceptionally strenuous. He was tired and overheated, though it looked now as if rain and hopefully a cooldown could happen at any moment.

Hugo reached the top of the hill and rounded the tower looking for the doorway. He was startled by Phillipe's body, swollen now against the tower wall, eyes missing, broken neck allowing his head to lie flat against his right shoulder, his corpse covered in blackbirds and crows. The body was starting to stink, and Hugo could not make himself touch it. The birds scattered.

"Oh my God," he said.

Hugo was certain he should not touch the body. The sheriff needed to be notified. Hugo decided he would try to find a way to do it anonymously. It was important for no one in town to know he and his son were there.

X

Hugo decided they would spend the night in the house. In the morning, he made Octave take a bath; he took one also. He washed their clothes by hand in the sink. When the clothes had dried in the sunshine, or nearly, he filled a gunny sack with as much relatively non-perishable food as he could carry. On the back of a scrap of paper containing a grocery list, Hugo wrote a note with a pencil he found: *Phillipe Labardemont dead from fall at his farm.* He pushed the paper into his pocket. Hugo found his Uncle's car keys on a shelf. There was a pack of Luckies next to the keys. Hugo had quit smoking a year ago, but he took the pack of cigarettes. He tried to start the Ford, but it would not turn over.

Hugo then took his son's hand, and they walked up to the road and began to make their way toward Ste. Odile.

The road into town ran mostly through woods. Anytime Hugo heard a car or truck approaching, he pulled Octave into the bushes or behind trees to avoid being seen.

In the early afternoon, the dirt road became gravel and Hugo knew they were getting near to Ste. Odile. At the edge of a rocky glade, Hugo and Octave sat on a granite boulder out of sight from the road. From this vantage point, the town and the Great River were visible and to the south.

"Why are we stopping here?" Octave asked.

"We will wait until tonight to go further," Hugo said. "No one must know we are here. Eat something. We will rest for a few hours."

Later in the night as the moon rose, Hugo awakened his son and they returned to the gravel road. Quickly the gravel was replaced by cobblestones and the road became Rouen Street. At the corner of Constantinople Street, they turned north. They stopped at the corner of Constantinople and Endymion, at the great stone and brick and iron gate of Phrygia House. "I want you to wait here for me for just a short while," Hugo said.

"Wait? By myself?" Octave replied incredulously.

"Just for a few minutes. I will be right back. Sit on this stone in the shadow. No one will see you here."

The boy sat as he was told. Hugo continued north to the end of the block where Bucephalus Street intersected. The city jail and police station were there. A dim light in a front window illuminated a deputy, feet on his desk, reading a newspaper. Hugo watched the deputy for a full minute until he decided that the man was actually asleep. Hugo took the folded note he had written at the farm and slipped it under the office's front door. He hurried back to Octave's hiding place.

"Anyone see you?" he asked the boy.

"No. Just a big dog."

"All right. Let's see if we can find a way into this old building. We will hide out in here for a few days and decide what to do." A heavy rain began to fall as Hugo led his son through the dark avenue of cypresses toward the gaunt and imposing buildings. Hugo was surprised to find the heavy front door of the convent open. He slipped inside first then helped Octave step over some rubble into the vestibule.

Octave looked frightened. "This isn't a good place," he said. "Bad things have happened here."

"It's all right, son. No one will know we are here, and I can decide what we will do next. For now, it's shelter. Let's find a room to sleep in." The rain was falling more heavily now, and thunder clapped in the distance. "Let's hope the roof is in good repair."

Stepping through the vestibule door, they found themselves in what appeared to be a large sitting room. The walls of the dark room were starting to show the effects of dampness. Much of the wallpaper was peeling, and spots on the dark wainscotting that were illuminated by the weak streetlights outside showed scattered mildew. An old bronze and glass fish tank sat against the north wall, nearly full of murky water. "Odd there would still be water in that," Hugo noted. "After all this time. I hope it's not from a leak."

Octave clutched his father's hand tightly. Hugo noticed that his son watched the tank closely as they walked past it out into the hallway. "We'll go to the second floor," Hugo said. "Must be the bedrooms up here. Downstairs are common rooms, I would guess." A great stairwell ascended into the cobwebbed darkness past a landing with a stained glass window that must have been eighteen feet high, rising above a window seat.

At the top of the stairs, the corridor of bedrooms extended to the right as another flight of steps disappeared into the darkness of the third floor. The first bedroom on the right was drenched as rain from a broken window splattered in. The room across the hallway overlooked Constantinople Street. It was dry and secure. Hugo found a candle on a small washstand and lit it with one of the dry matches he kept in his vest pocket. The room was scattered with cobwebs and dust but was still somehow inviting. The bed against a wall was unmade but looked clean. "This will do, don't you think?" Hugo said.

Octave nodded in agreement. There were a few papers and books on the floor, partially under the bed. Octave picked one up that appeared to be a child's primer. Primly dressed children played on the front cover, accompanied by a shaggy dog.

Hugo closed the shutters in the window to hide the candlelight. He then sat in a corner chair to sort through his haversack for their dinner. A sudden shriek from Octave startled him. The boy, trembling in fear, held open the picture book on his lap. The pages were blank but for two words scrawled in pencil across them.
YOU'RE HERE.

XI

"To my mind, there is no doubt about it." Miss Adelina wiped the sweat from her forehead and cheeks. It was obvious to Iseult that the session had been very difficult for the medium and had drained her strength. "They remain in the South. South of here, as I saw yesterday." Miss Adelina continued, "The Great River is nearby. They have not moved yet, if my sense of it is right."

"Ste. Odile," Iseult said. "I *knew* it! Your sense is right. Hugo has some family there. An old uncle. That's where I need you to take me, Marigold."

Marigold, an old woman of eighty or more, toothless with thin white hair, was one of Miss Adelina's few followers. She smiled as she finished the biscuit and honey Iseult had offered her. "Ye know," she said, showing the food she was gumming in her mouth, "I wondered if ye needed a favor Iseult, ye rascal! I wondered why ye just invited me and not the whole group!"

"This is vital," Iseult snapped. "You have a car. I need to get to Ste. Odile. We have become close thanks to Miss Adelina."

"Close? That's the first I heerd of it!" the old woman cackled. "My old Durant ain't much of a car. Might not make it all the way down there."

"We will take the chance. More than likely it will be fine," Iseult said. "I don't have the carfare to take a bus or the train. I need the help of a true friend. I will pay you back for expenses... over time."

A serious look came over Marigold's face. "I had a bad feeling about this since the séance," she said. "Yer boy is innocent and blameless. Sadness has overtaken ye and killed yer sense of right and yer love fer 'im. I think ye mean to harm 'im."

"No!" Iseult protested.

"Ye don't know it yerself. Ye won't be able to hep' it."

"You see him as just innocent," Iseult said. "Something is at work in him, controlling him. Something that makes him do evil... or... at least block good."

"No!" Miss Adelina said. "His spirit has replaced your father's, but the boy is as helpless in it all as Pearse is."

"I've seen him looking at me," Iseult went on, "I've seen the look of triumph in his eyes!"

"I am not gonna hep' ye in this!" Marigold insisted. The old woman had left her purse with her car keys inside on a small table near the front door. Iseult moved quickly to the table and began rummaging through the purse. She withdrew the keys as Marigold attempted to grab them from her.

"No!" the old woman screamed. Iseult grasped Marigold's bony shoulders and smashed her body against the doorframe. Marigold's head hit the frame so hard, blood spurted onto the wall nearby. She fell senseless to the floor.

"Oh my God!" Iseult gasped. "Oh God, I didn't mean it!"

Miss Adelina checked the old woman's pulse. "She's in a very bad way," she said. "We have to get her to the University Hospital."

"She stood in the way... of something I needed to do!" Iseult cried. "I didn't mean it! I don't have time for this..."

Miss Adelina stood. She looked at Iseult. "She could die," she said.

"What are you going to do?" Iseult asked.

"You are a dear friend," Miss Adelina said at length. "You have become obsessed. You have been living in hell. This could kill you.

Actually kill you. I can't seal your fate. I can't. I must go with you, though. I cannot send you off on your own, knowing you as I do."

"Thank you," Iseult sobbed. "How awful this is. How awful it has become. I need to get her onto a bed. I will call the police, then we must go. Hurry! Hurry!"

XII

It took Hugo half an hour or more to calm his son down. "It's nothing," he said. "A coincidence. Has nothing to do with you."

"It does!" There were tears in Octave's eyes. "It was meant for me and me alone. Some of the gray people are bad. Bad!"

Hugo hugged the boy. He knew that the thunder, lightning, and violent rain were making Octave's state of mind worse. "This old place wasn't a good choice after all," he said. "I just didn't know where else to go."

Through the tumult of noises outside, Hugo thought he could hear the howling of a dog. He looked at his son. "I heard it too," Octave said.

"Poor old mutt," Hugo said. "To be out on a night like this." The sound was repeated. "Almost sounds like he is in the building..." Hugo stood and opened the chamber door. Octave followed him. They looked toward the north hallway. Another corridor intersected theirs about seventy feet away. Light from a streetlamp flooded in from an unseen window around the corner against the opposite wall of the intersecting hallway. The shadow of a large dog could be seen silhouetted against the wall. The creature's steps could be heard on the dusty floor. The shadow reached the corner, trotting at a brisk pace, but at the corner of the corridor, nothing emerged. Animal nails clicking on wooden floorboards could still be heard, but nothing except darkness and the gloom of the extended hallway were visible.

"Where did it go?" Octave insisted. "We seen it. *Where did it go?*"

Hugo gently pushed his son back into the chamber and closed the door. "Our eyes are tricking us," he said. "We are tired. We need to rest." He sat Octave on the edge of the bed and removed the boy's shoes. "You sleep on the inside, against the wall, and I will be on the outside, okay?"

Octave nodded. He crawled across the bed to the wall and lay down. "If this building dies," he said vaguely, as if speaking to no one, "everything in it, everything left here, dies too."

"Let's try to sleep," Hugo said.

Octave settled in. Under a sheet Hugo had found in a dresser, he became drowsy and began to relax. "Dad," he said after many minutes. "I am the reason Momma is sick."

"No, son. You mustn't think that. Everything will be fine someday."

"I can see Grandpa Pearse in a dark place like Momma says. He is afraid and suffering."

"Put that out of your mind. Your mother or her friends have put that idea in your head." Hugo pushed off his brogans and lay down.

"It scares me too, the dark place."

"Son, I don't want you to talk about it or think about it anymore."

"I don't want to, but I can't help it. Being in this place makes it worser."

"Well, I agree. As soon as the weather clears, we will find a new place."

"Dad... I'm not sure, but I don't think we *can* find a new place."

"Don't be silly. Lots of places we can go, so long as we aren't seen."

"Something put this place in my dreams."

"What?"

"I don't know if it was a person or spirits or God, but I had dreams about a place like this. It's afraid here, whatever it was. It wants help and protection. It might be a person. It might be a little kid."

"From what, son? What are you talking about?"

"It was crying. Crying because it was afraid of a dark thing. A dark thing in this place. I am the one who heard, but I don't know what to do."

"It's a coincidence. It's all in your imagination. I am sure I mentioned this place to your mother or somebody. It's nothing."

"All I can do is *be here*. That way whatever it is that found me... is not alone. It's like leaving Momma. Something tells me when I dream that if I can help stop the sadness and the fear, that I *should* help."

"Go to sleep."

The old building creaked and rattled in the storm for hours. Hugo slept intermittently but was grateful that Octave went to sleep quickly. Out of the sound of the wind lashing the trees and branches hitting the windowpanes, another sound slowly asserted itself. The sound seemed to grow out of the crashing of branches against the brick and stone of the old convent, but as time went on it became less abrupt and more *organic.*

"The storm is so noisy!" Octave was awake now.

"I'm sure it will settle down soon."

"What is that sound it's making? It sounds like a sound I have heard before."

"It's nothing, just the wind." Hugo laid his hand on his son's shoulder and coaxed him to lie down again. As he did, he noticed that the sound had changed—that it had become rhythmical, like a heartbeat.

Hugo lay back down. He knew he must not show any signs of concern to Octave.

In a moment, he heard what sounded like breaking glass and rushing water coming from downstairs. It seemed as if it were coming from the front entry room.

Octave had fallen asleep again. Hugo arose carefully and quietly slipped out their chamber door. He made his way to the staircase and down to the first floor. Water was spreading from under the vestibule door. A plant stand holding an empty pot had fallen over. Hugo pushed a tattered old rug against the door, blocking the passage of water under it. As he returned to the stairs, he thought he saw a flicker of light in the murky fish tank against the wall. He stared into the dark glass for a few seconds.

In an instant, out of the depths of the dark tank, a pale, calloused man's hand pressed itself against the glass. Hugo gasped and fell backward onto the wet floor. He scrambled to his feet and moved across the room from the tank, watching it intently. There was nothing but darkness, though the water was still disturbed and sloshing in the tank.

Hugo ran back up the stairs. His heart was pounding, and he was gasping for breath. Octave was undisturbed in the bed. Hugo removed his wet clothes and spread them across the floor to dry. He found fresh clothes in his haversack. He sat in the corner chair to calm himself. He found the pack of Luckies in the tow sack he had brought from the farm. He lit one and waited for dawn.

XIII

The morning was overcast and looked as if the rain would return at any moment. Octave slept past dawn. Hugo had sat up and watched over him all night. The street seemed to be full of people cleaning up trash and detritus from the storm. The front lawn of Phrygia House was littered with broken branches from the cypresses, and an ancient ginkgo at the northeast end of the property, just inside the surrounding brick and stone wall, had lost a low-hanging branch that had split away from the trunk.

"Can we leave here today?" Octave asked. "I want to leave. I'm supposed to stay but I..."

"We can't leave just now," Hugo said. "Too many people about. Let's see if we can find clean water and I'll make some porridge."

Hugo opened their door and glanced out into the hallway. The air smelled musty, but the streaks of light coming in through the great window at the landing cheered him a little. At the bottom of the stairs, Hugo glanced tentatively at the dark fish tank. The water was murky and still. The floorboards of the room were warping near the entry door.

Hugo guided Octave to the left, into the large assembly room. Octave sat at one of the long tables near the eastern wall. The glass in the window high on the wall was broken. Just below it, scratched into the plaster, among hundreds of other scratches and marks that had been there, apparently for decades, was the word *YOU*.

"You smoked last night," Octave said.

"Yes. Couldn't sleep. Believe me, we will leave here as soon as we can." Hugo wandered back to what was once a kitchen and found a sink with a still-working tap. Further on were bowls, skillets, and other kitchen items. "This looks like an alcohol lamp," he called to his son. "Looks like we are in business!"

Octave watched his father prepare to cook their breakfast. He drew his name in the dust of the table at which he sat, and a rough drawing of a dog. Without thinking, he drew another figure, a stick figure of a young girl next to the dog. The bench upon which he sat shook a little, then the table. Octave glanced up at his father. He had felt the movement too. As he turned back toward the window, Octave saw that next to the word *YOU* he had already seen, now were the words *ARE HERE.*

XIV

"I have opened a portal for you I should have never opened," Miss Adelina said. She was not used to riding in automobiles. Even though Iseult was driving very slowly, as she had just learned to drive when she married Hugo and they had never been able to afford a car, Miss Adelina was terrified. "Not everyone is strong enough to hear what the spirits tell them."

"I had to hear what you told me. Father needed to tell me."

"I shouldn't have come with you. I should have gone to the police. An old woman is injured, maybe dead."

"It was an accident. An *accident!*"

"I felt I needed to come to keep you from harming anyone else. I have brought this on you."

"I needed to know..."

"Nothing you do will bring your father back. Your son plays no part in that."

"My father's investigations into Theosophy and the spirits have cursed him. Octave is sent by dark agents. I have seen it in him, the look in his eyes, his little smile. And I have seen it through your help and in my dreams."

"So what do you mean to do?"

"You... you must help me. You must drive the evil one out of him. We must stop him from being a barrier to Father's spirit. My son may be saved if you do it."

"I cannot do that. I am sure it is beyond my grasp to do—"

"I wanted to harm Octave, to get him out of the way; I admit it. Hugo thinks that is what I mean to do still. Dark forces will rule him, make him an agent of the Evil One, if we don't stop them. I have seen it in my dreams. But now I know—I feel—we can drive the darkness out of him. I believe now we can drive it out, and once we do, I will go to the police... about Marigold. First, I must know if my son can be saved. If they are in Ste. Odile, we must find them before they move on."

The dark clouds under which the women had been traveling for an hour suddenly dropped a shroud of rain across the rolling landscape. Iseult slowed the car even further and could tell by the grinding sound that she must be in the wrong gear. A loud pop was followed by the Durant swerving and skidding. Iseult slowed the car almost to a stop and the engine died as she pulled to the grassy shoulder. She got out and examined the front end. The left front tire was flat.

"*Dammit!*" Iseult cursed.

"Well, that's it," Miss Adelina said. "We're done for without some help."

"I have seen Father do this," Iseult snapped. "I think I can do it." She walked to the rear of the car and loosened the bolt that held the spare tire. Under it were bolted a jack and lug wrench. "I think I can do this."

Iseult removed the jack and positioned it under the front of the car. She then placed the wrench on a lug but could not budge it. After a few minutes' effort, both women pushing on the wrench broke the lug free.

In another twenty minutes, Iseult had successfully changed the tire. She put the flat and the tools into the back seat of the Durant. She started the car. "I don't know if I can drive in this," she said.

"We should wait until the rain lets up," Miss Adelina said.

"I can't. I can't do that. If they are in Ste. Odile, I have to find them. If they leave town, I may never see them again."

XV

Octave moved away from the window and closer to where his father was preparing their food. He wasn't sure why, but he decided he didn't want to tell his father what he had seen. Perhaps it was because he could see that his father was full of worry already and doing his best to protect him. His father seemed to be wearing himself out, and Octave didn't want to make things worse.

Octave took a seat facing the kitchen. He did not want to look again at the wall of windows. "I want to leave here if I can," he thought. "Someone more afraid than me wants me to stay."

"Did you feel that?" Hugo asked.

"Yes. What was it?"

"Tremor. Small tremor. They have them down here now and then, Uncle Phillipe told me."

Octave ate the porridge his father placed in front of him, though he wasn't hungry. When Hugo had eaten, he walked across the room to the row of windows.

"Where are you going?" There was urgency in Octave's voice that startled him. Hugo looked back at him and seemed a little surprised.

"Looking to see if we can slip out of here."

As Octave watched his father move toward the wall, he made himself look at the scrawl scratched into it. The words Octave had seen were no longer there.

"We will probably have to stay here tonight too," Hugo said. "People will be cleaning up this mess for days."

"Do you think Momma is worried about us?"

"I think she must be. I am not sure I did the right thing here. I panicked, I think. When we find a place to stop, I will get in touch with her and see...."

Octave insisted he didn't want to spend the day in the assembly room. A short hallway near the kitchen to the west side of the building attracted his attention. Hugo and Octave walked to the end of the short passage and looked out through a latticed window.

"What is that little building in the hillside?" Octave asked.

"I think it's a chapel. An old chapel half buried in the hill."

"Can we go there?"

"Let's wait until dark."

Further down the first-floor corridor, they found the gothic oaken door of another chapel, a larger one that appeared to have been for the entire population of girls who lived in these buildings when it was a Catholic academy. Octave ran to the front row pew and Hugo followed him. Statues of Jesus and the Virgin were still in place, each frozen in a hallowed gesture high in the web-draped gloom of the nave. The altar was white marble. Colorful stained glass windows were mostly intact on the north and south walls, one separated from the other by painted plaster Stations of the Cross.

"They had their own church here!" Octave exclaimed.

"Yes," Hugo agreed. "The girls here had to go to church every day."

Octave lay on his back in the front pew and stared at the vaulted ceiling. Very quickly, he fell asleep.

As the sun was setting, the heavy rain began to fall again. Octave awakened to thunder. His father was dozing in the pew behind him. Hugo stirred as Octave tried to climb on wainscotting high enough to see what he could of the outside. "It's almost dark and raining hard."

"Yes. We will stay another night, if you can do it."

"I guess I can."

"All right. We need to find something to eat."

"Can we go in that little church in the hill? We're just sitting here..."

"We'll get wet."

Octave shrugged.

"All right," Hugo continued, "Let's go."

The stone and brick pathway to the Reliquary Chapel was overgrown nearly to the point of obliteration. Large, mature trees towered on either side of it, as did boxwoods, holly, and many other bushes. The façade of the small building was all brick and stonework with the same tracery and quatrefoils as could be found on the larger buildings on the property.

Three limestone steps led to a small but heavy front door. With some effort, Hugo pushed it open. There was a vestibule and a small main chapel that might comfortably seat a hundred people. There were three stained glass windows on the north wall and three on the south wall. The room was damp and smelled of mildew.

"There's something... here," Octave said. "What's that?"

Octave and Hugo walked down the central aisle toward the front of the chapel. There seemed to be three altars in place there. Octave kept his eyes on the left altar as they approached it. A sense of uneasy familiarity and fear grew in him as he slowly realized what was behind the glass front they were nearing. Hugo walked ahead of his son as he, too, recognized what they were seeing in the altar.

A small standard of gold foil rested inside the front wall of the altar. Hugo read *Corpus Sanctae Aureliae, Martyris*. The desiccated corpse laid, withered and grotesque, on a bed of silk, dressed in rich fabrics and brocades with gold foil embossing. Dried, stretched scraps of gray flesh still clung in spots on the skeleton, and all exposed areas of the face, feet, hands, and arms were covered in a film of milky gauze.

Octave looked up mournfully at his father. Hugo picked the boy up. "These are relics of an early church martyr," Hugo said. "There is another over there," he indicated the glass altar on the opposite side of the main altar, "And an alcove with bones. *Berencis in Pace*. I think we shouldn't have come in here."

"No more spirits here," Octave said. "Just bones."

"Would you like to go back upstairs?"

"Can we stay here a little while? It's quiet here."

The two sat in the front pew. After a moment, Octave ran to the far casket and examined the body inside. He then returned to his seat.

"I thought this would upset you. So, all is quiet here?" Hugo asked.

Octave nodded his head yes.

"An odd thing for a church to do, don't you think? Keep dead bodies on display?"

"I think it is to show we remember them," Octave said. "They were hurt by bad people who killed them. But they aren't alone. They have someone with them—each other. That made them feel better and have gumpfort, like Momma says. They are happy again."

"You mean *comfort*? I suppose that makes sense."

"Can we go to our room now? And lock the door?"

XVI

Octave held his father's hand tightly as they passed through the entry room to the stairs. At the foot of the staircase, Hugo stopped suddenly. He stooped and picked up the bottom half of a broken plaster statue of St. Christopher, and to Octave's astonishment, smashed it into the fish tank. The murky water spread across the already wet floor.

"Why did you do that?" Octave asked.

"Upstairs. Let's get upstairs."

In their room, they stripped off their wet clothes and Hugo found them both one last dry change of clothes. The storm had strengthened, and thunderclaps rattled the mullioned windows of their chamber and the outer hallway. Hugo lit their candle. Octave climbed under the sheet of the bed. "I don't like the rain," he said.

Hugo stood to button his shirt. The room suddenly shook, east to west, violently enough that he stumbled. "That's an earthquake!" he said. "Definitely an..." He ran out of the room down to the landing on the staircase. Octave followed. From the large window they could see that several large trees had fallen, and a portion of the property's front wall had collapsed.

"We need to get out of the building!" Hugo said. As he moved, another sound could be heard above the falling rain. A deluge of water washed through the buildings on Constantinople Street from the northeast. A great wave pushed through the alleyways and streets, crashing against the perimeter wall of Phrygia House, shattering large sections of it, then washing in against the buildings themselves. Another torrent crashed in, and the violence of the water did not subside until the buildings were surrounded by water up to the very edge of the second floor.

"Great God!" Hugo said. "This isn't just a flood. This much water... the whole river has shifted! The earthquake... has changed the course of the river. I don't know how we can get out."

Octave started to cry. He hugged his father's leg.

"It's all right, son," Hugo said. "We need to get higher in the building. We will have to get our things and go to the attic."

Above the sound of the rushing water, Octave heard the plaintive sound of a dog howling. He helped his father gather their things from their room, and they rushed to the staircase, past the third floor and on to the attic. "This should be high enough," Hugo said.

The attic was dark, hot, and humid. "I wish we had something besides these candles up here," Hugo said. The floor was rough and splintered in many places. In the limited light, the only piece of furniture visible was an overturned wooden stool. Hugo turned the stool upright, and when he stood, he made a little gasping sound.

"What's this?" he held his candle up and saw a rope, which had been cut, dangling from a ceiling rafter.

Octave stepped forward slightly and his foot hit something that made a metallic sound. "Look at this," he said as he stooped to pick up an old signal lantern.

"Well, that's lucky... if it will still light!" Hugo said. "Must have been a railroad man or sailor here at one time. Let's hope it works." He found a match in his vest, and to Octave's relief, lit the lantern.

Hugo shined the light around the attic. The room was huge. It contained a few boxes, bits of broken furniture, and a Franklin stove at one end. Against the west wall there was an old settee. Hugo guided his son to it. "You can sleep on this, and I will sleep on the floor," he said.

Octave sat on the cushion. It smelled musty but was comfortable. "Try to rest," Hugo said. "You are safe here. I want to see if there is a way we can float to shore, to the hill behind us, and get to higher ground."

"You can't swim," Octave said. "What if something happens to you?"

"I won't try anything crazy."

As his father left, Octave trained the light on the Franklin stove some thirty feet away. He thought of how the stove had probably never been used in all the time he had been alive. He lay back on the cushion and in a few moments, his eyes drifted shut.

XVII

"We can't go any farther in the car," Iseult said. The tires had sunk five or six inches into the muddy road. The heavy rain, which had subsided and restarted overnight, had made the dirt road completely impassible by car.

"Do you know where we are?" Miss Adelina asked.

"The tower is familiar," Iseult said, indicating a dim pinnacle rising from a hilltop through the downpour a quarter mile away. "Yes, this is it. Not much farther." The two women ambled out of the car and hurriedly made their way toward the pinnacle of the hill on the side of the road. When both were quickly soaked, they slowed their pace.

At the top of the hill, the farmhouse was in sight. A roan horse was standing on the farmhouse porch out of the rain. "Look at him there, poor thing," Miss Adelina said.

"I saw him once," Iseult said. "Hugo's uncle gave him to a neighbor when he got rid of his livestock. He must have gotten lost in the storm." The roan raised and lowered his head several times as the women approached. They both stroked his nose as they stepped onto the porch. "Phillipe!" Iseult called. "Uncle Phillipe, it's Iseult."

No answer. The two women entered the house. The roan stuck his head in after them. Iseult searched the house. She saw her telegram lying on the kitchen table. "He's gone," she said.

"We can wait out the storm here," Miss Adelina said. "I see a car by the side of the house. Useless now, in the mud."

"No, I can't delay. I have to go now. The horse won't like it, but he will make it easier."

Miss Adelina's expression sank. "Then I will have to go too," she said.

XVIII

The wick in the signal lantern was burning very low. When Octave opened his eyes and glanced over at it, it had only a few minutes' burning time left. He was still alone. He sat up on the cushion. He turned the lamp to the right to find the door.

The white face inches from his was an evil full moon. The lips were black, swollen, and dripping, the eyeballs red, with drops of blood falling from them. The eyes were hellish augers of murderous intent and squinted slightly in a verminous and stinking smile.

Octave screamed. He ran in the dark in the direction of the door. After flailing uselessly for a few seconds, he found the knob and threw the door open. He meant to cry out for his father, but he could not find his voice. He began to cry uncontrollably as he ran down the steps to the third floor. His father could be anywhere in the huge and complex building. Octave felt suffocated by the inability to utter any sound. He gasped for breath as he ran through the north corridor.

He stopped when he saw something moving on the floor. Some indistinct shape writhed in the shadows. The shape divided into two segments and Octave saw it was a pair of black snakes, probably escaping the flood. The snakes moved away to the right and Octave ran past them. The north staircase was just ahead of him.

The heavy rain had stopped, and the streetlight was lighting the base of the stairs. Motes of illuminated dust swirled and then began to congeal into a form. Octave heard growling and slowly understood that he was looking at the image of an enormous dog. Octave stopped. The dog was huge, as large as he had ever seen. Its fur, excepting nearly bare spots, was coarse and brush-like. The spectral creature quieted and sat motionless, watching Octave for many moments.

The moan of a child seemed to float down from above. The illuminated motes high in the stairwell descended, and the whimpering grew louder. A childish face made ancient and wizened by suffering congealed in the midst of wafting light. The girl was nearly bald, and her eyes protruded grotesquely from their sockets, on the very verge, it seemed, of falling out. Sounds were emitted that seemed to be from her. As a wave on a shore, Octave was suddenly awash in her pain and fear and in the secrets she kept. In a moment he felt he knew her better than anyone in his life. She was terrified.

"Virginia..." Octave said. In that instant, nothing was left to be seen. Even so, Octave sensed he was not alone. He turned and looked back into the dark corridor of the south hallway. He heard no sound but the rushing river water outside.

"Dad?" No response. "*Dad!*" he yelled. Still nothing.

Octave felt a waft of freezing cold surround him for a brief moment. His eyes were drawn upward. High above him in the stairwell, staring down, was the same pale, ravenous face he had seen before. It bore the same dripping smile. Octave could not move or utter a sound. He could do nothing but stare upward, transfixed.

XIX

It had been years since Iseult had seen Ste. Odile. She and Hugo had visited once just after Octave was born. If she remembered right, the muddy road they were on, whose name she had forgotten, turned into Endymion Street in town and was near the old academy property Uncle Phillipe owned.

The rain had subsided a little. Old Vern the roan trudged along dutifully, allowing himself to be reined by his mane, and the two soaked women on his back were grateful he needed little encouragement.

It was well past dark as the horse topped a hill. The moon had risen, and Ste. Odile could be seen in its entirety.

Iseult was shocked at what she saw. "Oh, my God! Everything is flooded!" The great dark island that had once hidden the town from the main channel of the river now sat in a plain of moonlit mud as the river had shifted westward.

"The river changed course," she said. She heeled the horse forward. The river's edge reached as far west as Thermopylae Street, several blocks from Phrygia House, visible above the other buildings. Dozens of townspeople stood huddled in groups at the water's edge. Many were crying and all looked at the panorama before them in disbelief. As they watched, several of the older Creole houses on Constantinople Street collapsed into the water, as did the northern wall of a brick warehouse nearer the submerged riverbank.

"We can't get to Phrygia House," Iseult said.

"Why would they still be there?" Miss Adelina asked.

"They may not be if they had advanced warning, but I have to check there first. I just feel they may be there." Iseult looked to the north toward the high prominence over the town and the curve of the river below it, scarcely visible in the dark. Following the new flow of the river, she noticed the hill that sloped westward behind Phrygia House.

"If I can get to that hill," she said, "I may be able to find something to use as flotation past Phrygia House."

"The current is terrible," Miss Adelina protested. "You'll drown."

"Let's go," Iseult said.

XX

River water was just starting to spread across the floor of the laundry room. Years ago, someone detached the galvanized laundry sink from the wall for removal. The sink looked to be about ten feet long, and Hugo had managed to plug the drain with rags and wood slivers. If he could maneuver it to the second-floor landing and out the large window, it might float long enough so he and Octave could get to shore in it, or to the hill behind the building.

The laundry room was at the far south end of the second floor. Hugo didn't intend to move that far away from where he had left his son, but at least he had found something to use for a makeshift boat. With some effort he pulled it through the laundry room door and out into the hallway. Toward the stairwell, the floor became dry as the settling of the building over the centuries had sloped the planks downward slightly at that end of the structure.

Hugo was startled to see a mass of garter snakes wriggling near the stairs. As he approached them, they scattered into the darkness of the north hallway. Hugo pulled the sink loudly to the stairwell and slid it roughly down to the landing. Standing on the window seat, he looked out the window. The water was only about eight inches below it and flowing at a rapid rate. "It must be about eighteen feet here," he said.

The hill of the Reliquary Chapel was about two hundred feet away. Ten or fifteen feet of the hill rose above the water. The branch of the new channel the river had cut that now flowed behind the building became frothy, rushing water, made so by the narrowness of the passages through the buildings to the north of Phrygian House.

Hugo hurried up the stairs behind him connecting to the third floor. He ran along the corridor to the north end of the building. "Octave!" he called, though he doubted that the boy could hear him in the attic at that distance.

As Hugo neared the north staircase to the attic, the light filtering in through the tall window illuminated an impossible eidolon: Octave, in a seeming trancelike state, was suspended in the air some ten or more feet from the floor.

"Son!" Hugo called, but the boy was insensate. "*Octave!*"

Hugo ran to a spot under his suspended son. He feared the boy could fall at any second. After a moment, he climbed the stairs to the landing to see if he could reach into the void far enough to grab him. He could not. Hugo slipped over the banister and stood on the small outer edge of the landing. Stretching his arm as far as he could reach, he could not touch Octave. As Hugo's weight pulled against the banister, he felt it move. Feeling that the wood could give way any second, he pushed off the ledge upon which he was standing and leaped toward his son. He grabbed the boy and then twisted so his body would take the impact. His left leg was more extended than he thought, and as he landed on it, he felt his ankle shatter.

Hugo writhed in pain on the floor. Octave roused himself from his trancelike state. "Dad..." he said. "Dad, you're hurt!"

"We have to get to the window. Downstairs to the window."

"It was the bad man. Pettibone. He came for me."

"We have to get to the window. Let me lean on you a little. You're not safe. You're not safe."

"But you can't walk! Virginia is afraid. She wanted me here. She is so scared I will leave."

"Please son, we need to hurry. I don't know how much this old building can take."

"But she is lost, Dad. Spirits can't wander too far. Not a person's spirit."

Hugo's pain was immense. He balanced himself lightly on his son's shoulder and guided the boy down the hallway toward its opposite end. Hugo hopped on his right foot and found in just a few feet he was exhausted. A tremor shook the old building; plaster crumbled to dust on the wall and rained down from above them.

Hugo fell to the floor from pain and exhaustion. His fall brought Octave down upon himself. Octave tried to help his father up. Hugo swooned as he stood and nearly passed out. In another twenty minutes they'd made it to the stairway. Hugo slid himself down to the landing and Octave helped him as best he could.

Hugo was almost too weak to lift the end of the empty galvanized sink. He wasn't sure how he would manage with his son inside. "We just have to push across here and hope we make it to the hill before we get swept out to the main channel. You climb in and I'll try to push this thing out the window." Hugo picked up the board he had found in the laundry to use as a paddle and tossed it into the sink.

Octave climbed up onto the window seat and slipped into the sink. The boy looked out at the raging water swirling in the near darkness. "Momma!" he said.

XXI

Iseult was lying across a wooden plank bench in the swirling water. She was anchoring herself, holding on to the dead branch of a bare maple tree near the north end of the building, about twenty feet from where Octave in the sink was emerging from the window.

"*Octave!*" she cried. "I knew you were here. I felt it."

"Momma!"

"I don't want to hurt you. I *never* want to hurt you!"

"Momma, be careful!"

"I wanted to find you and bring you home..." Her grip on the branch failed.

Hugo pushed the sink completely out onto the raging water and tried to hold it tight. He heard his wife's voice. He caught a glimpse of her slipping into the water. He gasped. The bench Iseult had been floating upon turned end to end and floated past in front of the sink.

"*Momma!*" Octave cried.

"Son, you must sit! Sit down!"

"My momma..."

"I'm climbing in now. No... I'll have to push and hold onto the back. I can't climb in. Sit down. Get down lower!"

Octave heard his father but did not respond.

"It's the comfort," the boy said, as if in a dream. He turned and looked at his anguished father. "Momma said comfort for the afraid ones. The ones alone. If I can give the comfort, I must." Octave looked high up on the outer wall. His expression brightened as if he saw a familiar face watching him from the third-floor window far above Hugo. Smiling, he stepped over the edge of the makeshift boat and dropped into the raging water.

Hugo lost his grip on the sink. He grabbed for it but couldn't hold on. He stood, bearing the pain of his broken bones, teetered against the windowsill, and then, with the germinating dread of future remembrance of his regretful impulse, with the thought of the immurement of his shame crushing any chance of comfort for empty decades to come, fell back onto the floor.

Baby Monster

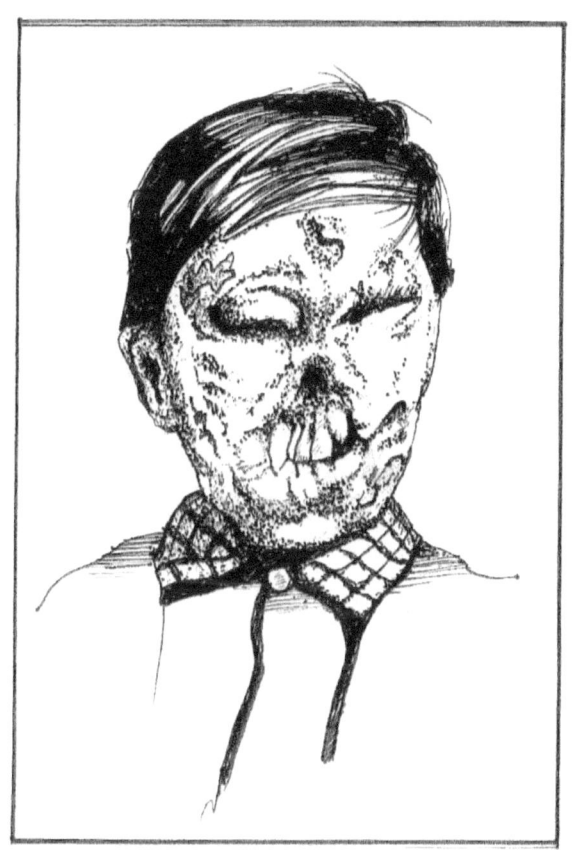

"You are ten years old, Beau-Garçon," Florette said. "Old enough by now to see that I am not well and in a hurry."

"I'm sorry, Mamma," the boy responded. "I couldn't see you very good in the shadow. I am not well either. My head hurts today." A steamboat whistle sounded down on the landing and the boy shrugged in pain.

"That's *every* day with you. I told you this morning I will get more headache powder when I can afford it. And you don't have to ask me about it every time your brother cries. You watch him enough. I don't know what to do for him any more than you do."

"He got so sick so fast. I just don't want to do nothing wrong for him. Sometimes I don't hear him cry and I can't always see..."

"Stop that!" Florette screamed. Beau-Garçon was startled, but his swollen and red-blotched face could no longer carry expressions. "When you make your little suggestions, I know what you're doing and I think you must be the devil! I know an accusation when I hear one. You little devil...you look the part!"

"But Mamma..."

"And stop *spitting* when you talk. If I get close enough to understand you, you spit all over me."

"I can't help it. You know I can't," the boy whimpered. In the months since Beau-Garçon's upper lip and the tip of his nose had fallen away, he had essentially needed to learn to speak all over again. He could not tell when speaking caused him to spray through his exposed upper teeth.

"I know I am to blame," Florette went on. "God is punishing me through my children. I don't know why my symptoms have gone away and I feel better while you and little Roland just get worse. God is torturing me."

"I'm sorry, Mamma. I'm glad you're feeling better. Roland and me will someday too, I think."

Florette looked at herself in her small, inadequate mirror. She then continued packing the open bag on her iron-frame bed. "I guess I don't look too bad considering all I been through. What's a seventeen-year-old girl supposed to do when her husband dies? What choices did I have? God put me in a terrible situation and then punished me for surviving." She looked at her son with a glimmer of compassion. "I am a person who wants to be happy. Some people who have an easier life than me will never be happy, no matter what they have. They will be happier dead. They are ignoring what God has given them. They are better off out of the way so those of us who want happiness can have more. Remember that. And if I am better off, we all are. Remember that, too."

"I know God loves us and will make it all better someday."

"God helps those that help theirselfs, which means sink or swim. That's why I got to go to Ste. Odile. It's an opportunity I must go after. Maybe something will come of meeting Mr. Demarest."

"You mean you might get married?"

"It's possible. Well, it ain't *impossible*. Just met through a notice in the newspaper. Anything's possible."

"That would be so *good*! Does he know about us? Me and Roland?"

"No. Not yet. I thought about putting you back in the orphanage again. Both of you, just until things get decided. They would take good care of you until things get decided."

"No, Mamma... no!" Beau-Garçon insisted. "They will be mean to Roland... and me. They will put him in a toddler cage, that wooden cage for him to stand in with a hole in the top for his head. Please don't send us there."

"Nonsense. He can't even *stand* yet. I got to do what's best for us all," Florette said. "Time for me to start walkin' if I'm gonna get there in time. You take good care of Roland. I'll be back tomorrow or the next day."

"All right, Mamma."

"I will be at Herve's restaurant early this evening. They wouldn't let me in there alone last time, but now I look more presentable and less whorish, and I am meeting a gent. Later tonight... I don't know where I'll be."

"All right, Mamma."

Florette closed the front door and began her long walk north to Ste. Odile. Beau-Garçon watched her from the front window of their room but could not see her clearly for long.

He and his mother had moved down to Belgique to this rooming house from Ste. Odile just before Roland was born. Beau-Garçon's symptoms had started to show by then, and the townspeople recognized these and had started to shun the family. They were forced out of their rooms in town, and the shabby Bruges Boarding House was all they could afford. Many times, Beau-Garçon heard his mother mumbling about how Aunt Estelle and Uncle Louis back in Ste. Odile were ashamed of her and her ugly, diseased children. Beau-Garçon did not understand why his family would feel that way about them. Uncle Louis seemed to have kindness in him. Beau-Garçon and his brother would surely get better with time as their mother had, since, according to Dr. Treves, they all had the same disease. And Florette was out in the evenings trying to find a new father for them, as she often repeated. If she succeeded, they wouldn't be so poor. If he and his brother ever got well, they may never look normal, but at least they wouldn't be so poor.

Roland started to stir in the bed he shared with Beau-Garçon across the room. Roland was just over a year old but was developing slowly. He could not stand on his own. His skin was wrinkled and splotched with rashes, and his eyes and nose wept constantly. There was often a filmy membrane present inside his mouth. He whimpered and cried a little. Beau-Garçon stood at his brother's side, both warmed and pained by the love he felt for the helpless, suffering child.

"Mamma got better," he whispered. "We will get better because we will be *grateful* for our happiness. That pleases God. A person who won't be happy just takes up space, like Mamma said. It's just a waste. We will pray to get better."

He carefully picked up his brother and carried him to a pillow placed on the floor in a corner. He sat the child on the floor, leaning him back into the corner. "I will warm up some milk for you," he said.

Roland ate very little. Beau-Garçon spread a tattered quilt on the floor and lay his brother on it: a short while on his back, then on his front. He sat next to the child and talked to him about traveling on the river someday, about riding horses, and about how their neighbor in The Bruges, Mr. Vickers, was a veteran of Antietam who had lost both his arms and learned to live with his disability. He had made a good life for himself after his wife left and always looked on the brighter side of things.

Late in the afternoon, Beau-Garçon cleaned his brother, washing him as best as his impaired vision would allow. After his bath, Roland fell asleep, and Beau-Garçon knew the child would sleep until morning. As Roland had seemed to grow weaker in the last few weeks, Beau-Garçon's sleep had become more intermittent as he lay next to the child listening for his faint breathing.

Florette had left little food in the house. There were grits left from two days before, a few apples, and two potatoes with buds starting to sprout out of them. Roland ate a little of the warmed grits and Beau-Garçon ate two of the apples, dismayed as he always was at how the juice ran out of his mouth from between his exposed teeth.

By the next morning, Florette had still not returned. Beau-Garçon was hungry and he had little solid food left to give Roland. He would wait one more day.

Florette had told her son never to accept food from Mr. Vickers, the only other boarder in the house. She said it would be spoiled and unsafe, and her boys' delicate health may not tolerate it.

On the second morning, Roland would not eat the grits anymore. His teeth were not strong enough for the apples or potatoes, so Beau-Garçon knew he would have to walk to Ste. Odile to find his mother.

A year ago, Florette had taken a small canvas haversack Mr. Vickers gave her from the war, and she cut two holes in the bottom as a means of carrying Roland on her back when she went to the marketplace. With a great effort that nearly drained all his strength,

Beau-Garçon managed to put his brother's thin legs through the holes and secure the haversack to his own back. The day was clear and rather warm, and he felt he could walk to Ste. Odile in a little more than an hour. He usually put a cloth sack with eye openings over his head when he went outside. He found this on the tabletop and pulled it on.

The Belgique Road was dirt and rock in some places. It became a street in Ste. Odile, but Beau-Garçon could not remember which one. He had not been to the town since he was a little older than Roland. The warmth of the day made the cloth sack even more uncomfortable than usual, and Beau-Garçon had difficulty keeping the eyeholes aligned. His poor vision made this situation worse, and he found himself stumbling over rocks and into ruts he did not see in time to avoid.

Roland complained a little, whining and whimpering, but soon seemed to settle into and accept the heat and discomfort. An old man driving a mule cart passed them, going south. The old man barely noticed them. Beau-Garçon was grateful he had encountered no children his own age on the road yet. He had faced their cruelty before.

Beau-Garçon was hungry and slowly growing weaker. He felt his brother must be hungry too. After nearly two hours of walking, the forest bordering the road opened, revealing the river and the town of Ste. Odile.

Beau-Garçon had to decide where to look for his mother. She had mentioned she was going to Herve's, a restaurant, but she wouldn't still be there. Maybe she went to a hotel in town, but which one? He knew his Uncle Louis and Aunt Estelle lived on a corner just down from the Church of the Holy Mandilion. He would walk there and see if he recognized the house.

Beau-Garçon had never been to school. He knew that his aunt and uncle lived on a street with a long name. When he saw a street sign that had many letters on it, he suddenly remembered his mother had told him the house was on *Constantinople* Street. That was surely a name with very many letters. The large house on the first corner he came to looked very familiar.

It was a stone house of three stories, smaller than its neighbors, but still impressive. He cautiously climbed the stone stairs at the front porch. He hesitated to knock, terrified that a stranger would open the door. He would be ashamed of his appearance and slurred speech with a stranger.

He knocked faintly on the glass. In a moment the door was opened by a thin, graying woman. Beau-Garçon could see well enough to tell this was Aunt Estelle, and she had an appalled expression on her face.

"Oh, my Lord!" she gasped. "What in the world...?"

"Hello, Aunt Estelle," Beau-Garçon said. She didn't seem to understand him. "My Mamma is Florette."

Estelle frowned. *"Florette."* She partially closed the door. "Louis! Louis, come here!" she called.

"What *is* it? I have two dead rats to get out of the pantry!"

"Come right now!"

Louis came to the front door mumbling.

"Look," Estelle said, pushing the door open.

"Oh," Louis said. "Florette's boys. What are you doing here, son?"

"Mamma came to town a couple of days ago," Beau-Garçon said. "I thought she might come here. We ain't got no more food at home."

Louis stepped out onto the porch. He removed Beau-Garçon's hood. Louis and Estelle stifled a gasp.

"Good God!" Estelle whispered.

Louis looked at Roland. He glanced at his wife, then at Beau-Garçon. "This baby is dead," he said.

Beau-Garçon's swollen and splotched face remained involuntarily expressionless. His eyes moistened but he could say nothing.

"This is wonderful...*wonderful.* Now it is our responsibility." Estelle said. "Contact the orphanage. Put this one there until his mother comes back. I'll get a message to Napier to remove the body."

"No... no." Louis carefully removed the haversack from Beau-Garçon's back. Roland's small, limp body had slumped down into the interior. "This is my family. I will take the baby to Napier and then talk to Sheriff Aubuchon. You give this boy something to eat and put him in the guest room. And contact Mr. LaPointe, the monument maker."

"His name is Roland," Beau-Garçon said.

Estelle seemed angry as Louis left. "Sit in that chair and don't move," she said to Beau-Garçon without looking at him, indicating a chair in the entryway. She went into the kitchen.

Beau-Garçon sat quietly. He did not try to take in his surroundings. He thought only of Roland. He wondered if carrying him to Ste. Odile was too much and had caused his death. He wept. A wave of guilt came and went in his mind. His little brother would suffer no more. Everyone was happier in heaven, and this was the way Roland had left his disease behind.

"Damn these rats!" Estelle screamed from the kitchen. Beau-Garçon ran in to her.

"What's the matter?"

"These damned rats! It's an infestation since people started dumping their rubbish across the alley." A large rat skittered along the baseboard and into the pantry. "Your uncle poisons them with strychnine, but they keep coming..." She opened a cupboard near the wooden icebox and removed a bottle containing white powder. She quickly replaced the bottle among many others in the cabinet. "I'll leave that to him," she said.

Estelle ordered Beau-Garçon to return to his chair in the entryway. She warmed some onion soup for him, and he ate it alone in the dining room. Afterward, she led him upstairs to a small bedroom.

"You stay in this room," Estelle said. "Do not move out of it. I must go talk to the monument maker. I don't see why this should be our responsibility. Your trashy mother will never come back. She may not even be alive, knowing the types she took up with. You can't stay here. Understand that. I won't have you around. And if you had stayed home and got help there, your brother would still be alive, I have no doubt."

She slammed the bedroom door as she left.

"It's sad to see her so unhappy. I would hope she could be glad for everything she has. Maybe she will be, one of these days," Beau-Garçon murmured to himself.

Beau-Garçon was also told by Uncle Louis to stay in the guest room unless told otherwise. He had a comfortable bed to sleep in and food to eat. He was grateful, though it was obvious that his aunt and uncle did not want to see him or speak with him.

On the third day, Roland was buried in a tiny wicker casket in the northeast corner of the Ste. Odile public cemetery, known as the pauper's section. Louis took Beau-Garçon to the burial. Estelle stayed home. A young traveling priest was the only other person present. The gravestone Estelle had commissioned had not been set yet.

"What was this child's name?" the young priest asked.

"*Roland!*" Beau-Garçon said, more loudly and angrily than he meant to. "His name was Roland."

The priest said a few prayers and the service was quickly ended. Louis and Beau-Garçon began the short walk home.

"Aunt Estelle is a nervous person, very frail," Louis said at length, never looking at his nephew. "She has many complaints of the stomach. Having you in the house makes her worse. It affects me, too. You are my nephew, but I can't help you. Your mother disgraced us. She suffered for it and so have her children. We don't want to be a part of her sins. You must go. You can go to the orphanage here or we can put you on the Orphan Train, which will be stopping at Belgique in a few days. I don't want to treat you bad, son. I know you have seen a lot of that in life, but this isn't my responsibility. Don't expect the kindness to last too long."

"Thank you for explaining it. I am sorry Aunt Estelle is so sad." Beau-Garçon said. His body still hurt from the long walk from Belgique days before. "I don't want to upset her."

Beau-Garçon was happy enough, keeping to his room. It was almost as though he had a space all his own that no one in the world could violate for the first time in his life. He was sorry it wouldn't last. He found some illustrated books for children on a shelf and remembered Uncle Louis and Aunt Estelle had lost a child to measles a few years before. Studying the pictures, he guessed that one of the books was about a hedgehog who owned a cobbler shop. He could see the pictures if he held the book at a certain angle. Another book appeared to be about a troll who lived under a bridge who fell in love with a shepherdess. That one was his favorite.

Twice on the day after the funeral, he heard Aunt Estelle moaning in pain downstairs. When Beau-Garçon could summon the courage, he would peek out his bedroom door, even though he could see very little. Over the next two days, Aunt Estelle's condition seemed to improve and worsen again every few hours.

As Beau-Garçon sat in his room in the evening and after he had finished with his books, he wondered if he could climb out his window late one night and walk a little, unseen by the town. To walk among fine houses and well-kept yards would be wonderful. He could not imagine the thoughts he would have about taking all of it in and how happy it would certainly make him. There were no gutters or trellis near his window though, and he knew if there were, he would not be strong enough to climb down and back up again. His imagination alone was free to walk the streets.

On the third day, Beau-Garçon vanished into his room wordlessly after dinner, as had become his custom. He sat on the floor near the bed with his picture books. After a few minutes, he could hear his aunt's voice screaming words he could not make out. It sounded as though she was holding a cloth to her face. Then he heard vomiting. He hurried downstairs to see what was happening and found Uncle Louis ministering to her at the dining room table.

"Get back upstairs!" Louis screamed at him. "I told you to stay in your room."

An hour later, the commotion repeated. Beau-Garçon peeked out his door and took a few steps into the hallway. He was startled and terrified when a vase crashed into the wall next to him.

"I told you stay in that room!" Louis screamed from downstairs. "You're the cause of this. I'm putting you on the Orphan Train tomorrow. I want you far away from us!"

Beau-Garçon slipped back into his room and closed the door. He sat on his bed and wondered what the rest of his life would be like. Surely, he would get better as his mother had. He wondered if his mother was still alive. If she were, he hoped she was now happy. He would miss her, as he missed Roland. So much of the sadness he experienced around him seemed unnecessary, and it must not be allowed to destroy happiness, wherever happiness could be found.

He lay back on his bed. Sometime later, he realized he had fallen asleep. He was awakened by a crashing sound downstairs, and his Uncle calling, "Boy... boy!"

Beau-Garcon cautiously opened his door. He crept out to the top of the stairs. Aunt Estelle was lying on the dining room floor and Louis was holding her head. She was groaning faintly.

"You want me, Uncle?"

"Come down here. I need your help."

Beau-Garçon hurried down the stairs, holding onto the banister so he wouldn't miss a step and fall. He felt himself step on a pliant strand of something on the step. A squeak. He wondered if the rats, up to now only emboldened to come into the kitchen, were now moving into the rest of the house.

"I don't want her to choke," Louis said. "I have to hold her up. I just made a solution of bicarbonate in the kitchen. Go fetch it. I don't know what else to do for her. Then go two houses down and get Dr. Treves. Hurry!"

Beau-Garçon rushed into the kitchen.

"Hurry up in there!" Louis called. "Can't you see it on the countertop right in front of you? Hurry!"

Beau-Garçon brought in an open jar full of the mixture. Louis took it from him impatiently and held it to Estelle's' lips. "Drink it all if you can, Estelle. Drink it all."

She struggled to swallow and grimaced at the unpleasant taste. She moaned and scowled in pain. Her body started to quiver. Her arms and legs became rigid. She gasped for breath, and her spine contracted into a hideous arch on the floor.

"My God!" Louis gasped. "My God, Estelle... What is happening?"

In another few seconds, her rigid body gave no signs of breathing.

"I will go get the doctor," Beau-Garçon said. He hurried out the front door.

The night was clear and warm. The village was quiet and the streets scantily lit by the few streetlights along North Constantinople Street. A beautiful night for walking, for appreciating the lovely life these people had. Beau-Garçon felt more at peace now than he had earlier in the day, knowing there was a little less unhappiness in the world. He was startled as a dog barked at him suddenly from behind a fence as he crossed Mal Ardents. He thought how in a moment, the dog would forget about his passing, go lie down and be happy again.

In another half-hour, he reached the Ste. Odile public cemetery. Even in the dark he easily found Roland's grave. He sat beside it on the damp ground and thought of how accepting and kind Uncle Louis might be to see his only remaining family member when he returned home. He knew Uncle Louis would be someone he could depend upon to protect him and be kind to him, as he learned to accept things as they are. Accepting things as they are, after all, is also important to gaining happiness.

Beau-Garçon saw the gravestone had been placed. There was an inscription on it, a collection of marks that meant nothing to him. A breeze blew through the trees and the moonlight illuminated the words:

BABY MONSTER
1897

Editor's Note

If you're already a fan of John's incredible work, welcome back. If you're new to it, then welcome in. I truly hope you have been as affected by John's vision and prose as I have.

For John's first collection, *The Dark Walk Forward*, he insisted we use a specific photograph of a real man on the cover. He was Second Lieutenant Henry Ralph Lumley, or H.R. Lumley, a pilot in World War I. He had just received his pilot's license and was taking off for his first mission when the aircraft caught fire. Lumley was severely burned, particularly on his face. Dr. Harold Gillies and his surgical team, who were just beginning the painstaking process of reconstructive surgery, used a skin graft from Lumley's chest to create a new face for him. The photograph is of him as his skin grafts are healing. However, the size of the graft itself and his weakened state caused him to pass from heart failure in 1918, two years after the accident.

The cover for this book, John's second collection, is from a real daguerreotype, a type of photograph produced on a silver plate or a silver-covered copper plate. And again, John strongly proclaimed he wanted to use it. It's of a boy with severe facial deformities from congenital syphilis, taken circa 1880. Syphilis is a sexually transmitted disease that was rampant during the Victorian era. This child was born of a mother who had the disease and passed it on in utero. We don't know the child's name, nor who his parents were, nor who took the photograph. But he was the inspiration for the title story of this collection, "Baby Monster." John contacted artist of the macabre Gabriel Augusto to create a painting of the boy in his own vision. It is indeed an effective introduction to this dark collection.

John has written about his fascination with the novel *Frankenstein, or the Modern Prometheus* by Mary Shelley. It's clear he admires Shelley's ingenuity and imagination when it comes to combining science with horror and romance. The time period, the tragedy of the creature's life, the study of who is the man and who is the monster, all come together flawlessly in her groundbreaking manuscript. The story seems like a cliché now, but the themes truly remain timeless.

John consistently explores these same themes in whatever he writes. He understands that extreme intelligence can lead to a lack of empathy, that discovery through experimentation can override morality, that endemic horrific conditions will lead our fellow humans to unspeakable acts none of us could ever imagine.

He also memorializes the forgotten, like 2nd Lt. Lumley and this afflicted child. He helps us find pity for the downtrodden, understanding for those who have no choice. He praises medical breakthroughs while lamenting the torment of its subjects. He gives dignity to the maimed and deformed, pride to the terrified and outcast. He helps us remember humanity's past and its triumphs and failures, and knows that if we don't listen to history, we are doomed to repeat the most horrific and darkest portions... and that is probably the most terrifying notion of all.

All in all, whether you find morality, justice, empathy, or any other philosophical consideration in John's work, the truth is his fascination with the morbid and mysterious is infectious, drawing us in with curiosity and trepidation. I am never sure what I'll find as I turn each page with anticipation and dread. And I hope you as a reader were just as conflicted as I was.

Andrea Thomas, Editor
Arizona, 2024

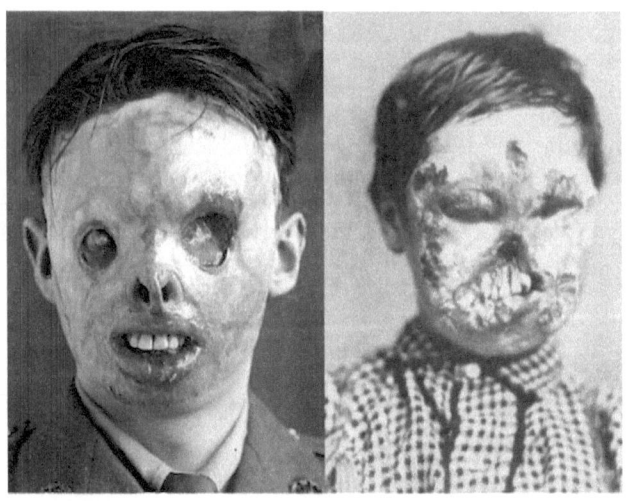

*2nd Lt. H.R. Lumley after his skin graft, c. 1918,
and boy with congenital syphilis, c. 1880.*

About the Author

John S. McFarland's short stories have appeared in numerous journals, in both mainstream and horror genres. His tales have been collected with stories by Stephen King, H. P. Lovecraft, Robert Bloch, and Richard Matheson. His work has been praised by such writers as T. E. D. Klein and Philip Fracassi, and he has been called "A great, undiscovered voice in horror fiction." McFarland's horror novel *The Black Garden* was published in 2010 to universal praise, and his young reader series about Bigfoot, *Annette: A Big, Hairy Mom*, is in print in three languages. His story collection *The Dark Walk Forward* was his first and will appear in a German-language edition this year. *The Black Garden* has been selected by world-renowned publishing company Zagava for a special edition print run. All of John's books are currently available through Dark Owl Publishing.

McFarland's gothic stories of the macabre begin...

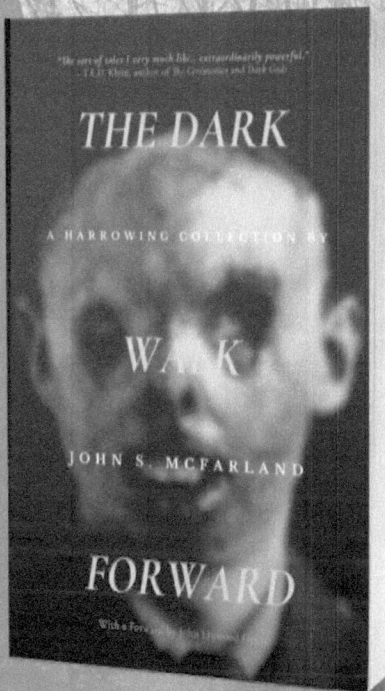

"The sort of tales I very much like... extraordinarily powerful."
~ T.E.D. Klein, author of The Ceremonies and Dark Gods

THE DARK

A HARROWING COLLECTION BY

WALK

JOHN S. MCFARLAND

FORWARD

With a Foreword by

"McFarland tempers his frights with the mercy of
familial love and sympathy for outsiders and victims.
Horror readers will be riveted."
~ Publishers Weekly

 Available from Dark Owl Publishing
www.darkowlpublishing.com

The shocking story of
Ste. Odile is unmasked...

"An engaging,
intricate horror
tale that feels
ripped from the
pages of a
penny dreadful."
~ Kirkus Reviews

Available from Dark Owl Publishing
www.darkowlpublishing.com

More dark secrets of Ste. Odile are revealed...

The sequel to The Black Garden

"Masterfully written with the perfect blend of
historical setting, folklore, suspense, and horror.
I couldn't put it down."
~ D.L. Andersen, author of Across Unstill Waters
and That Far Distant Country

Available from Dark Owl Publishing
www.darkowlpublishing.com

You met
Annette
as a
big, hairy mom...

Now spend time
with her
as a big, hairy
grandma!

Annette: A Big, Hairy Mom
and
Annette: A Big, Hairy Grandma
written and illustrated by John S. McFarland

Chapbooks for young readers
that adults will love, too!

Both now available from Dark Owl Publishing
www.darkowlpublishing.com

www.ingramcontent.com/pod-product-compliance
Lightning Source LLC
Chambersburg PA
CBHW021006260626
47169CB00006B/1969